My Dear Watson

Elm Jed

ELM JED
Author - Creator

To my best friend Leah,
You'll always be my sunshine on the darkest days
Thank you for believing in me and Autumn

Contents

Content Warnings

This book contains:
Heavy depiction of PTSD flashbacks, anxiety and panic attacks, thoughts of self-harm, and depression on page.
Discussions of sexual assault and rape, domestic violence, homelessness, death, family loss, and hospital/surgery trauma.
On page, characters are stalked, physically attacked, yelled at, and bullied.
Mental health is heavily discussed in various scenarios.
Aspects of BDSM is shown & discussed.
Major cliffhanger

Chapter 1

Coffee, Aisle One!

The battered case of *Howard the Duck* is tossed into the growing heap of my other cult classic films. I quickly pile some of my hoard of DVD cases, trying to clean up after accidentally knocking over a stack. I really needed to get a shelf or rack for them. I'd gotten used to just stacking the hundreds of movies against my wall. It's cathartic some nights, though.

As I snag a specific movie, glancing at the clock, I snatch it and put it on top of my old box television set to watch after work. Good enough for who it's for, AKA my messy ass. I jog over to the counter to grab my bag, hat, and jean jacket. My arms are pulled through the sleeves as I run down the stairs toward the back hallway of *Nan's Bookstore*. Instead of going through the rear exit, I go to the front entrance where Nan sits at the register. Her warm brown eyes catch mine as I pass her, waving. "Gotta go! Don't want to be late!"

"You always have plenty of time. Being twenty minutes early isn't being late, dear," she muses as I get to the door.

"Tell that to my anxiety."

"A talk with your therapist then?"

"Really, Nan? Already hitting me with therapist comments," I groan, my hand on the door handle. "That must be a great sign."

Nan laughs at me as I escape outside and jog down the street, taking a few turns until I reach my subway stop. Sweat drips down my forehead as I head down the stairs. Once at the platform, I check my bag for my current romance read; safely tucked away. I feel the cool breeze of the subway train as it approaches, jumping onto my train, and staying near the back of the car as I hold onto one of the rails.

Pulling out my book the train starts to move, I smile to myself as I start to skim the passages. A classic tale of an English Lady and Scottish Laird, who's determined to make her his wife. I hum while reading, vividly listening to the noise of people talking around me, someone playing the saxophone, and the clacking of the car itself. I let the sounds ease me, reminding me of the familiarity.

Do I know Nan is right? Yes. Does that mean I'll change my anxiety that easily around time? No.

Someone coughs loudly, and I glance at them briefly, pushing down a different kind of anxiety. My awareness heightens when something clicks nearby, but the saxophone drowns it out. The train comes to my stop while I shake it off and exit to the subway platform.

Even after years of therapy, some things just don't change.

Well, they do, but not with the wave of a magic wand. Like anxiety around being late or not showing up on time. Then again, this particular "tick" wasn't even close to as bad as some of the others I spoke to my therapist about. Didn't exactly take precedence. Besides, I'm just being punctual. Good work ethic. Blah, blah, blah.

I come out of the subway greeted by Lower Manhattan; blasted by the heat of the summer and noise. The city is always awake, but damn is it loud in the mid-morning. Weaving through people, I make my way toward work which feels barely a stone's throw from Wall Street itself. Speaking of, I almost run into a couple of businessmen, which I duck my head and apologize as I continue on my way. The familiar street I've traveled to work the past two and half years is cramped with people and glowing with the summer sun. I adjust my flat cap, moving past more well-dressed businesspeople who are yelling on their phones or carrying coffees before I make it to the side street. I step around some garbage and slip through the back employee entrance of *Blue Java Café.*

The clock says I'm fifteen minutes early, but right on time in my head. A smile bursts over my face as I head through the kitchen, where Phoebe is cleaning up before her shift ends. She gives a quick smile as I duck into the employee backroom to drop my bag, jacket, and hat off.

"You're early," she says, passing me to grab her stuff. Her dark curly hair is pulled back into a bun, complementing her fair skin and heart-shaped face. I wink at her as she unties the apron, she starts to say, "Have a good shift. But just so you know—"

"Autumn," Yuki, our general manager for the café, calls out my name.

I give Phoebe a look, and she gives me one back. "Should I be worried?"

Phoebe whispers before heading out, "Bailey destroyed five pastries and spilled three drinks already. Have fun."

Phoebe walks out with a wave, while I snatch my apron.

Yuki comes out of her office, looking already exasperated. Her shoulder-length black hair swishes over her shoulders as she grabs my elbow and pulls me toward the kitchen area. We don't cook anything back here, but do heat up quiches, sandwiches, and pastries already made by the parent company that we pre-order from. You'd think that's easy until there's an order of twenty egg and bacon sandwiches at once.

"I need you back here," Yuki tells me. "Bailey still doesn't know how not to burn quiches or use the toaster oven."

"Okay, I may suck at cooking, but you have to admit she's got a talent. Even I don't burn quiches." My idea of a well-balanced meal was takeout, specifically Chinese or Thai food.

"I may join you back here just to get away from the crowds of grumps this morning, which may go into this afternoon." She rolls her eyes as she crosses her arms.

"Already that bad? It's only Wednesday." I tie on my apron for the back.

"Don't get me started on phone calls from the owner and other calls to the distributors," she mumbles. My hand pats her shoulder caringly, and she smirks at me.

I've worked with Yuki the entire time I've been at *Blue Java*. She's risen into the general manager role, and I just stayed where I was. Preferred it that way. Go-to barista.

"I also had three 'manager' talks due to men telling Mabel how to make their drinks properly," Yuki continues. "And another woman on the difference between oat milk and two percent."

Batten down the hatches then.

I glance past Yuki into the coffee shop where there's quite a line forming. Bailey is a tall blonde with deep blue eyes and a chest that doesn't quit. She's what every fashion magazine cover wants, always with a flirtatious sweet smile; bright like nothing was wrong in her little world. Even while she gives away free drinks to *every* customer she thinks could be a potential date. I'd have never thought of using my barista status as a replacement for *Tinder*, but we all have our hobbies.

Mabel, the café's assistant manager, is a bit shorter and curvier in other places like Phoebe, but with light brown skin and a shaved head. She always wears colorful tops and earrings to match, and today's color was turquoise with some silver. Mabel could make latte foam art with one hand tied behind her back and both eyes closed.

Almost three years and I can make a decent heart outline. Kind of.

"If nasty customers are still here, I can kick their asses or say they have a small dick?" I propose and Yuki snorts. "How about pointing out bad haircuts?"

Yuki laughs under her breath. "Maybe if it was a Monday. But if it gets any worse out there, Mabel will come back here and help you."

"Fine, but if there's any more business assholes, I'm letting Mabel lay into them and record the whole thing...*then* I'll say they have a small dick."

"That's what I'm afraid of," Yuki mutters as I get to work.

Being a barista at 28 wasn't the most glamorous of jobs, but I did love it. Even on days like this. It was one of the best things to have happened to me in the past five years of my life, probably longer than that. I work full-time, but now and then I work at the bookstore, especially when Nan goes out of town. Okay, living above the bookstore was the best thing to have happened. Nan took me in when I needed a place, even though we weren't related by blood, but she's always treated me like a granddaughter.

My life was simple. I'm pushing thirty soon and I'm the happiest I've been since I was seventeen.

The early afternoon dragged on and at one point Mabel did join me in the back, due to her almost wringing Bailey's neck. Didn't blame her.

The young girl, barely twenty, has only been here for six months, and although she can get drinks right most days, Bailey clearly had her focus on anything but doing her job. Her father owned a law firm, while her mother was a housewife who did charity work. Typical new money. She'd told me more than that, but I always seemed to zone out during those conversations, especially after hearing about her "daddy's" work for the fifteenth time and how she had this job because he wanted her to get *real* life experience. Since she refused to go to college, this was her parent's other way of getting her to be an adult, I guess.

Things begin to slow down, and Mabel and I exhale loudly as the mid-afternoon crowd dwindles. Thank goodness. Yuki leaves before three, and then Mabel begins to leave as I clean up some of the kitchen.

"How dare you leave me early today," I chide Mabel.

She chuckles, tossing me a small bottle of her lotion. I snatch it and put some on my hands and forearms before I throw it back for her to use.

"Have fun closing with Bailey," she tells me as she starts to leave through the back door. I glare at her as she laughs at me, groaning as I briefly check the front. I'm about to stay in the back when I see a hoard of customers come in. Well, crud.

I head out into the fray of the coffee shop. The cafe is on the corner of a building, with windows covering the front and side walls.

There's a bar along one of them, while the other has square tables lined up against the other. The café's pick-up station is near the threshold to the back kitchen area. Where we make drinks takes up most of the back wall, whilst the food and pastries sit on the opposite side of the pickup station next to the wall dedicated to the coffee beans we sell. The door, smack dab in the front, opens as a couple of well-dressed people walk in.

Showtime.

I stay out front with Bailey, before everything calms down again, and I head back to the kitchen to restock and organize. I'm close to blissful as I get into the rhythm.

"Autumn!" Until now.

I finish up the dishes, going out to Bailey, who's standing in front of the espresso machine looking frustrated with her manicured hands on her hips. It's late afternoon, so only a few people are in the shop. The place is mostly filled with regulars on their laptops or chattering college students.

Bailey's nose scrunches at the machine like she's never seen one before. "Something is wrong with it," she says, pointing at a group head on the machine.

I move the metal demitasse cups and hold back a groan. "Baily, you need to replace the grounds for every drink. All of this is burnt." Cause Wall Street guys *totally* love it when that happens.

"Well, I didn't want to waste time grinding beans. It takes *forever.*"

"How many shots have you made with just this?"

"A few," she shrugs, not meeting my eyes. I picked the wrong movie to watch tonight.

I pull out the portafilter of the espresso machine and try to keep from rolling my eyes. Nan would even be able to notice the difference between this espresso, and she only drinks drip coffee. "How many orders do you have with espresso?"

"One for the gentleman over there." She waves her fingers at the man in the white button-up and tan slacks. He doesn't even look up from his phone.

"I'll get some shots ready for you, but you finish the rest. I still have a few things to clean up in the back." I dump the grounds and quickly grind some fresh beans for her, then attempt to go to the kitchen again. She whines about needing help with another thing and I find myself making most of the drinks behind the counter.

I'd rather make it right the first time than fix everything she makes. Gotta keep us from getting yelled at for it tasting like shit. Honestly, wouldn't blame them. I do what I almost always do when it comes to working with Bailey: doing most of the work myself.

At this point, I don't mind, rather than listening to her whine. And I like making drinks. Plus, sometimes her 'cutesy' behavior gets us good tips. Sometimes. Take a win when you can.

A woman in a jean vest retrieves her drink from the pick-up station. I smile at her as she flicks her gaze to Bailey, who is unabashedly flirting with another customer. She leans a bit over the counter, pushing up her breasts as she speaks with the taller gentleman next to another woman. Jeez, that girl really needs to get laid.

"That was an Americano and non-fat sugar-free vanilla latte, both mediums?" Bailey asks as I head back to the grinder.

"Yes, and don't make the coffee too hot," the woman replies.

I keep back my snort, but my grin doesn't falter as I keep my back to them.

"Coffee is supposed to be hot, Juanita." A deep voice responds with a smooth undertone that makes my skin tingle. The man should read audiobooks.

The drinks are already being made by my hands as I hear the woman, Juanita, mumble something as her heels click on the tile.

"We can bring the drinks out to you if you want to sit down. Unless you want to...*linger* here a bit longer." Bailey's voice practically drips like honey.

My grin gets bigger as I try to concentrate. Haven't even seen the guy and I can already bet he's at least a decade older than her from his voice alone. It sounds like he walks away, and Bailey sighs. Maybe she has some unresolved...? Okay, not going down *that* road, but it would explain *a lot*. I chuckle low as I turn around, almost bumping into Bailey.

"I'll finish," she blurts, snatching the Americano from my hand.

I hold my hands up in surrender, and another chuckle escapes as I head for the kitchen. I pull on my apron for doing dishes, tying it as I glimpse at Bailey. She's scrambling to collect the two drinks as she adjusts herself to deliver them to the man at the pickup station, whose back is turned. I'm about to let her have this fantasy with the customer when I see the crumpled carpet right where she's headed.

Shit. Not good.

I rush forward to intercept Bailey before her foot catches the fold in the rug. Her eyes flare at me, but she trips over the rug just as I jump in the way of the splash zone. My body takes the brunt of the falling liquid, standing between the drinks and the man. Down my front goes the Americano and the non-fat, sugar-free vanilla latte. Heat hits my skin as the coffee spills onto me. Bailey's mouth gapes as I hear others in the shop gasp at the sight of the barista covered in coffee and non-fat milk. I look down at the mess all over me, noticing the man's shoes directly behind me "embellished" with foam on them. The smell of vanilla and fresh Ethiopian grounds drift into my nose and I start to laugh under my breath. My hand covers my mouth as I laugh at the ridiculous predicament. My giggles only worsen as Bailey's eyes widen in shock.

Not sure why I find it funny, but I do. That and screaming sure ain't gonna change the fact I'm covered in coffee from a customer who didn't want it "too hot." Guess I should thank her later.

I attempt to suppress my laughter as I turn to check on the gentleman behind me. I'm met with a tall man, probably in his early thirties with upswept dark hair and golden undertone skin. As I raise my gaze, I find deep hazel eyes now filled with confusion, brows furrowing together in concern. I notice his squarish jaw and the shadow of a beard on his face, and then finally that he's wearing a suit with a black button-up and no tie. My eyes flash down to his chest where his shirt could've been delightfully paired with an Americano and vanilla latte.

Too bad, his loss.

A grin breaks out at the thought, and I swear he almost stumbles back from me.

Yup, I'm officially the neurotic barista. Eh, been called worse.

"Are you alright?" He asks.

I look down at my soaked apron, then with a finger, swipe some foam off my chest and bring it to my mouth. I lick it off, trying the leftover bit of coffee with a grin still on my face. "Not bad, but better in a cup."

His brows remain furrowed together, staring at me with bewilderment and shock. Huh, he's kind of adorable looking like that. Although I doubt *anyone* would describe him as such to his face. Handsome, maybe striking—

"Sir, I'm so sorry! Are you okay? Are you hurt?" Bailey asks a million questions as she grabs a towel to start cleaning up the pick-up station which is still pretty clean.

"Oh my god, Mr. Luciano are you alright?" Juanita walks over, fawning over the man. Her long brown hair, slightly curled sweeps over her shoulders, matching her flawless copper skin. The silk blue blouse, pencil skirt, and tall heels tell me enough to back away from the man. Either he's her boss or boyfriend, and I ain't getting in the middle of that.

He brushes her off, giving her a stern look. "I'm fine, Juanita."

"There's coffee all over your shoes!" She screeches. "They're practically ruined…those are Italian leather!" She yells at, I'm guessing, me the barista covered in her coffee. "Do you know how much—"

"Enough," he warns.

"But, sir, they—"

"*Enough.*" The tone of his voice deepens, changing suddenly as she quiets.

I ignore them, picking up the cups and snatching the towel from Bailey, who looks stunned. I plaster on a pleasant smile, my laughter now long gone. Not my first rodeo. Mr. Luciano, as I now know him, has his eyes on me. I see another wave of surprise flit over his harsh expression as I speak.

"I apologize for the inconvenience; I'll make you new drinks right away. So sorry for the trouble." I turn around, not waiting for a response.

"There's no—"

I wave him off flippantly, going about doing my job and pointing for Bailey to head to the back. She seems to be on the verge of sobbing, and I wave her off as she cries like *she* just became latte foam art.

Hugs are probably off the table.

Juanita still talks and complains while I promptly make their drinks and deliver them. The woman takes them both, the man already near the seating area on his phone. I glance over at him, finding his gaze solely on me, before I turn away to clean up the rest of the mess. At some point, I grab Bailey and get her to concentrate enough to take care of the front while I change. I go into the back, shuffling through Mabel's cubby, and pull out one of her extra shirts as I take off my tank top.

I text her that I'm borrowing it and will bring it back tomorrow. She texts back, asking if I'm alright and if I have any burns. Well, someone cares. I tell her I'm fine and go back out to the shop. The man is gone along with the woman. *Blue Java* is back to its usual. More tips are in the jar, too.

Bailey doesn't apologize once or ask if I'm okay. Not at all surprising, and I don't care. She does make a few scenes throughout the afternoon over the espresso machine, and an hour before closing I've had enough. I send her home early, leaving myself alone to close and I lock up the shop.

I lean against the door and let out a long exhale. "Was that the start of my villain origin story? Get coffee spilled on me, laugh like I'm Harley Quinn before they drag my ass to Arkham?" I shrug to myself and start mopping. "After everything else that's happened, may be my best way out in life. Maybe I'll get hyenas."

If there's one thing I've learned in the last three years: laugh when you can, because you never know when you can't; smile even during insane moments; give people compassion, even if others may not give it. I'd seen enough destruction and hate, all I wanted to do now was see the brighter things in life.

I turn on some 80s music, Bonnie Tyler's voice blasting as I finish clean-up duties and dance away today's frustrations after I've pulled the shades down. By the end, I find myself thinking about those hazel eyes.

I'll probably never see him again. Who'd come back after a disaster like that?

Chapter 2

Not Yet Your Usual

"Okay, for once, I don't smell like this due to being clumsy." Nan blinks quickly as I enter through the backdoor of the building, near her apartment entrance, and lock it behind me. "*But…I did find out that catching coffee is a difficult thing to do. With bare hands.*"

Her face scrunches as I drop my bag, sitting on the steps that lead up to my own apartment. I pull out my tank top, showing the stains, and point to my jeans. She takes the top from my hands and smiles as she looks over my pants, which I've been wearing all day. They've got stains on them from years ago, it'll add more character. The wetness has been annoying me all day though, pretty sure I started chaffing.

The warm lamplight above her apartment door shows the wrinkles around her eyes and makes her snow-white curls glow. She's a bit shorter than me and has the curves of an older woman who's lived her life to the fullest, not caring what people told her what to eat or do. Then again, her late husband always made sure she did exactly that. Break the rules and fuck society and all that jazz.

"What happened?" She asks with amusement in her tone.

"Bailey almost dropped two drinks on a Wall Street guy, so I jumped in before I'd get a splitting headache from being yelled at for ruining his Italian suit."

"How do you know it was Italian?" She pats my head before I stand.

"Woman he was with mentioned Italian leather shoes, and they usually come in matching sets…right?" Nan starts to laugh a bit harder. "I'm only guessing, but come on, isn't there some dumb rule about brown belts and shoes or whatever? Something tells me if the shoes are Italian, the rest has to be."

She shakes her head at me, kissing my cheek. "Perhaps, dear."

"Night, Nan."

"Get some rest, and I'll have this washed in no time."

I walk up the stairs to my apartment and enter the mess that I left earlier today, the small living space filled with books and movies. It's mostly clean, given its size. I didn't have much, never did. My living room is to the left, while the kitchen is to the right with a short hallway to my bathroom and bedroom. I head into my bedroom tugging off my clothes and folding up Mabel's shirt neatly for tomorrow. A quick well-deserved shower is taken once I peel off my jeans. Pulling on baggy shorts and an ACDC t-shirt, I go heat up some pizza and grab the movie I'd picked to watch tonight. I debate putting in something else like *Friday the 13th* or even *Heathers* but decide to stick with my morning choice. Settling into the small couch, I click play and munch on my dinner.

Kiera Knightley walks through the early morning light on screen, perusing through a book as *Dawn* plays in the background. The music lulls me. I slump back with a sigh and my mind drifts. My thoughts flit back once again to those hazel eyes. There were small lines above them and crevices like he was in deep thought. My mind still wanders as Mr. Darcy appears on screen, commenting on Elizabeth's appearance.

"Barely tolerable," I murmur around some pizza. After today, I'm pretty sure that man thinks the very same about me.

He came back.

My head cocks to the side, watching through the doorway as he stands on the other side of the counter. Thankfully, he's alone and ordering from Mabel. No chances of getting into the splash zone. He nods, keeping a very stern expression, almost cold, as Mabel turns around to get his order. I glance at the clock, noticing he's here the same time he was yesterday. Maybe I accidentally made him into a regular in hopes of more comedic showings.

Honestly, I'd understand that.

I stay in the back as he collects his drink, checks his watch, and then walks out the door. Expression never changing. I move to the front, watching him through the windows as he disappears down the sidewalk. Curious.

"What's with that face?" Mabel comments.

"That was the guy I…well, saved from the coffee-tastrophe."

"Really?" She looks in the direction he disappeared. "He was nice, grumpy looking, but nice. Even knew what coffee beans he wanted."

"Well, it *was* his female counterpart who gave the crocodile tears about his shoes. And pants. Pretty sure all of it was fine, at least he seemed to think so." I knew nothing of fashion or how it worked, it was two years ago I learned suede shouldn't get water on it. Why was it popular as a jacket if it's just gonna shrink?

"Long as he didn't come back all snotty or some shit," Mabel murmurs as she cleans up some coffee grounds. "He even tipped with a twenty. Maybe he was hoping for an encore."

I glance at the tip jar and snort. "Well, that'll be extra and if you dump iced coffee on me, I do the macarena."

"Oh, if he comes back, I'll let him know. Probably makes the big bucks, he can be your benefactor."

"Every dude in a suit who comes in makes big bucks," I chuckle, but keep my voice down from other patrons hearing.

"Yet, none of them spend nearly enough on us." Mabel grins, making an over-the-top dramatic gesture to cup her face in grief. "I should see what happens if I throw an iced coffee on you instead."

"Then I do the Cupid Shuffle," I say deadpan.

Mabel laughs, shaking her head which makes her blue beaded bangles chime with a wonderful sound. The bright blue compliments her orange outfit for the summer. Wonderful against her skin, while I'd look like something Gondor would use to call for aid. Dark hues were my friend, along with band t-shirts I've found in thrift shops. Such as the black *Pink Floyd* shirt I'm wearing today.

"Hey, can you switch shifts with me next week, by the way?" Mabel asks sometime later as I come back to refill the espresso.

"Can't. I won't be on my regular schedule starting in two days for like a month."

Her eyes widen. "If you're leaving me alone with Bailey, I swear—"

"I'll be back," I laugh. "I'll just be opening instead of closing, but I'll be gone before that for like four days." She stares at me. and I stop.

"*You're* opening?"

"Hey, I can do early mornings."

"Uh-huh."

"Yuki asked, and I wanted the afternoons to help Nan. She's gonna be out of town seeing her grand-nephew." Mabel makes a sweet face at the mention of Nan's best little guy. "I'll share the pictures she sends, don't worry."

"You better. Leaving me alone with Bailey for like a month? I should put holes in your shoes." I blink at her. "I'll think of a better revenge comeback later." She heads to the backroom and returns with some pastries to replenish our case.

"I believe in you." She narrows her eyes at me before I pull out a small bottle of lotion from my cargo pocket. "Make her work in the back or something."

She takes the same lotion, puts some on her hands and forearms, then tosses it back. "Oh, and deal with burnt pastries from the *microwave*? Come on, Autumn, that girl doesn't even know how to boil water."

I put lotion on my hands and glance over my shoulder at her.

"That's when the water bubbles, right?" She laughs, flinging a towel at me and I giggle. "Okay, fine, then just help her date the next guy she makes googly eyes at and maybe she'll quit." Mabel's expression doesn't look impressed. "To live her lifelong dream of being a Finsta-influencer since it's all the rage."

"You're terrible," she giggles.

"Am I wrong?" I raise my hands innocently as I go to the kitchen, and she pauses. She sighs and nods. See, I'm not the only one Bailey has spent copious amounts of time explaining her big life plan to.

The rest of the day goes smoothly. I have Mabel leave early, so she can check in with her mother in hospice. She moved there about two months ago, and I've been handling most closings by myself so Mabel can spend time with her. She calls out her thanks, the shirt I borrowed yesterday in her hands, as I take care of the last of the customers for the evening.

Fifteen minutes before closing, dumping out grounds, I hear the doorway open. Oh, come on! I groan inwardly push down a grumble and paste on a smile for, hopefully, the last customer of the night. I turn and freeze when I see him.

He's wearing the same black suit from earlier this afternoon, almost as dark as his hair. His gaze watches me carefully as he adjusts his jacket casually, and I can practically see his arms flex under the jacket. It's only a moment before I notice, now, how broad his shoulders are. It feels like his entire presence sucks the air out of the place as he approaches the counter slowly.

I come to the register, my smile turning more genuine, "First time wasn't enough?"

Confusion flits over his face, and he glances around the empty shop. "For what?"

"Well, either the drink you got today was *soo* good you needed more or…" I purse my lips, and he raises a brow, "…you need a pick-me-up before returning to Gotham to stop a canary with a machine gun."

"A canary?"

"Six ounces and dangerous. Blame the Riddler not me." Smooth, Autumn. Not. His brows furrow. "You know from *Batman?*"

"Batman?"

Please tell me he knows who Batman is. "Yeah, as in 'holy cabooses Batman!'"

"I know who he is."

We stare at each other a moment, and I clear my throat when he remains silent.

"Just checking," I say with a shrug, unperturbed by his uncertain, rigid expression. "If you want, I could just spill coffee on you; show you what you missed out on."

Once I mention the fiasco from yesterday, something in his eyes shifts. He doesn't smile, brows still furrowed, but his gaze softens. Ah, found a tender spot.

"Are you alright from that?"

I wave the question off logging into the register "Don't worry. Had worse things happen in my life than having coffee spilled on me."

"Such as?" His head cocks to the side, coming closer to the counter.

"Like the kind of stuff I shouldn't tell a customer." The shine in his gaze fades, going back to assessing me. He finally reaches the register, but keeps his distance, not leaning in. His hands go into his pockets, watching me with interest. "Americano?"

There's a quick flick of his eyes to the register, to the espresso machine, then back to me. "You remembered."

"Hard not to. Practically imprinted on my skin," I tease, but his face darkens as the last of the softness in his eyes disappears. "Joking by the way."

"I'm conflicted on whether to thank you or tell you never to do that again. To not place yourself in harm like that in the future."

I scoff. "Only harm I was in was being within the wrath radius of your date."

I ring up the Americano and start making his drink. "She's just an associate."

"Is that what the kids call it nowadays?"

"I wouldn't know. Never keep up with the modern new terms," he replies coolly. I glimpse back as he dips his head. "However, she's not my girlfriend."

"Dodged a bullet," I murmur, but I think I hear him snort. Ignoring him, I continue to work on his drink.

"What is your name?" He asks after the silence stretches for like ten seconds.

I pause, unsure about replying, but realize there's no point in not telling him. Apprehension ticks at the back of my neck, warning me of the potential dangers, but I ignore it. Not the same. He's just a customer. Besides, if he became a regular and I gave a fake name… yup, don't want to have that hypothetical conversation.

"Autumn."

"Autumn," he repeats quietly. Finishing his drink, I stop at the register. "Like the season?"

"Uh-huh, and my favorite time of the year, too."

"Won't have to wait much longer, should be thrilled about that." Although he's making small talk, his tone sounds very aloof and serious. Like he's in a business meeting or I'm interviewing *him*.

I place the Americano down between us. He looks down at the coffee and then back at me with surprise flicking over his expression. I smile at his realization that I've finished his drink already. A smirk *almost* comes over his, while my own smile grows seeing a bit of whatever mask he wears withers away. Definitely a business guy who doesn't know how to quit, even at 9 pm.

"Five dollars, mister…" he pauses pulling out his wallet, eyes meeting mine and I clear my throat, "…what's your last name again?"

"Luciano."

My brows pull together, hearing a hint of an accent in his voice and the 'ch' sound of where the 'C' is in his name. I repeat it out loud, "Luciano."

His eyes soften again. "Correct."

"So…Mr. Luciano—"

"Leonardo."

"What?"

"Only those I work with call me Mr. Luciano."

"Your full name is Leonardo Luciano?" My gaze catches his as he pauses, nodding stiffly with the cash in his hand. It feels like time drags on for the next half minute as I wait for him to say something more or give me the cash. But he remains in place like I've caught him in the act of doing wrong. Do people call him a Ninja turtle or whatever?

I break the silence, shrugging. "Nice ring to it."

He visibly relaxes, holding out a fifty-dollar bill. I start bemoaning inside, wanting to ask for anything smaller. "That's the tip," he says. "This is for the coffee." He pulls out five dollars, placing it on the counter.

"You don't need—"

"It's the least I can do after you took the…*hit* from the latte and Americano. Perhaps, help with dry cleaning." I snort loudly. His brows furrow together. "I am trying to be considerate here after what happened, not trying to minimize your predicament—"

"Oh, shit that's not why I snorted!" I wave my hands in front of me. Giggles erupt from my throat. "You brought up dry-cleaning and I've never owned anything that needed it. Those clothes have already been thrown into the washer. And my jeans have stains on them from years ago."

"Ah."

"It's one of, well, many reasons why I jumped in the way. My stuff can be replaced by going to a second-hand shop, whereas yours would be ruined. And make a gaggle of women cry, I'm sure," I explain, but the pinching of his brows deepens. "Look, I deal with a lot of assholes throughout the day, and it's just easier to take the hit. I'm not gonna cry over my shoes having stains on them or my jeans. Never been a worry. By the way, not calling *you* an asshole…just, others."

Leonardo's face suddenly warms, his brows ease and the face I'm left with is filled with compassion. "You shouldn't feel the need to ruin your own clothes. To take the brunt of such anger, accidents happen. And it's just coffee."

"I'm gonna tell you a secret," I say, leaning on the counter, and wiggling a finger for him to come closer. He flicks his gaze down at my hand, but he slightly bends down. "Comes with the job. Most who walk in here don't see us as people, just those they can yell at or put their worries or rage on. It's in the fine print for customer service."

"You should have someone checking your contract."

"Ah, well maybe next time I won't when I sign the dotted line." I smile, standing fully and trying to be cheery.

He doesn't seem convinced because he holds out the fifty to me again. "Please take it from a customer who does not see you as a person to…place my rage on."

My thoughts slow as I stare at him. I'll admit I've had some good customers come through, even Wall Street guys and politicians here and there. Most were regulars, getting to know us over *months* coming in. They talked to us like we were human and not someone who was placed on this earth to screw up their frothy drink.

None of them have ever offered to pay for dry cleaning.

My chest warms a little as I carefully take the fifty from his hand. I don't touch his skin, placing it in my pocket then take the five for the coffee. He takes the cup to sip and makes a content, humming sound. He begins to leave but pauses at the door. "You work here full time?"

"Yup, but not always trying to catch coffee with my bare hands. Other days I use a net. That's your tip for the night, Leonardo. Get yourself a butterfly net."

"I'll keep that in mind," he muses. "But call me Leo or I may be forced to trip another barista for attention."

"Do I get to choose the barista?" The shine is back in his eyes again. "Have a good night…Leo."

He nods once, leaves the shop, and walks down the sidewalk. The coffee stays in his hand, even as I wait for him to drop it in the trash. He doesn't, sipping from it again. Huh, he actually wanted coffee.

The warmth in my chest spreads further, moving down as I lock the door and pull the shades down. Butterflies come alive in me, but I quickly squash them when I realize what's happening. No. Not gonna happen. There's no use getting those kinds of hopes up. Just a kind customer who I confused with a very niche Batman joke. That's all.

I swallow hard, rubbing my hands together harshly as I recall that softer expression of his. I shake off the fluttering emotions, no matter how good they feel. Even while concentrating on my tasks the fifty dollars in my pocket weighs heavy in my pocket.

Chapter 3

Punctual Sessions

The new cookbooks are stacked with the rest before I move down the aisle toward the history section. I shelve the next set of books as the quiet afternoon drags on. It's mid-day and like most weekdays before the rush of people getting off work, the foot traffic is pretty slow. It's always slow, but having the bookstore all to myself, I can't help but feel grateful.

Nan's been gone for two days already, and in another two days I'll be opening *Blue Java Café* at 5am…for almost three weeks. Not the greatest thing in the world, I'm usually a night owl. I like mornings, but waking up that early to make coffee for those who *do* hate mornings? Not on my favorite things to-do list.

My phone dings, and I open a message as I approach the front. A smile forms on my face as I see a picture of Nan's grandnephew, Jeremy. He's still toothless, but cute. I send the picture to Mabel and other friends. My best friend, Leanne, texts back gushing over how cute he is. And that she'll see me after my session, wishing me good luck as always. I glance at the clock, shrugging as I go to lock up the shop a little early. It's empty anyways.

Besides, without working at the coffee shop, even for two days, the bookstore can't keep me busy enough. The tactile work helps, but

I need more to keep my thoughts under control during the slow hours.

I leave the store, heading toward downtown with the brilliant sun shining above. The warmth spreads over me as I smile, running my hand through my short hair. It's been a shaggy pixie cut with a reddish brown color for almost three years now. Passing some shiny buildings, I glance at my reflection to see the jean jacket I wear covers most of my lightly tanned skin and smallish figure, not to mention the faint few scars on my arms. I'd be considered average, not much in the boob department and not fit, just some muscle from wrangling the espresso machine on busy days. Still pretty healthy, running around a coffee shop does that, and I'm pretty sure I drink enough water.

Maybe.

I make it to my therapists' office at the *Luna Stella Women's Center* with twenty minutes to spare. Skipping steps, I get up to my floor and open the door to the reception area. There's a counter, which is mostly bare except for the sign-in sheet, and a few doors lining the back wall, along with a small hall to other offices to the right. Just as I go to scrawl onto the paper to sign in, one of my best friends, walks out of her office.

Patricia Fuller's, Trix, face lights up when she sees me, sparkling copper eyes catching mine as I lean on the counter. Her short dark afro matches the deepness of her skin, accentuated by the mint green dress she's wearing today which hugs her lean frame.

"You're early," she says with a smile.

"Maybe I wanted to talk to you," I retort.

"Uh-huh," she snorts, putting paperwork into some folders at the desk behind the counter. "Thought you were working on the time anxiety thing?"

"Hey, nothing wrong being punctual."

"You once arrived at an event an hour early."

"Bet you won't complain when I'm able to snag us a table at a busy restaurant or getting the good spot in a bar." I lean on the counter on my elbows, smiling playfully.

"You don't go to bars."

"I could though."

"You could, but you don't. Not really." She laughs, folding her arms as she tilts her head at me. A bright smile breaks out and she comes around to give me a quick hug. "How's your week been?"

"Slowish. Covering the bookstore for Nan, so no coffee shop schedule for like…four days. Two more to go."

"Already not liking it?"

"We may have determined I'm not a workaholic, but I may be turning into one. Is there a group for that?"

"They convene the same time as shopaholics," she teases, walking back behind the counter. "But you can talk to Dr. Wilson about that." She pauses, checking the computer and looks up at me with a soft expression. "Coming up on your anniversary with her, by the way."

I let out a long exhale and nod slightly. "Sneaks up on you, huh?"

"Well, you were just busy living life again. That's a good thing."

"I know, Trix."

My entire life was turned upside down, and then around, and then again three years ago. For the better, even if it took time before I believed it. After the worst moments of my life passed, I started therapy a few months after, moved in with Nan, and started the barista job. Before most of that, I found Trix, well, she found me, technically, in that hospital room. I'll be forever grateful it was her who was assigned as my original case worker. Over that first year of recovery, Leanne, Trix, and I started hanging out and becoming a trio of best buds.

Trix knew every horrid detail of what happened to me *that* night, stood in the aftermath of it as part of her job. I was reassigned someone else a month later. Leanne and Dr. Wilson knew only what I was willing to give. Nan barely knew, and I hope she never would find out.

Well, that and I hoped to never face it on my own again. To have those memories expunged from my mind. Except, there's no way to do that. Apart from a lobotomy, but they're frowned upon these days. Not worth having something plunged into my skull anyways.

"Autumn?" Trix's voice trickles into my thoughts. I shake my head. "You good?"

"Yeah. Just thinking about…I guess, progress."

"You should be proud of yourself. How far you've come." She reaches for my hand on the counter, squeezing it. "Even on the bad days."

"I am proud. Really."

"Good." She lets go and starts heading to her office door. "Still on for dinner after?"

I start to say yes, when Dr. Wilson's door opens. Trix gives me a hopeful wink as I nod instead, then stick my tongue out at her playfully. She giggles as I grin and head into the doctor's office.

The room is painted a light green, trimmed with cream with a small desk and chair in the far-left corner. Her usual armchair and sofa are on the right with a bookcase filled with self-help books. The coffee table between the seat has water, magazines, pens, and notepads to "write down your feelings" if needed. Lastly, her tall plant still looks like it needs water.

I take my place on the sofa across from Dr. Celine Wilson, who has light curly brown hair, pulled into a messy bun, and porcelain white skin with barely a freckle. She's wearing her usual thick rimmed glasses, blue pale blouse, and skirt. She sits with notepad in hand. I take my jacket off, settling in as we do our usual check in for the session. It's the same every time. Check in and see what new issues have arisen from nightmares of being chained to a wall or discuss about the asshole who yelled about his cappuccino.

The nightmare was more pleasant.

We started with sessions three days apart, then to five, then to a week, and now I see her about every two to three weeks. I start off like clockwork about any meltdown's, triggers, or nightmares. Thankfully, not much in those departments lately. Unfortunately, assholes about coffee don't come in short supply.

"Well," she says, putting her notepad down in her lap. "If nothing else there, has anything exciting come up?" I stifle a laugh, and she looks at me peculiar, I pause, then explain about the coffee incident. "You're, okay?" She asks.

"Oh, yeah. Coffee wasn't that hot. I've had worse tossed on me like puke, frying oil, and blood. This was nothing. Smelled a whole lot better, too."

She chuckles, causing her blue eyes to crinkle at the corner. "I'm glad you got a smile out of it. Or, at least, saw the positive side of things."

"Yeah, and who I saved from the spillage was nice about it. Better than most."

"Who did it almost happen to?"

I purse my lips and shrug. "He's just a...um, new customer." Don't pry further. Don't pry further.

"He? A newcomer you said?"

Shit. Come on. "Well...no, not really, well yeah...it was actually the...haven't seen him before that day. So, probably new."

"Yet you jumped in front of him."

"Not exactly the most heroic thing ever. Part of the job. Protect customers from clumsy baristas. Who knows how many times Mabel or Yuki made sure I didn't make a fool of myself while working. It's nothing. Just another funny work story," I say quickly.

She assesses me a moment. "Did you learn his name?"

"Does it matter?"

"It matters because although the substance didn't hurt you, it could've. We both know how dangerous hot liquids can be." Where is she going with this? "And it's the act itself that was very unselfish. You don't normally put yourself out there for strangers, beyond that counter, especially over the past two years. You've kept your distance, mainly from men, and yet this time you didn't."

"Because I didn't want to deal with the aftermath if *he'd* gotten the coffee all over him. Easier to avoid confrontation. Isn't that part of the trauma responses I have? Avoiding confrontation? Take the easy route, *away* from potential danger?"

"But you didn't." My brows pinch together. "You put yourself *in* danger this time. And you mentioned a woman who yelled at you, so you had to deal with some confrontation. Even though it wasn't him who stomped his feet, you had to face a difficult situation. You could've left it all to Bailey to take care of. Let her take…well, the fall."

"That'd be a dick move." Even if she rubs me the wrong way, not gonna be that malicious.

"It wasn't your job to protect the customer or to take the blame for what happened with her tripping."

"Yeah, but—"

"You can't keep taking the brunt of everything for everyone, Autumn." She stops me, and I frown. "No matter how much you think you deserve it, you don't. You don't deserve to be looked at or feel as if you're—"

"I'm broken? Insane? Poor? Not good enough?" I interrupt, and her face falls as she shakes her head. "I know I'm not most of that. Or to feel ashamed with my situation, I get that. Really…I do. These last couple of years, I'm not embarrassed for where I am, but…but the world isn't going to think like that. People will make their own snap judgements, and I'm fine with that because I don't have this need to please them. I've worked too hard to feel free again to give that up."

"Autumn, I'm not—"

"And most of the time, I don't know what customer I'll get. So, I judge them, too, once I see them, make that decision, cause they'll do the same with me."

I take a deep breath, rubbing my face a little as she watches me quietly. "I didn't stop him from being dipped into latte foam art because I thought I deserved it. I was just trying to be helpful and not have to deal with a bigger mess than it would become. The guy was very kind afterwards, even offered to pay for dry cleaning."

For a moment, I realize he also commented about me taking the brunt of issues or misuse. Maybe I'd met her sibling or something.

"Alright." She settles, putting her notepad to the side. "I'm just checking in because you have done this in the past; slipped back into old habits. Dangerous ones. I want to make sure we're not dipping back into those again and lose progress."

"No worries." I wave it off, leaning into the couch.

Quiet comes between us, and she smiles faintly. Yeah, not at *all* suspicious. "Was he handsome?"

I snort out a laugh. My heartbeat quickens, remembering his deep hazel gaze, dark hair and strong jaw. Confusion on that strict face about my niche joke attempt. The way he watched me, trying to figure me out with that furrowed brow of his as I tried to reject the money. I still haven't spent it yet. It may have not been much to him, but it was to me. To feel seen again, even if for only a moment.

I shake off the feelings, forcing a smile. "He was okay looking."

"Autumn."

"I'm not ready yet."

"I won't push," she sighs. "There's no definitive amount of time it takes before ever feeling that again. Don't dismiss what could be a chance or even some small talk. Maybe not him, but with someone else? Perhaps, getting out there again, nothing serious, just talking to people. Creating more friends and relationships."

"I talk to Trix and Leanne."

"More than just them."

"Nan, Mabel…"

"Not who I'm talking about, and you know that." I huff and nod my head in compliance. "It'll be scary, but maybe you should try opening your social circle more. Being open to the possibility of a relationship again."

"What if I don't want one?" I ask suddenly, regretting saying it already. Full on lie. She knows it's a lie, too.

We leave it mostly there and the session soon ends. No more prodding, but she suggests once more that I try talking to others, going out with my friends more. Try another friend group. I get that she thinks I'm scared of being out in public or being social, I wasn't… not really. It's the thought of being out *there* again. I didn't want it. At all.

Life has pushed me down and I wanted to stay in my little corner of the world. Comfortable.

Then again, maybe that's what she was pushing for. Me not

staying in "comfortable, safe, squishy land" forever. We both know why I don't want to leave it. An unspoken truth that hangs like a painting behind me.

I walk out, seeing Trix waiting at the doorway. She catches a glimpse of my gaze and plasters a smile on her face. Fucking bless her, and knowing my little tells. She waves to Dr. Wilson as her next patient walks in. Trix doesn't ask how it went until we reach the first floor.

"Fine," I answer. "Other than, I think I may have a savior complex. Or could just be masochism."

"Oh, could've told you that," she teases, and I shove her lightly. She squeezes my arm gently. "Well, I may not be a doctor or therapist, but I've been a social worker and have known you long enough. Autumn, I understand you outside that room more than she does. What I do know is that you'd rather see people smile than cry or be hurt. You always make sure others know they're wanted unless you don't truly want them around."

I shrug as we walk out onto the street, heading toward our usual Mediterranean restaurant to meet up with Leanne. "Bet you'd change your mind if you knew how many times I've thought about wringing some of my co-workers necks."

Trix laughs brightly. "We all want to shove a co-worker off a rooftop at some point, comes with the territory." I laugh with her.

We're about half a block away when I catch sight of Leanne. She stands outside the entrance and turns to give us a gigantic smile. Her hair is in tight twists, she's been growing her hair out which almost reaches her shoulders without a relaxer. Her brown eyes still dazzle me every time with their kindness, ever since we met in college all those years ago. She's the real MVP in my life, apart from Nan, the only one who stayed through *everything*. She's taller than me, folding me into her chest as I fall against her like she hasn't seen me in years.

It's been five days.

"Ohhh, I missed you!" She exclaims.

I giggle against her. "It's been less than a week."

"An eternity!" She pulls back, smiling at me and kisses my cheek.

I do it back, hooking my arm through hers. Her dark skin contrasts with mine, more so when winter comes when I'll get paler.

We head inside, getting our regular table quickly and settling in for dinner and drinks. We catch up on some things as they talk about office stuff. Trix is an advocate and social worker who helps people through domestic violence situations, while also heading programs outside of the *Luna Stella Women's Center*. Leanne's a program coordinator for public-school systems. They both love their work, but I'd go insane if I had to wear business casual stuff every day. Leanne at least has the legs for a pencil skirt. I do not.

Leanne and I met at Stony Brook University, freshman year. She's my longest time friend, who stayed in New York with me, and we lived together for a short time before I moved out to live with my ex. The biggest mistake that trickled into tragedy.

I'm pulled out of my thoughts as Leanne brings up the girl that Trix has been seeing on and off the past few months.

"You should make it official," Leanne comments, looking at Trix knowingly.

"It's just…a…well, a…." Trix tries to defend herself.

"Please don't say crush," I mumble over my glass of water.

"Does anyone hear muses singing? Statues dancing and talking about getting on your case, cause she won't say it?" Leanne looks around dramatically. I lean back and laugh, while Trix scowls at us.

"You know what? How about you? How's the romance thing going, Leanne?"

"Nowhere, duh," Leanne snorts, and I chuckle. Yeah, that wouldn't have gotten her.

She loves her job, has for years. Everyone that's tried to get with her haven't yet survived the hassle of her job being first and the strict schedule she follows. Dedicated and being great at her job, made it hard for dating.

She has a valid excuse for not regularly dating or trying new relationships. Too bad I can't copy off her for Dr. Wilson. Lucky.

Leanne turns to me, grabbing her amber beer. "What about you, hun? See anyone at the coffee shop who grabbed your attention because they asked for a simple coffee instead of an elaborate drink."

"Those *elaborate* drinks can be fun to make."

Trix snorts. "Until you have to make a cappa, cappa, half-non-fat latte with caramel syrups and milk from that *one* cow in Massachusetts."

"Massachusetts?" I ask.

"Fine, Pennsylvania."

I hold onto the table, laughing hard. "We're not that kind of shop."

Leanne joins in and says, "Sometimes I've walked into one of those vegan or 'craft' cafes, and their drink menus scared me."

"Was it the grass shots?" Trix asks.

"Probably the non-alcoholic drinks that *definitely* should have alcohol in them. How else you gonna make dirt taste like spicey chocolate?" I say.

Trix points at me with an over-the-top expression. "I think I've had that!"

We laugh, letting the conversation steer away from dating. I think briefly about answering, but do I want to tell them about Leo? Was there any point? My schedule changes in two days for a while, even if he did come back, we won't be there at the same time. Even if he was attempting to flirt, which I doubt it, he'll more likely give up. Or won't come back at all. Or do what the rest do and date Bailey.

Sure hope he's smarter than that.

I finally decide it's not worth mentioning him, continuing my friend date and letting thoughts of Leonardo Luciano...Leo drift away.

Chapter 4

Strangers Through the Night

Screw this waking up early for work shit. A week has gone by, and I already regret my life decisions. Totally wishing to go back to evening like a bat into its cave.

My second alarm goes off as I groan, sitting up to smack it to shut up. Grumbling, I get up and know I'm gonna tell Yuki I'm never doing this again. She can make Bailey or Daniella or Phoebe or whoever do this early morning rise thing. I pull on a shirt, jeans, and sneakers, quickly eating some cereal before I head downstairs. I slip out through the back, heading toward the subway as the "city that never sleeps" keeps its nickname intact.

One pro of being up so early, there are options for seats on the subway. Once seated, I skim parts of my romance book, another novel of an English Lady and Scottish Laird, this one planning to take her away from London socialites. Degree in English or not, I don't regularly read Austen, Emerson, or whoever in my off time.

I have more refined taste.

More people stream into the subway just as I'm leaving. The sun shines through the city buildings, casting morning shadows as I walk toward the café. Sunlight begins to glare, reflecting from glass buildings across the street. I slip through the backdoor, opening up and getting everything ready for the day. Sita arrives shortly, another barista I barely see who always works the morning shifts and because she refuses to work with Bailey. Don't blame her. Sita plays the summer hits to wake us up, which works, but if I have to hear *Call Me Maybe* or *We Are Young* a dozen more times today, I may go bananas.

Sita's long brown hair is pulled into a braid; her dark ochre skin appears warm as the sunlight washes over her while she works the front. The day is started with a large group of customers, needy and ready for caffeine. One of the few good things about opening is that the earlier shifts go by in a flurry, even if Calvin Harris seems to be on repeat. It's almost 1pm, my shift almost over, when Yuki comes in. She stops me before leaving, waving me into her office.

"What's up?" I ask as she tosses her bag onto her small desk.

"I know I asked you to do the morning shift for another two weeks," she starts. "But I need you back for the closing shifts starting tomorrow. So…surprise! You get to sleep in again."

My jaw drops. Huh, my wishes never come true.

"What, why? I mean, I'm not upset about going back to closing shifts sooner than we agreed, but what happened?"

"I shouldn't bring you into it. I'll be opening for the next few weeks instead, so you and Mabel will oversee shifts for the afternoon and evening." She pulls her hair back into a ponytail, making her short-sleeved shirt show off some of her ink, which consists of cherry blossoms floating on invisible wind. A remembrance tattoo she'd gotten for her grandmother when she visited Japan after her passing. Her sister got the same one.

I've never been bold enough to get my own tattoo. Something about those needles make me queasy.

"Okay…not at all worrisome," I comment. Yuki huffs and goes to close her door before she leans on her desk. "Oh, gee, the mood got better."

"You have to promise not to tell anyone or higher management what I'm about to tell you."

"Only higher management I talk to is you." She gives me an exasperated look. "I swear! Unless they offer a way for me to take over a chocolate factory, but I don't think Nan wants in on that." Her expression worsens. Alrighty, someone is *not* in a lighthearted mood. "Won't say nothing, promise. You know me Yuki, whatever you tell me in here, stays in here. So, what happened?"

She sighs, "Three times the back door of the shop was opened *after* the security system was engaged, and then the front for two days."

"How? When I came in it was locked—"

"Because after twenty to thirty minutes, it was re-engaged. Only noticed an issue when Sita brought up a discrepancy yesterday morning when she was checking her hours. But someone…was coming back into the shop."

Her eyes meet mine and I automatically know who'd be dumb enough to do that. I pinch my forehead with my fingers. "Bailey."

"Yup."

"Please tell me she wasn't stealing. Or just really surprise me and say she was making blue suede shoes."

Yuki snorts. "Oh, I wish. But when you came in, did you or Sita notice any messes when you came in? Trash or what have you?"

"Apart from dishes stacked, grounds not cleaned out, and trash not taken out? Nah, just the usual late shift putting work off on early shift staff, but Mabel would never do that."

"That's because Mabel wasn't closing with Bailey."

"Daniella?" Shakes her head. "Phoebe?" Another shake. "Who?"

"New guy we were training." Everything clicks and my jaw opens. Bailey didn't. Yuki nods her head with a knowing look. "If you'd gone through the trash, you'd have found condoms." She did.

"What the…*why*—?"

"Oh, he gave every excuse in the book," she sighs. "Laid off the guy last night."

"What about her?"

"Gave her a warning. And to never use the shop for her own… personal use. That's why I need you locking up."

"Ummm, there a reason…" My voice trails off as Yuki meets my gaze. It's hardened and tired, and before she explains I already know the answer even as she explains.

"Her *daddy* made sure she keeps her job. Won't go into details, you get the gist. He contacted the owners and said to make sure she stays. So, I'm giving her the week off until I figure something out on scheduling or a way to keep any potential male employees."

I shake my head, running my hand through my partially greasy hair. "I'll close. No problem. Let you take care of…*that*."

Thank goodness we didn't have any scheduled inspections. Here's where we keep the pastries, don't worry they're fresh, along with these condoms!

"Thank you, Autumn. You're always a lifesaver." I shrug. "Don't come in until two tomorrow. You work long enough hours. Again, no telling anyone." Yuki instructs, pointing at my chest.

I salute her a little. She laughs, waving me away. "See you tomorrow."

"Get some sleep or something." We walk out, both toward the front, but she stays with Phoebe at the counter. I skim through a group of women laughing loudly, coming out into the glorious sunshine.

Ruffling my hair a bit, I glance down the sidewalk, debating my choices for the afternoon. Usually, okay always, I go home. No matter when I left the coffee shop. The only times I ever go out to lunch is with Leanne, Trix, and rarely Nan. My growling stomach makes the decision for me.

A part of me debates hailing a cab, but the twist in my gut tells me otherwise. I turn away from my usual route, holding my over shoulder bag close as I head down a few blocks to stop at a small deli I've passed before. I pick up a pastrami sandwich and chips, then make the short distance to one of the Central Park entrances. The park is bursting with people and color as I walk a little into the park, my heart rate quickening at the idea of being in the open. I take a few breaths, pushing to calm myself and head to a bench to sit and eat. My head is on a swivel as I watch people as they pass, going about their day. Slowly, my heart rate goes back to normal, and I take a long breath as I chew. The twist in my stomach changes into relief as I eat, focusing on the delicious quick meal.

Not only do I have a thing of hating being late, but I abhor crowds; large open areas. Again, not scared of the outside world, just…wary. In the coffee shop, I can control where I am and who can get to me most times. There's a counter and the kitchen and doors to shut the people out. Outside? Shopping? Alone? Nope. There's nowhere to hide. Well, *there* is, but not readily.

I toss my empty sandwich paper into the trash when I finish, when there's a pricking sensation at the back of my neck. The hairs on my skin stand on end as my skin tightens over my arms. I spin on my heel, searching for what's causing it as I look around frantically. People pass, not paying attention as my chest begins to feel like sand is being poured into it.

It hurts to breathe, and I have to concentrate as the sensation over my skin doesn't stop, worsening. *Calm down. Nothing's wrong. Just anxiety…everything is fine.*

I gulp, the feel of it scratchy from the chips I ate. Still trying to breathe without a struggle, I walk briskly toward the exit of the park. There's a chill down my spine, forcing me to start jogging and heading for the street. The constant feeling like someone is breathing down my neck, like someone's about to grab me doesn't relent. My body shudders as I run, my heart pounding in my ears.

I race across the street for the subway station, disappearing into the chilly depths and out of the summer sun. Without double checking which train I'm hopping onto; I get on and find a corner that's not as crowded as I clutch a handle. Only when it's pulling from the station does the chill disappear and the prick of my skin loosens. My heart pounds as I try to focus on my breathing, shutting my eyes.

He's gone. No one there. He's…

Quietly, I start reciting *The Raven* under my breath, going through each line deliberately. I concentrate on the inflection, the set-up of the poem, and each break. Slowly, my breathing becomes more leveled as I restart and recite it again. Halfway through the second time, the train pulls into a station close to home. I walk out with somewhat shaky legs and my chest still tight.

Yeah, screw trying to meet people and going out. Even without reason, I still have these random panic attacks when I'm in public. Fearful he's there. *Any* of them are there. Park is off limits. Noted. Get an exit buddy next time.

Once I've made it back to the bookstore, Nan is checking out a couple with a stack of books. A few kids are near the fantasy section and another couple are near the self-help books. I nod at Nan, tightening my jaw and I disappear through the back and into my apartment. Dropping my bag, I slump onto my couch and then call Leanne with still trembling hands.

"You're not gonna believe what happened." I rub my face.

"Shit, I know that tone," she murmurs. "Panic attack?"

"Uh-huh."

"Where were you?"

"Oh, just really dangerous stuff, you know, eating a sandwich in Central Park," I grumble.

"Did you see, smell, or hear anything that may have triggered you? Sound of glass shattering? Maybe the smell of that cigarette brand…wasn't it Newport?"

"Marlboro," I mumble, wincing as I remember that damn smell on my own. "But no, none of that, not that I know of." I lean my head back, and glance at all my movies. "You busy tonight? I don't want to bother Nan, she just got back…and—"

"My place or yours?"

"Yours. Back to closing duty, so I can sleep in."

"Deal." There's a moment of stillness and some tears gather in my eyes. Once again, my best friend to the rescue, the one whose sat with me through hell over and over again. Trix may know most of the sordid details, but only Leanne knows how deep the betrayal went. "He's gone, hun. You're safe."

"I know," I whisper.

Now just to get the rest of my body to know that.

I spent the night at Leanne's. Most of my college days I'd end up in her bed or vice versa whenever life got hard. Years later, almost a decade, and we still do it whenever life gets overwhelming. We didn't talk about what happened in the park, just watched reruns of *Family Matters* and *Full House.* She drank suspicious looking wine from her fridge, while I nabbed some of her good blueberry tea.

It's late afternoon and I feel better already being back with my usual schedule at the shop. Thankfully, it'll only be Mabel and I working together until next week. Otherwise, I may have wrung Bailey's neck for pulling the stupid stunt she did. No idea if that former employee will try to lash out, but who knows.

"Do you know how *terrible* it's been without you?" Mabel asks as she restocks the pastries. I roll my eyes at her, cleaning the machine given the down time we have between crowds. This late, there's barely anyone in the shop, apart from those doing work on their laptops or reading.

"It was like two weeks, Mabel," I chuckle, cleaning up some spilled coffee near the brew station.

"Yeah, longest two weeks ever. New guy was worse than Bailey when it comes to making drinks. I half expected to see him trying to froth water. Or pour lemonade into lattes."

"We don't have lemonade."

"Exactly!" I snort laugh at her.

"Well, he can now go apply at a big ole' coffee shop down the street. Show off his skills there."

"Thank goodness for those or this place would be crawling with hipsters and college students and 'Karens' for hours." She shivers and I giggle.

Blue Java Café got enough foot traffic, but with places like Starbucks on every corner or bigger, fancier shops, sometimes business dipped. I'm with Mabel. Fine with the smaller crowds.

Mabel suddenly gasps as I make a latte for myself, coming up next to me and whispers, even though there's barely anyone here. "That guy came back and asked for you."

"What?"

"That *guy*. The one you saved from the Bailey Hurricane."

"What do you mean asked for me?"

"Will you open your ears?" She folds her arms over her chest. My brows pinch together in confusion. "As in asked for you. But he asked Bailey, and she said you weren't going to be here anymore. I was going to correct her that you still do but wasn't sure if *you* wanted him to know and he was already leaving, not to mention two guys were with him. Practically escorted him out on their phones."

"That's weird, why would she….oh." I shake my head as Mabel raises her brows, tilting her head in agreeance. We both know why she did. Even though she was screwing the new guy in the back. Or maybe it's part of the reason why she did.

I'm almost impressed with her chess playing…almost.

"She really is a snobby 21-year-old, isn't she?" I ask. "Screwing one guy while staking out another and lying to him. He's also gotta be a decade older than her. To each their own, but…"

"She'd drive him crazy with her immaturity." I laugh under my breath. "Hey, got the proof, 'cause he hasn't been back." She crosses her arms as I turn toward her perplexed, finishing making my latte. "He asked about you the day you switched shifts. So, I think he was into you. Not even the men he was with have been in the past two weeks."

"Or it was just a passing fancy anyways," I mumble. "Lost interest once I wasn't conveniently here." Oh, wow there's a small punch to the gut. Mabel grabs my cup, beginning to make a swan in the foam. "Besides…saving him from the coffee maelstrom was a one-time thing anyways."

She snorts. "You'd do it again in a heartbeat." I glare at her. "I've worked with you long enough. And he's hot."

"That's it, I'm making my own latte foam art." I try to grab for my coffee, but she blocks me. "Hey, I'm like the Monet of latte art…or Picasso."

"Keep telling yourself that."

I get my drink when she finishes, grinning at her as she winks. The afternoon goes by slowly with the evening just as quiet-paced. The shop is near empty as closing time approaches, and I send Mabel off, closing on my own again. My entire body thrums with normalcy again. It's quiet as the last customer leaves and I start to mop, taking my time to clean as I hum Bon Jovi to myself.

My mop makes it over to the far left of the shop, near the windows, as I look outside and go still. There are a few parked SUVs on the street, including…

Leo.

The beating of my heart picks up pace as I recognize his figure and facial profile. The lights outlining his firm jaw and well-tailored suit. He speaks with a few other men, some dressed in suits like him, and they shake hands with nodding heads. I watch as the gentlemen leave in the cars and Leo turns to two men who stayed behind. They're on their phone, probably assistants or something as Leo adjusts his jacket and watch then pauses. He slowly swivels his head toward the coffee shop.

All breath leaves my body as I stand like a freaking statue with mop in hand.

I can't see his eyes this far away, but I know he sees me. Even from the distance I notice as he stops fixing his attire, staring in my direction as I look back with wide eyes. Unsure what else to do, feeling caught doing my job, I bring a hand up and wave a little with my fingers. Maybe he scowls, I'm not sure, but he turns away.

Whelp. There goes that. Interest is gone.

He goes back to the other two gentlemen, and I untense. Shaking my head, I go back to mopping and work on settling the fluttering in my stomach, then pull down the shades of the windows. It's been weeks since he came in and I disappeared, what did I think was gonna happen?

The stern, polished businessman would wave back? Nah.

I take the mop and bucket to the back and come back out. Looking up I halt with a jolt and almost yelp as I clutch my chest.

Leo stands at the doorway. His eyes of forest greens already on mine as he unbuttons his suit jacket, stepping carefully around where I've last mopped. He stops before the pick-up station that I'm standing behind, and I swear it is like he's sucked the air out of the room. As if he owns it. I breathe in deep to settle my shocked lungs and get a whiff of his cologne. It's musky with a hint of spice, reminding me of a suave, speakeasy lounge.

Shit, get yourself together, Autumn.

I plaster on a smile, shaking myself out of my weird stupor. "Hi."

My originality is unmatched.

"I was told you left."

I sigh, running my hand through my hair. "Yeah, no…sorry, you fell victim to a jealous 21-year-old. My hours changed for a bit, but I never left."

"To when?"

"Opening. You know, the opposite of closing shifts." I stand there, staring and frankly shocked he came in. I would've thought he was passing by. It's also kind of late for coffee. Speaking of. "Do you want a drink?"

He tears his gaze away, glimpsing past to the machines, and then back to me. "Of course."

"Americano?"

"Perhaps something without caffeine. It is becoming late." The sultry undertone of his voice is back, and I nod stiffly as my stomach flutters again.

Hey! Get a grip! What's wrong with me?

I shake myself mentally, walking over to the register. "How about tea? We have green, decaffeinated black tea, or just decaf coffee if you're not into the tea."

Leo follows me from the other side, his gaze staying on me like I'm going to disappear. The furrow between his brows is partially there, a shadow of his concerned expression. He wasn't actually concerned about me…no…well…maybe?

"What's your favorite?"

I look up, grinning fully at him. Suppressing a laugh, I say, "You're drinking it, not me."

"Then what's the easiest for you to make?"

I struggle not to laugh at him, staring into the *very* serious expression I'm met with. Not a glimmer of a tease. "Did you really just… you know what, you're getting decaf coffee. You don't strike me as an Uncle Iroh."

"I don't understand that reference."

Can't say I'm surprised.

"Fantastic kid show." His brows furrow further. I sigh, grumbling inside about my horrendous small talk skills. "Just…you're getting coffee."

"Very well." I turn away, unsure if I heard amusement in his voice as I go to the decaf coffee pot. There was some left from the late crowd, but it's a bit old.

"Do you want what I have left or a fresh cup?"

"If it's easier—"

"That's not what I asked." This time I don't suppress the laughter in my voice as I grin back at him. "You know what. You're getting a fresh cup of decaf, whether it's easier for me or not. And until it brews, you'll just have to be stuck with me. Maybe then you'll learn to just order whatever you want."

His eyes widen slightly as I talk, but after a moment his expression softens. The attempt of a smile comes over him and he nods. "Whatever you wish then."

"Good." I turn away, putting together another pot to brew enough for a cup of joe. I clean up, multi-tasking as the quiet starts to annoy me. I can feel him watching me, practically can sense the furrow of his brows. When I realize I want the summer hits to be playing again, I break the silence. "So…how have you been, Leo?"

I look over my shoulder. He tilts his head and answers, "Very well. Yourself, Autumn?"

"Long days, but good. The work hour change was a little warpy, but I didn't mind it too much."

"Why did you change shifts?"

I pause, wondering if I should tell him anything personally about me. Dr. Wilson's words float around in my head along with my friends. Talk, and try. Open your social circle. They'd all be ecstatic that I was talking to a man at all again, and alone. And no panicking…huh, that's new.

Doing a few more mental calculations, I decide to say fuck it. Perhaps being triggered by grass yesterday has made me slightly salty over life circumstances. I *can* talk to the Italian shoe wearing man.

"My Nan had to leave town, so I watch over her shop when she leaves. Then I switched shifts to help my manager out but had to change back due to new employee stuff."

"Nan, wasn't it?" I nod. "What kind of shop does she own?"

I wipe down part of the counter. "Bookstore."

"Do you like books then?" I laugh to myself, waving it off as he looks at me with questioning eyes.

"You have no idea." The coffee finishes brewing, and I pour him a cup and take it over to the register. As he starts to pull out his wallet, I hold my hand up to stop him. "On the house."

He raises a brow. "I am quite certain I can pay for a cup of decaf coffee."

"Oh, I know. I still have the fifty you gave me in my pocket." Both his brows shoot up. I chuckle at his reaction and shrug.

"Why wouldn't you—"

"Saving it for a rainy day," I interrupt, and his jaw snaps shut. "I'm not doing this because you may not be able to pay for it, no intention to bruise your ego." I wink and he continues staring at me. "I'm doing it because you didn't walk where I mopped." I lean to the side, sure enough seeing he'd taken the small dry paths I'd made. "So…thanks for that."

He looks back and that ghost of a smirk returns. I do wonder what he'd look like fully smiling, although the wrinkling at the corners of his eyes and the lines over his brows tell me not often. It's not like he's struggling to smile, but as if it's… foreign to him. There's a bit of a glimmer in his eyes, turning back as he continues opening his wallet. He pulls out another fifty-dollar bill, placing it on the counter.

"Add it to your rainy-day fund."

I take it without protest, knowing I'd probably lose. Or he'd just slip it somewhere else in the shop. I hold it up with flourish, putting it into my pocket with dramatic flair. His hazel eyes brighten, making my stomach tighten and go topsy turvy with butterflies.

He takes the drink, beginning to leave before he stops at the door. "You'll be here tomorrow? Perhaps, I'll come back earlier for one of your Americanos?"

I grin. "Yeah, I'll be here. No disappearing this time, but if I do, I'd look into the blonde barista. She's got the money and motive."

His expression falters, a quick tension in his jaw. "I'm sure you're safe."

"Probably. And just so you know, if you come back ready to tip another fifty, you should give it to another barista. Otherwise, I'll think you're playing favorites."

"Perhaps, but it's not every day that someone takes a…*coffee* for me," he says, and then adds quietly to where I almost can't hear him. "Or gives me one."

I tilt my head with curiosity at the comment, but then he gives a half grin, and it makes my heart skip a beat. It's tiny, not even close to a full one, but enough to make me grip the counter. He nods, leaving the shop.

I slump onto my elbows, watching as he walks down the side-walk. Moving quickly, I get to the windows and peek out past the window shades. As I continue to stare, he doesn't dump it as he joins the other two gentlemen still standing out there. They all start moving, both following in step behind him.

Still doesn't let go of the coffee.

"Well shit, maybe he is playing favorites." This time the butterflies in my stomach make me giggle as my chest warms. It's a feeling I've not felt in forever, and I don't fight it this time. Welcoming it.

He'll lose interest…right? They always do. The moment I open up and show everything I harbor inside. Until then, I don't want to let go of these fluttering, warm feelings.

I walk to the door, lock it and pull down the shades, pausing to stare down where he disappeared. Deep down, I hope he doesn't lose interest. For the first time in years, the way he looked at me, made me feel a bit more alive than I have in years.

Chapter 5

Maybe This Time...

He came back. Every day. For a week.

Thankfully, he left his fifty-dollar tips in the tip jar, easier to add it to the end of day tips for everyone. Yuki and Mabel took it as a wealthy businessman trying to puff out his chest, while I kept quiet. Honestly, I didn't think he was trying to impress me, but maybe wanted to be helpful. Or just being…nice.

I'm working in the back when I hear Mabel make a noise to catch my attention. I look up, seeing her move away from the doorway then notice Leo by the pick-up station. His intense gaze finds mine, and a knowing expression comes over his face. I smile, going to say hi, when I notice our old friend and "associate" Juanita join him at the station.

Swiftly and with no class, like a terrible Bond villain, I fumble over my feet and bodycheck the table's edge, almost falling as I try to get out of sight. I grip the table-top, breathing deeply from the pain that hits my torso. Wincing, I rub my side.

Okay…maybe, just maybe, I do try to avoid confrontation sometimes.

Not my fault the last time I saw the woman she was screaming about leather shoes and pants or whatever. And although I've had some good banter with Leo all week, albeit quick, her showing up just brought up some *wonderful* memories.

"Crud muffins, Autumn, not like she's gonna start yelling at you…okay she *might*, pattern could stick," I whisper to myself. "No, come on, stop being a wuss."

I take a deep breath as I stand up and head to the front. Juanita is gone when I get there, sitting at a table near the front window speaking on her phone. Leo remains in the same place watching me with curiosity. Mabel comes up behind me, handing me Leo's drink with a wink as she goes to help another customer. I bring his drink over, placing it on the counter with a tight smile.

"Did you see—?"

"Are you hurt?"

We talk over each other, and I chuckle, wincing in embarrassment as I thread my fingers through my hair. Damn it. I peek up through my lashes and whisper, "Can we pretend that you didn't see me almost fall on my ass because my feet decided to do the cha-cha?"

"Is that the reason why?"

"Depends. Is it a good enough excuse without me sounding like a wimp?"

"Why would I consider you that?" I flick my gaze past him to his associate, and he follows my gaze. "Ah."

"Didn't want to accidentally hurt your *expensive* footwear."

He snorts, shaking his head. "You're not a *wimp*, I assure you."

"Promise?"

He slowly slides his coffee over the countertop. "Hmm, perhaps, although it may cost you for me to make such a promise."

I laugh under my breath, crossing my arms. "Like what? Getting another Americano on the house?" I check on Mabel and the lack of customers at the register. Her curious eyes watch us as she pretends to be busy with the pastry display.

"That you give me your number." I swing my gaze to him, shocked as he still looks at me with a very serious expression. Did he just—?

Suddenly, I burst out laughing and try to keep it from ringing through the coffee shop as I cover my mouth. I hold my side where I hit it, looking up to see a frown form on his face and I quickly straighten, but still choking down giggles. Mabel gapes at me and Juanita scowls toward us. Calming my laughter, I swallow hard and whisper, "I'm not laughing at you."

"Doubt it."

"No, no…it was just surprising, and it was actually smooth. *Really* smooth. Not something I thought you'd do. Besides, this is how I show I'm impressed."

"If you think you could convince me that you didn't fall back there, you can't expect me to—"

"No, really," I interrupt, and his brows pinch together. "I'm not laughing at you."

"Sounds like you are."

"Great, instead of hurting your footwear, I've hurt your feelings," I mutter under my breath, and rub the palms of my hands into my eyes. The line on his forehead shows up as it has every time he scowls deeply. Which is frequent. "Leo, just…crud muffins, your expression is making it worse."

I divert my gaze from his, not at all scared from the scowl on his face. It should scare or worry me, but the line on his forehead can be really amusing. I find it endearing. He doesn't show joy often, speaks in a manner that's almost monotone, but it has a touch of sincerity. It would appear to others he's unfeeling or just grouchy, but he's just expressive in his own way. And I don't think he knows it either.

I breathe through the last of the giggles and find his surprised face. Another expression that happens a lot around me. I flash a look to Mabel, who's helping a new customer. She gives me a look, and I roll my eyes at myself as she gives me a small grin. Bless her and trying to give me more time with him. Cause I'm pretty sure I just bruised the fuck out of his ego.

"It sounds cliché," I finally say steadily. "But it's me. Not you. Really, really."

"You have a…peculiar way of showing it."

I snort to myself. He has no idea.

His eyes meet mine, and thankfully I don't see much hurt. "Leo, I think it's—"

"I'd like to speak with you without orders, coffee, *associates*, or other prying ears around, Autumn."

"So, not a coffee date huh?" I try to joke, and it doesn't really land. His expression falls completely and shut off with disappointment beginning to seep into his gaze. Shit. I calm myself, taking a step closer to the counter and lean in, whispering, "I appreciate it, but I don't think…I think this is fine…how it is." My chest begins to feel tight, and I hold my hands together to keep from trembling. "Please, don't be mad." I swallow a little, not liking the upset in his eyes. "Please. I find it nice every time you come in, it's just…I…I…"

My voice falters, then falls away as I hope he's not gonna turn into a dick. A part of me starts to run through my head if I've given the wrong attention to him. If I showed signals to make him think… fuck, no Autumn. Not your fault. *Not your fault.*

Leo takes a sharp intake of breath, and whispers, "What's wrong?"

"Not you," I blurt, and his eyes widen. I take a shuddering breath. "I went through a bad break-up, few years back. It's made me…careful. So much, I feel better behind a counter from a guy than in front of it." I wave to the fake marble between us. "And anxiety. Out the wazoo to boot."

All of a sudden, his expression softens and the upset in his eyes disappears. "When you say bad, what does that entail?"

"Police were involved. And the hospital." I avert my gaze to customers at tables. "It didn't end well, and it's not because I think you'll…you'll be like that, I just…I uh, need more time."

"I see."

"Look, I get it if I never see you again," I mutter, stepping back. Yup, this is always when they walk away, might as well prepare myself mentally. "Or if you think I'm lying, so I don't go out with you. Think whatever you want."

"Autumn." There's a strictness in his voice, a tender command that makes me meet his gaze. "I believe you."

This time it's my expression that turns to shock as he casually adjusts his wristwatch, then grabs his drink. "I'll see you tomorrow, if you're working that is?" Stiffly, I nod my head. "Very well. I'll wait until you are ready. Until then have a good day, Miss Autumn."

"Watson." My last name tumbles out of my mouth, and I blink rapidly, surprised I said it at all. I've always had a closer connection to it than my first name.

The small glimmer in his eyes comes back, and he nods. "Very well then…dear Watson, I'll see you tomorrow."

He turns away, motioning for Juanita that he's leaving. She passes me a glance, following him out into the street as they turn left down the sidewalk. Briefly, he looks over his shoulder toward the shop.

The warmth in my chest comes back as I swallow hard, rubbing my clavicle. Mabel comes over and whispers, "What happened?"

"He asked for my number."

"Did you give it to him?" I shake my head, and she lets out a frustrated groan. "He's obviously into you! Come on! Came back regularly and everything, why not go out with the rich guy with a fascination for Americanos?"

My head shakes again, moving toward the back. "Not that simple."

"Yeah, it is," she scoffs. "Look I may be a bit younger than you but come on, dating doesn't change *that* much in getting numbers. I mean, I've never even seen you date—"

"Please, Mabel," I interrupt. My gut wrenches as I look at her, and she stops.

Sighing, she says, "Fine, fine. Can you get more coffee beans, and restock the chocolate pastries? Running low."

"Sure." I set to work, ignoring the pain in my chest and hollow feeling. My mind becomes fuzzy a moment as I grab a bag of coffee beans, and I stop to clutch the tabletop. Inhaling deep breaths, I remind myself where I am as my heart rate picks up and my hands shake.

"It's fine…you heard him. He believes you. He—"

Elm Jed

Except, in the far reaches of my mind, where I've stored certain things in forgotten attics a voice says, *he's lying*.

I stand outside the women's center, looking up at the cloudy sky. I've just finished another session with Dr. Wilson, and I didn't tell her jackshit about what happened with Leo. Kinda didn't want to go down the unrequited love route with her or hearing "just try" again. Otherwise, I may just scream.

It's been four days since then, and Leo did come back. He hasn't asked for my number and has kept it cordial between us. I'm not sure if I should be annoyed that he takes up so much of my thoughts lately, but it's hard not to with those damn eyes of his. Furrowed brow. Lightly stubbled chin. Stupid, tall, broad shoulders....

My entire being shakes, trying to get my thoughts under control. Exhaling harshly, I start heading home, but stop when I see *him* down the way. You gotta be kidding me!

Leo speaks with a taller man with dark skin and a bald head, dressed in business casual. There's another man who's almost just as tall with copper tanned skin, and he's wearing a suit that's similar to Leo's. All three seem to be in a deep conversation as I turn around, and scramble to dive behind the cement stairs next to the center.

Oh, good, I'm hiding now. Fantastic.

I lean back against the stone, wincing a little as I slide down the wall until I'm sitting on my butt. I bring my knees up, holding them close as the pounding in my chest gets worst. A shiver wrecks through my body as I lean against the wall, so I huddle forward away from it. Fuck. My anxiety spikes, wondering what I should do. I mean, a normal person would just go walk past or say hello. Not like he's gonna kidnap me. Or worse, what if he ignores me? What if he *doesn't* ignore me?

Yup, no win-win situation in my head right now.

"Why can't I 'people' normally?" I grumble, lightly hitting my head against the stone behind me. "Come on, just get up…don't be a scaredy-cat."

I take a few more long breaths, trying to get the shaking to stop. It doesn't. It worsens as I peek around the corner. My breath stalls out as I catch him walking towards the women's center. And just like that, I hide again. I bite down on my fist as I try to breathe, but it's like all the air is caught at the top of my lungs.

Hide. Don't be seen —

Why am I hiding? Why am I even—?

He's not him. He's not any of them.

I shut my eyes, trying to keep the barrage of old emotions away. My body trembles, holding myself close as I resemble a lost orphan missing their dog, Sandy. All I'm missing is snow and Miss Hannigan.

What seems like forever, I stay put, but finally open my eyes and pull my head up. Carefully, I stand and peek over the stairs again and don't see him anymore. I rub my forehead as the trembling in my hands doesn't stop and start briskly heading for home. The thundering in my chest doesn't relent as I get on the subway, trying to recite *The Raven* again and not finding much relief. Every turn I take, there's a prick to my skin and it's like someone's breathing over my neck. The panic attack makes my eyesight blurry, and the edges of my vision go dark as I make it to the bookstore.

It's empty apart from Nan who comes around an aisle. "Autumn, you're home late… what's wrong?"

I drop my bag and go into her waiting arms. She folds me into her embrace, rubbing my back as silent tears streak my face. My breath is ragged as she hugs me close, kissing my cheek with a calming hum.

"I just had a panic attack seeing a guy I may or may not like on the street," I rasp, holding her tight. "I hid behind some stairs for I don't know how long. It felt like being caught again. Being stalked…"

"Shh, baby, shhh," she murmurs, brushing my hair back. "They're gone, dear. Won't find you. It's okay to be scared. It's okay. But it's just us, deep breaths…you're okay."

I hold her tighter, wishing that the panic will subside and that I could've said hi. Could've at least waved or asked if he wanted a coffee or even tripped like some rom-com. Been *normal.*

"Every time I feel like I'm getting better, it's like I take five steps back. I just want to move on," I whisper.

"I know, dear, I know." She continues to rub my back. "You can move on, dear. You can. Just a small step at time. It may feel like you haven't reached far, but you're not where you were before. And *that's* progress. Would you have even talked to this man two years ago?" I shake my head against her neck. "A year ago?" I shake it again. "But you've spoken to him before?" I nod. "There. That's progress. Even if it doesn't feel like it right now."

"Hiding from someone you're crushing on is progress?"

"For you, having a crush and admitting it is." I snort lightly. "Steps are steps, Autumn, no matter how small."

I swallow hard and nod my head as she pats my shoulder. "Thanks, Nan."

"Why don't you head into my apartment and get some tea started? I can shut down the store early."

"No," I say, shaking my head and stepping back to wipe away the tears. "I'll go watch a movie or two. Get a breather, you need the shop open."

She waves a hand in the air. "Oh, pish, this shop is fine. Don't worry."

Nan goes to lock the front and turn the "Open" sign to "Close." She hugs me close to her as we head into the back, and she gets me to calm down with some tea and some of her cooking. Later into the evening, I go up to my place and fall into my bed and stare at the ceiling.

I'm a twenty-eight-year-old who hid from someone I like on the street.

Yeah, safe to say I'm a wimp.

Chapter 6

Heroes Drink Coffee

Fine. Not a wimp. Because there's no way a wimp would calmly stand across from a grown ass man as he berates and belittles you about how much foam was in his coffee. Okay, it may have been about espresso or temperature, but I've forgotten how I got here about three minutes ago.

The blonde businessman with huge shoulders and what looks to be two class rings on his hand, points at me from across the counter. He frowns as he continues with his gruff voice as I nod my head, biting back everything I want to tell him. Phoebe stays off to the back after I sent her there, not wanting us both to receive the brunt of this. It's been about seven minutes now, and some customers have given looks of disgruntlement or just left. Must be nice.

I concentrate on keeping my breathing level, trying again to get the man to leave or just buy another damn coffee. He keeps telling me he wouldn't want anything else from here, yet he doesn't leave. Phoebe watches with a pursed mouth and worry in her eyes. The man has gotten closer to the counter and the hand pointing at me is barely inches away. There's a twist in my stomach, which makes my legs wobbly, and my hands shake as I stare him down. Shaky or not, this is *my* job and I'll be damned before crumbling before him.

"Sir, I've told you—"

"I don't fucking care, you incompetent girl!" Oh, yeah never heard *that* before. "Can't even make a simple cup of coffee correctly, where the fuck is the—"

Simple? The guy had like a triple shot, two pump vanilla latte with almond milk and said some random nonsense about consistency of the foam. Not to mention saying he needed a specific blend of coffee beans that we don't even have, which I've told him multiple times.

"Sir, please leave if you're—"

He comes closer to the counter, leaning towards me and I become frozen. I can smell his cigarette-tinged breath with stale mint that didn't do its job. He brings his hand up, and my eyes widen as he brings it up to possibly shove me. My body flinches, tensing as I await getting hit as Phoebe gasps, "Autumn!"

There's a grunt, and I open my eyes to see the hand clutched by another. The man strains, puffing out his cheeks as he glares over at the one who's holding him back. The trembling in my body stops, but my heart pounds in my ears. Leo grips the man tightly, forcing him to take a step back as Leo scowls at him with such fury that makes my stomach plummet.

"Touch her or any of the employees here and it'll be the last time you ever use your hands," Leo warns under his breath. His voice is lethal. His body is rigid, not showing an ounce of strain in holding the guy back. Even as the man tries to pull from his grasp and shove him, Leo holds firm.

"And why..." The guy looks at his face, sneering, but his expression begins to falter as Leo gets closer. He whispers in the man's ear, and I see the blonde guy go pale, eyes widening. "I...I..."

"Go. *Now*." His words are a final command as he lets go, and the guy stumbles back.

He tries to adjust his jacket, glaring at Leo and then tries to look at me. Leo steps in his way, shaking his head once before the man finally leaves. I glance at the doorway, seeing a couple of guys outside dressed in jeans and black shirts rolled up at the sleeves, both with facial hair and tattoos, following the man quietly down the street. Probably bikers ready to intervene if Leo hadn't. Not the first time. We've had a few bikers come in and rough up people to get out. Leo just got here first.

I take a long breath in, centering myself as I focus on the present. He didn't touch me. I'm safe. It's fine…

"Autumn," Leo says calmly. Hazel eyes find mine, the same ones I hid from the day before. Suddenly, it's like a wave is crashing against my chest and that long breath wasn't enough air. I shake my head, trying to plaster on a smile, but avoiding his gaze. Fuck, I feel sick.

"Thank you," I murmur. "I appreciate the help."

"Autumn, are you—"

"Phoebe will help you with your order," I state, trying to keep from blacking out. I turn toward her, and she comes up to rub my arm a little. "His drink is on the house. I'll be back in a few minutes."

"Yeah, sure."

I clear my throat and give a tight smile back to Leo who's watching me with a stony expression. "Again, thank you. Have a good day."

Not waiting for a reply, I step away and disappear into the back room. I close the door and break down into tears. My hands shake as I try to regulate my breathing, hating these past two days and feeling like a shell of a person and a coward.

"Fuck…*fuck*," I mutter, hitting my hand against the wall. My fist throbs as I tremble and tears stream down my face. My breaths are heavy as I try to get the tears to stop, rubbing at my eyes and then stopping as I realize it'll make my eyes worse. My fist hits the wall again, and the pain that jolts through me pierces the panic in my brain. I gasp as I step back, rubbing my hand as I go to sit down.

My throat feels tight, aching as I try to hold back the tears and wipe away those that have fallen. Fucking customers. Fucking men. Fucking…

I take a long breath, grabbing my phone and start playing some music. My rock playlist begins to play, and I start to breathe easier, switching to a Queen song and shake off the last of the tears. My hand scrubs through my hair as Queen sings about people biting the dust, and it helps me imagine the man falling into dust, too. The song moves to *Bad Reputation,* and I choke back a laugh.

Finishing the songs, I put my phone away and check my face. I don't wear make-up, especially at work, but don't want puffy red eyes either. Looking tear free enough, I meet Phoebe at the pick-up station as someone takes their tray of coffees.

She meets my gaze and comes up close to squeeze my arm. I notice her nails are a bright pink with long tips and sparkly glitter. Cute. "You okay?"

"Yeah, better, haven't had that kind of...*conversation* in a while."

"Tell me about it. I was about to call the cops." My stomach sinks, trying not to let my mind go there. Instead, I just nod. "The guy who intervened left, but said he hoped you're okay."

I look around the shop to see there's barely anyone here now. Well, fuck. "Was he mad?"

"He looked frowny, but then again he basically told that guy to go shove it where the sun doesn't shine." She points to our tip jar. "Also left a big tip, told him he didn't have to, but he looked pretty decided already."

I stare at the jar for a moment, swallowing hard. "Right. Um, I'll work in the back for a bit, okay?"

"Yeah, I'll take care of the front," she squeezes my arm again, then heads to the machines. I glimpse around the shop once more, hoping he'd just show up magically for me to say thank you but not through an oncoming panic attack. When I'm sure he's not hiding within the pastry display, I go to the kitchen and stay there until closing time.

He doesn't show. For three whole days.

Each day my anxiety spikes more and more, replaying those short moments after he threw the guy out. How I spoke to him and how he spoke to me. And then my mind reels to the day before then, hiding from him. Maybe he saw me? Noticed I'd hidden from him? Or maybe—

I groan, trying to turn my brain off as I lean forward on the counter. It's almost time to shut the café down, and there's only a few people left. Mabel thought about staying, but I shooed her away to go see her mom. Taking another deep breath, I start cleaning the espresso machine and putting coffee bags away. I hear the door open and close, glancing behind me to see the last few couples leave. The shop is empty, but suddenly the prick at the back of my neck comes back.

I go still, my breathing becoming shallow. My eyes flick over to the windows. I see a man in a brown jacket standing just down the street. A group of people are chatting near him, but he doesn't seem to be with them. Even with it almost being nine, there's still some light from the sun, casting long shadows. I notice the man is just watching the shop and I start to feel sick.

Everything in me goes on high alert. I just *can't* catch a break this week, can I? Trying not to bring attention to myself, I check the clock and notice I've got ten more minutes. Yuki won't care if I lock up early, right?

Carefully, I put down the bags and grab a pair of scissors by the cash register. Not the best weapon, but it'll pierce through someone's balls or eyes in a pinch. The man begins to head to the door but stops short and walks past and down the street.

I slump back and rub a hand over my face.

The door opens, and I get ready to throw the scissors like a throwing knife until I see Leo. I exhale with relief, dropping the scissors on the counter. "It's you. Thank goodness."

His brows pinch together as I push my hair back in exasperation. I'm so done this week. I need ice cream and a good-bad movie pronto, preferably *Reefer Madness: The Movie Musical*.

"Generally, I feel I'd be humbled hearing those words from you, but your tone worries me," he says.

"Rough week. Asshole after asshole. How's yours going?" I say roughly, putting the scissors back in their proper place. I head to the back to grab the mop and bucket without waiting for a response.

He still stands there as I come back out, prepping to clean after he's gone. I stop with my back turned to him when he says, "Am I one of the assholes?"

I straighten, turning slowly and realizing I'm on the same side of the counter with him. Funny, he looks taller than the first time I saw him. Course, I saw him the other day, but this much closer without the counter, somehow, he looks more imposing? Larger? Not sure.

"No," I answer. "Honestly I thought *I* was the asshole to you."

His brows scrunch together, taking a step toward me. Something in me tells me to run, sprint for the back as he gets closer. Except it sounds like the voices are responding to just a week of yelling, creepy assholes and panic attacks brought on by memories of the ex-asshole.

In other words, I've landed in *Spaceballs.* I'm surrounded.

"No, I presumed I overstepped when I told that man to leave. I just...he raised his hand to you, and I reacted. After you told me about your ex, I only wanted to—"

"Can we sit?" I ask gesturing to one of the tables, and his mouth snaps shut with a harsh intensity in his eyes. "Sorry, I have a habit of interrupting you, don't I?"

His jaw muscles relax and shakes his head once. "It's fine."

I gesture toward the chairs again, and he does as I request, while I move past him to finally lock the front door. I feel him watching me as I wait for my skin to prick, but it doesn't as I sit across from him at the small round table in the middle of the café. He unbuttons his suit jacket, leaning back with that suave assertiveness that always seems to surround him.

Does he know when *not* to be a business guy? Relax a little?

I snort to myself, smiling and he gives me a curious look. Shaking my head, I start, "I'm very grateful you stepped in. I did mean it when I said thank you, I just wasn't in a great head space. Panic attack, to be honest." He keeps his gaze with me, nodding lightly. "I could pretend that I could've handled it, I mean, I have in the past, but, well..."

"Rough week," he finishes, and I nod. "Perhaps surprisingly to you, I have those, too."

"Not at all surprising, we're all human." I fall back against my chair as he furrows his brows once again. I snort to myself, trying to hide my amusement. I sigh heavily and ask, "You didn't avoid the shop the last few days cause of me, did you? Or is that me being too…main charactery?"

His brows, somehow, pull together more, and I can't help the smirk this time. "Should I understand what that means?" I shake my head. "Well, I can tell you it wasn't because of you. I had business that took up my time this week. Couldn't get away."

"Does that happen a lot?"

"Most times." His voice is succinct, glancing out the windows. "You said assholes in plural, who are the others?"

I wave it off. Might have just been a potential customer and decided no coffee and walked away. My mind has been on high alert lately, which means scenarios that don't exist will pop up in my head. Or I overreact.

"Normal asshole customers. I mean, there's only a few regulars I like who come this late. Speaking of, want a decaf?" I get up, flipping the chair onto the table. Leo stands, doing the same with his and I grin at him in appreciation.

"Actually, some of that business will continue into the night. I could use one of your Americanos."

"If you still had business or whatever that's been keeping you busy, why'd you come in then?" I ask, walking around the counter.

"I wanted to see you."

I almost trip over my feet and grab the counter. Trying to play it off, I swallow hard and peek over the tall divider. Leo watches me with an amused expression.

"What is with you being so smooth?" I mutter under my breath as I set to making his drink. A few minutes pass in silence as I get the water for his drink, and he finally speaks.

"I'd like to ask you a question, dear Watson." A shiver goes down my spine when he calls me that. I glance over my shoulder, noticing his hands in his pockets as he inclines his head. "A few days ago, were you near the *Luna Stella Women's Center?*"

Busted.

I swallow hard and nod. He makes a low humming sound, trying to assess me again. "From your expression, I will assume you saw me as well. Except, you disappeared quite swiftly."

"I panicked," I blurt. "I saw you, freaked out and hid behind some stairs." His eyes widen as his posture tightens.

"If I've done anything to scare you or to think—"

"No, no!" I set up the espresso to go and turn toward him, holding up my hands. "You've done nothing. It's me and my thoughts and background and...not you. Just like how I wasn't laughing at you? Close to the same." Green eyes flecked with gold and earthen brown stare into mine, while brows come together as he's clearly thinking. I lick my bottom lip, and I notice his eyes shift down before coming back up.

I clear my throat. "You haven't scared me. At all. There have been moments, I've waited for you to disappear, be angry, or get all...ego bruised. But you haven't. You've been kind, I appreciate that. You would get customer of the year award, if we had that."

"If I receive a customer of the year award, you should receive an employee of the year award," he counters lightly.

"For giving you coffee on the house or catching coffee without oven mitts?"

"Perhaps both."

I snort, hearing the machine finish the espresso shots and turn away to complete his drink. Once done, I turn back and place the Americano down in front of him. Leo starts to pull out his wallet, giving me the cash for the Americano and then another fifty. He holds it out for me to take, and I stare down at the bill in his hand. My heart clenches a little. I reach forward, but instead of taking it, I fold his hand back over the money. His hand is warmer than I thought it'd be and there are calluses I haven't noticed before. I press both of my hands over his and I think his breath hitches.

"Keep it," I whisper, staring down at our hands.

"Autumn."

I look up with a small smile. "I appreciate it, a lot. But I don't want you thinking I like having you around just for this."

"I don't think that."

"Still. Keep it. Save it for a rainy day."

He tilts his head, his expression open and line free. Leo inhales deeply, clenching his fist before he pulls away from my grasp. I watch him put the money back into his wallet. He takes his drink, pausing for a moment. "Thank you."

"Sure. Uh, let me unlock the door for you," I say, moving around the counter to meet him at the door. I unlock it as he approaches, towering over me as I realize I barely come up to the top of his chest. "See you tomorrow? Unless business takes over again?"

"Busy or not, I'll see you tomorrow. I promise. Good night, dear Watson."

"Good night, Leo."

He steps out and I lock the door behind him as he goes down the sidewalk. I watch him as he disappears into the summer evening, fading into the light crowd. I pull down the shades and clean the shop for the morning before I stop and pause at the backdoor. My memory flicks back again to the guy I'd seen earlier, and I dip into my bag to find my pepper spray and k-bar. Locking up and walking out into the city evening, I keep those items clutched in my hand, but there's no one suspicious. I breathe easier once I get to the subway, sitting on a rare vacant seat and remember how warm and inviting Leo's hand felt.

Chapter 7

Summer Rains

"Another lavender latte, but with almond milk," Mabel tells me as she places the cup next to the other two. I quickly dump out the old espresso grounds, putting in fresh ones. "Rush almost over."

"Thank goodness, I've wanted to nab one of those chocolate croissants before everyone took them." I hand over a latte to Mabel to create some foam art. Mabel eyes me, and I wink at her. She giggles, before giving back the drink for me to place at the pick-up station. Coming back to start on the rest, I feel her bump my backside. Turquoise earrings swish past my vision as she bumps my butt again with hers. About to ask her what's up, I notice Leo walk up to the register, the last of the customer rush.

"Americano. Medium," I tell Mabel, going back to the other drinks. There's a low chuckle and it lights up my tired bones.

He's laughing. Leo's laughing. Wow, miracles can happen.

I hear her taking his order, and then whispering something that I can't catch over the whirring machines. I finish the other three drinks, taking them down to be picked up, and then finish Leo's drink. While setting it down, he meets me at the counter with a glimmer in his eye.

"Not too busy, today?" I ask.

"Unfortunately, I am, but this should help get me through it."

The door opens, and I groan when a group of girls walk in, chattering eagerly. My gaze flicks up to the darkening ambiance outside.

"Be careful out there," I tell him, and he goes still, jaw tense. I gesture to the outside. "Heard it'll be storming later, looks like it's coming in sooner than expected."

Leo exhales a sharp breath. "Yes. Will you be alright?"

I wave him off. "I'll be fine. Stay dry."

"Autumn!" Mabel calls, and I turn to see about four cups already lined up. Whelp.

"Not the only one busy today. Stay dry yourself, dear Watson." Leo nods once, taking his Americano and walking past a few of the girls who blatantly ogle him. One of them bites her lip.

I go back to the espresso machine, getting ready to start the next drink when I see one of the chocolate croissants off on a napkin next to my station. I narrow my gaze at Mabel as she gives me another clear cup. "What's that?"

"Your *favorite* customer may have heard from a little birdie that you were craving one," she says slyly, and I gape at her. "And he put two fifties in the tip jar. I swear, Autumn, if he ever stops coming here...I'm gonna cry."

Yeah, his tips do make up for those who don't leave any or have thrown .25 cents at us.

I laugh, continuing making drinks. About an hour later, I'm able to munch on the croissant as the rain starts to come down and the crowd lessens. Some people shelter from the rain out front, while others dash in from the wet. Both Mabel and I grumble at the soggy mess we'll have to clean later as the evening wears on.

The storm has barely let up as closing time nears and Mabel leaves a bit later than usual but was smart enough to have brought her umbrella. She leaves as I finish the last of the closing duties and pull my jacket collar up as I lock the backdoor. Entering the code, the beep goes off and I set off for home as the rain pours down. I pull my flat cap harder onto my head as I start walking but pause when I see the man who approached the coffee shop last night appear. He stands near the corner I take toward my subway stop. A car passes, spraying some water on my legs, but I barely notice.

My skin pricks, warning me as my stomach twists in worry. I keep my head down, trying to act nonchalant as I rummage around in my bag, turning away from my usual route. The rain comes down as I come to the intersection and turn left instead. The sidewalk mostly deserted from the storm. I chance a look behind me, and see the man beginning to move towards me. Shit!

I did *not* want to end my week as a Hitchcock cliché.

Quickly, I hurry down the street, trying to act like the rain is getting to me as I cross to the other side. Continuing down the opposite direction of home, I decide to find a way to divert his path and aim for the flashy hotels up ahead. I'll walk the entire city before I give this guy a chance to know where I fucking live.

My lungs tremble as I continue rummaging in my bag and finally brush my hand against my k-bar and pepper spray. I nab the pepper spray, peering through the rain as I glance over my shoulder to see he's even closer. He holds his jacket close to his body, but he's plowing through the few people out on the street and straight for me. Once I get to the next crossing, I sprint, not waiting for the signal after a car comes around the corner. I rush down the sidewalk, coming closer to a large hotel that has gold plated walls and crystal-like windows.

I'm engrossed in my thoughts of where to go, subway stops, bus routes, anything to evade him and while looking back I bump into someone and stumble back. I fall against a building, letting go of the spray in my bag to catch myself from falling. The man is there, pulling a knife from his jacket, moving for me.

He rasps against the rain, "Was just gonna steal your bag, but I think I'd rather have fun with you."

"Fuck off," I respond, trying to find the spray.

"Behave, little *barista* bitch." He steps closer as I take a small step to the side and find it. He laughs darkly, taking another step and I pull out the can and hit him square in the face with the spray.

He screams as I kick his leg, making him howl as I run past. "You fucking cunt! I'm gonna—!"

I'm knocked to the ground, and I spin to kick at anything, which I do. His groin. He yelps, trying to yank my jacket off and I punch him. As his head whips to the side, I get up and throw the empty can at his head. It bounces off his temple as I run, panting as I look for any escape and see the gold-plated hotel. The rain is pouring down, there's no one else in sight.

Fuck it.

I bolt, practically feeling his fingers skim over my shoulder. More water splashes over me as I sprint toward the hotel. I race through the revolving glass doors and burst into bright light. My wet shoes slip causing me to trip over my feet, and I skid and fall into the hotel lobby. People gasp as I slide across the marble floor, panting as I look at the still spinning door. The guy sneers as he starts to come in but stops when there's commotion behind me.

A young man dressed in black vest and slacks, kneels beside me. "Miss, are you—"

"Guy…there…tried to assault me… attack me with a knife…" I gasp, pointing to the man who's now turning on his heel to run.

My head begins to swim as there's more commotion and the man calls out for me, while two others run outside into the rain after my attacker. I feel woozy as my head tilts back, my vision going blurry and darkening around the edge as I strain to breathe. Memories drift forward. Images of knives, broken glass, and rough, cold hands. I'm choked by the stale smell of beer and drugs, and then the ghost of a kick to my stomach makes me gasp. I curl into a fetal position, trying to breathe through the trembling and attempting to forget the flashing memories that rampage me. A sob starts to build as the images in my mind start to conquer me, until I hear his voice.

"Autumn!" There's a warm hand on my shoulder. It's not cold and unforgiving. "Autumn, can you hear me? Autumn!"

I lift my head, shuddering at the touch and fight with my instincts to flinch away. My insides scream at the contact. Blinking, I look up to find familiar hazel eyes. "Leo?"

"Are you hurt? What happened?"

"Followed," I whisper, and I flinch this time as he moves his hand over my shoulder as I sit up. My lungs burn and tighten as a group of people gather around us, causing my heartbeat to race along with my twisting stomach. Too many. There's too many people seeing this… seeing me lose my shit.

Keep it together. Keep it together.

Leo gives orders to someone and, I think, it's the man who was next to me earlier. All I hear is mumbling, combining with the roaring in my ears and the spinning of my head while I shake, trying to gain control of the panic attack arising.

Three years of damn therapy. Wouldn't know it with the week I've had. Damn it.

My arms shake as I try to get up, but Leo catches my arm and we both go still. His gaze comes to mine, saying something that doesn't register. A moment passes, and I'm moving suddenly with one of his hands on my shoulder as he leads me out of the crowd, out of the lobby, and down a hallway. I'm taken into a large office, where I'm given a seat on a leather couch with my bag set beside me. Leaning forward, I hold my head as I try to calm my breathing as the air in my lungs still burns. Water drips down my face and I shiver slightly. The tightening of my skin makes me queasy as I listen to doors open, close, people talking. The present meshes with the past as I remember sitting in the police station. The hospital bed. An empty room—

I squeeze my eyes shut, and I start to recite *The Raven*, rocking silently. Someone approaches me, kneeling, and I continue the poem, thinking I'm muttering low enough not to be heard. The stanzas falter as I recognize the cologne.

"Is that Edgar Allen Poe?" Leo asks.

I nod, quickly losing track of where I was. Fumbling through the words, I try again, but then Leo finishes the stanza, "…- *Darkness there and nothing more.*"

I blink up at him, finding eyes deep in color resembling summer forests now filled with concern. Inhaling deeply, I gulp past the lump in my throat before I release a loud huff.

"I recite it whenever…whenever I have panic attacks," I murmur.

"Quite long."

"Enough to help come back to reality. Remind myself where I am." He nods and I notice he has a blanket in his hands. He unfurls it, bringing the soft, warmth around my shoulders and my breath catches with how close he gets. He doesn't touch me, his hands a breath away.

Leo stands fully, walking over to the bookshelf behind a large wooden desk. He comes back with a glass of water, handing it to me. I give a small smile, taking a sip, and murmur, "I'm sorry."

"You have nothing to be sorry for." His response is quick, startling me. His expression is stern, stoic almost, but the sympathy in his eyes hasn't left. His jaw tenses, a muscle flickering as his brows come together. "Are you hurt? Physically?"

"No, just fell a few times…and wet. Probably get some bruises later, that'll be it."

He grunts, frowning as his hands go into his pockets. "Did you know the man who attacked you?"

My eyes widen. "How did you know—?"

"One of my valets said you were followed by a man, who was caught by one of my security guards with two large knives on him and pepper spray covering half his face. He was half a block away from the hotel before they caught him. Not to mention, I have no doubt, he was caught on our security tapes chasing you into the hotel." Leo doesn't move his gaze from mine, tilting his head ever so slightly as he regards my reaction. "The police are on their way."

Fuck. *Fuck.*

I go through the precinct numbers in my head, trying to remember if this hotel would fall within a particular one. No, he's on the other side of the city. Unless he moved. No…he wouldn't get close to me. He wouldn't risk it. I hold my head, trying to reign in my rambling worry.

"Do you need anything?" Leo asks, pulling me from the chaotic thoughts.

I stare down at the water, taking another sip and hoping it'll calm my nerves. "Apart from a bottle of scotch, or maybe drugs to take off the edge," I laugh with an empty sound. "How about a memory wipe instead? Something tells me that's not as doable."

Leo moves back to the same area he grabbed the water, and I notice the small wet bar with different liquors and crystal glasses. He pours something, bringing it over, and offering the amber liquid to me. I look at him, and then the drink in his hand.

"I doubt you need a full bottle, but we can start with a glass first." He keeps the drink held out for me and I continue to stare at the glass. "Although, you should know, I won't condone drugs with alcohol." I snort at him.

Well, this week has already gone to shit, might as well break my damn rule.

I take it with less shaky hands, putting the water down as I sip the liquor and groan at the smooth familiar taste. "Is this Dewar's?"

His brows move up slightly in surprise. "White label. Impressive."

"I, uh, used to really like it, but Ardbeg was sometimes a favorite." Until I could barely stand the taste of alcohol cause I kept drinking myself into a stupor to make the memories stop. Didn't need AA to tell me I had issues.

With that thought, remembering tonight and other assholes, I take another sip of the scotch. Was I going against my rules of drinking where I should be under supervision with friends? Yes. Did I care? Nope. It's been a fucking unnerving week. My nerves are shot, and my head won't stop spinning. I just had to get chased through the rain at night after being followed from work. I was beyond a cliché at this point; a start of a bad 1930s film.

If Humphrey Bogart walks through that door, I'm calling it quits.

I take another sip of the drink, realizing how good it is and there's no sick feeling in my stomach. I look back up at the man who watches me, and I try to smile. "Do you take tips? I think I have fifty in my pocket. Probably wet though. Shit…I'm getting water on this couch!"

I mutter under my breath, standing up on shaky legs when Leo puts his hand on my shoulder. "Don't worry about it. Sit. It's just a couch."

"But I don't—"

"Sit," he instructs with a faint command in his voice. "Please, Autumn."

I swallow hard, moving back down to sit as he opens his mouth to say something else, when there's a knock at the door. His expression becomes harsher as he walks over, opening it to reveal, I think, one of the men he was with outside the women's center. The man flits his eyes toward me, then back to Leo. "Police are here."

"Good. Send them this way." Leo looks over to me. "We have the man in custody, and the police are here. Will you be alright if they come in here for me to talk with them?"

I nod numbly, and he gestures for the man to go. The door closes as Leo walks over to the desk, taking his jacket off to set over the chair's back behind it. My mind starts to catch up, clicking words and details into place such as Leo being in the lobby…bringing me to an office…giving me scotch and a blanket and not worrying about a wet leather couch.

"Leo…did you say one of *your* valets?" I stare at him.

He takes off his tie, opening the top button of his shirt. "Yes, because this is my hotel."

I feel my chest hollow out as my stomach drops. The glass of scotch goes down my throat in one fell swoop. "Autumn—"

The door opens and Leo practically growls at the intruder, who pauses before Leo eases his expression and in walks a police officer. The officer, broad shouldered and white pasty skinned with blondish hairs, shakes Leo's hand. I watch as a switch within Leo flips, similar to moments in the coffee shop. Now *very* stoic and reserved. No sympathy in sight.

"Officer. Thank you for arriving quickly."

"Of course, Mr. Luciano. Came as quickly we could when we heard it was your hotel," the officer replies, then turns to me with assessing eyes. I'm still sitting here a bit dumbstruck from the events of the past fifteen minutes and finding out that I fell into *Leo's* hotel with *expensive marble floor*. And I know that cause I slid across it.

In the words of Rick…of all the places in the world.

"Officer Grotsky," Leo continues talking, and my mind comes back to reality. "There should be footage for you to look over. You can see what occurred, but the man was apprehended with illegal weapons on him after attacking one of my guests." Excuse me? "Miss Watson here was about to check in when he attempted to assault her." I stare at Leo, trying not to gape and wonder if the alcohol is already kicking in. Did he just say that? A night here would cost me three weeks in wages! "She fell into the lobby asking for help, which one of my valets and security guards can confirm."

"Yes, that's what I was—"

"Given the circumstances, and the ordeal that Miss Watson has endured this evening, I think it'd be wise for the man to be arrested and taken to your station for the night, at the very least. All evidence can be given over quickly, give you a short night." Leo walks away, pouring another glass of Dewar's. There's a starkness in his voice that's not to be trifled with, swallowing up the confidence around the officer. I'm blinking rapidly as the empty glass in my hands is replaced with the new drink.

I have to be dreaming. Can't be a nightmare, otherwise I'd be in a tea-length dress serving drinks with pearls around my neck. Dreams for some, nightmare for me. Maybe I started taking drugs again and forgot I had. Nah, Leanne and Nan would've kicked my ass.

"The cooperation is appreciated, Mr. Luciano—"

"Luciano," I repeat, emphasizing the 'ch' sound. I surprise myself when both men look at me. I clear my throat, correcting Officer Grotsky on his pronunciation, because even with my head pounding, I'm worried about how a police officer says a last name. "It's pronounced Luciano."

Leo stares at me, his rigidness faltering for a moment. The policeman clears his throat. "Anyhow, we'll need a statement from you, Miss *Watson*," he says with a tightness.

Oh, isn't he cheeky.

"I doubt you need it," Leo interrupts, his voice severe. "She's been attacked, that's all you need to know. You have witness accounts. There's no reason to batter my guests when there's a dangerous man to be taken into custody, Officer *Grotsky*."

The officer and Leo stare at each other, and I see the policeman shift on his feet under Leo's unforgiving glare. Not liking the tension in the air, I say, "I can give a statement."

Leo shifts his gaze to me, looking me over and nods once at the officer who clears his throat again, coming over to take my statement. The next fifteen minutes or so, I'm on autopilot answering questions. My body is going numb at this point, the aftershock of the attack and information that buzzes in my mind settling in. I add to Leo's small lie, saying I was checking into the hotel.

"Yet, you work down the block from here?"

I adjust in my seat, pulling the blanket more over my shoulders before folding my hands in my lap as I look up at Leo. His gaze is dark, watching the officer like *he's* the one who chased me into his hotel.

"Wanted a special night," I answer. "You know spa night and all with a good breakfast with feather pillows? About once or twice a year I save up for a night like this, to just relax and all. Though… don't think the spa part is gonna happen now."

Please let there be a freaking spa here.

"All of that can still be available to you, Miss Watson. It'll all be taken care of." Leo's voice is sure as I keep myself from rolling my eyes. Course he freaking would.

"Very well, that'll be it then." Officer Grotsky stands, while I grab the last of the scotch to knock back. I nod to him as he leaves the office.

"Why did you make me a guest?" I ask when Leo shuts the door.

"For any legal matters which may arise with the man who attacked you," he answers briskly and now it's my turn to furrow my brows. "I now have the ability to provide full legal counsel to you, as a means to protect my guests and reputation of the hotel, of course."

"Of course," I mumble.

"Autumn, if I'd said you were just a passerby, I wouldn't be able to give you my full protection, which you will have. Trust me," he explains, putting his jacket back on. "And to stick with our story, you'll need to stay here for the night to keep up the ruse."

"Hold on, wait." I put the glass down, standing as I bring my hands up to motion him to slow down. "I'm soaking wet, no extra clothes—"

"Amenities will be provided to you, including clothes for you to sleep and leave in." I gape at him. Hotels have that? Who am I kidding? I have no clue what a five-star luxury hotel like this provides for guests.

"I can't stay here."

"Yes, you can."

"No, Leo, there's no way I can pay—"

"I meant it when I stated everything would be handled. And given I did start the little *white lie* then it only makes sense for you to stay on my dime. Anything you want, including those spa services, food, and whatever else you need will be provided. No cost to you."

"You actually have all that, huh?" I wave my hand in the air as he raises a singular brow. "Right. Course you do and would know, 'cause you own the hotel…oh, damn, fucking crud muffins."

"It's not that bad of a hotel," he says gruffly. "I think that's the first time I've heard you swear that much."

"Usually not this frazzled, frustrated, and in need of…fuzzy slippers!" I fling my hands in the air, running them through my hair. The anxiety now vanishing, replaced with aggravation and weariness. Yup, bad humor is next for me. "You got those, too? In your provided list? Actually, could you just please throw a latte on me reminding me how I got here in the first place?"

Leo is silent as I take another long breath, then close my eyes to think. How could this have happened? I know better than this. More careful than this. After all I've been through, how did I get followed from work? *Stalked* at work? And land here? Why was fate this cruel, hadn't I given enough?

I rub my temple, scrambling through my thoughts and coming to the conclusion it's best to stay. Don't exactly want to go home, risk being followed again until I get more pepper spray or a sharp umbrella.

"Fine. I'll stay here," I say, picking up my bag.

"Autumn."

"I'm not mad at you or grumbling at you. You're not the asshole. You're just trying to be nice…I know that." The blanket drops onto the couch, causing me to shiver. My bag is thrown over my shoulder, and I look up at Leo. My head leans back, remembering how much taller he is as he takes another step closer. The butterflies in my stomach come back full force, aching to be held suddenly as tears press at the back of my eyes. I rasp, "I thought I was done…done with…never mind." I shake my head.

"You're safe here, Autumn. I assure you."

His words clang through me, and I have to swallow hard to keep my composure. "I am grateful that it was your hotel that I fell into. Thank you for helping me. I appreciate it, truly, I'm just…just…"

"It's alright," he says with a gentle voice as he comes within a foot of me. Taking a deep breath, I feel myself wanting to sway into the chest before me. Steadying my body, I force myself to remain still as the need to cry presses at the back of my throat. As I peer into his gaze, a small part of the worry slips away. "I'll get you settled for the night, but I'd like to request something of you. Your answer won't determine if you get to stay or not, please understand that."

"What is it?"

"Have breakfast with me tomorrow."

Chapter 8

Summer Nights

Leo's words echo in my head as I lie in the soft bed, staring up at the ceiling as I debate his request for breakfast. I didn't answer, just gaped at him like he'd grown wings. He said I didn't have to reply until morning, taking me to the front desk and everything became a blur. Somehow, I end up in clothes that aren't mine, but are soft and comfy. They tried to take my own clothes to wash, but I refused as my anxiety spiked of losing my jean jacket. Now, my wet bag is drying next to a fake fireplace with my hat on top, while I lie here wondering how the heck I got here.

I thought of taking a shower but opted to just make the borrowed clothes smell like rain, coffee grounds, and dishwater. Hours tick by as thoughts swirl in my head and sleep evades me. I toss and turn more until I check the time. Only 2 in the morning. Groaning, I sit up and turn the lamp on to illuminate the room with warm light that bounces off the pale cream and green blankets, and pictures of farmsteads, and gold trim on the walls. As I rub my head, I get out of the bed to stumble to the kitchenette area in the next room. Why the man put me in a suite, for which I'm not paying for, I have no idea. Could've just put me in a regular room. This suite is bigger than my apartment.

I fill up a glass of water, swigging it back in hopes to ease my thoughts. Nope.

Sighing, I walk over to my things and sit by the fireplace to stare at the flames for a few moments. I rummage through my stuff, finding my wallet and pull out my emergency card. There should be enough to pay for the room. The plastic is clutched tightly in my hands, knowing that's not why I have it in the first place. My skin pricks remembering, and I shiver even next to the heat. Putting the card back, I start pacing as old instincts tell me to check every cabinet, shelf, and drawer. To jam a chair under the door handle, leave a light on, and put a knife near my bed.

The old survival mechanisms I learned from my ex make me shudder.

"Three years and I feel like I'm back to square one cause of a bad week," I mumble to myself.

Deep down, I knew it wasn't the same as years ago. I've made progress and have learned, being more myself and living. Except moments, like these alone in the dark after ordeals reminding me what I escaped, it feels too much. Triggering coping mechanisms and thoughts, ones I didn't want anymore. I physically shake myself, go to the bedroom and snatch up the socks they left for me. My shoes are still soaked through. "Maybe wandering will help."

I made a promise to myself two years ago, that if I ever slipped into the never-ending well of despair, I'd go do something that made me smile. Just a small reminder that I'm free and alive. I can make my own choices. Usually, I'd grab a favorite movie or book, but I'm not home.

Pocketing the room key, I slip into the bright hallway of the hotel that's luxurious in its design. There are suite doors down the hall from me, most looking very posh with dark wooden doors and golden trim. I glance around, moving down the hall as I notice security cameras, where the hall turns toward the emergency exit and see no elevator. I turn, heading back and find one around another corner and hum as I glance at the pictures of hillsides of foreign countries, mountains, and cities. Pressing the button to head down, I examine a deep blue vase with elaborate painted flowers before I step onto the elevator and narrow my gaze at the list of floors.

I'm on the 24th floor of what, at first glance, is a 34-story building, but there are three floors above that don't light up. The 35th says *Private* while the other two say *Offices.* Huh, he has more offices, which makes sense given how big the damn place is. Ground floor office to deal with guests, I guess. I snort to myself. Okay, that's actually kinda smart and funny to me. What I wouldn't give to have entire floors between myself and certain customers.

Skimming down the list of buttons, floors are marked for restaurants, salon and spa, and…bingo. I press the button for the ballroom floor, and head down to have a hall revealed to me that's quiet and filled with grandeur. My toes press into the carpet beneath me, covered in intricate designs, as I come upon the first door. Each ballroom on one side of the great hallway is named after a flower, *Orchid Room, Geranium Room, Dahlia Room,* and the last one I come upon is the *Narcissus Room.*

I frown. These aren't exactly common flower names, that I know of anyways. Most rooms I've heard of were named after roses, daisies, pansies, or even cacti. These were…swanky.

I scrunch my brows, folding my arms in thought. Who the heck names these rooms anyways, now that I think about it. Perhaps a question I'll ask Leo if I decide to go to breakfast. With that thought, a nervousness settles over me and I quickly press open the door of the *Narcissus Room.*

The door is silent as it opens, and I freeze not exactly expecting it to be open at all. I glance around, tiptoeing into the large ballroom filled with tables covered in blue and light pink cloth, the entire place an extravagant set up. Giant vases of flowers are on each table, illuminated from the faint light above from the chandeliers. I'm guessing the next event is a wedding as I look at the chairs lined with satin ribbons and placement cards adorned with silver. In the middle of the room is a large dancefloor, laid out for the main event.

I peer over my shoulder at the closed door, then back to the dancefloor. Briefly, I peek around the other two doors near the back, probably for kitchen or cleaning staff and hear and see nothing. I should go. I should…

Instead, I head to the dancefloor and tap the wood with my sock covered foot. Once more, I check around the place and shrug. "Just don't disrupt anything. Break nothing. And never give a sense you were here."

Swiftly, I run backward and pull my pants up a little as I hype myself up. I take a running start and stop just as I get to the edge of the wooden floor. My feet slide across, and I don't go as far as I'd hoped. I race back and do it again, skidding further than I had before and find myself giggling. They erupt from my chest each time I do it, going further than I had, adjusting my stance and lean into the skid. A smile breaks out over my face as I challenge myself again and again. Until I slip too far and land on my butt and start laughing at myself.

Breathing hard, I get up and do it one more time, making it the furthest I have. I start skating around in circles, scooting over little lips in the floor and spinning as I go. I'm careful not to damage anything or grab at the elaborate tables near the dancefloor. Every few minutes, I pause, listening for anyone who may have heard. Nothing.

Time passes with me skating around like I'm six years old again in the skating rink, before stopping in the middle. Catching my breath, I hold my arms up into a dance frame and I start waltzing as I play music in my head. Within moments, I'm that 21-year-old who's dancing part-time at a community center, glittering across the floor with my partner. The sway of the blue dress I always wore twirling around me as we glided with the music. I hum out loud the melody of *Moon River*, echoing around me as I become lost in the dance.

Practically hearing the chorus entering the music, I stop in the middle, feeling a bit dazed as I open my eyes to the ballroom. My hand rubs over my head, realizing it's been years since I've even thought of dancing. It was all before him. Before…

I gaze out at the sparkling décor, my heartbeat settling as the tremors of earlier feel far away. My mind eases and I remember why I do random little things like this. Silly, yes, weird maybe, but worth it.

Checking the floor for any scratches or scuff marks and find none, I leave without a trace or sign I'd been inside. The door shuts behind me, and I lean back against the solid wood. A smile breaks out over my face, and remember what Nan told me after I came back from the interrogation room, after hours in the police station, the hospital, when it all seemed hopeless.

"Happiness can be found in the most unusual moments, even when it feels the darkest."

I make my way back to the elevator, glancing at the other side of the room to see two larger ballrooms. The *Coliseum Ballroom* and *Pantheon Ballroom*. Humming to myself, I get on the elevator to head up a few floors and arrive at a hallway similar to where I'm staying, but less fancy in how the doorways are adorned. I tiptoe down the hall, looking at the paintings and vases of flowers on random tables. The flowers are real because I check every vase. How often do they have to replace them?

I get to the end, finding the stairwell, and open the door to glance down and up. It's carpeted and the walls are bare with just white concrete. I step back into the hall, and turn to head back, when I notice another doorway and peek to see it's just another stairwell for employees.

"This place feels like a maze," I mumble, going back to the elevators and deciding it's probably time to try to sleep, *actually* sleep this time.

I get back up to my suite and shut the lights off as I slip into the comfy bed and take a long breath. The soft bedding and pillows help me relax a little. Inhaling deeply, my mind drifts finally as I hum the waltzing melody in my head again and think of mansions and castles. I smile, falling into the quiet.

It's still dark when I wake up screaming. Cold sweat covers my body while my head pounds as I gasp. A strangled noise erupts from my throat as I clutch the bedding. My stomach convulses as I switch the lamp on, looking to see it's barely 5 in the morning. Damn. I wipe the sweat from my brow, sitting up as I regain my breath. Even dancing and fancy hotel distractions are no match for the inevitable nightmares.

"Well, almost two months without a nightmare was a record at least," I mutter, crawling out of bed. Stumbling into the bathroom, I find tired eyes, mussed hair, and skin that's flushed with sweat, not at all a flattering shine. I'm a mess. No other way to describe it. I look down, tugging at the soft pants material that's now been soaked through with my sweat.

I splash cold water on my face, taking all the clothes they gave me off and tossing them into the hamper provided. I grab my clothes, still partially damp, and pull them on with a shiver. Pulling my cap over my head and picking up my bag and shoes, I start heading for the door. Even if Leo's invitation to breakfast was real, no way am I going looking like this or in borrowed hotel clothes. Usually, I could care less that I look like I'm coming from playing rugby, but I'm not in the mood of batting off stares at some classy breakfast place.

I shove my wet shoes on, wincing at the feel as I walk down the hall. It's just as quiet as it was three hours ago, but just before I get on the elevator, someone comes around the corner from the stairwell down the hall. A woman with a tight dress, heels in hand, and hair pulled up walks up to a suite and slips in.

Guess I'm not the only one trying to avoid the morning-after walk of shame. Except I'd spent the evening with nightmares, not a person.

I press the button for the ground floor, staring at the carpet. Perhaps it's from lack of sleep, but in my mind's eye I see Leo's firm jaw. The small smirk he gives from time to time, hinting at an actual smile. The smell of his cologne, which I can't quit place. The warmth of his hand. My heart kicks up in speed as I remember having that hand between mine, strong and gentler than I'd have imagined. A warmth rises as my thoughts wander to those hazel eyes, and the deepness of them I could easily fall into and be lost in their intensity. Calming and grounding me like a long-lost friend giving comfort as the rest of the world falls away.

My body jolts when the elevator dings, opening its door as I shake my head from my daydreams. The lobby is almost silent as I step off and aim for the front desk where a woman stands with her dark hair pinned back with pearl clips. She smiles pleasantly, and I glimpse at her name tag. "Good morning Chiari, I'm checking out."

"Early bird, my kind of person," she replies, typing into her computer, barely glancing at my rumpled attire. "The name?"

"Uh, Autumn Watson, but I was staying as a guest of the… owner?" I ask tentatively, ready to pull out my emergency debit card. A random thought in the back of my mind awaits her judgement, but it never comes.

Her smile stays as she says, "Ah, yes, Mr. Luciano mentioned you. Everything has been taken care of, were the clothes and other amenities provided to your liking comfortable?"

"Clothes are in the bathroom hamper, but yes. Everything was perfect."

She flicks her gaze over me. "Did you want to wear another set out? Mr. Luciano said it would be fine if you had. No cost to you, per his instructions. I can send someone to retrieve a fresh set of clothing for you?" My mouth opens a moment, unsure of what to say. "Wouldn't want you catching a chill this early in the day."

"I'll be fine," I muster out, giving a tight smile. "I appreciate it though."

"Is there anything else I can help with before you leave?"

"Uh, yeah, if it's not too much trouble." If I'm leaving early, I may as well be an adult about it and not try and slip out like a cat with the family hamster. "I'd like to leave a message for Mr. Luciano. I just need a paper and pen to write it out, and to make sure it gets delivered. I was supposed to meet him this morning, but I have…I have a thing to get to."

"Of course." She reaches under the counter, pulling out a fountain pen and stationery with the hotel's name embossed in gold. Chiari gives me a reassuring smile before she picks up the ringing phone. I grab the materials and write out: *Thank you for helping and allowing me to stay. I appreciate it. Your coffee is on me next time.* I snort to myself and ponder a moment. Gathering what courage I have this early in the morning, I write my number down beneath the message and add: *If you need anything for the cops, Autumn.*

I fold the note neatly as I place it on the counter, writing Leo's name on top of it. Chiari catches my eye, still on the phone, and swiftly takes it with a small nod. I mouth thank you and walk out of the lobby.

Chapter 9

Muffins, Books, and DVDs

My damp clothes slump onto the floor as I step out of them, then charge my phone, which is practically dead. I silence it as I pull on an over-sized shirt and lounge pants to go lay down on the couch. After a quick nap, I awake with a knock at my door. My muscles ache a little and I grumble, hearing the doorknob jiggle before opening. Prying my eyes open, Nan comes in with a plate of muffins.

"Tired, dear? It's almost nine."

"Is it? I got some sleep then," I mumble.

"Perhaps you should take an actual day off today," Nan mentions, shutting the door as I stiffly get off the couch. "You don't need to help with the bookstore today if you barely slept. That's what days off are for."

"I'm fine, just need coffee and your muffins."

Her eyes flit over to the pile of wet clothes on my floor. "Get in late last night?"

"This morning," I mumble, grabbing for my bag of coffee grounds. "Didn't stay here last night." As I say it, I can feel her stare into my back as she hums, putting the muffins down on the small kitchen table.

Most days I have off work at *Blue Java* I end up working downstairs, but not without starting my day with Nan and her muffins. We'd have breakfast and chat before she opens *Nan's Bookstore*. Cinnamon permeates my nose, mixing with the aroma of fresh coffee as I collect mugs for us.

"Did you go to Leanne's? I don't recall you saying anything about going to her place and it was storming last night."

I let out a long sigh, muttering to myself. She'd be worried to hear I was stalked, followed, and attacked. Not exactly events I want to burden her with, and it's all been taken care of anyways. For now.

I also wasn't ready to answer questions about the reappearance of the man I told her I hid from earlier this week. Unfortunately, I can't say I was at a friend's place, because then I'd have to make Leanne or Trix lie to her, too. Well, don't I feel like a rebellious teenager?

"Crashed at Mabel's, was late due to deep cleaning of the café's kitchen and she doesn't live far from the shop." The lie feels sour in my mouth. Nan has never met my coworkers or know about where they live and such.

"Oh, and came home this morning?"

"Didn't want to overstay. Nightmares again." I shrug as the coffee begins gurgling in the pot.

"I'm sorry, dear. Do you want to talk about it?" She comes up, rubbing her hand over my shoulders. I grab hold of it, shaking my head. "Well, if do, I'm right here. I'll be fine without help today, too, if you need to relax."

"I'm fine, and I'll need the distraction of the bookstore." I step away, pouring coffee into our mugs. "And I gotta keep learning how to live with them, along with the panic and anxiety attacks. If I can't do that, I'll…"

Nan huffs lightly, grabbing the mugs from my hands and doctors up each one with cream and sugar as she nods her head for me to sit. I do as she gestures, grabbing a muffin from the plate as she sits across from me. Mugs are placed down, and she folds her hands before her.

Aw, son of a nutcracker, I'm in for a talk.

"I may be old, dear…" Yup, this is gonna be fun, "…and I do believe you've had nightmares again, but I don't believe you were where you said you were. You can lie better than that. We *both* know you can."

I glare at her slightly and she smirks. Mischievous woman. I slump back in my chair, taking my coffee and holding it close as I take a sip. "I lied worse in college. Never got anywhere with it."

"Oh, Leanne's told me plenty of times," she chuckles.

"Don't ask her about the science class debacle or the Dean's list," I mutter, pulling a piece of muffin top off to chew on. "I just don't want to worry you, Nan. Already came home crying and blubbering this week."

"Panic attacks happen. It's alright. And I'm going to worry over you no matter what. I love you and I want you safe and happy here." She reaches across the table, placing her hand over mine. My chest constricts at the tough love in her tone, warm eyes staring into mine as I let out a long breath. Ever since I wandered in here senior year, looking for specific editions of books, it's always been a safe place. That and her baking. I take another sip of coffee and explain what happened the night before.

She nods along and giggles with me as I tell her about "breaking in" to the ballroom to dance and slide around. We eat the muffins and drink most of the coffee once I finish. I feel some relief telling her.

"So, this is the man you hid outside of therapy from?" She asks, looking over her mug knowingly.

I groan. "Please don't remind me. And yes. And he knows I did." She raises her brows. "He saw me."

"Ah, and what did he say?"

"Thought it was his fault," I mumble. "Told him it wasn't, but… wait, that's what you got out of that? Not that I was attacked or—"

"You said everything was taken care of?" I nod. "And you said *you* were, too?" I nod again. "Then I am not worried. You got back up, are safe and was in a secure place last night, even with nightmares. No point to keep hitting the brick with our heads. With that and what you've told me…do you like this man?"

I groan again, rolling my head. My mind flits back to his gaze and touch, the way he was there last night for me, and the commanding tones in his voice. My memory flits back to him handling the awful customer, and I clear my throat.

"He asked for my number, and I turned him down. And then a few days ago, he helped throw an unruly customer out."

Nan's brows go up. "Oh, he seems to have an affinity for helping you."

"You're not helping."

"But he is."

"Can you not be so sassy right now?"

"Dear, what are you holding back?"

"Nothing."

She quirks a brow, and I frown at her. "I'm not…" I huff out a breath, and get up to refill my mug, "…what if I'm not ready? What if I make the same mistakes and…it's only been three years, Nan."

"You can't punish yourself for admitting what you feel." I look over my shoulder, and she smiles at me. "Nor should you punish him for a past he was not a part of."

"I'm not punishing him."

"Then how'd he respond? When you told him no?"

A faint smile rises on my face, remembering the concern on his as I mentioned my ex and the police. The way he called me "dear Watson" the first time. "He said he believed me. That I needed time. And to know that he'd come back, and he did…and now I think I may have told him I'm working today and I'm not. And I just ghosted him for breakfast." I bring my head down to the counter, lightly banging it with an aggravated noise. "Okay, I really do suck at all this. We'll go with me punishing myself. I'm a menace to dating."

"You don't deserve to be punished for what someone else did to you."

"I know, Nan."

"And I think he sounds like a gentleman, and you should try talking to him more. Give yourself a chance and him."

"Sassy and giving dating advice this morning, huh?"

She gets up and puts her mug in the sink, patting my arm. "You won't know if you're ready until you do try. If it's not now, that's fine. But you cannot wait forever for a perfect person to come around. The perfect time doesn't exist. It's the imperfect ones that are magical. You've done so well these last few years, growing and healing, and I think it's time you finally went after your own happiness. No matter how scary that is."

"I can find that here." I point at the small apartment and the book-store below. "I'm content and happy. It's far better than anything before, and I don't want to lose this peace for something that…if I…"

Nan touches my cheek, and whispers, "But what if you gain more? To discover a joy you deserve? There are all kinds of peace, which *can* include a relationship, even if you haven't been given that in the past. Because that my dear, can elevate your peace and hope for the future more than clutching the sands of time."

Not only is Nan sassy and giving dating-advice this morning, but she sounds like an old philosopher on life.

"With a guy from a coffee shop?" A rich, stern, brow-furrowing hotel owner who looks like he could toss me over the Empire State Building. He's hiding muscle under that suit I just know it.

Nan chuckles, beginning to head downstairs. "I met my dear Finn in a bar. Never supposed to happen, and even though my life changed, I never regretted it. Forty years of happiness and having my best friend was worth that odd moment in the bar. What could I have missed if I said no? Especially if your heart yearns for them."

"I'm not yearning for him."

"Then why are you moaning about not staying for breakfast?"

I frown and she winks, leaving with the door closing behind her. I rub my head, walking to the bathroom to take a quick shower and clean off the chaos away from last night. Pulling on my bathrobe, I walk over to check my phone and see it blinking with messages. I pick it up, heading to my closet for something comfy to wear and pause when I see three missed calls from a number I don't know.

My heart begins to thunder violently. Thoughts race, going into damage control as anxiety rises and my chest shudders noticing a voicemail. My hands tremble as I press the button to listen, fearful of who's on the other side and hoping it's not a ghost from the past.

I almost drop the phone when I hear Leo's voice. The low, sultry tone is calm and collected with a hint of worry. The words don't register as I listen, entranced for a second by his voice before I recall writing my number down in the note. If he found out I lied about working today and vanishing this morning, how pissed off could he be? Was he angry with me? Not answering his question after him giving me that suite and the clothes? Would he never want to see me again? Boycott the coffee shop? Throw paint on the windows?

Okay thoughts are running wild now.

Maybe I'm not ready for seeing people yet, outside of friends, because I can't be setting good examples for dating material. My mind continues spiraling at the idea that I fucked up any chance, when I hear the final words of the voice mail, "Please be safe. Call me and tell me that you're safe."

I pull the phone away, staring at the device. There's three people in my life who check in with me and my safety. Others assume I'll take care of myself or are clueless to what I battle with daily. Last night, he saw that part of me and didn't flinch, didn't back away. He recited the poetry, finishing the stanza for me. He got me out of the crowd, tried to safeguard me from the police.

Alright, Nan. Game on.

With determination, and also not wanting to be a scaredy-cat, I steel myself and push the dial back as I start to pace into my living room. After one ring, he picks up, "Hello?"

The quick response catches me off guard, and I trip over my rug. Stunned, I land on my carpet as a stack of movies fall around me. "Ow! Son of a nutcracker!"

"Autumn? Are you okay? Autumn?" His worried voice comes over the line.

"I tripped over the rug and then part of the couch." I hear him sigh, and I think, suppressing laughter. "I'm not clumsy, I swear! You picked up the phone and it startled me."

"Except you called me."

"I am fully aware of this, yes," I mutter, allowing my head to fall back onto the rug. I glance at the movies strewn across the floor. "I'm gonna have to restack those. *Again.*"

"Restack what?"

"Really want to know? After I ghosted you this morning, lied, and now tripping…the third or fourth time around you now?"

"Depends. What did you lie about?" I freeze. I make a few grumbly noises under my breath, apparently my brain cells have gone on vacation. Why'd I have to admit it? I blame the lack of sleep, last night's attack, nightmare, and talk with Nan. And the man on the other side of this phone call.

"I think I told you I was working today, but I'm not. I forgot. Unless I didn't say that, then metaphorically in my head…I lied to you. Either way I was reminded by Nan."

"Nan? The one with the bookstore?"

"Uh huh, she lives below me, behind the bookstore. Whenever I have days off, we spend mornings together having muffins and coffee. Like the little old ladies we are."

He's quiet for a moment as I stare up at my ceiling, noticing some weird cracks. When'd those get there?

"Is that why you declined my breakfast offer?"

"Well, kinda of, okay no," I admit quickly. Guilt trickles its way up my spine as I get up and sit on my couch. There's some ruffling noise on the other side of the line and a drawer being shut sharply. My stomach twists at the idea of him being angry with me. I inhale quickly, and say, "Can we try again? Well, me…can *I* try again with you? Since I keep having this habit of rejecting you, and honestly, most would have walked away or hung up the phone by now, which I get. Cause by now, between tripping, coffee spilling, disappearing, hiding from you…my track record ain't great."

"You are quite intriguing, aren't you?"

"Is this the part where I say 'I'm not like other girls'? It feels like that part. Have we already reached that part of the rom-com?"

He chuckles lightly and some of my anxiety wanes, while my heart flutters at the sound. Not mad. Thank goodness. I wasn't sure why I even cared if he was, apart from trauma, but it gives me warm feelings whenever he hints at a rare smile or laugh.

"I don't watch romantic comedies, so I wouldn't know."

"Course you don't."

"Is that judgment?"

"No..." I feign innocence, walking to my bedroom.

"I'm beginning to think you're a terrible liar, Autumn."

"To each their own. Depends on the day, so don't test me. I may give you Genovia's secrets." I attempt to tease, flinging pants and a shirt onto the bed.

"Is that a real country or city?" I pull the phone away and stare at it. Precious, precious man.

Putting it back to my ear, I respond, "In my heart it is."

There's more noise on his end, and there's muffled voices, including Leo's which sound like orders of some kind. He comes back on the line, and speaks in a more casual tone, "I have a meeting in twenty minutes, may I see you later today?"

"Not working at the café. Remember?"

"Then where may I find you?" I stop as my mind blanks out. I think of nowhere to meet because I never go anywhere. A bit of me struggles to tell him where I live, old warning bells ticking at the back of my brain. "I have time around two, if that works for you to get some sleep beforehand. I wouldn't want you to keep falling over me."

"Oh! That was *smooth*!" I smile, chuckling at the line he's given. "Big hotel owner using lines like that? Okay, you've got me sold, mister."

"You haven't told me where, yet."

I sit on my bed, sighing to myself. Okay, Autumn, just do it. "It's called *Nan's Bookstore*, but I'll text you the address. But any funny business and you'll have to deal with my Nan."

"Very well. I'll see you soon, dear Watson."

Fifteen minutes before two Nan leaves the shop for some errands. Conniving old woman. She learned I'd invited Leo, and *suddenly* she had places to be.

I huff out in exasperation, putting away books as jazz music plays in the quiet ambiance. Even when there's customers, it's always like this. Nan's late husband, Finnigan O'Malley, bought out the lease for her apartment and mine, but the bookstore wasn't fully paid off. I helped whenever I could for payments, but she always tells me she can take care of it like she had with Finn. Worked well for me, meaning no high rent or bills while trying to pay off old debt. I was lucky…now. I knew that. And I *did* prefer this simple life over life before.

I ruffle my short hair, going over to the cash wrap and crank up the music as Dean Martin begins crooning. I dance a little as he sings about loving somebody sometime. A grin stretches across my face as I move around the floor, twirling as I come to the register, grabbing a few books from the shelf behind. With those in hand, I head down the aisles to put them in their designated spots in the history section about the Vietnam War. The door chimes open, and I call out, "Welcome to *Nan's Bookstore*. If you have any questions, please—"

I come around the corner to find Leo standing at the entrance, his gaze finding mine instantly as he adjusts his cuffs. My heart thumps a bit harder as a small smile pulls at the corner of his mouth.

Sammy Davis Jr. starts singing, and Leo turns his attention to the stereo. I walk over to the stereo when he asks, "Do you normally listen to jazz? Or is that on special days when you're not listening to 80s music?"

"I listen to all kinds. Nothing quite like the Rat Pack, though, right?" I don't turn it off but bring the volume down a few notches. I hadn't realized how loud it was until he'd spoken. "Sorry."

"For what?" He walks closer, stopping a few feet from me.

"I could say for the loud music, but honestly…" I wrap my arms around my waist but drop them to not hide myself, "…I'm sorry for breakfast."

He looks me over briefly, and then he walks over to a shelf and picks up a book on Italy and its influence in WWII. He flips through some pages, humming to himself. I tilt my head at him, noticing a warmth coming over his expression as he skims a few pages.

"Are you mad at me?" I ask.

"No, Autumn. I should apologize instead, for suggesting something like that after the ordeal you'd had. You staying the entire night at the hotel was gracious enough of you. And leaving a note." His eyes flick up at me, keeping the book open. "Do you work here on all your off days?"

"Usually. I find it calming to be amongst stories." He raises a brow. "I like movie stores, too. People really aren't my, well, thing." I move closer, trailing my fingers over a couple more book titles.

"What about being a barista? You're around people all the time."

"Sure, but I have a counter between us to stop most interactions. Not always, as you saw, but I'm often working in the back if you haven't noticed."

"I have. A few times, I thought it was because of me." His eyes shimmer mischievously, putting the book back on the shelf.

"Here I thought you weren't conceited like other businessmen," I chuckle, dropping my hand as I look up at him. The butterflies come full force, but I don't feel the need to run as he stands before me. Little bit by little bit, I find myself more comfortable being around him. Just like those moments in the coffee shop, I find it easy to talk to him. Tell him how I feel and think.

He scrunches his brows, wrinkling his forehead, which makes me smile. "I don't think you are by the way."

"Why not?"

I hum, walking over to the next aisle as he follows me. "Well, the fifty-dollar tips for one. Most who want to flaunt they're worth double it and do it in front of a crowd. *And* they'd do it once. Two, when the coffee maelstrom happened, you were the only one who asked if I was okay. And three, you didn't blame me for disrupting your hotel lobby or your evening."

"It was that man's fault, not yours."

"I know." I stop in the poetry section, turning toward him as I pull out a collection of Poe's works. I hold it up. "You also recited the next line of *The Raven*, not to show off you knew it, but because you knew I needed it."

He reaches forward, taking the book from my hand as his fingers brush over mine. I stop my breath from hitching at the touch, something sparking down my arm and into my chest. He flips each page carefully, and asks, "How do you know I wasn't? Showing off that is."

I cross my arms as I lean against the shelf, staring at the book in his hands. A part of me wants to lie, just stroke his ego to protect myself. Except, I want to give him a chance and me. Not matter how small.

I inhale deeply before I explain, "I've been around many liars and manipulative people, enough to know when someone is genuine or not, Leo. Sometimes I question my judgement, 'cause I didn't catch it in the past, but the café makes for good practice. You see patterns and can notice behaviors in people, but I once lived with those whose deceit, selfishness, and just plain cruelty was never ending." Both our gazes move up, his tearing into mine with such rigidity as his jaw muscles flex. "As I said, I didn't catch it in the past before, but I do now. I try to scope out if someone's a good person or not, or at the very least if they mean me harm."

"And what do you get from me, dear Watson?"

Leo stands as if he's in charge of a room filled with people, conducting business not perusing through Poe. Commanding, yet not overbearing, just making his presence known. Standing in front of him in the bookstore, instead of the coffee shop, I realize it just comes naturally to him. Who knows why, but between the lines of that presence he's careful and thoughtful of his surroundings. He was someone I *wasn't* used to. Leo was foreign to me in many ways. I keep wondering if it's a trick. A ploy. Except, deep down I believe there is no trick.

"I think you are kind, perhaps due to your job and what you, well, own and manage, you don't get to act on it often, yet it comes naturally. You hide your emotions behind stern and rigid expressions, getting people to listen to you like unruly customers or…screaming business associates. You're considerate and sweet, just not often and it's very genuine when you are." I clear my throat, practically hearing my rapid heartbeat. "That's why I think I hid. Ran. You scared me."

"Scared you?" He closes the book, and I nod. "Why?"

"I'm not used to it."

He lets out a long breath, taking a step forward to put the book back on the shelf. Leo comes in close, and I take a deep breath to inhale his cologne and the drift of his own aroma with it. My body relaxes at the closeness, remembering that first time I spun around to see him staring at me perplexed. Except now, he doesn't step back, inches away from me as he looks down at me.

"Funnily enough, Autumn, I'm not used to it either. Kindness that is." His voice is low, and I notice one of his hands flex at his side. I wonder if he's holding back himself from touching me. The thought of him doing so lights me up inside. Anxiety be damned, I wanted him to.

He says quietly, "For me, the kindness I've seen in your eyes has me…confused and fascinated."

"Why?"

"I've had people willing to take a bullet for me, but not a stranger who was willing to take a coffee for me. Protecting me from embarrassment." He brings up his flexing hand, about to push aside some stray hairs of mine, but stops. His gaze stays on mine, and I nod with silent permission. "Or laugh in front of an associate who's screaming about shoes I don't give a damn about."

His hand brushes back the hair from my face, and I stop breathing. The warmth of his fingers rushes over my skin as I focus on the touch that sparks down my spine. I remind myself to breathe as his hand comes down slowly, all while his eyes staying on mine with a concentration of fascination.

"Could say it's the job, but you're the first I've done that for," I whisper.

He smirks. Leo takes a step back, and then asks with that assured voice, "I still have other meetings to attend today, but would you join me for dinner this evening?"

"Uh, like a date?"

"Exactly that."

I blink rapidly as my breath picks up slightly. Old fears ripple over me, bubbling to the surface as I fight them down. I already know I feel things for him, why not try more than chance encounters and bookstore chats about kindness? Except, those fears tick at the back of my neck, and I ask, "This is going to sound cliché, but why? I don't care about class roles or whatever, people are people, but I *really am* just a barista who got coffee spilled on her. Hid from you."

His head tilts partially, curious. "You're more than that and I wish to see more of the person within."

I smile a little. "Hmm, well, I guess there's more to you as well, Mr. Luciano."

"That reminds me, why did you correct the police officer concerning my last name?" My expression pinches in confusion. "I could've, but I've learned correcting people costs me valuable time, and someone within my employ will do it for me. But why did you?"

"Learning how to pronounce a name correctly isn't wasting time, it's showing respect."

"Even if they wouldn't think so? Or may never see them again?"

I shrug. "Especially then. And I was upset and wanted something covered in chocolate."

He regards me a moment, nodding. "That can be arranged for this evening if you'd like. The chocolate that is. Are you saying yes?" I smile, suddenly feeling nervous and can only nod. "I'll have a driver come pick you up. Dinner at my hotel. Seven-thirty." There's an absolution in his voice, and I see a glimpse of that commanding, stern man from the night before.

"So, no jeans?" I ask teasingly.

"Whatever you decide to wear is fine. It'll be an Italian restaurant, so most of the patrons wear suits and heels I should inform you," he answers matter-of-factly, adjusting his watch. He quirks a brow in interest, doing that head tilt thing again. I hold back a smile at the small tells hidden beneath his words.

"Alright, but if I arrive and we're both wearing the same dress, I'm not changing. You better have a second option."

For the first time, Leo gives a full smile, and it almost knocks me back. Surprise fills me seeing the genuine expression, almost gaping at how handsome he is. And that it took an offhand dress joke to do it.

"At seven, the driver will pick you up, dear Watson."

He walks around me and the air passing between us gives me a chill. I turn as he leaves the bookstore, and at the curb, I see a man and car waiting for him. He nods, and they get into the car before he turns toward the store to look through the window. The smile is gone, but there's a glint in his eye, promising me something I wasn't certain of yet.

But holy moly, for the first time in a long time, I wanted to find out.

Chapter 10

Pinot Noir

"**B**e open. Be honest. Be you," Leanne gives advice over the phone.

"And what if I get *too* open and honest?"

"Then he sees you, and you'll see if he's right for you. Better to have things out in the open right away, rather than weeks down the line. Remember that girl I dated a few years back? Would've been nice if her family knew she was gay *before* we visited them. Eight months after being together." The last part is muttered.

"Alright, alright, I get it. Honesty *is* the best policy." Leanne huffs as I laugh. I've spent the last hour on the phone with her, trying to decide what to wear. I still had one of her nice cardigans I could wear, and we both agreed on my grey slacks and black dress shirt. My hair is somewhat smoothed back, and no jewelry. I was half-tempted to wear my Doc Martens. Leanne said no.

"You better give me some details when you get home," she warns. "And if you drink—"

"I won't." I haven't told her or Nan that I drank the night before. Besides, I think I had good reason to.

She sighs longingly as I grab a small handbag, checking for my small pocketknife, phone charger, and wallet. Putting on plain flats, I head down to the bookstore and find myself fifteen minutes early. Leanne talks as I lock the back door. "Got everything you need?"

"Yup, even got my emergency pocketknife."

"How you don't own a taser, I have no idea."

"I'm better with a knife. And spray."

She chuckles. "Well, I think you'll be fine since you'll have a driver and be at a fancy hotel." I lean against the register counter, watching cars pass the shop. "And it sounds like you like him, which you owe me info on. I feel forgotten, best friend is growing up and didn't say anything."

"I wasn't sure how to," I murmur, not wanting to admit that I did like him and that I ran from him, rejected him...ideas itch of him being disappointed when he learns more about me, driving him further away.

"Hun?" I remain quiet, staring at the sunlight that casts long shadows. "You can say it. Say that you like him."

"What if I jinx it?" I start pacing, feeling myself spiral. "What if I'm wrong again, and he's no good? What if I tell him and he finds me broken or too much?"

"If he thinks that way, he's not worth it." Leanne's voice calms me, and I slump over the counter as I hit my head against it. "Stop hitting your head, step away from the hard surface." I do as she says. "He's not Steve, hun." I go still, barely nodding. "And you're worth having someone who cares. So, if he doesn't, then move on. It's okay."

"I don't want to keep starting over and over again."

"Is that why you've taken so long trying dating again?"

"Somewhat." And terrified of being ridiculed again.

"I bet it'll be fine. Just be yourself, full heartedly, cause that's the woman I love dearly. He should to."

"Have I told you how much I adore and appreciate your honesty, even when I hate it?"

"Not lately, so I think you owe me a drink or two."

I laugh, "Fine, next outing and I'll buy your drinks." She gives a victory laugh and I see a car pull up, similar to the one I saw earlier when Leo left. "Driver's here."

"Early, like you. Match made in heaven. Go have fun! And I'm proud of you!"

"Love you."

"Love you, hun." We hang up, and I go outside to meet the driver.

He's huge, built like many of the wrestlers I've seen on WWE. He's tall, very broad shouldered and burly, with a gut I imagine made from throwing trucks. His skin is tan and weathered with wrinkles near his eyes, and he has light brown hair that's full and brushed back. And some of the lightest blue eyes I've ever seen.

An adorable giant. Inconceivable.

"Miss Watson," he says with a deep tone that makes me blink as he opens the car door. I nod, getting in to sit on the posh leather seating. Oh, this is very new and different for sure. There aren't even any holes in the seat.

I sit quietly as the driver gets in, taking us to Leo's hotel. Fiddling with my fingers, I look outside and run my hands over the black leather and finished wood paneling. I've never been one to know anything about cars, I wasn't allowed to drive growing up and the city isn't the best for car owners. I was better at navigating the subway system and ferry anyways.

We arrive, stopping outside the front entrance which I "slid" into last night. I go to open the door, but the driver beats me to it, and I look up sheepishly as he gives me a quick nod and grunt. Not sure where else to go from here, I turn to the large man and ask, "Do you know where I can find the restaurant inside? He never said, apart from Italian."

He gestures toward the doors. "Second floor. You'll see signs for the *Giglio Giardino.*" Oh, he has an accent. Polish? German?

My brows furrow. "Is that Italian?" He nods. "For?"

"Lily Garden." Damn flowers again, at least it's a more common flower.

"Thank you, what's your name?" He starts to round back to the driver's side but stops and looks at me curiously. Rarely anyone ever learns my name at work, so I'm guessing most don't ask him either.

"Rudolf, Miss Watson."

"Thank you for driving me, Rudolf. I appreciate it." I give a small wave, before I walk into the hotel and begin to pass the front desk. A shorter man with freckles and copper hair smiles, ushering me over and nerves kick up.

"Miss Watson, Mr. Luciano left a message that he is a bit delayed, but the maître d' will take care of you until he is free to join you."

"How did you—?"

"Mr. Luciano makes it a point to give precise instructions when it comes to his guests." I'm hoping that's a good omen.

"Oh, thank you," I say, glancing at his name tag. "Oliver." He nods toward the elevators, and I walk over and get on.

The doors close, leaving me alone for a minute and I whisper to myself, "Did he give out my freaking photo or something?" I shake my head and limbs. "Oliver probably saw Rudolf drop me off. Guy would be hard to miss. Or Leo's a bit more bossy than I thought. Not sure if it's a rich thing or hotel owner thing…"

My mutterings stop when the elevator opens its doors to reveal a hallway that breaks into two directions. A few couples wait to get on, and I step off to let them through, but not before catching two of the women's snobbish looks.

They're in heels, satin looking dresses and long curled hair to complete their stylish outfits. One of them murmurs to the other as I continue down the short hall, trying to ignore them as I glance down at my borrowed cardigan and shirt from some thrift store. Yeah, yeah, I should be working here not dining.

I huff, and look between the two hallways, seeing a restaurant at each end. One appears to be like a steakhouse, *Sole Blu*, with dark wooden framework that contrasts against the gold and luxury of the rest of the hotel. Down the other way I see a sign for *Giglio Giardino*, and head for the large archway of ochre stonework coated in vines. I walk up to the host counter outside the doors, with velvet chairs nearby.

A tall man with dark, upswept hair greets me, "How may I help you this evening, *signorina*?"

"I'm here for a reservation with Mr. Luciano." My voice comes out smaller than I want it to be, but the ticking of self-awareness is on high alert because of those two prissy women.

"Ah, you must be Miss Watson. Welcome to the *Giglio Giardino*. Please follow me. Mr. Luciano will be joining us soon. That's a pretty sweater you're wearing."

I follow him. "Thank you."

We weave through tables of dark wood, illuminated by candle-light and chandeliers from the crossbeam ceiling. Stonework pillars are scattered around the restaurant, and my jaw about drops at the warm haven hidden within the hotel. The yellowed walls are quaint, complimented by fresh flowers on every table and the smell of bread and wine. This may be the most beautiful restaurant I've ever been in. I'm taken to the back, into a private corner, away from most patrons and next to a fireplace. Not sure if its fake, but I bet its real.

Once I'm seated, the maître d' asks, "Is there anything I can have brought to you while you wait?"

"Water is fine. Thank you." He nods and walks away. Once gone, I turn around and wave my hand near the fire. Fake. Dang. Tsk, well there goes the yelp review.

I lean back into my seat, fidgeting as I begin to feel overwhelmed by the glittering decadence. I've always been the one working in the kitchen, not sitting out here. This was something entirely out of my league and not really what I thought of when I first met Leo. Sure, I could tell he had money, that was easy, but this was a few levels above my…well, paygrade.

It feels odd.

I'm pulling at my sleeve when my water is brought over, and the waiter leaves before I can get a name. I go through the other names in my head, not wanting to forget their hospitality. All of them have been nice, and I can tell they're not faking it. All service people have faked it at some point. They haven't. Good sign.

A few minutes pass and I fidget more in place, turning my attention to the lily on our table and I pull it out of the vase gently. The white petals have small freckles clustered in the middle. It's soft in my hands, and I become mesmerized as I smile at the simple little beauty. The lily keeps me distracted, pushing out any other thoughts, until I hear a light commotion. Glancing up from the flower, I see Leo a few tables away, standing still as he watches me.

Was I not supposed to touch?

I move to put it back, but he shakes his head once as he walks toward me. Unsure what the etiquette is, I go to stand, but his head shakes again. Remaining in my seat, Leo comes over to the small round table I'm at. He unbuttons his suit jacket, sitting fully in the seat next to mine before reaching for my hand that holds the lily and raises it to his lips. My heart skips a beat as his soft lips press against my wrist, igniting warmth along my spine. A shy smile comes to my face.

"You look lovely tonight, dear Watson," he murmurs against my skin.

"We didn't wear the same thing, thank goodness, I left my backup at home," I whisper, captured by the firelight which catches his eyes, the gold in them like stars.

Leo releases my hand, his fingers lingering against my skin as I carefully put the lily back into its place. He straightens as the waiter approaches, and Leo speaks before he can put the menus down. "The Pinot Noir, Lex." The man nods and leaves.

"Menus don't appeal to you?"

"Not when you know the whole menu."

"Ah, so then you already know what to have," I smirk.

"Owning the restaurant and approving the menu does give me slight advantage in choice." He leans back confidently.

Ah, Mr. Luciano is in his element, I see.

I settle more into my chair. "Well then, *Mr. Luciano*, what were you thinking of having us try tonight?"

"I'm delighted whenever you say my name, Autumn, but please not in that manner." I can't tell if he's teasing or not but decide best to listen to his request. "Are you allergic to anything I should be aware of?"

"Such as seafood or steak?" He raises a brow, and I grin shaking my head.

The waiter, Lex, comes back to place a bottle of wine and two glasses. My stomach plummets as I suck in a breath, wanting to decline the drink, but Lex is already pouring as Leo orders for the both of us. The twist in my stomach worsens as I try to concentrate on Leo ordering something with salmon and salads. Lex leaves and I want to crawl into the fake fire.

Leo grabs his wine glass, holding it up and says, "To a wonderful evening."

His eyes flick to the other wine glass and, yup, I want to disappear. I'm completely out of my element here. Not just being in an expensive restaurant, but a date in general with this confident man beside me, which doesn't make sense in my head. It seems as if the walls are caving in, and I grab my water and chug half the damn thing. I start wishing it was alcohol, but that's what got me here in the first place—hyperventilating over wine. I struggle inside to either just take the damn wine or stick to my guns.

Leo places his glass down. "Autumn, what's wrong?"

"I don't drink," I blurt.

My breaths come out ragged, trying to find a normal rhythm as I hope he won't be disappointed or angry with me. *Don't hit me. Please don't—*

Squeezing my eyes shut, I try to find the right words, but nothing comes to mind. Fuck, just say it. "Last night was a rare occasion, 'cause I went into freeze mode, which consisted of needing a drink. I always stick with water, tea, or coffee. The only time I drink, if ever, is at home with friends keeping an eye on me. No public drinking. For…personal reasons."

Leo is silent as he reaches across to grab my wine glass, placing it on the other side of the table away from me. He sets his own next to it, and although the gesture is sweet, it makes me feel worse.

"I'm not upset if you drink, unless, okay if you decide to down three bottles, but that's a different conversation. I'm sorry, I should've said something before, but I don't know what I'm doing. Here. Overly snazzy place. Date. And the last week has been screwing with my—"

My mouth clamps shut when his hand cups my face, making me come full stop in rambling. His palm rests against my cheek while his thumb caresses my skin. Hazel eyes meet mine. My breathing slows as he holds me there. All other noise of the restaurant fades away as I stay there, swiftly becoming entranced by him.

"It's alright," he whispers. "There are other nights to drink, with or without you, and you must tell me if there's anything you need or want. Or don't need or want. I'll make it happen."

"That's a hefty promise," I rasp. The touch of his hand is warm, comforting.

"I'm a man of my word, I assure you, Autumn."

His head tilts while his gaze dips toward my lips. With that tiny movement, I want him to kiss me. A feeling I've not had in forever, swallowing me up into a yearning as I lean into his touch. It builds in my chest and core, devouring the worry once there as my own eyes give me away as I peek at his mouth. So close.

"Dear Watson," he murmurs, leaning closer while his thumb strokes in such a tender way. My entire body falls into that gentle hold I was so unfamiliar with, and I relish in the foreign touch. More of it. I want more of this safe feeling as the calm washes over me.

Leo's face becomes almost an inch from mine. His breath drifts over my skin, and I breathe it in as I close my eyes. I can't move as he stays there, holding still as I concentrate on the wanting. I swallow hard, opening my eyes and say against a dry throat, "I want you to kiss me."

He inhales sharply, keeping hold against my cheek as he responds, "So do I."

Leo's lips meet mine. Everything within me sparks with relief and joy. I lean into the kiss as he tenderly caresses my lips with his, all the while keeping my head still. My breath hitches as I inhale, and he kisses me a bit more deeply. Soft and exhilarating. A moan grows in my throat, but he breaks away, which causes my eyes to flutter open. Thrill flutters in my chest, down my spine as I'm elated with warmth.

Leo pulls further back, urging me to look up into his gaze. There's a softness in them I hadn't seen before, the low light causing the colors of his eyes to darken.

I swallow hard, reaching up to place my hand over the one that's still cupping my jaw. I whisper, "I haven't dated in a while, but I don't think that's supposed to happen until the third date."

"I don't play by the rules." He leans in, placing a kiss on my cheek. A smile grows on my face as he does. He pulls back completely, including his hand upon my cheek. Coldness sweeps over my skin where he'd been. He sits backs but keeps himself angled toward me. His hand grabs mine, his thumb moving in small circles over my wrist.

"How long have you wanted to do that?" The question slips out before I can stop it.

He smiles gently, bringing my hand up to kiss it. "Since you turned to me with a latte on your front, and you tasted it with the most endearing smile I've ever seen."

Chapter 11

A Waltz For Autumn

After the, well, best first kiss of my life up to that point, I was able to relax. We talked for the next hour easily. I learned more about him. This isn't the only hotel he owns because he owns a five-star hotel resort franchise basically. This was one of several. He had others in San Diego, Los Angeles, Miami, Chicago, and St. Louis. There were even three in Europe: Brussels, Madrid, and Rome. This one, the *Italian Lily*, was his newest of less than five years under his ownership.

"So, everything here is Italy inspired?" I ask, taking a bite of the salmon dish, which is delicious. I didn't touch the salad. Sue me.

"All of the hotels are inspired from specific regions and cultures, a way to honor them," he answers, sipping his water. He insisted Lex take the bottle of wine and glasses away. "This one is in honor of my own heritage and lineage. The ballrooms are named off of famous monuments in Rome, while the others are flowers found in Italy. If you were wondering."

My fork stops mid-way to my mouth as I peek over at him. A knowing smirk is there, and I know I've been discovered. Of course, he had cameras in there.

"Who outed me?"

"One of my security guards this morning. After you left, they contacted me and said they hadn't bothered to interrupt your…dance session, given you were a personal guest of mine. And they found you entertaining."

I put my fork down, folding my hands on the table. "I can explain."

"You barely made it halfway across the floor." I gape at him. "I'd have thought you'd have made it further, in all honesty."

"Hey, I had to use what I had, and they were the hotel's. So, better up *your* sock game."

"I'll make it top priority."

"May I suggest fuzzier ones?" I gesture to under the table. "Fluffier the better." I pause as I go to grab my water and pinch my face together with confusion. "Hold on, you're not mad?" He shakes his head. "How about thinking I'm a little nutty for doing that?"

"Autumn, you were attacked a few hours before. If you'd have slept like a newborn baby, then I'd be more concerned. And you disrupted nothing." He leans forward, tilting his head. "Although, I am curious as to why you chose the Waltz. I'd have bet Cha-Cha."

"You know which dance it was?"

"I've taken quite a few lessons. Part of my upbringing."

Noted for the future.

Reaching for a bit more of the salmon, I move pieces of it around as I try to think of a way to explain that makes sense. Biting into the dish, and chewing to think, I settle on one.

"The last few years I've made it a point to do things that make me happy, even if ridiculous to others. Help me find joy again in darker moments. I've been blessed with friends who encourage it, telling me that whenever I spiral to do something that make me smile. Feel alive. Sometimes it's sliding around on socks. May seem rather silly or obnoxious, but it helps."

"Would that include laughing when coffee is spilled on you?"

I shrug. "Better than screaming, especially since it won't change anything, and it was an accident. It happens. I'd rather focus on the good the best I can, sometimes it's hard, I struggle, but I try. It's easier when it's simple joyful things."

"Such as you reciting, *The Raven*?" I nod. Leo takes my hand in his again, slowly stroking his thumb over my wrist. "You mentioned it helped you think, come back to reality."

"Grounds me when I have panic attacks when I *can't* do the happier moments. It's complicated enough to distract, but simple enough to remember. I've always liked his poems." Leo's face becomes serious, his jaw muscle tensing.

I exhale deeply. "I should tell you about them."

"You don't have to."

"Except if I want to go forward with…whatever this is…" I gesture between us, "…I need to listen to my friends and tell you. Be honest." I glance down at his hand holding mine. Well, honest enough. "And I don't want to be unfair to you if I don't tell you now."

"Why?"

"Because I don't want to disappoint and waste your time." The words fall out of my mouth as we both go still. His hand doesn't leave mine, clutching a bit harder as my chest constricts.

"You would *never* be a waste of time, Autumn," he murmurs.

My heart thunders in my chest, echoing in my ears as I stare at the hand around mine. I swallow hard, and whisper, "I know the baggage I carry can be too much for others. I'm not broken or need to be fixed. The things that happened to me aren't me, but they're still a part of me. Lots of therapy taught me that." His thumb brushes over my skin. "So, for me, I'd like to know upfront if this is worth…worth trying."

"I understand."

I try to steel myself to talk, but the dread in my gut weighs heavy. It makes me ache as I even think about the past, and my hands tremble a little.

"My…my ex," I try to start, and inhale sharply, trying to keep it together. Why was this so hard? If he doesn't want to deal with me, I'll just move on. Right? Except, I don't want him to let go and am afraid he will when I open my mouth. Fuck, it was easier being alone and not dealing with emotions at all. How much do I even tell him?

"Once upon…" Leo begins, and I look up at him with wide eyes. His expression is composed, but there's a calmness about him as he prompts me again. *"…while I pondered…"*

"Weak and weary," I finish the first line, continuing the poem with Leo as he speaks it clearly with me. About halfway through, I squeeze his hand and feel more relaxed and less like a vice grip is around my chest. I nod, and he stops.

"My ex was a drug runner," I say quietly, and he barely blinks. "At some point, he did the drugs himself. We met after college, and were together a while, and I had no idea. He did a lot, and I found out. He…he physically hurt me for…for a short time, keeping me quiet. When I couldn't take it anymore, I threatened to leave and it resulted in a…a…" my voice chokes as I swallow hard, "…nasty, harsh altercation. Put me in the hospital. He's been locked up, but the scars are still there. I started over, with therapy…moving, and the trauma just…resulted into anxieties. That's why I rejected you. Hid from you. It's been three years since I've been like this with anyone, and I can't stop thinking…waiting if…"

His hand tightens around mine as I quickly give what details I can. The rest, I don't have the fortitude to tell him yet. I can't voice it. Not everything. I finish in a murmur, "He abused me more ways than one. And I'm left with the mess he created."

Leo's other hand moves, gently stroking strands of my hair back from my ear, brushing his thumb along my jaw. I realize he's wiping stray tears that have fallen down my cheeks. I hadn't known I was crying at all.

"I deeply appreciate you telling me. I don't think any less of you because of what happened. You're not broken, if you haven't heard that from other people besides yourself."

I loosen a shaky breath. "Thank you. You don't think I'm…too much? I haven't made it easy for you."

"I don't want easy, Autumn."

"Leo…"

"But I do want you," he states, and I freeze. Not what I was expecting after telling him all that. Maybe an *I'm sorry*, like everyone else, and *oh you poor thing*, but uh…I didn't have spark notes for this.

"What?"

"You gave me honesty and opened up, so I will, too," he says, brushing his fingertips over my hair again. "I won't fake pretenses with you. I am a CEO of multiple companies and hotel owner who would normally engage in casual sex and hook-ups. I work, build, and manage everything within my life, controlling every aspect. It's all I've known and focused on, nothing more."

Oh, so this is his form of rejection then.

My chest hollows out, beginning to pull back but he clutches my hand firmly. Leo leans closer as his darkened gaze pierces into my stunned one. "I *thought* that's what I wanted when I saw you. Another who I'd know casually. I went back that night with full intentions of asking you to come to this hotel…to *my* suite." Holy shitballs. "But then you made a terrible batman joke and had no idea who I was. What I owned. For the first time in a long time, I wanted to simply talk."

"Hey, the batman joke wasn't *that* bad. You were ordering an Americano at like 9pm."

His eyes brighten, and I relax again, but my heart pounds mercilessly. "It was somewhat amusing."

"And that's what changed your mind?"

"Not only that." His voice deepens and I almost shiver. I'm not sure whether to feel treasured, aroused, confused, or like a potential conquest at this point. "You disappeared, and I thought it was because of me and something I'd done. Or worse, another catastrophe happened, besides coffee, and I worried. An emotion I've only felt for close family overwhelmed me. So, when I saw you in the shop that night I was filled with relief. It was then I swore I wasn't going to let you slip away, not without talking more with you."

"You barely knew me."

"I didn't care," he whispers, putting my hand down. "Whatever baggage you carry, it won't stop me from being near you…dear Watson."

My body is still, apart from the thundering of my heart as he moves to kiss me again. He stops abruptly, a few inches from me. I reach up into his soft dark hair, gently bringing him to me. He tastes sweeter than before, and I lean into him as he cups my face carefully. The last of the dread is gone, evaporating. Safety, although foreign to me, washes over me as his lips brush against mine. It feels too soon when he pulls away, stroking down my jaw to my neck. He whispers, "Stay with me."

A half giggle comes out of me, and I clamp my mouth shut. "Didn't you just give a spiel about this being different? Or did I actually dream that?"

He puts space between us, leaning into his chair. "That's not what I meant." I give him a look to continue. "I meant as a formal relationship, stay with me."

"In comparison to an *informal* relationship?" I smirk. His expression falls a moment.

"If it bothers you I've had a past of being a—"

"Playboy?"

His brows furrow a moment while his expression becomes strict, but no hint of shame. He's absolute in the decisions he's made, and the man I've seen glimpses of comes back. The one not as gentle, but stern. I giggle again, putting my free hand over my mouth as I realize I'm not the only one with walls up. His brows furrow more.

"Autumn, if you don't believe me—"

"Aww, shit it looks like I'm laughing at you again." I hide my face completely behind my hands. I sense him go still across from me, and I try my best to keep my nervous giggles under control. "I'm not laughing at you again, I swear, really. Give me a minute."

I hear him grab his glass, bringing my hands down as he places it back on the table. He's severe almost, walls fully back into place as a stoic air surrounds him. Even his body straightens. I tremble; he goes rigid. Perfect pair.

We can both be honest. The sickening feeling of talking about my ex has already left, and I know I can talk with him. He's listened so far. Unfortunately, my little quirks may be my Achilles heel.

"Leo, I don't give two shits about your past." His brows shoot up. "Meaning, obviously like me, if there's parts you want me to know, then yes I'll care. Otherwise, decisions you made like flings or *informal* dating, I'm not going to fault you for that. You're human. Some people need or want that, but just know I don't want that. If you're serious about wanting to try and date, then sure, I'll try, however scary it is to me."

"You believe me then?"

"If you only wanted sex, Leo, you wouldn't have come back so often for an Americano. Coffee ain't *that* good at the shop." He visibly relaxes, but the surprise stays on his face. "I've seen the hook-ups of businessmen, frat boys, and whoever wanted a good time, but not you. Not what I've seen. *But*…if you're lying, I'll find a way to toilet paper your hotel. Not the slightest clue how to start, but I'll find a way."

Leo leans all the way back in his chair now, watching me with confusion. Brows fully pinched together with those little lines on his forehead. He rubs his chin a little in contemplation, and I now know I wasn't the only one worried about their past.

"Look," I clear my throat. "You don't see me as something broken or wrong due to my past, right?" He nods. "Then I don't with yours. People have baggage and red flags, but what makes things work is working through them. Even when it's scary. It's hard, talking and opening up, except maybe for us now the scariest part is over."

"How so?"

"We talked, and the other person didn't flinch away. And perhaps, seeing that both of us are willing to work through those things."

"And you're willing to look past it?"

"Not look past but accept it's part of getting to know you."

"It may be something you'd have to help teach me."

I shake my head, a smile growing on my face. "It's not my place to teach you, cause I'm no expert. Trust me." Especially since I panicked over grass.

"But I could learn from you, just as you can learn from me." Leo stands suddenly, buttoning his jacket and comes to my side, holding his hand out to me. "Would you do me the honor of walking with me, dear Watson?"

My hand goes into his, getting up to follow him out of the restaurant. I don't question about paying the bill, given he more likely has a tab. He keeps me close as we head down the hall to the elevator. We're quiet as he presses a button for the next floor, and I raise a brow at him.

"The first thing I learned from you, Autumn, was to smile. Even in the most peculiar moments."

Not sure what he's getting at, but I play along. "First thing I learned from you is to not wear expensive shoes in a coffee shop."

"Quite dangerous," he murmurs, a grin pulling at his mouth as the doors open. We're met with the familiar floor of ballrooms, and he leads me down the peaceful hall. "My family has always been wealthy, but I made a name for myself after I left home. One reason was to build something of my own, to protect myself and keep control of what was mine. This thinking was in part from being abducted and held for ransom when I was five."

My steps falter, trying to keep in stride with him as he continues talking, moving steadily like he didn't just say that.

"I was with the kidnappers for six days, longer than most perceive any abducted children could survive. It haunted me on how long it took for my father to help. To give the money over, days later. After both my parents were gone, years later, I left New York planning to never return."

"Why did you come back?"

"Hotel business and family tie-ups, that even I couldn't ignore." He stops before the door of the *Coliseum Ballroom*. He stares at the door, muscles flexing in his neck as I watch him earnestly. He clears his throat suddenly. He turns toward me, brows brought together to reveal the lines on his forehead and near his eyes when he concentrates. Thinking. Assessing. I squeeze his hand, and he exhales sharply. "I'm 33, and I still have nightmares. You're not the only one haunted by other's actions."

Tilting my head a little, I say, "I get nightmares, too. And thank you for telling me."

"It seemed only fair after what you divulged with me."

"Wait, hold on a minute, next *lesson* to learn I think." I try to keep my giggles back as his brows furrow deeper. Why does he have to look adorable doing that? It's becoming my kryptonite. "There does need to be some give and take, but it doesn't mean telling me things to even the score. It's not a scoreboard of how vulnerable the other is that day. Tell me when *you're* ready, that's all. Just like I hope you'd be patient with me talking with you."

"I'd never ask you to talk if you weren't ready."

"Then I won't either." I grin, watching as he relaxes, and that small smile comes back.

"For someone not an expert about relationships and keeps falling for me…" I roll my eyes at him, "…how do you know how to handle relationships so well?"

"Even though I obviously don't date?"

"Not what I asked."

There's a lightness in his voice that makes me giddy, and I swing our joined hands a little, liking the weight of it between us. "Well, good, healthy friendships can show you that. Then there's consistent, heavy therapy. Quit stalling, why'd you bring me back to this floor?"

"To the scene of the crime?" He smirks.

I jut my thumb over my shoulder toward the *Narcissus Room*. "You're off by a few doors."

"Or thought to give you a bigger dance floor."

He opens the doors, leading me into the gigantic ballroom. There's loads of tables and chairs set out, but no decoration. A stage is set up with a stereo system and a long table for where I presume a bride and groom would sit. My eyes flick to the stack of decorations in the corner, ready to be dispersed. Leo guides me through the vast array of tables toward the dancefloor that is indeed bigger than the one I slid across.

He stops us in the middle, taking his jacket off to reveal the dark-blue button-up he's been wearing underneath, while taking my bag to set to the side. He folds his jacket and places it onto the back of a chair, then goes to the stereo and presses a button. Orchestral music begins to play, but I don't recognize the piece as it fills the space with its soft tones.

Leo walks back to me, while casually undoing another shirt button to reveal more of his chest. My breath hitches, noticing what could be a tattoo hidden under the fabric before he takes my hands. Delicately, he holds the one up and places his right at my back as I place my free hand on his shoulder.

"Shall we have this dance?"

"Most people ask before getting into frame," I chuckle.

"Reminder, I don't play by the rules."

A new melody plays, a gentle theme and Leo sways us for the first few beats. My eyes don't pull away from him as he starts to lead us across the floor into a waltz. After a moment of dancing, I recognize the music. *A Time for Us* plays as our steps become more intricate, while his strong hold leads me easily around the floor. He's easy to follow with a firm frame that guides me across the large dancefloor. I can't help the smile that grows on my face, feeling a sense of peace. Floating is what it feels like as we dance, twirling and gliding together as the music plays. He spins me a few times, and a laugh escapes me as he catches me before I spin away from him.

My hand clutches his shoulder as the song ends and we stop in the middle of the floor. He doesn't break out of frame, staring down at me as my stomach flips and my mouth goes dry. Slowly, Leo lets go to completely cradle my face with his hands. He leans down, bringing his lips to mine into a tender kiss and I have to choke down the feelings bubbling up. There's a careful ease in which he handles me, not like a porcelain doll in fear of breaking me, but as if I'm that lily I held before, as if he's learning every delicate petal he touches.

He deepens the kiss as the music changes to another romantic theme, but I'm lost in his kiss. I'm lost in the moment as Leo sweeps me away into another world I didn't know existed where I'm floating and safe. Hands beginning to tremble, reach up to hold onto his arms to steady myself. He tastes divine. I fight back a moan as he starts to pull away, clutching at him almost to come back.

Leo's gaze is almost molten, his voice a deeper tone. "Come back tomorrow."

"Is that your way of asking for a second date?"

"Yes." The sureness in his voice makes me smile. So, I nod.

Chapter 12

Cold as Scotch on the Rocks

Even though I'm washing dishes, I'm smiling nonstop. *Blue Java* is busy as Mabel and Bailey work at the front making drinks. A few times I'm so dazed, that I end up walking into the freezer, the table, and almost drop some plates. Each time, I laugh at myself for daydreaming like a teenager and losing focus over a guy.

It feels *awesome*.

Rudolf drove me home last night, Leo not allowing me to go home alone. I agreed to meet him tonight at the hotel after I finish closing. Leo said where we'd be going for dinner wouldn't matter what I wore, so to just come in my work clothes. Fingers crossed, no coffee dumping on me today.

Last night I'd dreamt of dancing, remembering how it felt to be kissed. It hadn't been since my college days that I've felt even this close to giddy and flustered. It was new and I wanted to fall further into the sheer joy of it. It kept the nightmares away, which is a great sign in my book. And feeling that elated, I called Leanne when I got home who squealed with delight over the night I had. She kept telling me how proud she was and how wonderful it all sounded. Her words echo in my head, *"Finally! You sound like you again!"*

As late afternoon approaches, the crowd begins to dim. Mabel whispers for me as I wash more of the dishes, peeking over my shoulder to see her poking her head around the corner. "Autumn!"

"What? I can barely hear you."

"I can't yell because jealous pants over there is making drinks. I don't want her hearing."

I lean more to the side, catching sight of Bailey, and then quirk a brow at Mabel. "She'd be jealous of a plant, Mabel."

She giggles, shaking her head at me. Her mouth opens, but Bailey practically whines for her and Mabel frowns at me in exhaustion. I wince as she rolls her eyes, going back to the front. I move some of the dishes and notice the shortening line when I see him at the register. Leo orders his usual Americano, placing a fifty in the tip jar with a cool air about him. I snort. Should've known he'd still show up today.

Baily flaunts herself at him, batting her eyelashes and smiling flirtatiously. The twist in my stomach is hard to ignore as I watch the "blonde bombshell" make her moves on him. It worsens, including the forgotten wallflower feel, when I see Juanita and another well-endowed red-headed woman with flawless freckled skin touch his arm. Leo remains collected, barely passing a glance at the touch as he pays for all the drinks.

My breath shudders as I try to fight back the sickening response of self-doubt I feel. Suddenly, the giddiness I felt all day is practically gone and replaced with the sense of feeling small. I'm rethinking running away, hiding in my apartment tonight with my movies, when the two women go to a table and Leo comes down to the pick-up station. Although he's frowning, his expression lightens when his eyes meet mine.

More people come into the shop, adding noise to those already ordering. Mabel is quick with their drinks, and I sense Bailey before she comes to put the drinks down before Leo. It's all a blur as I watch him, biting my bottom lip as I remember that last kiss.

He smirks, perhaps noticing the little tell and mouths, "Dear Watson."

Juanita comes up behind him, saying something as she helps take the drinks and the other woman approaches next. I turn away, not wanting to feel the pang again, and go back to work. Grabbing some cups to wash, I glance over my shoulder as Leo leaves with the women.

I shake myself, trying to get rid of the unwelcome emotions. "Believe in him," I whisper to myself. "Have some faith, Autumn… including with yourself."

The whispered promise sounds faint against the noise of the kitchen and coffee shop, but they clang through me all the same.

Thankfully, my track record gets better as I'm not stalked from work again. Except the entire walk to the hotel, my head is on a swivel and there's a constant prick against my skin of hyperawareness. Old habits have sunk in, warning me of every potential danger as I clutch my keys in my hands. Once I'm in the *Italian Lily*, I put them away and relax slightly as I head to the front desk.

If Leo doesn't start giving me directions within the hotel soon, the front desk workers and I are gonna become best friends. Speaking of, Oliver is working again, and he smiles warmly as I approach with a small wave. "Evening, Oliver."

"Good evening, Miss Watson. Mr. Luciano is awaiting you, if you could take the private elevator that's on the right side of the main elevators. Here's a key for you, which will give you access and is programmed to take you directly to your floor." Oliver holds out a card.

Huh, fancy. I take it, staring down at the heavy black plastic. "Private elevator?"

He nods as the phone begins to ring, and I thank him as he goes to answer. I head toward the elevators, diverting my path from the usual gold signs to the black plated ones that say *Private*.

I scan the card and the elevator doors open, revealing a small love seat against dark mahogany wooden walls. I step in and turn around to see what floor I'm being taken to, finding floors inaccessible in the other elevators light up. The doors close as I ascend to the first *Private* floor.

"Phew…there's going to be more and more, isn't there?" I ask myself, touching the lavish walls and crushed velvet seat. If it was bigger, I'd nap on it.

Adjusting the bag on my shoulder, the elevator stops, and the doors open to a short hallway and foyer directly in front of me. I step out amongst the soft cream walls. On either side are two large ebony doors and the floor is a dark grey carpet. Within the foyer there's an archway that invites you in with a shiny black table with a vase of lilies displayed beautifully in the middle. I move towards it, leaning in to take a deep breath of the sweet aroma and notice the geraniums mixed in with them. A smile plays on my lips as I touch some of the petals, tracing over the intricate details of each.

The door at the end of the foyer opens, and I freeze with my hand still against the flowers. Leo stands there, his gaze flickering to my hand. There's an intensity in them, smoldering almost as my stomach does flips and I inhale a sharp breath. I stand fully, clasping my hands in front of me as I try to steel myself and keep from melting under his gaze.

"More private tonight?" I ask in a soft voice.

"Yes." His voice is a rasp as he holds his hand out. I move, taking it and follow him into the suite behind him. Well, what *I* had stayed in was a suite…this was a *freaking penthouse*.

Leo leads me down a short hall with a doorway to the left, where I see a dining room. As we pass it, we enter a wide expanse of a room with an open kitchen to the right, bigger than my own apartment. There's another doorway as the rest of the space opens up to a sunken area of the living room and large 'L' shaped couch. There's a fireplace and the back wall is just glass, which leads to a patio overlooking one hell of a view of Central Park and the city. To the far right, there are more doors, including a smaller room with another couch and television. That's only what I can see from the kitchen.

"Holy mackeral," I breathe out, looking around the place. "What package do you have to get for this?"

Leo chuckles lightly, walking into the kitchen.

There's only one thing that's throwing me off apart from the size.

It's bare. Like bare, *bare*.

It has grey walls and ebony trim, dark wooden floors, and expensive looking furniture that doesn't appear comfy. Nothing hangs on the walls. There's some shelving, but it's almost empty with only a few books on them. No plants. No pictures. No knick-knacks. Not even a freaking candle. There aren't even coasters on the coffee table. It's extravagant, but empty and almost…cold.

I look over to see him pull out two glasses, filling them with water. I set my bag near the counter that divides the kitchen from the rest of the living room space. My hand moves over the cool grey marble.

"This is my private quarters at the hotel, where I stay most of the time," he explains, handing me a glass.

"You work that much?"

"Usually."

"You live in a penthouse in your own hotel?"

"Technically, it's a luxury apartment," he says coolly. "I have a place in the countryside, but I only use it when I take a hiatus from work."

"Not often, I'm guessing." I quirk a brow.

"No, but I also have an *actual* penthouse within the city. I rarely stay there. I find it more agreeable and productive being here."

Well, at least he didn't describe the place as being homey. But…agreeable?

I look at the dark bricked fireplace, stiff couch cushions, and crystal glasses in cabinets. There's another small hall past the kitchen, apart from a runner that's just a black rug, it's bare, too. The place was almost bigger than the coffee shop *and* the bookstore combined, yet it was so empty.

"Is your apartment a castle?" I comment. "Filled with the rest of your stuff?"

Leo pauses, beginning to frown. "Our lifestyles may be different, but my businesses are important to me. Expansive as this is, it gives me what I require, which is solitude and control. I achieve that in being within direct contact of the hotel. Minimize distractions."

"Sorry, that came off wrong... I didn't mean it like that," I apologize, feeling like a jerk. "What I meant is that at first glance, this place feels...cold? Yeah, cold. Compared to the suite I stayed in and what I've seen around the hotel. It's different and a bit jarring that it's not like the rest, just wasn't what I was expecting."

"Cold," he repeats in a whisper.

I see his strict, rigid side beginning to surround him. Shit. I loosen a breath, putting my water down. "Leo, you're not cold yourself. That's not what I'm saying." His expression remains stiff. "I've told you what I think of you, and that hasn't changed. But what you just told me of this place being where you want to be the most, well..."

I don't want to finish the sentence, unsure if I'll sound more like a jerk or just plain rude. Old anxieties ripple forth, warning me to be quiet. Behave. Shut my mouth. I push them down even as my chest squeezes a bit tighter than it should. *No. I'm not there anymore.*

Leo places his glass down. "Finish that thought."

"No, it doesn't—"

"Autumn." He stands erect, putting his hands in his pockets as he looks to me for answers. "Tell me what you truly think. You said this takes work and being honest, please do that."

I sigh, hating he's using my own advice against me. It gets me to talk, though. "It saddens me."

"What?"

"This is where you find comfort? A 'luxury' apartment inside your hotel with no personal things? I mean if you're a minimalist alright, but even so you said yourself it's more productive being here. To not stop working basically, and you mentioned being alone, and..." My voice trails away, seeing his expression harden more. I ramble, otherwise I'd run out of here instead of pacing toward the living room.

"You told me that all you've practically known is working and taking care of your hotels. And I knew that the moment you walked into the coffee shop, you were probably someone who spent every minute working. Then last night, you said you only ever slept with women, casual stuff that's it. And, well, all of that tells me either you absolutely *love* solitude and want nothing emotional or…or you think you deserve it." There's a quietness to my tone as I look at what should be a gorgeous view of the park, instead I see it as fake freedom. A tease of life. "You're a very successful man, worth millions and you're alone, *choosing* to be alone. In a space that's empty…and cold."

He's silent behind me, and I brace myself for what I'll see when I turn around. I do so, and notice how his eyes have gone wide, filled with shock most likely from me going after his damn ego. He's also breathing heavier, neck muscles twitching.

"No one has ever told me that before, not even the women who I've invited up. Let alone those kinds of words." His voice is a whisper, and I swallow hard. Shit. What have I done?

My fight or flight kicks in, screaming at me to run for the door.

He doesn't move, staring at me in disbelief. Him not moving helps me keep control of those instincts, instead, going all out anyways since we're here. Too late now.

"Let me guess," I say. "They all presume you're just a fuckboy with a want for nothing else? Seeing you only for sex and only come back for that or your pocketbook? Cause I know plenty of people who'd easily overlook another's needs for those things."

I hug myself a little, while his brows scrunch together as he nods stiffly. I let out a sad, raspy laugh and look out the window again. The Leo I had a date with last night was not who I thought would be living in such solitude. I'd have bet all my money on a place that looked like *Giglio Giardino*, the way he spoke about his passion in sharing cultures and his own. A refuge from the outside. Yet, he didn't live within the beauty he's created below.

He's gracious, patient, and at times, funny, in his own way. There's an awareness about him, noticing small details, and he has quirks that people miss within small movements of his expressions. The mask he wears is well done, hiding in plain sight within what he's created. No one is going to admire a Monet painting up close.

It'd ruin the experience of the art. The whole creation must be taken in completely to enjoy, not up close where the small brush strokes jumble together where the imitation hides. It was something I knew all too well.

Keep close. They'll never find you.

"Leo, I'm going to tell you what Nan told me some years ago," I say steadily, dropping my arms to my sides. He stares at me, still near the kitchen, and the distance between us feels heavy. I can tell this was nowhere near how he expected the night to go. Neither did I. "You don't deserve to be alone."

His body loses tension, while his breathing comes almost to a halt. Even as my nerves shake through me, I glance out the window one more time before I more toward him and stop close enough to grab his hand. He glances down at the touch between us. Conflict sweeps over him with unease and shock.

"I'm not insulting you, just trying to say I think I get it. I remained alone, too. At one point, thinking it's all I deserved after what happened to me, and I have stacks of books and movies to prove it. You have empty walls." My voice is a whisper as I glance around the grey apartment. "You've been extremely kind to me, when a large portion of my life, others have not been. I could count on one hand those who've been nice to me as you've been. Patient. And I'm sad because, something tells me you could do the same." I clear my throat. "You don't deserve an empty home."

Leo brings his free hand up, and I keep myself from flinching as he places it against my jaw. I inhale, feeling the warmth of him as he steps closer and the assurance he gives eases my ticking anxiety. His eyes search my face, trying to find something. "Where did you come from?"

I shrug. "Ohio."

A gentle smile comes over him, and the walls built up come tumbling to the ground. All the harsh strictness pretense is gone, and I see the man who's been alone. Believed whoever told him that in the first place. Kept his place devoid of feeling.

"With you, I don't want to be alone anymore," he murmurs suddenly.

I'm not sure why, but those words drive me to make the first move. Letting go of his hand, I reach up to grab the nape of his neck and pull him down. His breath hitches as my lips crash against his, threading my fingers through his hair and I moan at how soft it is. Leo's arms move around me, holding me close to him as I wrap my arms around his shoulders. My body becomes electrified as we kiss. His tongue trails my bottom lip and I open up.

Leo takes the cue, deepening the kiss as our tongues dance over each other. I focus on how wonderful he feels, heat flooding my skin as he holds me tightly. I sink against his body, feeling him as his hands caress me. He begins to step forward, backing me up until I come against a wall, and he encages my body. A jolt runs through me as the pressure of the hard wall shocks me from the inside.

My eyes spring open, not seeing Leo kissing me, but another's face. Dread sinks into my stomach and my heart pounds. I feel foreign hands, gripping and holding me in place as I screamed for escape. Pain. My body shakes as I try to fight off the memory, not wanting to ruin this. *No. No.* We just got over a hurdle, no more!

I can't let them take this from me. Not Leo, too.

Not like the rest of them. *Please.*

My lungs become frantic, searching for air as I grip onto his shoulders, muscles quaking in fear while memories pass through like reality. A whimper releases from my throat as I try to stop the panic attack, squeezing my eyes shut. No. *NO.*

Everything hurts as horror digs its way into my brain.

Leo pulls away suddenly, breathing heavy and I feel hands clutch my face. "Autumn? Autumn."

His voice is desperate with worry. The muscles around my chest quake, tightening as I gasp for breath and begin to get light-headed. I can't breathe, air catching at the top of my lungs. I want to scream. I want to run. I want to—

Suddenly, I'm picked up and sat down on the couch, but I barely feel the soft suede layers. I rasp, gasping for air as I clutch the soft material and feel Leo kneel before me. His hands are back to cupping my face as tears stream down my cheeks.

A sob escapes me as I tremble, wanting the flashbacks to stop and the pain to leave.

"Autumn," he whispers. I continue to shake without response, tears continuing down my face as I whimper again. Flashes of the pain come back, my body remembering what it endured. "Autumn." No. No, not that name. Not what— "Dear Watson, look at me."

My eyes fly open at the nickname. I see hazel eyes, blurred through my vision, but there's calm in them. I hug myself closely, beginning to rock a little as my body continues to shake. Worry flits over him, but his voice is steady as he begins reciting *The Raven*.

He pauses, nodding at me. My voice is a strained whisper, "...*pondered, weak and...and weary...*"

Just like the night before, he recites the poem with me, guiding me. Almost through, he forgets lines, which tempts a smile on my face as I finish the rest of the poem by heart. By the end, I loosen a deep breath as the tears stop and the shaking eases. Quiet comes over us as he holds my hands between us, still on his knees.

"Do you want anything?" I shake my head. "Let me rephrase that, do you *need* anything? Do not lie. I have tea or water I can get you."

A watery, empty laugh escapes me. "Tea is fine."

"Stay here." He kisses my hands, before getting up to go to the kitchen as I listen to him gather supplies. I pull my legs up, wrapping my arms around them as I lean my head against my knees.

Why couldn't it have been different than before? Everything else had. This is why *I* was alone, because anytime I tried intimacy this seemed to happen. Memories flood back without remorse, playing back like a horror film I couldn't turn off. This time, feeling how I did with Leo and talking, speaking my mind, I hoped I'd be fine. Apparently not.

If I could throw my ex into the Atlantic to drown I would. After tying cement blocks to his feet.

Leo returns with a mug, which billows with steam and a glass of scotch in the other. He gestures next to me. I nod and he sits, handing me the mug as he sips from his glass. Yeah, don't blame him. I'm half-tempted to drink a whole bottle.

Silence stretches and the only noise is the crackling of the fireplace, which I now notice has been on the entire time. Unlike my suite, it's real. I sip the hot tea, glancing over at the man who sits quietly watching me. I open my mouth, but he speaks before I can. "Do not apologize." My face falls. "I know you were about to."

My chin quivers at the sudden gentleness of his voice. Fuck. I feel like a wreck. Worse than the rest of the week has been.

"It wasn't your fault," I choke out.

"You mentioned understanding being alone, was that a reason why?" I nod stiffly. "Do you want to talk about it?"

I stare at the flickering fire, watching the shadows move over the dark areas. Bringing the tea up close, I breathe in the light lavender tea and allow it to ease some of my tired muscles. Leo shifts, not attempting to touch me and keeping enough distance. I could choke on a laugh, different memories flashing of Trix doing the same those early months. Or Leanne sitting across from me or Dr. Wilson reaching, but stopping. Always close, but don't touch.

If the man didn't have such a stoic, harsh mask most times I'd have pegged him for a social worker or therapist. Someone who knew how to handle meltdowns.

"Autumn—"

"I prefer it if you call me the other name," I interrupt, still staring at the flames. My throat feels tight, not wanting to hear that name. "No one else ever calls me that."

"Very well, dear Watson," he says quietly. We sit for a bit in silence. "Was it something I did that triggered you?"

The question makes me blink at him. In the past, I've never gotten that kind of response when these happened. Then again, he's done a lot that others haven't, such as reciting the poem with me or sitting with me *after* a flashback. "It wasn't you, um, that I know of. I don't know. It just happens. I thought I'd be fine. And yeah, why I get preferring being alone."

"You hide behind jokes and laughter; I hide behind work and solitude."

The simplicity of how he says it surprises and eases me. An understanding. Both of us have a crap ton of baggage apparently. Unfortunately, I think mine is covered with caution tape.

Holding the mug close to my chest, feeling it's heat, I say, "You know for meeting through chance encounters and two dates...I'm beginning to think we understand each other a bit more than others would at this point."

"Don't follow the rules," he responds. I smile sadly, watching him as he sips his scotch then places it on the coffee table. "I can have you taken home."

"I don't want to leave." The sentence leaves before I can stop it. The thought of going home, away from him makes my heart ache. I already know I'll be going home to nightmares, no sleep, and watching old cult classics in hopes of relief. Going back to emptiness. *My* emptiness. For once, I don't want that right now. Worry climbs up my spine, afraid he'll insist upon me leaving.

"You are more than welcome to stay," he whispers.

"Even after I insulted you?"

"You were being honest. Blunt, but honest." He glances around and clears his throat. "I cannot argue with you either on your observations."

I keep him in my gaze as my chin quivers. "It's not *that* bad."

A soft silence comes between us, staring at the other as the fire crackles. He then says in a gentle, commanding tone. "Stay."

I swallow hard, and nod. Then quietly say, "Thank you."

He remans still, keeping his attention on me as I clutch the mug. My chest hurts again, and I keep the warmth of the mug close to help. Going back to staring at the fire, I whisper to him, "I want to tell you what really happened. The rest of it."

"Are you sure?"

"Apart...apart from four others, no one knows what...what almost broke me. N-no, it did break me. But know I didn't tell you right away, cause…I, uh, just was hoping for more time. That the past wouldn't rear its head…again."

Leo inhales sharply, and nods. "Alright."

"Even after I called you cold?" I check again, feeling guilty.

"My apartment, not me. Remember?" I softly snort. "I'll listen."

I jut my head at his drink. "You, uh, got more of that stuff? Cause you may want it. After I tell you, and then you can determine if you really want this to be a…*formal* relationship."

"Dear Watson—"

"What I went through…I know, it can change a person's view on someone. It's just reality. I'm prepared for that. Please understand, I'm just…readying for the worst."

My gaze meets his and his jaw tightens. He inhales deeply, getting up and walking away. He opens a cabinet and comes back with a bottle of scotch and places it on the coffee table with another glass. He takes his, sitting and nods for me to continue.

I steady myself, taking in a long breath as I start to explain the horror I lived through. Forcing myself to go numb, as I had taught myself years ago.

"My ex, as I told you was a drug runner. He did the stuff, too and went out all the time. At first, I stayed, thinking I could help him. Save him. I loved him and didn't want to find him dead, and he was my…my first love. How could I have left? Now I see the stupidity of it." My voice becomes a murmur, staring down into the tea. "I went to the clubs with him. He'd get high. Drunk. Then he'd beat me, and I never fought back. I was too scared. Scared to leave him, scared to walk away…where it got to the point, I *couldn't* leave. It wasn't…wasn't a life at that time."

My stomach clenches and I think, *fuck it.*

I put the mug down and grab the scotch and pour myself two fingers worth. The entire thing is knocked back and I huff against the quick burn. Leo fills my glass again, and I give him a sad smile. I trust him enough to keep me from overdrinking, going too far.

The liquor doesn't help much with the downpour of emotions that come next. My throat tightens as my chin quivers. "One night…

he brought me to an apartment…with other men. I tried to leave. Tried, but they wouldn't let me. And Steve, he didn't…didn't stop them. Kept saying I owed them. Clear his debt for…for *him*." I choke out the word, gripping the glass hard. Leo places his hand on my shoulder, steadying me as I grab onto it like an anchor.

I didn't want to say it. The word. The horrible, brutal word that makes me shake and want to scream. Swallowing harshly, I push it out with a shaking anger, "They…they *raped* me. *He* raped me. *Hours*. Over and over again. I screamed, and they gagged me. I fought, and they tied me up. And they…they drugged me. It…it was relentless until late and they left me. I…I dragged myself to the hospital. Bruised. Bleeding. In shock. I can't tell you how long I was there… until I felt…felt human again."

"What happened to your ex?" Leo's voice is harsh, lined with wrath. I glance over, seeing his attention on the fire while his jaw muscles flex and his upper lip curls with a fury that could create its own flames.

"My, uh, best friend helped me file charges. He's in jail, but uh… shit," I knock back the second glass, putting the empty on the table. "The others weren't charged. Steve wouldn't say their names. They haven't been found since then. That I know of."

Leo's head snaps to me, wrath flaring over his gaze. I flinch a little, barely remembering he's on my side. "How the fuck were they not found and charged?"

"Police got their assailant. My ex. Most of the…DNA on me was his. And they, they weren't in the system for any matches," I explain, holding my knees close. "I've taken defense classes ever since. Learned to shoot. Wield a knife."

"Coming into a public space. More witnesses," he adds. I nod. "Don't take numbers from strangers. And stay behind the counter."

His gaze pierces into me, still rolling with anger, but it calms as what I see isn't pity. It's just sadness.

I clear my throat and point at my hair. "I cut my hair short. Harder to grab. Cover up, and not wear anything too revealing. Don't date, as you've noticed. I don't go out, just work. Get to places early. Carry pepper spray…"

"Defense tactics. You've been protecting yourself."

I nod faintly.

"You're afraid they'll come for you again." I clutch myself more, and nod again. "Fuck, Autumn."

"Probably not tonight," I whisper the retort. His eyes widen in surprise, and I shrug weakly. "Humor helps."

"Obviously."

"I've moved on, well, as much as I can. Sometimes, I have these panic attacks. Anytime, before, I've tried being intimate with someone or told them a piece of what happened, they left. I tried to date two years ago, but every person didn't want…want to deal with me. Honestly, after tonight I wouldn't blame you if you didn't either." My head hangs down as the last of my muscles give out, and my legs fall down. I slump back, staring down at my hands and awaiting the inevitable.

I've fucked up so much tonight, wouldn't be surprised if he banned me from the hotel.

"Ban you from my hotel?" Leo asks suddenly. Did I say that thought out loud?

I keep my gaze away from his, now slightly embarrassed.

Leo finishes his glass, clinking it on the table. "Please look at me, dear Watson."

Slowly, I lift my head, and he holds his hand out to me. I stare at the invitation before me, gesturing for me to come to his side. He's offering safety and comfort, and the simple gesture with how he looks at me causes a sob to rise in my throat. Every negative expectation I've had of him becomes shattered by every word, movement, and gesture he's given. Did I deserve this kindness? Was it real? Even with those questions, I ignore them as I reach for his hand that's there for me.

Leo pulls me into his lap, holding me close against his chest as I wrap my arms around his neck. He breathes deeply, running one of his hands up and down my spine in a soothing motion. "No, I will not ban you from my hotel."

I whisper against his neck, "Thanks. But I...I don't know if I can give you—"

"I will replace every touch that has wronged you, any part of your body and soul will be replaced by my own, dear Watson." His voice is deep against my ear, causing shivers down my spine as I listen. "Over time, it'll disappear into mist. Where there was pain, there will be pleasure; where there was fear, there will be comfort. I promise you with everything that I have, your body will *never* be harmed by my hands, only protected."

I clutch onto him. "How are you able to make a promise like that? If I haven't even agreed to a...a relationship."

Leo pulls back, stroking back some of my hair. "Doesn't matter if formal or not, I know enough. Someone tried to steal your smile from you, which you've given me freely again and again, along with that sympathetic, beautiful view of life."

I stare at him, confused and entranced. He strokes the side of my face, bringing his forehead to mine and murmurs, "I'd gladly give up so much within my life to never feel the loneliness I felt when I thought you were gone. If I don't deserve to be alone, then neither do you, Autumn Watson." My throat tightens, and I grip him with trembling hands. "And I'm a man who keeps his promises."

Chapter 13

Marshmallow Cereal

Leo slept next to me all night.

He gave me a shirt and pants, both smelling of him and were comfy, even if the pants had to be tied pretty snug to stay on. He remained on one side of the bed, not daring to touch me throughout the night. Quietly, I wake up to the first rays of morning filling the bedroom. I glance at Leo, noticing his calm expression as he sleeps.

I step out of the bed, careful not to wake him as I pad to the kitchen. I stand in the vast space, narrowing my gaze at where the coffee supplies might be. He *had* to have something here. Silently as I can, I search for what I need, even though it takes a bit longer than I care to admit. His elaborate coffee machine works, and he has *really* dark roast beans. That's not surprising from the man who drinks Americanos black.

My elbows lean on the counter as I watch the coffee pour, thinking about last night.

The last time I tried telling a guy what happened, I barely got to the worst part before he started victim blaming. And the few before that, only wanted sex. Really knew how to pick them. I tried barely eight months after the event, going off advice from Dr. Wilson. She wanted me to move on; I wanted to hide in my bedroom. It was easier being on my own, and not deal with constant rejection or feeling like a crumpled piece of paper ripped to shreds. And all those other stupid expressions.

Leo didn't falter though.

An anger, I've rarely seen before, a murderous kind of rage was his response; at those who hurt me. A shiver runs down my spine, but I knew deep down Leo would never hurt me. I believe his promise, not only from what he said, but how he handled the situation. He was concerned, genuinely.

The coffee beeps, and I go still, hoping it doesn't wake him. It's barely 7 in the morning, even I'm not sure why *I'm* awake. No movement.

I pour myself a cup, adding what sugar I can find and glance around the large "luxury" apartment. It's a penthouse, he's not changing my mind. Albeit, one that I think *at least* needs a plant. Even a fake one.

I head toward the windows, the bright sun coming over the horizon and I sit on the top of the sofa as light reflects through the city. Letting out a light sigh, I feel hopeful.

There's a stirring behind me, and I turn to see Leo leaning against the bedroom doorframe, watching me. He changed after I got into bed, and now I'm blessed to see his pajama pants hanging low on his hips. My gaze moves up to his t-shirt, and I'm met with a sight that makes my jaw drop.

He has tattoos. Not like tattoos, but like…*tattoos*.

His bare arms are covered in ink to midway down his forearms. My gaze goes to his chest, seeing a bit more of what lies underneath.

"You have tattoos," I blurt.

He glimpses at his arms, and back up to me. "Are they a problem for you?"

"What?" I blink rapidly at him and notice the weariness. How about don't stare at the man like he's an alien, Autumn! "Oh! No, I didn't say it 'cause they bothered me, just surprised. Would've never guessed that for you, well that many, and especially since given the art styles…you're *covered*, aren't you?" He nods slowly. "You make up for the both of us. I've got none."

"Now *that's* surprising."

"I'm secretly a wuss with needles." I shrug as he walks over, and I swear my heart jumpstarts as the light pours over him, catching the dark strands of his hair. He stops next to me, and I point at the sunlight coming in. "I'll admit, not too cold when the sun reaches in like that."

He smiles softly as he caresses the side of my face. "Nor is it when you're here." A giggle escapes me, and his brows furrow a moment before a singular brow raises. "Not laughing *at* me, are you?"

"You really do have some smooth lines."

"Working on them. Have you eaten yet?"

"Just coffee. Really like it dark, huh?" I bring the mug up, sipping it with a teasing look.

"I don't have a sweet tooth."

"Hmm, noted. I can make some breakfast." I get up, heading to the kitchen.

"You don't have to. I can have food brought up."

"How about, let's ease into your higher living standards or whatever, so for like the first few dates keep it simple." Setting my coffee mug down, I open the fridge and look for what I require.

Leo chuckles behind me, grabbing a mug for his own coffee and I glimpse over my shoulder to see him drinking it black. Smirking, I grab the milk and rifle through his cabinets. He only has two types of cereal, wheat grain and some kind of bran cereal.

I take it back, there are things I should teach him like what good tasting cereal is.

I grab some bowls, setting them up on the long counter about to pour the cereal in, when I catch Leo's gaze. "What?"

"Cereal is your idea of making breakfast?"

"I never said what *kind* of breakfast I was making. Sounds like you assumed something, mister." I grin up at him.

He sighs, putting his mug down and trying to hide a smirk. He takes the cereal from my hands. "Do you know how to cook?"

I cross my arms at the insinuation…that's not too far off from the truth. "Cereal can be very good breakfast food. Except, may I suggest not being so bland on the stuff itself? There's a whole diverse selection of sugary goodness with more color, and you decided on…" I grab the box, holding it up, "…whole wheat? Without sugar coating? Or marshmallows?"

"Are you judging my cereal choices?"

"Only slightly."

"Coming from the one who presumably doesn't cook." He takes the cereal box from me.

"Blame the city, everything is take-out or delivery. Does microwaving count?" He shakes his head. "Fine. I rarely cook…ever. It's just not something I've concentrated on."

His smile grows, and there's a twinkle in his eye as he puts the cereal, bowls, and milk away. I think about protesting, but it's not cereal worth protesting for. He points to one of the stools at the counter. "Go sit. Take your coffee."

I narrow my eyes as he starts to move about the kitchen but grab my coffee and walk over to sit where instructed. He pulls out eggs, bread, bacon, and potatoes. Well, alrighty then.

"Do you like cooking?"

"I don't get to do it often, but yes I do." He pulls out a frying pan, cutting board, and knives as he gets to work on chopping potatoes.

"Is it because of the busy schedule?"

"Most mornings, I'm up and off to business meetings with staff, video calls with investors, board members, or starting the day going over contracts alone." He glances at me with a smirk. "Boring business stuff."

"You want boring? I'll make you jump from the patio when I start explaining the difference between how coffee beans are grown around the world. Unless you're into that, and I'll save it for another date."

He laughs, and I grin broadly at the sound. It's loud, ringing through the space as it makes my chest warm. Leo grabs his coffee and leans across the counter. He kisses me gently on the lips, surprising me with the small gesture before he goes back to preparing breakfast.

I watch him as he easily moves from one task to the next, looking relaxed in front of the skillets, a towel thrown over one shoulder. I watch with fascination, glad I'm able to witness this part of him, which I know many may have not. The activity is just so…human, that it makes me sigh with content. Everything he wears for the outside world, physical or not, has been stripped away here and I get to see him, fully.

"Did you want to be a chef when you were growing up? Or was it always hotel mogul?" I sip from my mug.

He glances over, a pleasant grin tugging at one side of his mouth. "I loved watching my mother cook. Wanted to be like her. So, yes, I guess I did want to be a chef. Since her death, it's been a precious pastime of mine, but I became so busy…"

His voice trails off, giving all his attention to the cooking. He fixes our plates, putting everything on them as he sets one in front of me and another at the seat next to me.

"You stopped," I finish for him. He nods, sits, and clinks his mug against mine. "Thank you for breakfast."

"My pleasure."

We eat silently, and I'll admit, it's beyond good. Leo knows what he's doing and it's far better than cereal. Whether he's taken a break or not, I couldn't tell. Halfway through the meal, he breaks the silence. "I already told you what I wanted, and that hasn't changed."

I pause with a forkful of egg at my mouth, and slowly put it down. His hands become steepled before him, staring down at the counter. I'm unsure what to say. After a minute he brings his full attention to me. "I want you to only be mine. An exclusive, formal relationship. Boyfriend and girlfriend, if you'd prefer those titles."

Did I suddenly sit down in a business meeting?

I'm half tempted to look around myself to check my surroundings, but instead push my plate away from me as I put my elbows on the counter to think. He watches me carefully as I sit for a minute. "I know I could do something that's, maybe, not so serious? Without as much pressure, but…"

"You don't need to answer now, but perhaps in the next few days you could give me one."

"Leo, I told you a lot last night, are you sure you even want to consider it?" He tilts his head, and I can tell he's absolute in his decision already. "It's one thing of this being casual, seeing if it could go somewhere, but you're asking for full commitment. A kind of relationship I don't think either of us is used to. I'm not saying no, just… being practical."

He places a hand over mine, stroking his thumb over my wrist. "I do not like the idea of you not being in my life. Without your smile, laughter, or honesty. Perhaps we're different, more ways than one, but as you've said it's learning about the person and accepting them. And you, dear Watson, I very much want to continue learning about most of all."

"How can you be this certain, so soon?" He talks like we've known each other longer than a few weeks.

Leo looks to the bedroom, hanging his head a little. "I've never spent a night with a woman without sex." My eyes blink quickly as I glance toward the bedroom and then to him. "Every morning, I wanted them gone and would send them away. Never would I cook for them, dine with them, or dance." His gaze comes to mine, while mine widen. "I know what that makes me sound like, but in my line of work getting close to someone is difficult. People either want me for money, social standing, or…"

"Sex."

"I won't pretend I'm not conventionally handsome," he smirks slightly, and I almost roll my eyes at him.

"I won't pretend either." I smirk back. "They all sound like shitty people though, may I suggest new friends?" I attempt a joke.

He shakes his head, still holding my hand. "Seeing you wave at me through the window of the café, I wanted to never lose you. You make me feel…good."

"Pretty sure those other women did too, well, in other ways."

"No," he says, stroking back a few strands of my hair. "Everyone complies to my wants, decisions, and desires without a fight. Most days I do not mind that power, I've worked hard to be in this position. Yet some days, when everyone just agrees with you, because of who you are and what you own—you feel used. Unwanted in a way. A prop. But *you*, dear Watson, make me feel wanted."

"But we haven't…I mean, we didn't…" I can't find the words. I'm floored by his confession. I didn't know how much I've already impacted him, even after practically insulting him last night. He's definitely impacted my life already, this becoming a relationship or not.

"These last few weeks you've wanted me, to spend time with me, perhaps not in the same way as others have." I shrug not so innocently, and he grins. "Or yes, in some ways. But you've wanted to talk to *me*, learn about me and what I felt or thought. We may have known each other for a short period, but isn't that how it starts? An inkling, a chance because you feel tethered by a thread beyond your own fates." He brings me in closer, placing his forehead against mine. "Every part of you has intoxicated me, from how you smile, joke, and persevere. I don't want to miss a single thing."

I lean back and stroke my fingers through his hair, still as soft as it felt last night. Although I feel somewhat the same, the way he invades my mind and makes me feel safe. How he listens and makes me feel worthy. But something holds me back from agreeing. The small voice in the back of my head, telling me to run. Albeit faint.

"You're not like anyone I've ever met, Leonardo Luciano."

"Are you saying yes?"

"Hold on, cowboy, it's a 'I want to think on it,' but not a no. I just…I just need to talk to my therapist and see if she thinks I'm ready." I watch his reaction at the mention of her, it's not the first time I've talked about therapy, but not part of how some of my decisions hinder on it.

He nods, dipping his head to kiss me gently. I breathe deeply, tasting him against my lips. He pulls away, brushing fingertips against my cheek. "I'll wait however long until you're ready."

Elm Jed

The door closes behind me as I glance over at Trix's office door. It's closed, which means she's probably on a call. Damn. Swallowing hard, I walk to the table of tiny water bottles and take one to drink as I leave. I'll have to talk to Trix another time. Today wasn't a normal day for an appointment, I'd called in to come earlier than my scheduled one in a couple of weeks.

It's been a few days since I stayed at Leo's, and I couldn't keep his question from tumbling around in my head. Although I'm not sure if Dr. Wilson made it fully better…or worse. She seemed surprised that I was willing to date at all, and told Leo as much as I did so early in the relationship…friendship…acquaintanceship?

Dr. Wilson appeared more intrigued with how he helped handle my panic attacks and how open he's been. Oh, she was excited, while I was still worried and scared. Sure, Leo probably had an angry streak in him. I've seen snippets of it, but it's never been directed towards me. He's commanding, strict, and doesn't seem the type to give compromises. And appears to thrive while being in charge.

Sighing, I get on the elevator and slump back against the wall, replaying parts of the session in my head.

"He sounds like most business owners," Dr. Wilson commented.

"Yeah, but…none of that bothers me. Why am I scared? I want to, but why…"

"Because you've been neglected and abused. Your first instinct will be to reject that care, fearing its insecurity. You were like this with Nan, too. And Leanne. You holed up and had meltdowns and panic attacks, but you learned to open up. Similar situation here. Bad things can scare us, but good things can, too."

"You're kidding me."

"Remember when Roger got you the job at Blue Java? You didn't think it would work out, but it did. It ended up being a very good thing, to give you stability."

"Not to mention income," I muttered.

At the end of the session, she said it was my decision to make, not hers. I knew that, but some validation that I'm not making a major mistake would be nice. I grumble, running my hand over my face. "Scared of a good thing? Sounds like an annoying catch-22."

Getting off the elevator, I check my phone, no new messages since this morning. Leo has texted me every morning and evening to check in that I made it home. He still came into the coffee shop, that much of our routine hasn't changed. Except, I've been working in the back, while other women flirt with him out front. It was easier on my ego to stay out of sight, even if I ached to see him.

All kinds of emotions flit inside me. They pull in different directions, one part wanting to be with him. Another worried it'll just be this passing phase and I'll be alone again. And the last tugging at me to just hide. Stick with my old instincts. Except, like Leo, I didn't want him completely gone from my life. I don't think I can tell him no entirely. We've known each other a short time, but I felt safe with him. Although a few moments panic sparked at the back of my mind, but I wasn't wholly scared of Leo. Deep in my gut, something told me I can trust him. He'd asked where I came from, but I wondered the same about him.

I was just a jumbled mess of feelings.

I leave the building, tossing the empty water bottle as I walk out onto the hot, sunny street. Even with the heat, I'm wearing my jean jacket and flat cap, which does help cover my eyes. It's late summer, and I'm ready for fall to show up. I weave through the throngs of people, heading home as my mind continues to argue with my heart and gut.

Yes. I can tell him yes. Huh, see, wasn't too scary to admit.

I smile to myself, pausing at the crosswalk for the light to change. I allow the thought to come back, repeating to myself I can say yes. It feels more right each time. Confident I can tell him yes, I cross the street with a grin.

Elm Jed

Approaching a newsstand, there's sudden prick at my neck. The hairs on my skin stand on end, and I slow my pace to glance down at the copies before me. I pretend to browse as my eyes flit to the side. All I see are people, moseying about. Smiling at the owner, I shake my head and continue toward the park entrance and stop to glance at a map of the park.

Again, I peek behind me.

There. He's dressed in dark jeans, a button-up, and sunglasses with tanned skin and golden hair. He's a good enough distance away, but I recognize him as I left the women's center and when I stopped at the vendor. That's almost two blocks worth of trailing me. Shit.

My heart rate picks up as I head down a path into the park, forgoing taking the easiest route home as my chest tightens. People buzz around me as my throat goes dry. I don't have to steal another look behind me, knowing my instincts are right that he's not far behind. My mind goes through each defense tactic and route I can take as my heart pounds in my ears.

My sight stays before me as I wind down a path and rummage through my shoulder bag, finding only my knife. Damn it, I didn't replace the pepper spray. I could call someone, but it'll be too late, and no way can I walk home and let them know where I live. If they didn't know already.

Fear trickles down my spine. I squash it down, allowing my fight or flight response to kick in and fight wins out as frustration begins to bubble up. I'm moving on with my damn life and for some fucking reason in the past two weeks, I've been followed *twice*.

No. This is NOT happening again.

Fortifying myself as I gather up my courage, heading down long paths through the park and as I take a quick turn, I chance a look, seeing him still trailing behind. I round another corner, and sprint. Racing between runners and dog walkers, I run through the park and aim for a familiar part of Sheep Meadow. He's chasing me and it's confirmed when I hear someone shout, "Hey! Watch out!"

I veer to the side, and dive around some trees, then between some shrubs. Once I break through the brush, I skid to a halt and crouch behind a large bush to catch my breath. Keeping low, I watch through the leaves as the man rushes past and stops a few feet ahead of where I crouch. Silently, I stand and move behind him just as his head snaps to the side as my shoe crunches over a leaf. I kick at the back of his knee, making him lose his balance as I swing my arm back and punch him square in the jaw. He grunts, stumbling back, but not far enough for me, so I knee his groin and stomp on his foot before he falls. Pulling my knife out, I point it at him.

He groans on the ground, holding onto his dick with a heavy, pained grunt. The sunglasses have fallen off, and he looks up at me with shocked blue eyes. He holds his hands up in defense when he sees the knife. "Hold on! Hold on! I'm not going to hurt you!"

We're far enough away from the groups of people picnicking, no one will hear him. Then again, they won't hear me either. Great plan. Full proof, Autumn… not.

"Says the one who just chased me through Central fucking Park," I hiss between heaving breaths. I wave the knife in my hands, and his eyes bulge at the k-bar. "Why were you following me?"

"It was for your own safety." Is that an accent? "I had no intention of hurting you." Yup, that's an accent.

"Are you British?" I ask. He nods briefly. "Are you kidding me? I'm being chased through the park by a James Bond wannabe? And you're trying to convince me that you—"

"L—…Mr. Luciano was worried about your safety."

I freeze. I stare down at him, frowning. Leo what?

"I'm part of his head security team, and he instructed me to keep an eye on you," he explains, bringing his hands down.

My heart pounds harder as my head starts to whirl, feeling confused and a bit woozy from the sprint and this new information. "Alright…let's say I believed you. *Why* would he want to keep *any* eyes on me?"

His breath slows a moment, scooting further back into the grass and closer to the base of a tree. I scowl at him with a half snarl, and he stops. "Tell me."

"I can't tell you."

"Bullshit," I scoff. "If you're fucking following me, chasing me through a damn park, stalking me home because my safety *is* in jeopardy, you're telling me why."

"Miss Watson, I can't—"

"Don't say my name!" I yell, brandishing the knife again. "I know *exactly* how to use this. Don't give me a reason to."

"Please. Listen to me. If any harm came to you while under my protection, Mr. Luciano would be—"

"*Exceptionally upset?*" I mock his accent a little and he blinks in surprise.

I feel like I'm slipping; about to lose it.

Taking long breaths, I debate what to do and try to clear my head. I could call for someone, bring them over here, but then I'd have to explain why I'm carrying a military grade k-bar in my bag. Or worse he'd find a way to use the people against me. Unless he's telling the truth. Trying to push the panic away, which wants to rip its way through me, I struggle to concentrate on what I need to do. Confirmation. I *need* answers.

I inhale harshly, and ask again, "Why is my safety in danger? Give me that fucking courtesy at the very least."

He visibly swallows, sitting up ever so slightly. He glances at the knife, and then back up at me, before he loosens a breath. "The man who attacked you about a week ago skipped bail, even though he wasn't supposed to have it. The officer in charge of his case screwed up paperwork, not realizing he was a flight risk and had a criminal history."

"He had a history?" I rasp as my stomach plummets, then tightens.

"There were other warrants out for his arrest from other incidents," he answers, and he frowns. "You didn't know?"

"No, I had no idea he had…what kind of screw up was there, especially to miss something like that?" I'm beginning to feel sick, unease gnawing at my insides.

"I'm not sure, Mr. Luciano's lawyers were contacted and informed him of the situation. The police didn't contact you?"

"No." I shake my head, racking my brain as he looks at me in confusion. "Why wouldn't the police contact me if had—?"

My voice stops as my heart clatters in my chest. Fucker. I knew *exactly* who did it; trying to keep me out of the system even if it put me back in danger by doing so. The nerves twisting inside me worsen. I lower the knife, easing off my defensive stance. "Why didn't Leo contact me then?"

"He was informed only this morning. He didn't want to alarm you, until he spoke with the police on finding the man or hiring a bounty hunter."

I try to calm myself, trying to think a bit more clearly. It's a struggle to think past fearful memories seeping forward. Warning blaring in my head. The anger I'm feeling toward Leo seems to be pushing it back. I told him about how I worried about being followed. How I feared that others were coming for me. I *told* him. And then he had me *followed*. He took matters into his own hands without consulting me, when it involved *me*.

We weren't even officially dating yet!

Even so, you tell your partner if you're having them followed!

I glance over at the British man, and point the weapon back at him, still not fully convinced he's telling the truth. I won't risk it.

"Hand over the gun I know you're carrying, quickly," I instruct. Stiffly, he does as I say, pulling out a handgun I recognize as a Glock. He places it on the ground, and I walk over to snatch it up. "Next, proof that you work for Leo. Pull up his contact on your phone and call him. Put it on speaker."

He pulls out his phone as I take out the magazine of the gun, tossing it away from us. He hits speed dial and I step closer, listening as the phone rings three times.

"Isaac, you're late with your check-in." Leo's voice comes over the line. The man, Isaac, says nothing as he stares up at me, waiting for me to speak.

Fury flicks through me as the familiar emotion of being deceived hits me. Tricked. Lied to. Again.

Without another thought, I plunge the knife through the phone, splitting it down the middle just as Leo began to ask Isaac for a report. I take apart his gun, dropping the small pieces in the grass and pocket his firing pin.

Isaac gapes at me as I pick up my bag and put away the k-bar. I start to walk away, pausing to say, "Tell him he fucked up and broke his promise. And tell him I'd rather he'd have hit me. At least I'd have seen it coming."

Isaac calls out to me as I storm away, "Miss Watson!"

I sprint for home, taking an alternate route, making it harder for anyone to follow as my stomach churns. The deceit runs deeps in my veins as the tears begin to fall.

Chapter 14

Baggage We Carry

Nan has knocked on my door three times now. I was supposed to work a few hours tonight, but called and told Yuki that I needed the night off and apologized. She told me to have a good night. Too bad I've been spending the last hour sitting on my counter, staring at the door. There's a chair in front of it, and I double checked that my other knife is taped beneath the couch, while a kitchen knife stays beside me.

Stupid instincts and my brain thinking *they're* coming for me again.

Frustration and anxiety battle in my head, fighting for the upper hold.

I keep repeating *Leo isn't my ex* in my head. I should get up, use one of my coping mechanisms to calm my brain fog like watch a movie or something. I don't want to move, feeling like a child who's been told they're bad.

A few more minutes pass, and I'm able to slink off the countertop and spread out some movies on the carpet. Distraction, I need a distraction. I come across the case for *The Room*, staring at it a moment and shake my head, putting it back and find *Reefer Madness: The Movie Musical*.

"Hello old friend," I mutter, and get up to put it in the player, when my phone rings. The television screen goes to the movie menu as I go to grab my phone, seeing Nan's number. Sighing, I pick up, "I don't want to talk, Nan."

"Moping in your room isn't going to do any good, dear. Come down and have some tea, I'm sure that'll be more helpful." Her voice is sweet, and I can practically smell the cookies she more than likely just made.

"I'm watching a movie."

"Sweetie, you can't always hide in your movies." I get up, beginning to pace.

"Fine, I'll read a book then," I mumble. She exhales heavily, and I run my hand over my face. "Nan, I just…I don't know what to do… and I need…okay, I don't know what I need."

"Well, Leo is down here, and he's worried about you. Perhaps, *he* can help."

My feet stumble over themselves as I clutch the couch. "He's *here?*"

"Yes, he came in a bit ago because he couldn't get ahold of you." Probably 'cause I've ignored every single call since I ran from the park.

She continues, "He explained to me what happened, and it sounds like a misunderstanding, dear."

"A *misunderstanding?*" I almost screech. "He sent someone to follow me! He—"

"Knew a criminal was back on the streets—"

"Along with the rest in this city!"

"Let me finish, Autumn," she says, and I pinch the bridge of my nose as I slump against the couch. You gotta be kidding me. "He was trying to be helpful, given the circumstances. Help ease some of your worry."

"Except I didn't know the guy was out!" I yell, beginning to pace. "Even if I did, then it would've been worse knowing someone was following me. But I didn't know. *No one* told me the guy skipped bail." Or had a criminal record, which still causes unease to gnaw at me.

What *kind* of history?

There's a muffled sound on the other side of the phone, whispers being covered over. For a moment, I think Nan is scolding someone and I hear a door close. Nan comes back on the line, "He said he thought you knew, someone informed him the police contacted you."

"No, they didn't, Nan." My voice goes quiet.

She goes silent a moment, and whispers, "Caltz?"

I clear my throat, trying to shake off the nerves. "Not his jurisdiction."

"You don't sound convinced."

"I don't know, Nan, who knows if it was him, but the fact of the matter is that no one told me anything. And then I had the shit scared out of me while in the park. Again!" I groan, gripping my hair as I glare at the cabinet where the stashed scotch is.

Would this count as an emergency?

Nan hums, and I wait a moment, hearing no signs of mumbling in the background. She finally speaks, "You should talk to him."

I rub my forehead. "Why are you so insistent I talk to him?"

"Because you're an adult and so is he, if there's an issue or miscommunication, then you need to discuss it."

Am I really being scolded right now?

"Nan, what he did is almost no different than—"

"It is not the same, and don't condemn him for something another did without knowing the why." Oof, that hurt. Okay got me there. "You won't understand his entire perspective until you talk with him. Give him that chance to explain. Give *yourself* that chance, because I think he was truly trying to help you, dear." Her voice becomes soft. "If you still believe he'd done it maliciously *after* you talk, then I will help you kick him out."

I tap my head against the living room wall. I'm holed up in my apartment with no way out, maybe enough food to last me a week, but only enough coffee for two days. That's the clincher. My vision moves to the television screen. Fine. Talking is probably more productive than rewatching a musical about weed.

"Fine. I'll come down and talk. But you better have cookies, Nan."

She chuckles smugly. "Of course, dear." She hangs up, and I put my phone down.

Rubbing my head, I move the chair and open the door, almost jumping back with a scream when I see Leo standing there. His mouth is in a tight line, brows furrowed as he stares at me severely.

"Shit! Sneaky woman was distracting me!" I scream, pushing the door to close it, but Leo stops it with his leg and hand. He easily keeps it open as I try to shove against it.

My heart rate picks up, flashes of the past attempting to burst through. I focus on the weight of the door, ignoring it as Leo states, "Let me explain, Autumn."

"I take it back; don't want to talk! I don't care if I sound like a freaking child right now!" I push against the wood, not budging.

"Allow me to—"

"I just said—"

"I fucked up, I'm sorry, Autumn." His apology makes me freeze. My muscles are still locked in place against the door, but my heart rate slows. What?

I look up at him, noticing he's breathing a bit heavy as his eyes frantically search my face. "I was told you were contacted and I didn't know you had therapy today. I thought you'd be at the coffee shop and would talk to you *in* person instead of over the phone on what to do."

"Except I found out through your bodyguard, who *you* sent to follow me."

"Isaac was as safety precaution. He would've stayed across the street, given you enough space."

"He chased me through the park!"

"Because you ran—"

"Don't pin this on me!"

"He thought you were in danger."

"And *I* didn't know *he* wasn't the danger. I told you the other day about how I worry being found again."

"That's why I didn't tell you right away."

"What? That doesn't, uh!" I throw my hands up in the air, stepping back from the door as he pushes it open fully with his hand.

"You were never supposed to know Isaac existed," he says as I grumble at him, covering my face with my hands. "Autumn, if I had told you I planned to have someone shadow you—"

"I'd have said okay!" I interrupt, dropping my arms.

Leo is taken aback, stepping away as shock moves over his face. I exhale harshly with frustration as I see confusion on him while his mouth works. He reaches up, running his hand through his hair as he scowls. "What?"

"I would've said okay," I repeat.

The crease between his brows worsens, and a part of me is happy seeing the familiar expression. With that confusing turn of emotion, I throw my hands up in the air and walk into my kitchen in search of ice cream. Fuck the alcohol, I need sugar.

I throw open my freezer, pulling out a pint of double chocolate and grab a spoon as I talk. "Could I'd done the whole 'No, I'm a strong woman. I don't need protection. I'm independent.' Sure, but fuck that! I told you enough of what I went through, and honestly, fuck feeling like someone is *following me* everywhere I go. Feeling powerless if those five guys show up again. Or another stalker following me at work." The lid of the container is thrown off, and I shove the spoon into the ice cream. "These last few years I've hated going out because I'm always looking over my shoulder, hoping that a few defense classes will save me, but even with a weapon or pepper spray, that's never a guarantee. I keep *waiting* for them to show up. I can be a strong, independent woman while taking help, but I *need* to know *who* it is helping me."

I slump against my counter, shoving a spoonful of ice cream into my mouth. The chocolate helps a little as it melts on my tongue. Leo quietly closes the door and walks toward me slowly, stopping at my tiny kitchen table. "You honestly would've been fine with a bodyguard?"

"Yes." I flick my spoon in emphasis, and ice cream gets on the counter. We both stare down at the small mess. Inside, I bemoan that I must also look a mess. I put the dessert down, reaching for a towel, but Leo grabs it first and cleans it up for me. As he puts the towel back, he leans over the counter across from me, gripping the very fake granite top harshly. I grab the ice cream, moving the spoon around.

"I haven't felt safe on my own in over three years, Leo," I admit. He looks over his shoulder at me, his gaze somber. "For the first time in a while, I finally felt safe enough with someone, with you. Like I wasn't going to have my head bashed in or slapped or thrown down stairs. Sure, I have some panicky moments, but I honestly felt safe being around you. Today knowing I was being followed, I didn't feel safe."

His expression falls as he hangs his head, his chest expanding with long breaths. I go back to my ice cream, having a few more mouthfuls as the minutes pass. Leo finally stands up straight, turning to face me. "In my world, security is paramount. There's always a guard with me, even if you don't see them. It comes with the territory of what I own and who I am. I'm used to putting those guards in positions of protection with or without the consent of those they're tasked with. The hotels have many who visit who are required to have such security, and in the past, I've dealt with those who've rejected that protection and suffered the consequences. I did not want to take that chance with you."

"Well, you need to," I counter, stabbing my melting ice cream. "You need to talk to me, ask me what I think, and don't assume I'll automatically say no."

"I apologize for not talking to you before, truly I am. I should've spoken to you, even if only over the phone. If I had, none of this would've happened and..." his voice fades away, and he leans against the counter next to me, "...I wanted to keep you safe, and I did the exact opposite."

His apology eases my mind, helping the ticking of worry disappear. The genuine concern and understanding clashes with what I've known, which my past instincts scream at me that he's lying. That secretly he's waiting to yell and beat me for fighting him at the door, and I should cower. Flicking away those thoughts, I throw my spoon into the sink and put the ice cream back into the freezer as Leo watches me carefully. I stand opposite him, wrapping my arms around myself.

"Is Isaac alright?" I break the silence.

His eyes widen a moment, then return to normal. "Ego a bit bruised, but he's fine."

"Well, if he's going to be my bodyguard or whatever, he's gotta up his game. I took him down easier than the one guy."

"I ordered him not to harm you, under any circumstances, but I'll give him your review." Leo's expression is serious, even though I'm pretty sure he just attempted a joke. His strict posture does relax slightly. "Did you have that k-bar when you fell into the hotel?"

"Yeah, but the pepper spray was easier to grab. I forgot to replace it."

His gaze flicks to the knife on the counter next to him. "You know how to use a military grade knife, but not how to dice potatoes?" He asks, a shadow of a smirk on his face.

I respond in a deadpan voice, "Castrating isn't hard to do."

Leo coughs suddenly through a scoff, rubbing his jaw harshly as he tries to hide his grimace, while I smile smugly. "Am I in danger of your skills then?"

"No."

His brows raise.

I almost snort at him, but add, "I understand *why* you did it, and I'm still pissed, but I forgive you. Just…promise to talk to me first."

Leo nods, and holds his hand out to me. I take it easily, coming into his embrace as I feel his arms wrap around me. He kisses my head, breathing deeply while I hold onto him. The last of the anxieties from before, melt away in his arms. When he's not nearby, I feel confused and my thoughts run wild, but with him I feel safe. Most of the churning thoughts stop like he's part magic, and I'd hate to lose that.

"What is on your television screen?" He asks suddenly.

"Coping mechanism."

"And that includes watching a musical about marijuana?"

"Don't knock it 'til you try it," I grumble against his chest.

He hums, unmoving as we stay there together in silence. Leo breaks the quiet first, "Given the circumstances of meeting Nancy—" I groan into his chest, and he stops.

"What deal did you make with her?" I mutter.

"That sounds ominous, and now I feel I must be aware of any future deals."

"So, yes?"

"Is it a common occurrence with her?"

"The woman has tricks up her sleeves. She's wily and knows how to get what she wants." I lean back to look up at him. "Again, I ask, what did you agree to?"

"Dinner at a place of her choosing."

"When?"

"I'd assume if we came downstairs with my dick still intact given the information I just learned about your knife skills." His tone has a lilt of amusement, while his face is completely serious, which makes me giggle. I step away, taking the movie out of the DVD player and put it with the rest of the mess. I go to grab his hand.

"Come on, mister," I say, leading him out of the apartment and closing the door. "I've been to your restaurant, time for you to see mine."

When we make it downstairs, Nan's there with a plateful of sugar cookies and a smug expression. Not telling her she was right…yet.

We're herded out a few minutes later. It's amusing to watch Leo being practically "woman-handled" by her demands. Finn would be proud. He tries to offer taking his car, but Nan convinces him not to, given it's only a few blocks away. We arrive at Nan's favorite pub, a small place that Nan has been coming to since she married Finn. The servers give us wide eyes, not expecting Leo with us and I swear the manager gives us a side glance, too. Nan and I have never come with a guy before. Once we sit down, I barely get a word in, remaining silent as I watch Nan and Leo interact with amusement.

She basically gives him the third degree. Maybe I should feel sorry for him, but he appears to be taking every question she gives in stride. They even talk about stuff like stocks, real estate, and what else have you. They do try to bring me into the conversation, but some subjects just aren't my forte. Real estate is one of them. Nan handled the bookstore even before Finn passed, and it's not surprising that Leo would understand handling a smaller business. Near the end of dinner as they start on leasing contracts, I excuse myself and go to the bathroom. I skim past some cooks murmuring near the kitchen doors. After I finish and washing my hands, I stop and look at myself in the mirror.

A moment of sudden *existence* of the world hits me. Pieces of me trying to figure out how I got here. I stare at the woman before me, who doesn't seem too much like a stranger to me anymore.

My fingers brush back the short strands of my hair, the color a faded auburn and no longer showing signs of blonde. There's more color in my cheeks, along with faint freckles from being in the sun more, and I've finally gained a bit more weight. The frail, sunken cheeks, pale, bruised woman isn't here anymore. I trail a finger down the mirror, tracing my face, almost forgetting what I used to look like. For some reason, I'm just now realizing that I've changed.

Years ago, I'd have let Leo in with or without an apology. I'd have begged him to stay, said sorry for being rude, and pleaded for him not to hate me. I would've blamed myself, and said it wasn't his fault. Past me would've done anything to not be hurt worse. To behave. To make it through. Odd enough, hearing Leo's apology, without begging for one from him, I felt relief.

I smooth my hair back, smiling a little. Maybe, I'm more ready than I thought.

Apparently, I just need Nan to scold me.

When I walk out of the bathroom, I find them smiling, well, Leo's doing his attempt at a smile. I'm weary over the glint in Nan's eye.

Should've been faster. Leo pays the bill, of course, and we leave. Once outside, Nan gives the excuse that she needs to finish some errands, given that we had dinner early.

I try to argue with her, but she just pats my shoulder. "Nan."

"I'll see you in a bit. We'll have cookies and some tea later, Autumn. Leonardo, I expect you as well, I'm sure whatever business you had tonight, can wait, yes?" The way she quirks her brow at him, makes me think I should've never gone to the bathroom at all.

"Yes, ma'am."

I gape at his response, and she walks toward the small market down the block. Twilight about to pass, I glance over at Leo who watches her with a tiny glimpse of caution. What the heck did they talk about? "You two hiding something?"

"Nothing for you to worry about. I promise." He gestures for us to walk back to the bookstore, and I remain beside him as we head down the sidewalk. Just before we turn for home, he suggests, "How about we take a longer walk?"

Speaking of suspicious.

I peer across the street to the small park nearby, nodding towards it. We go into the tiny pocket park as the sun dips behind the skyline, coming upon a mostly deserted playground, apart from a small group of teenagers and occasional dog walker.

"Something tells me you want to talk," I say as we pass a swing set.

He puts his hands in his pockets, stopping near a bench as his jaw muscles tense. "You asked me why you, why I am choosing you, but now I feel I have to ask the same."

"Why you?"

"Why tolerate me?" His question throws me, and I stare at him. "After today, including your correct assessment of me being a loner, I feel as though these are things you would not have tolerated before. Intervening with that customer in the shop, with the man who attacked you, or even ordering your food. Not to mention tipping far more than the average person and dealing with the police on your behalf."

"You…you think I'm only tolerating all that?"

"You've mentioned red flags and baggage, I've seemed to bring some of yours to light without intending to. I've also exemplified some of those flags, especially today, yet you forgave me."

This is *nowhere* near of what I thought he wanted to talk about.

"No one is perfect, Leo. Not even multi-millionaire, hotel moguls. I'll hold you to the same standard as any human." The lines on his forehead deepen. "I've also shown not great qualities like hiding, skipping out on breakfast, practically insulting your home, and yelling, so are you just tolerating me?"

"Of course not."

I cross my arms over my chest. "Then do you think I'm staying around for the wrong reasons?"

"No." He shakes his head, pulling his hands from his pockets. "Money, business, and what I own or have doesn't seem to interest you."

"It doesn't, cause it's just stuff. It's not you."

"But they are a part of me," he counters. "Part of the…deal, package as it were, if you decided to continue with us."

"Maybe, but still not you. Just a *part* of you," I try to empathize. "You could walk away from it."

Leo averts his gaze, rubbing his hand over his stubbled chin as he exhales sharply. Kids have begun to play on the equipment, and there's a couple of nannies watching them from the other side of the park.

"I can't walk away," he says in a rough tone. "Not with the responsibility I have to others and their livelihoods. Companies under my control that provide their jobs, the cash flow under my hands which I alone am responsible. I provide security for many people. This far into my life and the businesses I maintain, all of it is a part of me, what I am. Which includes, being the sole decision maker. If I want to continue taking care of those under my authority." He clears his throat roughly. "I can't simply walk away."

I think I understand what he's trying to tell me. After a moment, studying his rigid posture, a light bulb goes off in my head. All the things he pointed out of what he thought I "tolerated" seemed to have a singular dominator—control.

Today won't be the only time he makes a mistake. I know that; he's human. But...

I hold myself close and I can practically sense those severe walls of his going back up. My memory flits back to years ago, thinking where I was would always be intricately connected to me. All the aftermath of my decisions, imprinted on my skin and at first it always felt like I couldn't escape it. It would always be me. Except, I got out. And realized it wasn't.

"Still not you, Leo," I say, and he goes to argue, but I shake my head. "You could sell it all, give it to someone else, obviously you won't, but you could. It would take time, like changing any major part of us. But when the doors close and you're by yourself none of that matters. No job, title, power, or assets can ever equate to just you." Leo cocks his head, his expression contemplative as I turn to watch the sunset. I release a soft sigh. "Maybe, part of why you think you deserve to be alone is because you think you're no one without it. I remember feeling like that after the assault."

I hold myself tighter, snorting softly under my breath.

"Autumn—"

"You've been building your empire for over fifteen years, it *would* be scary seeing yourself without it," I continue, facing him completely. "To then you just think that's all you'll be, so it *has* to be you. Am I close?"

He shifts his stance, putting his hands back into his pockets as his jaw muscles tick. "Perhaps."

"And like me with the assault—"

"I will not have you equate something horrific that happened to you with my...my work."

"It's not the same, but similar enough." Leo just stares at me, shifting on his feet again. "Cause sometimes if someone doesn't accept a certain part of us, this thing that's been there for so long, it feels like they don't accept *us*. But it's *not* us. No one is perfect. Each with a past and things that tie us to certain..."

My voice trails off and I exhale hard. I have no idea if I'm making this conversation more confusing.

He steps closer. "Certain what?"

"Pieces of us. Maybe even red flags," I answer, and his expression softens. "But it all depends on who we meet if they're willing to understand those pieces when together. And maybe, just maybe, both of us have found one too many people who only saw the piece of us we truly wished to walk away from." My voice quiets. "And then *they* walked away."

A breeze blows past as the sky darkens, causing the lamplights to flicker on and the kids start to disperse. The noise of the night life echoes around us. I close my eyes for a long minute, *really* hoping that I'm making sense, because I'm not entirely sure that I am. Breathing through the worry I open my eyes to meet his.

"I'm not just tolerating you, Leo. I understand a little where you're coming from today. It doesn't mean I agree with how you went about it, so I forgive you, truly, but that doesn't excuse what was done. I get why you are this way, and I can't really change that nor do I want to, but that doesn't make it okay to cross my bound-aries. To do something that involves me without telling me. It just turns into excuses, then lies, and then mistrust. I won't pretend that I'm perfect or won't make mistakes either, cause I'm sure there'll be times I'm sure you'll lock yourself away to keep from talking, while eating chocolate ice cream. Well…pretty sure you'll be in a mansion with something praline flavored."

He remains quiet, staring at me with a somber expression. I grab his hand and hold it firmly. "Leo, I care about you. I'm saying this because I accept who you are. And why you? Because you listened. You paid attention, been patient, and apologized. I see more than just some big wig hotel guy. So, if you promise to work on these baggage claim items of ours *together*, then I say yes."

"Yes?" He rasps.

"To your formal relationship proposition. Yes. But I need to trust you, so talk to me and I'll do my best to do the same. Give us a real chance at this."

Leo yanks me forward, bringing his mouth to mine. He clutches my face gently as he kisses me, and I smile against his lips. My body flares to life at the contact and I hold onto his shoulders for support. He whispers against my mouth, "I will for you. I'll try."

"I believe you."

He kisses me again, holding me close as I melt against his touch.

Lingering a bit longer, he releases me and places a kiss on my cheek. He looks at me with adoration in his gaze and a soft smile grows on his face as I stroke his hair back. I step back, offering my hand and he takes it, holding it firmly as we start walking for the bookstore.

"Since we're kind of discussing the subject of 'no-gos,' by the way, secret security detail is one of them if you haven't noticed," I attempt to joke, and thankfully he smirks at me. "You better not try to get me to quit my job or some rom-com bullshit."

His brows go up. "Have I even alluded to doing anything like that?"

"No, just covering my bases. Who knows, maybe down the road you'll get sick of my coffee making or whatever." He chuckles. "Or you'd want to keep an eye on me, which connects with the whole protective security thing with you."

His expression becomes passive, almost a blank slate...like I caught him. I gasp, and he says quickly, "I said nothing."

"Wow, I pinned you hard on that! You know that's like three times now with you." I try to hold back my laughter as he squeezes my hand playfully. "What was the suggestion gonna be? You got a coffee shop in your hotel that could try a new barista?"

He clears his throat, side-eyeing me. "Maybe."

"That's four. Let's see, buy the coffee shop? Offer up my dream job by buying it?" Each suggestion, I'm *this* much closer of getting him to roll his eyes. "Pay off my debt? Buy the building I'm living in?"

Leo suddenly clears his throat roughly, and I stop to stare up at him. There's almost a guilt in his eyes, and I want to laugh at how transparent he is with me. I've watched him remain perfectly stoic with others, but barely can keep a glower towards me.

"Your building is on a block—"

"Don't you dare!"

"It's not your decision, and Nancy wouldn't have to worry about her bookstore, due to the lease that's left on it. She's not completely in the clear, even if her late-husband paid off most. She doesn't own the building." His tone is pure business and my jaw drops.

Son of a nutcracker, *that's* what they were talking about.

I start laughing outside the park entrance, the absurdity making me keel over with the ridiculousness of it all. The sound echoes off the brick buildings as Leo stares at me. I wave my hands at him, speaking between giggles, "Fine, buy whatever you want, but not the whole damn building, please. I don't want you becoming my land-lord, too."

"Did you just agree with me buying *Nan's Bookstore*?"

"I'm not trying to change you, Leo, and definitely not in a day." I wipe away some laughing tears, calming down my giggles. "There's some things I'm not gonna argue, which includes Nan getting taken care of. And you already talked with her, didn't ya?"

His entire face is lined with confusion, blinking a few times and nods. "Yes."

"I'd have a chance against you, but not Nan. No way." I start walking, and Leo sweeps his arm around me, bringing me to his chest.

"You're a fascinating woman, dear Watson."

"Not easy though."

"No, and I quite adore you for that." He kisses me again, and I breathe in quickly to inhale his sweet, musky aroma. The kiss is quick as he pulls away, taking my hand to walk us back.

"Just no hiking up prices."

"Or what?" He muses.

I smile devilishly at him. "I'll make you watch *Reefer Madness* and eat marshmallow cereal."

Chapter 15

Not The Rain

Leanne pays for our sandwiches at the register before we sit down at a window table. It's slightly busy, which isn't surprising given the foot traffic that comes through. I sit with my back against the wall, glancing toward the entrance of the shop. Leanne puts down our waters, and I hand her our sandwiches.

"How's work been?" I ask as we start to eat.

"Gearing up for the start of the new school year." She bites into her turkey sandwich, moaning a little with content. "Oh, I keep forgetting how good this place is!"

I take a bite of my Ruben and agree with a hum and nod.

"I can't believe it's almost fall," she mumbles, before going into the programs she'll be heading for the semester. I nod along, trying to keep up with her as she goes through each of the syllabus requirements and numbers she'll have to reach. We're about done with our meal, when she finishes and asks, "So, any news on your front?"

I swallow hard, staring at her and wince a little. Right. It's been almost a week since I told Leo yes, and I haven't told her or Trix. Not that I was avoiding the conversation, I just wanted to tell them in person. Unfortunately, with fall around the corner, they'll both be busy as schools go into session. The only downside with friends that work in the education realm. So today had to be it in telling at least one of them.

"Uh, I actually have some news," I say with a soft smile.

"Oooh, what?"

"Well, Leo and I are officially dating. I have a boyfriend."

Leanne's brown eyes widen as her mouth opens in shock. "Are you serious?"

"No, I actually adopted an otter and named them Seymore." My expression is dead serious, and she lets out a sudden whoop. I brace myself for a hug, knowing it's coming as she stands up to do exactly that. I smile at her as she wiggle-hugs me.

"Oh, I'm so happy for you!" She sits back down, taking my hands and grinning. "That must mean the other dates went well."

"You have no idea," I murmur, moving my gaze toward the cloudy ambiance outside. It looks like rain is coming again.

"And that's suspicious," she says, pointing at me as she leans back in her chair. "What else happened? Spill it."

"It's a lot."

She shrugs. "Never scared me before. Lay it on me."

Letting out a long breath, I tell her everything over the last couple of weeks and the dates Leo and I had. She folds her hands under her chin, listening and nodding her head as I talk. It's starting to sprinkle outside as I finish telling her about the dinner with Nan, and Leanne purses her lips, humming.

"What's that sound for?" I ask her.

"Nothing."

"Leanne."

She waves her hand in front of her. "Just a thought, but I haven't met the guy, yet either."

"Just tell me."

Someone rushes into the bodega, shaking the water off them as the rain begins to come down harder. We both glance outside at the sudden rainfall, and I realize only Leanne brought an umbrella. Fantastic. Good thing I don't mind getting wet. Not.

"He sounds a bit overbearing." Her words catch me off guard, and I look back at her as she meets my gaze. "And a little on the controlling side."

"He's not, not really," I defend him, breathing in sharply.

"Having you followed?"

"He apologized, and we came to an agreement." I won't tell her that said 'agreement' is probably in a building or car across the street from us. He better not be in the dang rain.

"Maybe, but it's the fact he didn't even discuss it with you, and —" She stops, letting out a sigh and shakes her head. "I don't want you getting hurt, hun."

"I won't, not with him."

"You can't be certain about that." I give her a look, and she takes my hand to squeeze. "I'm sorry, I should be over the moon you found someone you like enough to be with. Instead, I'm picking on him."

"No, like you said, you haven't met him and hearing it from an outside perspective I get it. Really. And I know you just worry about me." She gives me a sad smile, and I tighten my grip around her hand. "I'm being careful, and he makes me feel safe. Like I can trust him."

"Really?"

I nod.

"Never thought you'd tell me a guy makes you feel safe." My face falls a moment, but I give her a tiny nod with a somber smile. "But I'm glad Leo does, even with unorthodox ways."

The rain comes down harder, and more people escape into the bodega with wet clothes and shaking off umbrellas. Thankfully not a thunderstorm, just a hard rainfall.

"When do I get to meet him?" Her smile becomes brighter.

"No idea. I want to take this slow, even though it doesn't feel like it. He saw I was about to watch *Reefer Madness: The Movie Musical*, Leanne. That has to be like seventh date material."

"Oh wow, and he actually stayed?" I smack her hand playfully, and she laughs at me. "At least you weren't watching a Nick Cage film again."

"Hey, those films are good."

"You have made me watch every single film, they're not that good, hun."

"They're not *supposed* to be good, but fun. What's more entertaining than Nick Cage repeating 'face off', 'you're the rocket man', or screaming 'not the bees?'" She gives me a bored expression. "They helped you stay awake during college."

She scoffs. "Yeah, I owe getting through sophomore year to Nick Cage hijacking an airplane."

"He wasn't the one—"

"You know what I mean," she mutters.

I purse my lips. "I should rewatch that soon."

"Well, now you have a *boyfriend* to watch them with you. Give him my condolences." I snort, looking down at our hands as my mind drifts to a thought. "Must be a serious relationship if you're actually thinking of watching a Cage movie with him."

"Yeah," I mutter as my thoughts continue to whirl. The way she said serious reminds me of something I *haven't* thought to tell him. Never been in this kind of a relationship to think about it. Leanne squeezes my hand, and I bring my focus back to her. She gives me a concerned look, and I purse my lips.

"What's up?" She asks.

"Just thinking."

"About?"

"When do I tell him?"

"Tell him what?"

"About me not..." I gesture to my body in a circling, wild manner, "...that I can't...have kids."

"Hun, your relationship is still pretty early," she says, rubbing my arm slightly. "You can wait with that stuff, especially if it makes you uncomfortable still."

"It's not that I find it uncomfortable." I let go of her hand, leaning into my chair as I wrap my arms around my stomach. I glance down at myself and back up at her, sighing as I let my arms drop. "Okay, maybe a little. It's just...usually, it's a deal breaker for most people.

And what if I wait too late? But then what if I speak too soon? Scare him off by mentioning the subject at all?"

"Again, don't bring it up yet and wait." She shrugs, grabbing her water. "You don't have to tell him *everything* about you." Her gaze meets mine with a steady look, raising one of her brows.

I huff in response. "Pretty sure this *is* something he should know about though."

"Fine, I'll ask you this, and understand that I love you, and not trying to be harsh." I nod for her to go on. "Do you plan on having sex anytime soon? If at all?"

My eyes drop to the table while my mind flits to the night of the panic attack. How harsh my flashbacks were with just getting "hot and heavy" while only kissing. Since that awful night three years ago, I've never been with anyone sexually since. I just couldn't. Got close to it, but…I never felt safe, waiting for the worst to happen again.

"I don't know."

"Then until that may or may not happen, the decision is up to you, not him. I don't think you need to bring it up. It's still pretty early."

"Coming from the one who said to just open up. Be honest."

"*Some* stuff can remain private, hun." She tilts her head at me with a kind expression. "You should tell him when you're ready, not when you feel pressured."

"But what if I do like six months down the way, and he feels like I've manipulated him? Lied to him? Used him?"

"Okay, that would only be true if you secretly got pregnant to entrap him. Not having the ability to, I don't think counts. And hun, your worth isn't determined if you can have kids or not, that's unfair to you."

"I know, I know…I know." I bring my head down to the table, knocking it a few times as I grumble to myself. Leanne pats my head, stroking my hair a little. "I sometimes already feel like this basket of issues, and I don't want to add more."

"And if he truly likes you, wants to be with you…he'll accept you. Like you accepting him even though he has some domineering, over-protective, stalking quirks." I bring my head up and give her a frown. "Just saying, the man went to the coffee shop every day to see you."

"He bought coffee."

"And overpays."

"Makes up for the shitty tippers."

"That's a whole other conversation on living wages."

I roll my eyes at her, sitting up as she grins a little. I slump back, staring out at the downpour. "You're right. I'm just worried, and my thoughts are everywhere trying to figure it out to not screw it up. While not falling back into old habits and letting my anxieties and depression take over."

"You won't, because my best friend is a smart, wonderful woman with a big heart."

I look over at her with a smile. "Ditto."

She shrugs. "Takes one to know one." We giggle when Leanne's phone starts to ring. She pulls it out to answer as I put my focus on the rain.

It bounces off the concrete and the tops of taxis. I tilt my head as people rush past with umbrellas or with newspapers over their heads. I can't help a small grin as I watch the city. After a few minutes, Leanne hangs up and scoffs.

"That's not a great sign," I comment.

"I need to go to my office, there was a mishap in some paperwork, and I need it fixed before Monday. I'd complain working on a Saturday, but you do it all the time."

"Not today," I smirk.

She gives me an exasperated look and I giggle at her as she throws her trash away, pulling her umbrella out as I hug her goodbye. "You staying here?"

"For a bit, see if it lets up out there. Otherwise, I'm making a run for it."

She hugs me tightly, and says against my ear, "I've got your back. Always."

"I know."

"Love you."

"Love you," I repeat as she heads out, opening her umbrella as she enters the rainfall. I sit back down, watching her rush down the sidewalk and disappear around the corner. Letting out a long breath, I throw my trash away and go back to people watching. Time passes and my leg begins to shake, and I tap my finger on the table.

Fifteen minutes pass and the rain shows no sign of letting up. Debating the quickest way to run to the subway station, the doors open, and my attention is brought over to the newcomer.

His blonde hair is wet as is the rest of him. Isaac comes over to my table, sets his umbrella against the chair Leanne was in, and goes back outside without a word. I watch him suddenly disappear around the corner, getting pummeled by the rain. My gaze moves to the umbrella, staring at what he left me.

Didn't know that was part of the bodyguard duties.

I get up, taking the umbrella and head out into the rain. It's a large one, opening wide as I stand out on the sidewalk and peer through the small crowd to look for him. Nothing. Oh, so he can hide better in the rain, huh?

I start walking for home, glancing over my shoulder from time to time, but don't see him. My skin pricks, but not from a worrying sensation, more from just knowing I'm being followed. I wait for the regular stomach clenching, spine twisting anxiety to come, yet it never does. I'm hyperaware that he's nearby somewhere, but if Leo trusts him, I can, too.

I make it down into the subway, and head to wait for the train within the thrall of people. As the car approaches, I swear I catch a glimpse of Isaac's blonde hair before I get on with the rest of the crowd.

Chapter 16

Country Roads

The soft purr of the car engine is the first thing I feel as I wake up. The second is Leo's chest expanding as he breathes deeply, speaking low. My eyes slowly open, seeing the back of Rudolf's head and the window to reveal the countryside. I swallow against my dry throat and flex my hand which is placed on Leo's thigh. Leo says something of getting reports and to move a meeting before hanging up, then runs a hand over my arm, moving up to brush the hair out of my face.

"Good nap?"

"Didn't realize how tired I was," I mumble, not moving from the warm chest against my cheek and side.

"You were asleep before we even left the city."

"Did I sleep on you the entire time?"

"No, but when your head starting nodding, I brought you over to keep you from straining your neck." He strokes my hair again, pressing a kiss against my temple. "Good timing, we're almost there."

"Great. Five more minutes, mom." I snuggle back into him, and he chuckles lightly.

A few days ago, Leo suggested taking me to his countryside

estate, wanting to show me something there. It's been a couple of weeks dating, and fall was just around the corner. Leanne and Trix have been busy lately, so I've barely seen them, but I've practically seen Leo every day. If not at the café for short moments, then it was me meeting him at the hotel or him visiting me at the bookstore. He's been working a lot, usually always on a phone call, talking about upcoming meetings, and working late at his office. So, when he suggested taking a day trip out to the country, I was excited.

Unfortunately, my anxiety said otherwise the night before and I was up almost the entire night due to night terrors. I was on my third rewatch of *Rocky Horror Picture Show*, looking probably exhausted, when Leo showed up this morning. I've not been out of the city since before I left for college, before I trekked to New York on my own. Maybe that was the reason for the nightmares, trauma before my ex.

I'll take it up with my therapist later. Not only do parks give me panic attacks, but country roads give me nightmares. Sorry, John Denver.

I feel the vehicle slow down, and I move away from Leo, rubbing my eyes. He leans over, kissing my cheek and I smile with my eyes closed.

"You'll want to open those. We're here."

They pop open to see his relaxed expression, his stubble a bit longer than usual with his hair swept to the side. I see gates pass in the window behind him and turn to peer outside mine to watch a vineyard go by, and then a few small barns before we come to a large open gravel driveway and roundabout. The car stops and my door is opened by Rudolf as Leo gets out on his side, and I step out to stare up at the…yup, *estate*.

He wasn't kidding.

The place is over three stories high with the front having a large stone arch and triangular shapes over the roof of logs. It's the color of honey and gold strung together, modeled off the cabins I've seen in magazines of expensive hunting lodges. There's deep grey stonework along the bottom, which hold the pillars up to an alcove and a few down along the large house. The great house spans out wide, connecting with a large garage that's almost longer than the house itself. I turn to see the vineyard that surrounds the property, small hills moving down to show off the larger ones of New York. It's a beautiful vision of the countryside and I wonder if I'm still asleep.

This can't be owned by the same man who lives in a bare luxury penthouse with depressing tones. *This* is what I expected him to live within.

"You like it?" Leo asks, moving his hand over my shoulder.

I gape at the place. "Leo. This is *gorgeous*."

"Better than the apartment?"

"Still haven't convinced me it's not a penthouse," I point out, staring at the few flowers under the windows. "And whoever designed this place needs to help you with your city quarters, 'cause something tells me your other *penthouse* needs their attention."

He hadn't been kidding about never being at his actual home, I've yet to see it.

"I'll consider it." He takes my hand, leading me up the stone steps and through the large entrance to enter the foyer, which also takes my breath away.

The entire inside is rustic décor, wood and stone create tall walls of darker wood. To the right is a hall with a catwalk over it, which a staircase to the left connects. There are some doors on the left, which I presume goes to one part of the estate, while the other hall goes to another wing. Before us and down a few steps, opens up to a living room with a bar to the right and a kitchen tucked in the far back. Everything is open, giving access to see wide glass doors that lead out to a patio. The sun shimmers through, lighting up the place with a warmth that's extraordinary. Leo walks us through the living room furnished in leather seating and there's a gigantic fireplace near the patio doors.

"One day, we'll spend an entire week up here. Perhaps in the late fall since it is your favorite season. Although my favorite time is in the winter."

"Is that when you usually visit?"

"When I can, not as much as I'd like." He stops us near the long counter, gesturing toward a barstool. I get up on the leather chair as he steps between my legs, rubbing my arms lightly. "I hope to change that soon. Be here more often."

I give him a small smile, putting my arms over his shoulders. "What plans do you have up your sleeves today, mister?"

"Do I sense concern there, dear Watson?"

"No, just curiosity. Since it sounds like you don't plan on us staying here tonight. So, what's the plan?" His response is a swift kiss.

"Stay here, I'll be back with what we'll need. Help yourself to anything at the bar or in the kitchen." He walks back through the vast living space and disappears up the staircase. I narrow my eyes at him as he crosses the catwalk, while taking his jacket off.

He's sneaky sometimes, but never for long. And he sure does like to surprise me.

I've learned the past few weeks he owns more than just a fancy hotel franchise but owns companies that imports goods and a lot of other real estate, too. Like *a lot* of real estate, focusing on rebuilding small businesses. Whenever he talks about it, he's strict and passive, moving into familiar behaviors I've noticed he's used with everyone, but me. It's almost amusing how swiftly he can go from "caring Leo" to "commanding Leo".

Even getting mostly the thoughtful side of Leo, there were still some things I couldn't yet open up to him about. In time, I'll do it in time.

I get off my seat, heading to the glass doors to stare out into the atmosphere of the countryside. There's an overhang above the patio, more than likely a balcony. The scenery is gorgeous, matching the rustic theme inside. Staring out at the hillside and vineyards, I hear a door in the foyer open and turn to see Isaac. He's next to a wall and two more figures walk in and disappear through other doors quickly.

I've not seen him since he left the umbrella for me, and I've not spoken to him since I knocked him down and kneed his balls. Hopping off the barstool, I walk towards him, and he turns to face me with a non-expressive look.

"Are you the one shadowing me still?" His bearded jaw tenses, and I wonder when he started growing it out. He nods his head once. "Well, thank you." No expression change. "And thank you for the umbrella. Did you get it back? I left it at the front desk of the *Italian Lily*, told Chiari to get it back to you. She said she would." He nods again, still no change.

Oh, gee this is going great. It's been almost a month since I pointed a knife at him, and I don't want to be a dick. "I'm sorry for kneeing you in the balls, by the way. And threatening you."

His mouth becomes a tight line, but he nods again. I let out a long breath, pinching my nose. "Look, if you're angry, I get it, but please tell me. I don't do well with silent treatments and will start speculating you're planning my death."

His eyes widen. "No, I'm not angry. Or planning your death."

"Good that shortens the list," I mutter, and he cocks his head at me. "Bad humor." I stick my hand out to him. "Anyway, can we start over? I know you were just doing your job, even if Leo was being a dumbass about not telling me."

Isaac looks up toward the second story, neck muscles tightening as I notice his hand flex. A smirk comes over his face, relaxing his shoulders. He brings his attention back to me, taking my hand into a firm handshake. "You don't need to apologize for defending yourself."

Halleluiah! Progress!

I cross my arms over my chest in a leisure manner. "Still feel bad about it though. Having fun shadowing me?"

"Not bad, shadowed worse. There's a coffee shop across the way I can do work while—" He stops abruptly, clamping his mouth shut as he glances over his shoulder.

I peek past, seeing no one. I then look where Leo disappeared, peering past the catwalk to the hall of the second story. I'm not sure if the guy is scared of Leo or doesn't want to disrespect him by telling me stuff. Except, it's stuff about me and we agreed about me knowing where I'm involved.

"I'm not gonna try to lose you or whatever, promise," I say, looking away from the stairs. "Honestly, it's more comforting knowing where you are. Helps the anxiety."

He readjusts his stance, facing me fully. "Anxiety?"

"I've been followed and stalked before, and attacked, more than what happened that night outside the hotel." I shrug. "And as a woman living in New York City, part of the criteria to live here at this point is to have your head on a swivel."

"I'm sorry you have to deal with that."

I wave him off. "Too used to it now." I listen to the rooms above, no movement yet. "Since you're shadowing me could we exchange phone numbers?"

Isaac appears taken aback. "Miss Watson, I don't think…that—"

"If anything happens, it'll be faster to contact you to come help. Leo or my friends may be too far away. Or let's say I change my daily route, and I can let you know of the change up. Starting next week, I'll end up doing that anyways. You won't lose me on the subway then." His brows furrow at me in confusion. "Something I've been doing for years, again…anxiety."

"Miss Watson—"

"Autumn." I correct with a small smile. He gives one in return, flicking his gaze up.

"We'll need to keep it between us. The boss doesn't like communication intermingling for safety purposes. He has to approve everything."

"Well, *I'm* approving this, if you're *my* security, I get a say." Isaac's eyes glint with amusement.

I hand him my phone, and he puts in his number, and I text him quickly. He pulls out his cell, showing me he received it and saves it. I'm not sure about *not* telling Leo, but I don't want Isaac getting in more trouble. The guy already had to deal with me beating him up essentially. Who knows what kind of reprimanding he got for me destroying his phone, outing him, and all that? Besides, not like I'm gonna try dating Isaac or whatever. Leo can't be that possessive…can he?

The wandering thought starts to take root when we're disrupted by the heavy sound of boots. I turn toward the stairwell, while Isaac steps back. My breath catches as my skin tingles with heat as Leo descends the stairs. He's wearing dark bootcut jeans, heavy boots, black v-neck shirt, and a black leather jacket. There's a pair of smaller boots in his hands, along with his smoldering gaze which he sweeps over me and then to Isaac. His jaw clenches, while his brows come together with a sudden serious look.

"I was apologizing to Isaac and thanking him for the umbrella he brought me the one day." My words make Leo halt in his steps, flicking his gaze over me. "Pretty sure he got soaked, so he better bring extra next time."

Leo looks at Isaac, gives a sharp nod, which Isaac takes as his cue to leave through the side doors. Leo keeps his attention on where Isaac left, before walking over to hand me the boots, which I grab tentatively. "Are you mad I spoke with Isaac?"

His hard expression softens, shoulders relaxing. "I have certain rules."

"About?" I raise a brow.

"My private life remains private. I prefer no interactions between those who work with me and those I…" His voice trails off, while his mouth becomes a thin line.

"Slept with?" His expression remains stern and now I feel a bit guilty for getting Isaac's number. I hold up my phone, giving him a half smile. "Okay, I'll respect your decision with your private life. Got it. But I'll need to communicate with Isaac if he continues as my bodyguard." His eyes flick down to the phone in my hand. "I have his number and he has mine, for emergencies. I talked him into it, so if you're gonna get mad at anyone, let it be me."

Leo's hard expression disappears as he peers over his shoulder and turns back to me. "I'm not mad. It's smart to have that line of communication. I apologize if I came off a bit possessive, I shouldn't have to make you feel like you can't talk to people."

"I won't share any secrets with him, pinky promise." I reach forward and wrap my pinky around his. He smiles, tightening his around mine. "Including your terrible choices in cereal."

He scoffs. "He already knows."

I let go of the pinky promise and sit down on the steps to put the boots on. "Should I be worried about how you're dressed and that it matches with the jeans you told me to wear?" I glance at the tabs of the boots. "Or that you know my shoe size?" What the heck?

"You'll see, and it's for your protection." Ah, yes, the constant conversation we have about me. I pull my tattered tennis shoes off, putting on the leather boots. "Nancy gave me your size."

"I'm beginning to think you two are teaming up, and I find it unfair." I lace up the boots quickly, finding them stiff, but comfy enough as I stand. I'm about a half inch taller in them, but Leo still towers over me.

He strokes back my hair, taking my hand as he leads us through the foyer to a door to the far right of the entrance. He leads me down a hall, through another door until we come to what looks like a mud room. There's a smaller black leather jacket that he pulls down, handing it to me. I slip it on, noticing it fits perfectly. When did Nan go through my closet?

Once on, I notice the worry line between his brow and the uncertainty in his eyes. My brows go up in surprise, unsure why he suddenly seems nervous.

"I'm hoping you'll accept this," he murmurs, his hand on the doorknob. "What's behind this door."

"Because?"

"It's a deal breaker if you don't." It's a statement, not up for debate.

"Beyond that door is important to you?" I gesture to the doorway, and Leo nods. Butterflies, not the fun kind, flutter in my stomach as I'm unsure what he's about to show me. I also hate that if I don't like it, this could be the end. Bracing myself, I tell him, "Might as well open the damn door then."

He turns the knob, opening it as he moves to flick on a switch as I walk in behind him. Bright lights flicker on to reveal the inside of the large garage I saw outside, and within sits a long row of motorcycles. My jaw drops as I count the bikes, coming to a dozen of them all lined up. Not a single car in sight. They're all different shapes and sizes, varying in types with long, tall handles, shorter ones, or even some with bodies that look to be made of wood. I walk down the line, staring at the chrome, leather, and varying colors. A couple seem tiny in comparison to those with the low riding bodies, handles high above them.

I'm in a state of shock. Never in a million years, did I think this is what he brought me up here for. Glancing down at the leather I'm wearing, I can easily assume he's a full-out biker, not just some collector. Remembering the tattoos I've seen, a few things click.

I turn to Leo, who watches me carefully with a pensive expression. His brows furrow deeply, while his muscles tick along his neck. I point at the closest one, and ask, "You ride?"

"Only in the countryside when I'm here. When I lived in California, all the time." I stare back at the bikes, taking a deep inhale of the metal and leather which mixes with oil and wood of the garage. "Autumn?"

I let out a loud whoop, pumping a fist into the air with a victory cheer. "Hell yeah!"

Leo relaxes, leaning against the garage door with relief washing over his features. "You fucking scared me."

"Sorry. Dramatics and all that." I run over to him, throwing my arms around his waist into a tight hug. "I've always wanted to ride. This is awesome."

He embraces me, holding me close in a tight hug. "Thank fuck," he breathes out, kissing me briefly. "Then we better get you on your first ride."

"Which one we taking?" I ask, spinning toward them and almost bouncing with excitement. I have no idea if it'll trigger me being on a bike, but I've never been on one, so luck is on my side.

Leo hits a button for the garage door to slide open, and he points at one of them. I follow the direction to a bike with a higher windshield and painted a deep maroon color. I walk over, skimming my fingers over the leather seating and the shiny handlebars. All the chrome seems to sparkle as the sunlight streams in. Leo taps my shoulder, and I turn to see a helmet in his hands. "What model is it?"

"Harley, Classic Heritage. One of the newer models." Leo puts the helmet on my head, securing it. He takes the bike, rolling it out onto the driveway, and I follow and look over to see some men milling about near the front entrance of the house. He stops the bike, turning back to me with a smile as he puts his helmet on. "I'll be getting on and then you'll swing your leg over behind me. Use the foot peg to help if you need."

He points to what he's talking about, and I nod as he gets on easily, straddling the bike. My body flares with heat watching him, and I remind myself to concentrate. I do as he says, swinging my leg over to sit on the seat pad behind him. He helps adjust where my feet go and places my arms around his torso.

"When I lean, lean with me. Not too much. You can keep your arms around me, don't hold too tight, just enough to keep contact. Otherwise, you can hold onto the sissy bar behind you." The what? I glance behind at the short bar that rests against my back. Alrighty. "If we stop, keep your feet up and stay on the bike, but once we get to our destination I'll park, and you'll get off first. Understood?" I nod. "If you need a break, tap my chest twice, I'll pull off."

"Got it, mister."

He chuckles, turning the engine on. The bike roars to life, making my entire body tremble with the ferocity of the engine beneath. It vibrates up through my body, making me shiver. He revs it, moves up the kickstand as I grip him. The grin I wear is gigantic, giggling at the feel of Leo's back against my chest and the rumbling of the motorcycle between my legs. Leo starts slow, moving down the driveway as I settle into the movement of the bike beneath and feeling how he moves with it. Before I know it, we're off on the road.

Leo turns onto the main road and laughter erupts from me as he speeds up the bike. Trees whisk past, while the breeze sweeps over us. Leo makes the bike go faster with a roar. I let out a whoop as we soar down the road, through the hills. Scenery passes quickly as I stare out into the still green hills, some leaves just now beginning to change into yellowish shades. We come to a couple of curves, and I do as he says, leaning with him and becoming in sync with his body. A thrill races through me, striking me with exhilaration and freedom as we continue the ride. I keep thinking of leaning away from him, grabbing onto the "sissy bar" like he said, but I don't quite feel brave enough yet. My arms stay wrapped around him, enjoying the feel of him and the rumble of the bike beneath.

I've no idea how far Leo takes us, winding us through the back-roads that weave through the country. I'm sure we've been out longer than I presume by the time he begins to pull off at a scenic overlook. My ears ring as he cuts off the engine, and I hop off the bike with wobbly legs as he fully parks it. He gets off, taking both helmets to set on the seats. Leo turns, and I think it's the happiest I've ever seen him.

"We're gonna test ride all the motorcycles, right?" I ask.

"Liked it that much?"

"Liked it?" I gesture widely at the road and the forestry around us. "Leo, that was *amazing*!" He beams and it makes my heart soar. "Pretty sure you're gonna turn me into, uh, biker chick. Is that the term?"

"Long as you're *my* biker chick." He tugs me close, kissing me deeply. I sigh against him, falling against his hard, leather clad torso. My arms fling around his neck, pulling him closer as he leans over to crush his lips against mine. Heat pools in the bottom of my stomach, growing as I clutch onto him for that kiss. My hips and thighs already tingle from the ride, and I feel my body clench at the blissful sensation.

After what feels like an eternity kissing, he breaks away and reaches into one of the saddlebags attached to the bike. He takes out a bag and thermos, nodding for me to follow him to the grass just past the parking area. We sit down over on a slope of a hill, overlooking the view.

He hands me a sandwich, and I grin as he takes his own.

"How'd a hotel mogul and business, city guy get into biking?" I ask between bites.

"We call it riding."

"Ah, riding then."

He looks out at the greenery and slow-moving clouds. "Began riding long before owning any business. Started when I was fourteen."

I do the quick math and gape at him. "You've been riding for almost twenty years?" He nods.

"How?"

"Never got along with my family, maybe cause of the abduction or just how it all seemed to fall apart when my mom died. I got involved with some bikers from Connecticut, they rarely crossed state lines. I spent almost every weekend with them, teaching me how to ride and take care of my own bikes. They were good to me."

"That young though?"

"Better than drugs, the guys used to tell me." Can't argue with that. "My family hated that I rode, and I did stop for a short time. When I moved out West, I found another group of bikers and started to ride again, became part of an official chapter for a short time, but couldn't keep up as my businesses grew. So, I created my own MC when the hotel franchise got to a certain point in growth."

"MC?"

"Motorcycle club."

"You owned a biker gang?" I finish my sandwich, leaning back on my elbows. He gives me a weary look, but relaxes once he notices my calm expression.

"Not all motorcycle clubs are gangs. Mine isn't official or an outlaw MC, but it's ours." I raise a brow at him. "Most of the men who work for me, like Isaac, are a part of it, too."

"Really?" He nods. "Huh, that explains a few things." Leo cocks his head at me in question and I shrug. "Ones I've met, seem pretty loyal."

"Most of them I've known for over a decade."

"Well, reading and watching movies are my favorite pastimes, but your hobbies are cooler."

"And I'm very fucking relieved you think that."

I smile at him, glimpsing at the tattoos on his arms. He had taken his jacket off from the heat, so had I. Honestly, it explains most of Leo now. The gruff expressions he has, not taking shit from unruly customers, and having this commanding presence. Maybe it was stereotyping, but I've read enough about bikers to know they aren't always fun and games, especially with society.

"Is that where all the tattoos are from?"

"Most. I wouldn't have gotten as many if I hadn't been riding. Got my first one when I was fifteen." I giggle and Leo looks at me.

"Sorry, not at you, not at you." I wave my hands in the air as he smirks. "If I told Autumn from that first week we had met, that you were a tattoo-covered, biker in disguise…she'd have, well…"

"Fallen over laughing?"

I shrug not so innocently.

He pushes his hair back, and I watch those muscles under his shirt flex and the ink on his skin move as he does. Well, that was hot.

He peers out over the horizon again. "I rarely show people this part of me. This world. If I mention it or show it, either people scorn the lifestyle, think it's a passing fancy, or want to do some heinous things on my bikes."

I grimace, glancing back at the one sitting behind us. "I never thought I'd feel sorry for a bike."

Leo lets out an empty laugh. "I've had some odd requests in the past, including one that involved a wrench and grease."

"I don't really wanna know," I mumble as I follow his gaze to the horizon. The afternoon is quiet, apart from rustling leaves and distant sound of cars passing on the highway. "Can you tell me about your family?"

He inhales sharply, adjusting his position as his face becomes solemn. "I have two brothers: one older, one younger. The younger is overseas, while the other is in prison."

"What for?" I ask quietly.

"He ruined lives and is now under firm watch, that's all you need to know," he says in a low tone. "My father died years back. He was a cruel, strict, repulsive man. When I left at seventeen, I stayed in New

Mexico for a while, met a few people and learned new trades. Before I knew it, I was building a luxury, five-star Michelin hotel franchise. I'd come from money, but I fought and learned how to make my own."

"You didn't want any of your family's money. Your father's."

"It felt wrong to follow in his footsteps. I wanted to prove to myself, my father, and my brother that I could be something without them. Without their name attached to me like a weighted chain."

"That's why your work is so important to you."

"And why it's all I am. Apart from…few other things."

Sunlight hits the trees, creating long shadows as the afternoon lengthens. More pieces of Leo click into place. He may be strict and seem rough, but he's not mean, not like his father. He's respected by his staff and others around him, but he's alone. He has all these people around him, yet he's closed off. Since I've met him, this is the most relaxed I've seen him. Riding and being away from the city are his only solace. Except, he doesn't get to do it often, and he was ridiculed for it by his family.

That's a heavy weight to carry. Being something your family dislikes. An outcast.

"My parents didn't like me," I say quietly, staring out at the scenery. I can practically feel his gaze on me, but I don't look at him as I speak. "I have an older sibling, who followed in my parents' footsteps of hating me. See, I wasn't planned, and they blamed me for how they were stuck with me. Small town in Ohio, nobody cared about anything but themselves, like crabs clawing out of a bucket. I left when I was seventeen, too. Out of twenty schools I applied to, Stony Brook was where I got a scholarship."

I clear my throat, shaking my head as I push away memories, and continue talking. "Leanne and I met, and she helped me figure out what I was good at. Somehow, I decided on studying Language Arts, English." I scratch my head, huffing out a long breath. "I went from one abusive relationship to the next. Maybe it's all I really knew or thought I deserved."

"You don't," Leo states.

"I know that now." I let out a breathy chuckle, finally looking at him. His expression isn't sad, but concerned and worried again. I seem to be receiving that look a lot lately. "What?"

"You deserve a good man, Autumn."

"Pretty sure I'm sitting with one." He looks away, jaw muscles tightening as his mouth becomes a thin line. He runs his hand though his hair, then rubs his chin.

"I want to do right by you. I promise I'd try, and I will continue to do so, but…" his voice drifts before bringing his gaze to mine, "…I ask for your forgiveness for what I can't tell you yet. You deserve honesty and trust, and here I am not able to tell you everything. I want to, but not yet. I'm not—"

"Hey, wait a minute." I move, sitting closer to grab his hand and kiss his knuckles. "Yes, I want honesty, trust, and to talk, but I know there's some secrets harder than others." The words feel heavy as my stomach sinks, knowing some of my own skeletons in the closet I don't want to speak of. "Some stuff you can talk about, and some you can't. Same with me, which I hope you can forgive me, too."

"There's nothing to forgive," he whispers.

"Well, two-way street here."

He reaches up, cupping my face in his palm. "One day I will tell you."

"You don't need—"

"Yes, I do." He clutches my face to bring closer to his. "I promise whatever truths I hold back, there's a reason. It's because I'm trying to protect you. Keep you safe."

"From what? You?"

"Perhaps." I stare into those hazel eyes, searching through the myriad of colors. Fear. It's similar to mine during those late nights, standing at the bathroom mirror. "I want you. This. These few weeks have been everything, but some things are harder to explain, to say out loud."

"I know, trust me, I know." I hold onto his wrist. "Just promise me something."

"What?"

"Be you. Even when you can finally tell me, please be you, cause that's who I care about."

"Of course, dear Watson." He presses his lips to mine, kissing me tenderly as his tongue lightly drifts over my bottom lip. He holds me close as I clutch at his chest, wishing I could say my own secrets out loud now. Although I've told him so much, it didn't feel like enough, that I wasn't going to ruin this. But I hold on with him.

He kisses my cheek, then cradles my head against his chest as we sit in the quiet. The breeze rustles the grass, bringing the late summer warmth. We drink in the scenery together. The silence a welcome, though unfamiliar, break surrounded by nature with Leo's arms wrapped around me. I want it to last longer, forever maybe, far away from the troubles within the city. Away from the shadows and worries.

Alas, it's only a moment in time.

He murmurs against my head, "Let's head back."

We get up, gathering the trash and tossing it into a nearby trashcan as we head to the bike. Leo says something about needing a minute, heading towards the trees. I grumble at his ability to piss anywhere, and I think he hears me, because he chuckles in the distance. I stay by the bike, grabbing my helmet as I examine the motorcycle. While inspecting it, I find inside the saddlebags, off to the side, the handle of a gun. I don't recognize the model, but glance over my shoulder to see Leo still gone and check the other bag. There's another large handgun, which I presume is a 9-millimeter.

No kidding on being protective. I bring the flap back down, securing my helmet over my head as crunching comes up behind me. I spin, loosening a breath as Leo approaches and checks my chin strap before putting his on. Before he straddles the bike, he pauses, touching the side of his helmet. He turns his attention down the road we came, mutters something under his breath, and taps his helmet harshly. Leo gets on the bike, nodding for me to follow suit. I settle behind him, asking before the engine is turned on, "Do you have a headset in your helmet?"

"Yes, it connects to my phone."

"Is everything alright?"

"Just have to head back. Hold on, sweetheart." The engine roars to life, drowning everything out as I wrap my arms around him. Leo squeezes my knee gently before he pulls out of the overlook, going the opposite direction we arrived from. He speeds up the bike not long after, turning onto a different road. I lay my head against his back as I become entranced by the buzzing tree line.

Chapter 17

Easy Riders

We ride up the driveway, turning past the estate and toward an open area. I peek over Leo's shoulder, seeing a helicopter sitting in the middle of a landing pad. If I'd said no to bikes, would he have just thrown me into that?

Leo stops us a good distance from it, cutting the engine after I get off. He follows suit as a couple of people approach, Isaac being one of them. A man with light ochre skin and stubble on his jaw, hands Leo a phone, then walks off without a word. Another juts his head at Leo with a frown. I think, he's one of the men Leo has been in the coffee shop with. Or I hid at the women's center from. I can't remember, and kind of don't want to. Leo takes his helmet off, shoving it at the somewhat familiar man.

"Your timing is shit," Leo practically growls, walking away with him, who straightens at Leo's remark.

I remain where I am as Leo walks away and points at the helicopter, then the house, and talks roughly on the phone. The man nods, heading back to the estate. Isaac is the only one left next to me by the bike.

"I thought I was grumpy going back to work after a vacay," I comment.

Isaac snorts, flicking his gaze at the bike and then me. "Enjoy it?"

A large smile breaks out over my face. "It was amazing. Leo said you ride, too."

He blinks rapidly, seeming perplexed. "Yes. His entire security team basically."

"So, all of you really followed him from California, huh?" Isaac pinches his face together, looking toward Leo. "He told me a bit."

"Such as?"

"About the MC, riding for almost twenty years, and that ya'll were loyal enough to come here with him."

Isaac adjusts his stance, nodding to a heavyset guy who takes Leo's bike and rolls it back to the garage. There's tension in Isaac's face, and he clears his throat. "He's a good man, Miss Watson. Even if others don't believe it."

I scrunch my face, and then look to Leo as he hangs up the phone and briskly heads over to us. He nods to Isaac, who gives a nod back before striding toward the helicopter. Leo pockets the phone with a serious expression. I'm saddened that the high of happiness is already gone. Weren't even back for two minutes.

"A matter came up that I need to address in the city," he says. "I had plans for dinner tonight, but it seems we'll have to take a raincheck."

"And apparently a helicopter." I gesture toward the large, flying machine.

"Are you scared of heights?" I shrug. "What about flying?"

"No idea. Never flown," I answer.

"How did you move to New York?" His brows furrow.

"Drove. Far cheaper and able to take everything I owned." Which was like two suitcases.

He exhales sharply, taking my hand to lead me to the landing pad. "You trust me?"

"Well, I did just ride through the countryside with you, never having done that before. So, for today, sure."

"Dear Watson, you do amaze me."

"What for?"

"For trusting me so quickly." We reach the helicopter, and he helps strap me into my seat and covers my ears with a headset. I'm half prepared for Leo to fly the damn thing, but no. Instead, it's Isaac and my inconceivable giant, Rudolf. Driver all around. His resume must rock.

Leo sits next to me as the doors are closed, and the blades begin to whirl above. I glimpse up through the front window shield, my stomach clenching at the spinning blades. Leo takes my hand, and a crackle comes over the headset. "If you need anything or get anxious, squeeze twice."

I nod, as the two in the front go through the controls, flicking things and pressing buttons. I look back at Leo, and ask, "Are all the headsets connected?" He nods. "Oh good, all of you can learn how colorful my language is *despite* an English degree if I freak out."

"Or recite poetry," Leo muses.

I fight off a grin as he looks smug. "Careful, smartass."

There's coughing in the headset, and Leo glares toward the front. My giggles can't be stopped as we begin to ascend into the air. It's a bit bumpy as we begin to climb, and before long we're in the sky. I stare out the window, my stomach doing flipflops as we turn and fly toward the city. Leo tightens his hold around my hand, and I give him a gigantic grin. His own forms, while his gaze softens, watching me become fascinated with this new world being shown to me.

"You rode a motorcycle? Nah, that would've been way too scary for me." I laugh lightly at Leanne's reaction to my retelling of my morning and afternoon.

"It sounds fun to me," Trix comments, sipping her margarita.

"Well, I prefer seatbelts, subways, *and* being on the ground." Leanne waves us away, sipping her own drink. Since dinner plans were cancelled with Leo, I called them up for a last-minute get together to have drinks at our favorite restaurant.

The helicopter ride ended on top of the *Italian Lily*, and he left me in the private elevator, kissing me goodbye and promising a weekend together soon. He disappeared on the top floor, joining a man with a digital pad in hand. I could see a few other suit clad men across the hall before the doors closed behind Leo. Only Isaac remained with me.

I glimpse over my shoulder, seeing Isaac sitting at the bar, within sight of us easily. I smile to myself, coming back to my conversation with the other two.

"I'm just happy you're having fun, Autumn," Trix says, clinking her glass against my water.

"I am, and fully prepared to become a biker chick."

"Just remember we're gonna need to meet him at some point." Leanne points her finger at me. I roll my eyes at her, and she scrunches her nose back. "By the way, I've realized we don't know his full name."

"Yeah, you've only called this big wig millionaire by his first name," Trix adds in.

"Oh, didn't think it mattered." They both give me displeased expressions. Ah, yes, I think I broke a girl code. "His name is Leonardo Luciano, although I thought I mentioned—"

"Wait!" Trix waves her hand in my face, and I freeze. "Did you just say Leonardo *Luciano*? As in Leonardo Durante Luciano?"

Is that his middle name?

"Definitely the first one she said." Leanne waves down our waiter, gesturing for another round of drinks. Trix's mouth falls open, staring at me in disbelief. I look to Leanne for help, who shrugs, sipping her mojito. The waiter comes back with two more cocktails and nachos, and my coffee is refilled.

"How have you been dating for weeks and *not* know who he is?" Trix asks once the server leaves. I shrug, while Leanne gives us wide, curious eyes. Trix huffs, laughing under her breath. "Autumn, he's not just a hotel owner, he's one of *the* hotel owners."

"I…I know…that. Hotel mogul, empire, whatever. Also owns other real estate and such, we've…*kind of*, talked? Anyway, your excitement bamboozles me." Leanne snorts. "What?"

Leanne chuckles, "I'm also *bamboozled*."

"Look, the guy came to New York five years ago, erected this new hotel, the *Italian Lily*, which within a matter of months became one of the most prestigious hotels on the east coast. He's a freaking genius when it comes to the hotel business, getting his up and running with a five-star Michelin rating within a matter of months. While being reclusive, he's clearly got good PR."

"How the heck do you know so much about him and hotels?" Leanne asks.

I grab a nacho, and mumble around it, "I'm actually kind of impressed."

Leanne shrugs. "Me, too."

Trix ignores our commentary and continues, "He came out of nowhere about ten years ago, but eight years ago his entire empire just blew up and became an international super star in the business world."

Leanne pulls out her phone. Oh, no. "He's not just some multi-millionaire, Autumn," Trix continues. "He's on the brink of being a billionaire from owning parts of California, Chicago, and Miami. He's been in *Time* magazine, and the *Business Insider* multiple times, not to mention other magazines."

I mutter, "If you tell me he has a Wikipedia page…"

"He does!" Leanne exclaims, holding up her phone to show a picture of Leo outside the *Italian Lily*. You gotta be fucking kidding me. Leanne brings her phone back, smiling knowingly. "Oh, he's hot. Best rebound ever for you, hun."

I hold my head in my hands, realizing why he looked so surprised the first time I hadn't recognized his name. I had no idea who the fuck he was, and all this time he hasn't fully divulged who he was either. Pot calling the kettle black there, Autumn. My eyes widen, wondering if this is what he was referring to earlier on the bike ride. How much the world knows him and what that can mean. Also explains not really going out and having dates at his hotel.

He likes his private life private. Beginning to see why.

"His hotels aren't why I know who he is," Trix adds, touching my arm gently. I look over at her in despair, knowing I may have to deal with media shit in the future. Ughhh. "He's the one who funds the *Luna Stella Women's Center*, including other shelters in the city. He has for almost four years now."

My jaw drops. "What?"

"I've met him," she says. "A few weeks back he visited the center, wanting to talk about allocating funds or something. He doesn't fund us personally, one of his companies sponsors us. Something in real estate, but myself and another looked him up after he left. We were curious, he was younger than we thought."

Somehow, my jaw drops more, realizing that must've been the day I hid from him. He was there for the center, and I almost bumped into him *in* the building. Why didn't he say anything? Again, my mind flits to our conversation this afternoon.

Whatever truths I hold back, they're for your protection.

Would I lose my sessions if they found out we were dating? Was that a conflict of interest? Holy mackeral, how did I not know any of this?

"And you met over spilled coffee?" Leanne asks. "Fate is weird."

I laugh nervously. "You really think its fate?"

Leanne's face softens, her gaze filled with old understanding. She reaches across the table, touching my arm as she strokes over the sleeve. "Maybe, after everything, this is a sign to move on."

"With a man who owns not just a hotel empire, but the center I have therapy in, and apparently cities across the U.S.?"

Trix shrugs, leaning back in her chair and takes her drink. "Is he good to you?"

"Yeah."

"Do *you* care what he owns?"

"No, I don't care, I'm just in shock I didn't know most of this, like *how* much I didn't know. He hasn't said anything apart from bits and pieces, but I never saw it as anything to dig deeper into. It's his life, and I'd hate having my life being pried into. Also, I struggle keeping up with it all, and he's just…Leo to me."

"Trust me, as part of my job, all that stuff is boring no matter what," Leanne mutters, sipping more of her drink.

"If he's such a big deal, how come I haven't seen paparazzi or stuff?" I ask.

Trix snorts. "We live in New York, darling. Most obsess over celebrities staying *in* his hotels instead. Not to mention he has strict security, when he came in, he had like three guys with him."

Two, actually, only because that moment is burned into my brain of embarrassment. I try not to glance over my shoulder at Isaac. Leo has mentioned that he's never really alone, that someone is always close by. I'm starting to understand why.

"He's good with his privacy, like *really* good." Trix sips her drink. I'm on the verge of wanting a taste. "When we researched him, we found very few articles, and he rarely *ever* gives interviews. Don't blame him, the man's busy, and yet he'll take you on a bike ride."

"Still want a seatbelt," Leanne says. "But if he has a friend with a Lamborghini or Ferrari, call me."

I roll my eyes. "Fine!"

We continue with our friend date, munching on nachos as I try to distract my worried thoughts. Once we finish, Trix leaves us to take a taxi home. Leanne and I watch her leave as we start walking arm in arm toward her apartment complex.

"Wanna stay the night?" Leanne suggests, and I'm tempted to say yes out of precaution, but remember Isaac is tailing me.

"No, I'll be fine going home. Didn't sleep much last night anyways."

"You sure? It's late, even for you. I don't want you having a panic attack this far from home, too."

"I'll be fine, and they've been tame lately. Went to the park a few weeks ago, *totally* kicked ass." We both laugh and she shakes her head at me. She didn't need to know the "kicked ass" was still following me around.

We're quiet as we continue toward her place, and I glance over at my usually talkative friend. A solemn expression on her face. "What is it?"

"I have more thoughts, but again, I haven't met him."

"That's comforting," I say deadpan.

"I just want to be honest, and again don't want you getting hurt."

"Well, tell me otherwise I'll think of worse things than what you're thinking. We both know my mind is quite creative."

"Oh, I saw your essays about cult movies, I know," she chuckles, letting out a sigh. "I really do think he cares about you, but...he should've told you about how well-known he is. What if news does get around and make trouble for you?"

"If Leo has been reclusive before, he'll do the same with me." Pretty sure he already has.

"But there's still a possibility."

"And maybe not."

Leanne stops, about to say my name, but closes her mouth. I look away from her, suddenly an old pain coming back to tighten around my chest. She lets out a long sigh, and says gently, "I don't want them finding you. If you get on television or a magazine, what if..."

"Let's be honest, Leanne," I scoff half-heartedly, almost empty. "They wouldn't recognize me. You know what I was to them."

"I'm still scared for you." Her voice trembles, and I look back at her to see tears in her eyes. "Some days, I'm still scared for you. Afraid of that phone call again, and I don't want that. And I know you're happy, but...can he protect you from them? Do you think he can?"

I swallow hard. "He's rich enough. And he did help take care of that guy who attacked me outside his hotel. So...maybe."

The guy is still missing after skipping bail. A thought that would worry me more if I didn't have a bodyguard trailing me everywhere.

She breathes in deeply, pulling me in for a hug as people pass and a few car horns blare. Although it's night, the city doesn't care. I hold onto her, burying my face into her shoulder. "I don't want them near you again. Ever."

"Survived them before, I'll do it again. Fuckers haven't found me since," I murmur.

"You gonna talk to him about what Trix said?"

"He'll tell me if I need to know anything, I really think that. He needs to be ready on his own time, not me, just like with my stuff. I knew what I was getting into with him, just...*more* than I first believed is all."

Leanne lets out a shaky breath, nodding against my head. She kisses my forehead and I kiss her cheek. We walk to her apartment, and as she asks again if I'll stay, but I shake my head. Leanne disappears through the doors as I turn away, heading for the subway station. I flick my gaze behind me to see Isaac not too far behind.

I keep my arms around me as I walk, my mind almost fuzzing out. Whether Leo was alluding to what I found out today, I'm not sure if I care if it was. Although I could be mad, he didn't tell me all that stuff, but he hasn't exactly hidden it. Who cares if a company he owns sponsors the center? Weird coincidence. Besides, I never took the time to look him up. It hadn't mattered before to me what he did, why should it now?

It's because his picture was on a website. A *public* website.

A prickling sensation moves up my spine, and I feel sick to my stomach. Just because he's on there, doesn't mean I will be. My head pounds as I reach the subway, going down the steps and getting on my train. It's late, so there's someplace for me to sit and I watch as Isaac gets on, staying on the far end of the train.

Stay out of sight. Stay hidden.

The ride feels too short, my head still a daze as I get off and head back to the surface. Before I know it, I'm back in my apartment, slumping my jacket off and sitting on the couch. I lean my head back, trying to concentrate on the good day I had. On the feeling of riding and how freeing it felt. I close my eyes, remembering the trees passing us. The rumbling of the engine and Leo's back against my chest. The revving of the motorcycle as we took off. The smell of leather and metal.

Tugging off my clothes, I change into a worn Metallica t-shirt and sweats then grab my newest tub of rocky road ice cream. I scatter my movies about, finding what I'm looking for. Snuggled with a blanket and dessert, I watch *Easy Rider* with a new outlook.

Chapter 18

Young Jealousy

The café bustles as another group of people walk in. Seriously? I grumble as about eight people file in.

"I'll take care of the back," Mabel says, taking some dishes with her and mugs in a bus bin. I'm left with Bailey at the front, making drink orders. After Bailey forgets *again* to change out the grounds for another espresso drink, I take over in fear she'd cause a riot of caffeine-deprived teenagers.

The minutes tick by as I concentrate on making drinks. We're almost blessed with a lull, when the door chimes and I want to throw something. If there's another group of women coming to get pumpkin lattes with no whip or sugar-free or whatever…I'm using pastries as ammunition.

I finish two more iced lattes, calling out the orders as I place them at the pick-up area. As I walk back to the espresso machine, I notice who came into the shop. It's Leo. He's on the phone, looking away from the register as he speaks succinctly. The man with the digital pad from the other day is next to him, and Isaac is already sitting at a table. Brought some of his Partridge Family I see.

Given that there's still a few people waiting on drinks, I won't be able to chat with him today. It's nice just seeing him regardless. I wave briefly at Isaac before I go back to the line of cups. Thankfully, the next few drinks are simple as I put them together. Delivering them, I peek around the corner at Mabel. "How you doing?"

"Fine, but how do you keep up with everything back here?" She hands me two plates of toasted pastries, and I turn quickly to put them with the drinks.

"Moon shoes," I tease. She gapes at me in mock surprise.

"Share next time!"

I laugh at her, going back to my spot as I chance a look to see Leo at the register. I start prepping for a medium Americano.

"Well, if it isn't my *favorite* customer," Bailey croons. "And handsomest."

"Americano, medium, and two black coffees," Leo states in an unimpressed, passive tone.

"Do you want any sugar with those? Or maybe cream?"

"Just the coffee, nothing else."

"Oh, but I'm sure you'd like something sweet?" I can practically feel her bat her eyelashes at him. "I think you secretly like sweet things, huh? It's okay I won't tell."

You gotta be kidding me.

"No, thank you," Leo replies sternly.

"Maybe a latte then?"

It's Leo's frustrated sigh, that doesn't sound too controlled, that makes me intervene.

I come up behind her, almost shoving her aside as I put his Americano down and put in the order on the register. "Here's your Americano, the other two coffees will be out shortly. If you do want cream or sugar, there's some over there." My gaze catches Leo's, whose frustration appears to ease. "Bailey, can you get the other two coffees? And then refill the pot? Thanks."

She huffs beside me, but I don't give her much room to disagree as I hold my hand out to Leo. Bailey walks away, and I loosen a long breath as Leo puts the cash in my hand. I get his change as he takes a fifty and puts it in the tip jar.

"Wouldn't blame you if you didn't do that today," I whisper.

He holds his Americano up in a small thank you gesture. "Except my favorite barista made my drink today."

I mock a gasp. "You *are* playing favorites."

Leo doesn't smile, but there's a shimmer in his eyes. He murmurs, "Thank you, dear Watson."

I wink at him, turning away to help finish the orders. I hear him walk away as I change out the espresso grounds, and Bailey comes up next to me. "That was rude of you," she hisses. "You made me look like an idiot."

"You weren't listening to the customer, Bailey. He said what he wanted, didn't ask for suggestions. How about *don't* make them uncomfortable with your flirting?"

She gapes at me, eyes flaring with anger. "Coming from the *forever* single one."

She turns, flipping her blonde hair over her shoulder to flick in my face. I blink quickly as she takes care of the regular coffees. Was I that annoying at twenty or whatever? Gosh, I hope not.

I grab a few things to take to the back, having to squeeze past Bailey who's taking up most of the space, unmoving. I sigh, putting the dishes down and hold back a growl, taking my apron off. *You can't punch her. You can't punch her.* I toss it in the hamper with the others, telling myself I'll put another on later.

Mabel grabs the dishes, and asks, "What she do this time?"

"Ignoring a customer's request. Borderline harassment. Normal stuff."

"I don't slut shame, people do what they want, but *that* girl…" Mabel whispers, glancing past me, "…she's another level of pretty privilege. I swear she flirts with every guy who comes into the shop."

"I'm pretty sure it's why we've lost a few regulars. They stopped coming back when she started working here. She creeps me out sometimes with that level of fake, flaunting sweetness. I feel like she's gotten worse lately."

"Too bad her father's rich," Mabel mumbles. "Otherwise, Yuki would fire her ass."

"Yeah." We both look out, seeing Bailey taking a few more orders. "The day she finally does, I won't be crying."

"We can get celebratory drinks instead."

"Just not coffee," I chuckle.

"Oh no, I'll need vodka. Yes, please." She winks at me.

I grin, walking back to the front, but as I turn the corner scalding, hot coffee is poured down my front. My body locks up as I hiss at the scorching liquid straight from the pot seeps through my thin shirt and pants as I stare at the mess on me. My bare arms scream in pain from the hot liquid. I bite my lip to keep from screaming, feeling the burn sweep over my skin.

"What the—" I wheeze out.

"Oops, my *bad*." Bailey is in front of me, putting her hands up with fake shock on her face. A small smirk comes over her as she drops her hands, including the *two* large cups in them. They tumble to the floor where the coffee drips, and she leans in whispering, "What? No laughing this time? Not *funny* enough for you?"

"Are you *fucking* kidding me right now?" My voice is a rasp. My skin hurts, tingling in pain. Anger builds inside me as it sinks in. Oh. My. GOD. She did it on purpose. My hands tremble, and my throat suddenly feels tight. I am *not* crying in front of her.

"This is a reminder of where *you* belong," she sneers, suddenly giving a fake gasp as she bends down to grab the cups. "Are you *okay*? You're *so* clumsy sometimes, Autumn!"

Am I really being bullied by someone almost a decade younger than me? Is that what my life has come to?

Mabel comes out, gasping at the mess and the coffee that is now staining my green shirt and jeans. People come into the shop, while others start murmuring from every corner and I want to curl up on the floor and disappear. My skin picks, hurting from the burn. Mabel gestures for me to head to the back, and says, "Bailey, take care of the orders. Autumn, you alright?"

I glare at Bailey, who has a small smile on her face. "Yeah. I should be used it, getting coffee on me because I'm so clumsy, *right*…Bailey?"

She narrows her eyes at me as I turn away, heading into the employee's room. I keep my head low as Mabel takes my place, slamming the door shut behind me. I breathe deeply, trying to keep myself together as I look down.

"You've gotta be fucking kidding me."

Tears press forward as I attempt to blink them back. Frustration builds with embarrassment. This isn't like other times having shit spilled on me. This was deliberate. Malicious. Irritation runs over my skin, and my stomach hurts as I start to feel sick. I press my palms against my eyes, trying to rub away the sensation of crying. "Come on, not that bad. Don't give that bitch your tears…don't…"

I glance down again, looking like I've gone through a mud run but smell of dark roast Guatemalan. Mabel slips into the room.

She gasps looking over my sorry state. "The one day I didn't bring extra clothes."

"Great," I mutter. "I'll stay in the back. Can't make drinks while looking like a line cook for the military."

"What happened?" I think about pulling my shirt off to ring it out, but I doubt it'll do much. My chest hurts, constricting, weight on my shoulders wanting to pull me into the ground.

"Bailey tripped." My voice is monotone and quiet.

"Autumn…"

"I'm fine. Head out front, wear an extra apron though, it's dangerous out there." I grab a discarded towel patting down my jeans at least. Nothing worse than wet jeans.

"It's slowing down. Take like a fifteen, okay?" Mabel suggests, and I nod.

Mabel leaves as I slump onto one of the chairs, holding my face as a few tears fall. My chin quivers as I try to hold back the tightening lump in my throat, aggravation rushing forward. I do what I can not to break down, not to lose it over something so stupid.

Suddenly, my phone chimes and I instinctively grab it, answering without looking. My voice is hoarse, "Hello?"

"Are you alright?" Leo's voice comes over the line, noise from the shop in the background. Shit he must've seen me get covered in coffee. Again.

I huff, trying to joke and not show signs of breaking down. "Yeah. Learned another way not to catch coffee."

"Don't lie to me. That was coffee straight from the pot, and a lot of it. Are you hurt?" He speaks in his strict tone, causing my breath to shake as I want to lie. Tell him I'm fine. A few more tears escape, and I stare up at the ceiling for help. "If you can't tell me, then I can come back there—"

"No! Please, you'll make it worse…I'm fine." Fuck, if Bailey saw him come back here, my life will turn into a living hell at work. I rub my chest, wondering what to do and wipe a few tears.

"Dear Watson—"

"Meet me outside at the back door," I tell him, walking out of the backroom and peering out at the shop. I look past a couple waiting on drinks, finding Leo at the window table. He turns when the door opens, eyes meeting mine and nods.

I hang up, heading out the back door for my fifteen. Even in the shade of the building, it's warm out as I grab a milk crate, propping the door open. I slump back against the wall. What am I doing? My hand rubs over my face, debating just running back into the kitchen to hide and try not to get red, puffy eyes for the rest of the day. The few people coming down the small side street, don't really pay attention to me. Thank fuck.

At the edge of my vision, I notice Leo coming around the corner, making quick strides. I straighten, trying not to look weak over such a dumb thing. The man has probably handled worse shit, and me being the target of a jealous girl has to seem frivolous.

I hold my hands up as he approaches. "Just trying new tie-dye ideas."

Leo grabs my wrists gently, beginning to inspect my arms with a serious expression. My breath hitches as he stands over me, moving his fingers lightly over where the coffee hit my skin directly. It's red and slightly blotchy, most likely the rest of my torso looks the same.

"It'll go away by tomorrow…probably," I whisper as the weight on my shoulders gets worse. I swallow hard, feeling that lump more and the ache it leaves.

Leo frowns at the redness on my forearms. His gaze moves to mine, while his jaw muscles tick. He comes closer, like he's going to hug me, and I shake my head. "It's still wet, I don't want to get it on your suit. My clothes aren't—"

"Fuck the suit."

Leo pulls me in gently against his chest, pressing me against him as I fold my arms against his chest. He moves a hand down my back, stroking it softly as he cradles my head. A few tears run down my cheeks. Its odd being comforted like this, over something trivial. Isn't it trivial? I've been ridiculed for crying in the past. Blamed. He should be telling me to ignore her or some shit.

Except, he doesn't say anything. He just holds me while the noise of the city continues on the street. When there's a group of people walking up, Leo eases us closer to the building away from them. He takes long, steady breaths as he soothingly moves his hand over my back. Leo presses a kiss to my temple, and then another.

My breath trembles as I inhale deeply, then murmur, "I need to go back to work soon."

"You shouldn't have to—"

"No, I'll be fine. Can't leave Mabel." He clutches my head a bit closer, continuing running his hand over my back. "I'm fine."

"I don't believe you."

A small snort comes out of me. He pulls back, wiping away the tears left on my cheeks. He searches my face, flicking down again to the red on my arms.

"I need to finish work, Leo."

He cups my cheek, stroking his thumb over skin. "Call Nancy that you'll be staying with me tonight. Isaac will walk you to the hotel."

"Leo—"

"Come straight from work. I'm sure you're closing again. I'll take care of everything."

I blink at him, heart picking up speed. "Do I get a say?"

He inhales deeply, still a serious expression on his face as he places a kiss on my forehead. "If you say no, then *I'll* escort you home."

"You seem very determined not to leave me alone tonight."

Leo's gaze becomes dark suddenly, flashing like a warning signal. "I don't like that *my* girlfriend may have been burned due to an insolent, jealous child. Given the state of your arms, I want to keep an eye on them, and I'm not too fond of finding you on the verge of tears. You were doing your job. She wasn't. You shouldn't have to be punished for that."

"Remember what we talked about? Not buying out coffee shops and jobs?" I narrow my eyes at him, except it's hard to remain serious.

I'm not sure why when Leo gets severe like this, my first reaction is to giggle. I know it's not aimed at me, and perhaps seeing him become strict like a Doberman on watch…it's endearing. In this moment, that is. So, naturally I want to laugh. Like an idjit.

A grin must be pulling at my mouth because Leo traces his thumb under my lip. "Smiling is a good sign. What do you say?"

I let out a long sigh, and nod. "I'll meet you at the hotel."

He leans down, brushing a kiss over my lips. "Be careful and I'll see you tonight, dear Watson."

"Thank you, Leo." He gives another kiss, straightening himself and turns away as I reach for the door. Over my shoulder, I watch his back profile as he adjusts his suit and briefly looks down at himself. His strides are even, unperturbed by what just happened before he disappears around the corner.

"If I could have a *semblance* of that kind of control," I mutter to myself as I head back into the kitchen. I pat myself off again, grabbing a kitchen apron to tug on and catch Mabel's attention. I gesture that I'll start the dishes, and she nods with a tight expression.

Before I turn around completely, I notice only Isaac is left with a mug of coffee and book. He lounges like any other patron. Unbeknownst to everyone, he's probably been given strict instruction to stab the next person who looks at me wrong.

I finally chuckle at how ludicrous *that* sounds.

Chapter 19

Carbonara

I put the code into the alarm system and close the backdoor with an exasperated sigh. The rest of the afternoon got worse, especially when Bailey "accidentally" bumped into me, smearing whipped cream on my front and the rest of a medium frappe. Not only were my jeans still damp and pinching, but now I was sticky down my torso. I pull my jean jacket close over my chest, turning and almost screaming when I see Isaac nearby. I clutch my chest, banging my back into the wall. His eyes widen, holding his hands up in surrender.

"Son of a nutcracker," I rasp.

"I'm sorry, Miss Watson, I thought you said to meet you back here."

"I did," I mutter, running my fingers through my hair. "I was in my head and forgot."

I shake off the scare, rubbing at my pounding heart and stop as I grimace down at myself. I'm one step away of looking like I'm part of the *Army of Darkness*. Not a role I covet.

I flick my gaze up at Isaac, who glances at the mess I try to cover with my jean jacket. The leftover of the frappe was harder to get off.

"If Leo asks, I ran into a customer." He looks away as I watch him practically debate in his head. "Isaac."

"Miss Watson—"

"Isaac, I will put holes in your socks."

He looks over at me surprised as I cross my arms, dropping them as it makes a weird sensation on my skin. It's not puke. It's not blood. Be glad it's only whipped cream and coffee, Autumn.

He exhales sharply, gesturing for us to walk and answers, "Very well. But don't assume I'll keep anymore secrets from him. I work for him, not you."

"Whipped cream is hardly secret material. Trust me." My voice is low as I walk by. He doesn't stay far back but remains just a few steps behind as we walk to the *Italian Lily*. Due to the nice weather, there's more people out and we weave through the evening crowds.

I hold my jacket closer around me as we enter the hotel, already feeling a few eyes on me. We start to head toward the private elevator, which I'm guessing Isaac already has a keycard for, but I see a familiar face at the front desk. My path diverts to the desk, and I hear Isaac quickly change course as I approach Chiari.

"Evening, Chiari."

"Good evening, Miss Watson." The woman looks up, smiling and her eyes flick down at my front. "Somehow your jeans look worse than the first time I saw you," she muses.

"You wouldn't happen to have washing machines here would you?" I ask, leaning over the counter.

"We do, although I think Mr. Luciano has other plans for you."

"If I didn't know him, that would've been an ominous response." She winks and I chuckle at her. "Thank you for getting the umbrella back to Isaac."

"I'm happy to help whenever." Her gaze flicks to Isaac behind me, and I turn toward him a bit. He's wearing a passive expression.

"Don't tell me he doesn't want me talking to hotel staff either?" His lips purse, and Chiari chuckles softly. "We've talked before. Her mom is in hospice, and she knows I have a thing for Scottish Lairds." She tries to hide her smirk, typing some things into the computer.

A couple of times coming to the hotel, I've stopped at the desk to speak briefly with Chiari. She's been nice to me since that early morning, like *truly* nice and not that bullshit customer service thing we all do. We've chatted from time to time as I waited for Leo, due to my early arrival quirk…thing.

I look over at her. "Or have I been breaking rules or something?"

"I'm a manager of his hotel, not his PR team," she answers, glancing at Isaac with a fast look of irritation. Interesting. "Being one of his top managers, I do understand how Mr. Luciano operates, including helping keep his private life, well, private."

"What does that have to do with…" I wave my hand between her and I, "…me talking?"

"*Other* people talk. Precautions, Miss Watson."

"Mostly relief there," I murmur mostly to myself. "How long *have* you worked here, by the way?"

"Since before Mr. Luciano bought out the original owner."

"Is this the part where you say he's improved quality of life or whatever?" I smirk.

She chuckles. "He has. I will admit the pay is better and the help with family financial benefits does make life easier."

"Well, damn there goes any chances for embarrassing anecdotes or uncouth secrets."

Chiari's smile tightens a moment, and there's movement to the side of the front desk. Rudolf comes around the corner, wearing a blue button-up and slacks that I think were personally tailored for him. He gives me a nod and looks to Isaac. "Situation on the top floor. Need you up there."

"Now?" Isaac asks, glancing at me.

"Boss is coming." Isaac nods a goodbye to me, leaving with that singular sentence from Rudolf. My usual driver turns to follow Isaac.

"See ya, Rudy!" I call after him, and he pauses to stare back at me. There's a hardness in his gaze, and I freeze, my heart pounding. Oh, shit maybe not a nickname for him. "Sorry, I mean Rudolf."

Isaac has gone still, keeping a wary eye between me and the big guy. Rudolf regards me, and tiny wrinkles appear at the edge of his eyes, smiling ever so slightly. "Rudy's fine, but only you can call me that, Miss Watson."

I relax a little. "Okay but figure out a name for me other than that."

"Hmm…good night then, *bärchen*." He winks, walking away and I see a look of astonishment on Isaac's face, before they disappear around the corner.

Well, now I'm curious about what he just called me.

I turn to Chiari, who also looks a little surprised. "Something tells me he doesn't do that often."

"Not usually. He stays to himself and doesn't interact with anyone aside from Mr. Luciano's personal security team. I *assumed* he had humor."

I scrunch my brows. "The bikers?" Chiari glimpses up from her monitor, and nods. Hmm, drives, flies' helicopters, and rides bikes. Was Rudolf part of the Fast & Furious gang? "I should head up."

"Mr. Luciano will be down…actually here he is."

As she says it, I turn to see Leo come around the corner in only a black button-up long sleeve shirt and slacks. A few buttons are undone, revealing his chest and the brief view of whatever tattoos he's hiding under that shirt. He strides across the marble floor, and it feels like the air has stilled as a few others in the lobby slow what they're doing to bring their attention to him.

His usual stoic expression doesn't seem to disrupt Chiari because she greets him warmly. "Good to see you this evening, sir. Miss Watson has been keeping me company."

"That doesn't surprise me," he says in a cool tone, stopping close. He reaches for my wrist, gently taking it and turning it over. The jean jacket covers where I was burned, and he raises it a little to look at the faint redness. His gaze flicks to the front of my shirt, and his jaw tenses as I try to pull my jacket together.

"Had a run in with a frappe. Didn't have my net to catch it." The joke lands flat as his expression doesn't change, almost worsening with concern. "I'm fine."

The air feels charged between us as his brows further come

together. Usually, I want to laugh at that look, but there's a roiling in my stomach that I don't like. I swallow hard, hoping he'll let it go.

"Were the garments you ordered up to your liking, sir?" Chiari asks suddenly, and I silently thank her.

Leo moves his attention to the manager, and says brusquely, "They were. I appreciate you obtaining them on such short notice."

"Always a pleasure to help sir, and if you need anything, I'll be here until midnight."

Leo nods, then takes my hand, leading me away from the front desk. Okay, guess we're going.

"See you later, Chiari," I tell her, waving over my shoulder. She gives me a small wave back as I follow Leo to the private elevator, the doors opening without him having to do anything. He presses the button for his apartment floor, and the doors shut as it becomes silent between us.

The tension grows worse as Leo keeps his gaze on the elevator doors, and the hand that once tethered me with comfort was doing the opposite now. My chest feels heavy, like I'm suddenly drowning as I feel the stiffness from him. Although his grip on my hand is gentle, the weight of it is dragging me under.

Did he have a bad day? Did I just fuck up by talking to Chiari? Maybe it's because I didn't tell him what happened, and he knows I lied. I don't want him getting involved, not with something as stupid as a jealous girl at work. I can handle it; I *always* handle it. Could it have been—?

The doors open and I'm practically hyperventilating. Anxiety yanks at my spine, making my stomach churn as my muscles tense. Leo's hand holds onto mine, and I start to follow him into the foyer when I freeze. My legs won't move, sudden fear of being trapped if I go through that door. The anger in the air around him, warning me to run. Leave. *Get out.* I want to puke.

"I should just go," I rasp, feeling my body begin to shake. I take a tentative step back, but his hold tightens, and I close my eyes, flinching.

"Autumn." His voice is low and soft, not at all reminiscent of the tension that emanates from his body.

"I...I need to...I can..." My throat is tight, and I start breathing hard, trying to concentrate. Heart pounding in my ears as I whisper, "I'm sorry...I'm sorry."

"Autumn look at me." My head shakes, taking another step back as my instincts scream for me to run. Muscles trembling, I want to hold myself close as Leo lets go of my hand. "Please look at me, dear Watson."

Shaky breaths come out as I open my eyes. He keeps his hands at his sides, watching me with worried eyes. "What's wrong? Talk to me."

I stare up at him, still trembling as memory flashes of yelling and pain. Anger and hiding. The memories make me flinch, stepping back a little. My arms come up to hold myself and I feel the stickiness, remembering my damp jeans, and feeling targeted. There's a drop in my stomach as I clench harder.

"I'm going to touch you, alright?" He says in a soft voice. My vision starts to darken around the edges as the panic through my body continues. Leo moves toward me, slowly moving his hand up to cup my jaw. I'm frozen in place as he takes my hand in the other, bringing it up to kiss my knuckles. "What was the promise I gave you? The first night we spent together?"

My mouth works against the dryness in my throat as I try to concentrate on the warm hand on my cheek. I struggle to breathe. "You, you...said..." my eyes close, and I shake my head, not able to concentrate, "...I can't..."

Leo presses his lips against my forehead. He places my hand against his chest where I feel his heartbeat. It's steady against my rapid one. His hand covers over mine, holding it there as he strokes his thumb over my cheek with the other. All I can do is stare at his chest and our hands upon it.

"Never will I harm you," he whispers. "You will only ever be protected by my hands. I promise you, dear Watson." I swallow hard, stiffly nodding as he holds us there. "What set off your panic?"

I inhale roughly, trying to make it less shaky. "I thought…I thought you were angry with me. I'd done…I lied, and you knew… caught me…and…shit."

Leo inhales sharply, continuing the soft touches. He steps back, keeping my hand against his chest while the other lifts my face ever so slightly. I'm met with concerned hazel eyes, not a flicker of the hardness from downstairs.

"I knew you were lying, yes, but I'm not angry at you," he says steadily. "I understand you want to handle your coworker on your own, but I also don't want you lying to me. I'm struggling to stay out of the way, but I will if you ask." The nod I give is small, my chin quivering. "Apart from already a long day of meetings, knowing you'd been hurt, and I wasn't there *did* make me angry. But not at you. Even if I am ever mad with you Autumn, I will *never* harm you because of it. Physically, emotionally, mentally…none of that. You're safe, dear Watson."

The last sentence vibrates through me, and a few tears escape. Damn, I seem to be doing that a lot today. "I'm not…I'm not used to that."

"I know, but please believe me. I'll never harm you, you're far too important to me."

Leo goes to hug me, but I place both hands on his chest to keep him from doing so. "I really don't want to get whipped cream and syrup on you," I murmur.

"Will you stay? Take a shower and put on some clean clothes?"

I wet my lips, which feel extremely dry along with my throat. I can only nod and Leo takes my hand leading me inside. The place smells like fresh pasta and a hint of bacon. Following him into the bedroom, I see clothes laid out on the bed as he has me drop my bag off in the corner of the room.

"Those should fit, from what I've seen you wear and talking to Nancy," he says as I walk over and check the shirt and lounge pant sizes. My voice still doesn't seem to want to work because my only reply is another nod. "Good. The shower is all yours. When you finish, there's ointment on the counter for you to put where you were burned. There's a hamper you can toss your clothes into, I'll have them taken care of tomorrow. After you're done, dinner should be ready."

I look toward the kitchen, noticing the billowing steam coming from the stove and other things set out. He was planning on taking care of me. He *is* taking care of me. Something squeezes around my chest, not sure how to process this. Most nights I go straight home, heat something up in the microwave, and watch a movie until I fall asleep. Usually, just me. Alone.

Some guilt that he's doing this starts to wiggle its way through me. Leo kisses my cheek briefly, walking out of the bedroom. "Call if you need anything or if the shower stumps you."

I let out a long breath as he closes the door behind him. Heading into the bathroom, I shut the door and see there are folded towels ready and a package of new underwear. My brows shoot up, staring at the cleanliness and there's a roiling emotion in my stomach. Shaking it off, I go to the shower and stare at the chrome contraption. A small glare doesn't get me very far and I'm too stubborn to admit it may have stumped me. After what feels like forever, I get it running and at a temperature I like. Finally peeling off the sticky, damp, and smelly clothes, I shiver in relief. Not having the disgusting sensations on my body, I can breathe easier and the anxiety goes down. The water is warm and comforting as I step in, hissing a little at the burns on my arms and bit on my chest. I ignore it, standing underneath the steam and the best rainfall of hot water I've ever had. My eyes close, taking time to let my body calm back down.

I'm exhausted. Physically, emotionally, and mentally taxed by bullshit and constant panic attacks. I'm tired and I realize I've not eaten for almost ten hours. Shit. No wonder I started to freak out and my vision went blurry. Leo could simply frown at me, and I'd start crying right now, thinking he hates me. Stupid anxiety. Stupid trauma. Stupid Steve.

The water runs down my back and I start washing, cleaning off the last of today. Once finished, I step out and dry off, tugging open the package of underwear. A flash of the hospital hits me, and I shove it away. Fuck no. Already panicked today, not adding those memories to the mix. Besides, these are much softer.

When I pull one out, seeing they're boxers, a giggle escapes me. I'll take them over lacey lingerie and thongs. I put on the comfy clothes, which fit great, and towel dry my hair. Standing in front of the steam covered mirror, I start wiping it away, but stop. Instead, I draw a smiley face. And then a heart. And then a coffee cup with steam. And then a star. I just keep drawing until it's filled with a bunch of things. Before leaving, I put the ointment on and admit it does help my skin feel better. If left to my own devices, I'd have put regular lotion on it, if anything.

The apartment smells and feels warm as I walk out, finding Leo in the kitchen with his sleeves rolled up. There's a towel over his shoulder again, and he moves a skillet over the stove. He cooks, moving from one station to the next. After he pulls, what looks to be bread rolls, out of the oven he notices me and smiles gently.

"Feel better?" He asks as I move closer, peeking to what he's making. "Carbonara if you're wondering."

"Which kind of dish is that again? And much better, thank you."

He comes around the counter, stroking some of my wet hair behind my ear. "It's a pasta dish with eggs and cured pork if that rings any bells."

"Oh, the one with bacon." Leo snorts, and nods before kissing me gently. The tender gesture helps melt away the worry.

Leo moves to set plates down on the counter and then water glasses. I flick my gaze toward the doorway of the dining room, wondering if it ever gets used. I'm half tempted to go eat in there but look down at my attire and figure the counter is the better choice. He finishes with dinner, putting our plates together and we sit down.

A few seconds I stare at the plate of the delicious smelling food, my brain feeling fuzzy like it's trying to recompute. I'm not sure how long I stare, until a hand comes to my back, rubbing in small circles as I look over at Leo. His gaze flits over my face, the line above his brows barely there, but enough to tell he's concentrating.

He says low, "You're alright." I breathe in deeply, smiling faintly. "Eat, dear Watson."

The first forkful I want to moan so loud I'll fall off the chair. Okay, may have been hangry on top of every other emotion today. The dinner is delicious as we eat, and more parts of me relax as the weight in my chest lessens. It's quiet and we're about midway through the meal when I can't take the silence much longer.

"What's your favorite food?" I ask.

"To make or to have?"

"There a difference?"

He hums around a mouthful, swallowing. "Is there a drink you prefer making versus what you like to drink itself?"

"Oh, taste versus process," I muse, and he nods. "Then, uh, both."

"Hmm, I enjoy making fresh pasta from scratch." As he speaks, I put a forkful in my mouth, and go still as he smiles faintly at me. He probably made this pasta from scratch. I'm about to compliment it, but then Leo reaches over and lightly brushes his thumb under my bottom lip.

My cheeks heat under the tender gesture as he wipes away some oil. His smile becoming affectionate. Leo wipes it off his napkin, leaving my brain in a flustered mess as he answers the rest of the question.

"And what I enjoy most to have are omelets. I can create them however I like, and make several different ones suited to my taste that day."

Both were very Leo answers. He could control and create what the end result is, being there from start to finish. I clear my throat.

"Yours?" He asks.

"We both know I don't really cook," I say quietly, concentrating on the plate before me.

"Then to have?"

An odd feeling comes over me. I stare at what's left of the pasta. Never really thought about a favorite. Food was usually just... survival. I shrug. "Whatever you cook seems to be my favorite of late."

Leo hums, not saying anything more as I finish the rest of my plate.

Once we're done, I help Leo clear the dishes, even after he tries not to take the help. Most of the dishes are put in the dishwasher, while the rest are placed in the sink for another time.

I stand in the kitchen, contemplating going home even though I said I'd stay. The guilt rises again of him taking care of me, wondering if it's too much. Uncertain, because it's late as well, but then Leo comes up behind me. My breath hitches as he wraps an arm around my waist, while the other comes over my chest in a strong, gentle hold. His chest presses against my back, and I want to melt into him as I hold onto his arms. Leo's head dips down, nuzzling his face against my neck.

Heat rises in my cheeks suddenly, while I feel my core tighten at the touch. My body becomes extremely aware that he's around me. Unlike before, the shortness of my breath doesn't come from panic, but an entirely different emotion. I don't want him to let go, feeling safe in his arms, even though about an hour ago it tried to be repulsed by his touch. Now, with a clearer head, I want to hold on and feel his skin against me.

Arousal. That's what I feel.

I blink suddenly, staring at the oven and backwash of the kitchen as Leo breathes in deeply. A quick pang of guilt for that emotion drifts, and I shove it away as I clutch his arms around me. I'm allowed to feel this. To cling to this.

"Stay tonight," he murmurs against my ear.

"Leo." Shame starts to dig at me, worried of what he's asking me. "I don't know…"

"Just to sleep. I won't push you for anything else. You've already had a long day."

"Are…are you sure?"

"I already told you to stay here, didn't I?"

"You did," I whisper.

"I just want you near, dear Watson. I need you."

He presses a kiss against my neck, and I clutch him, battling all the emotions inside. I feel overwhelmed, exhausted, unsure, and old feelings I never thought I'd feel again. Even with all this churning inside me, I knew one thing. I didn't want to go home. I didn't want to be alone. I wanted him to keep holding me.

"I'll stay." He squeezes me a bit tighter in response, and I almost smile.

"We can watch a movie, then bed. But I should warn you, I don't really know how to get my television or streaming service to work."

I snort out a laugh, moving my head to look at him. There's a glint in his eye, and I smile finally. "I'll figure it out, but that means you have to watch anything I want."

"Very well, dear Watson." He kisses me, letting go and I want to yank him back around me. "I'll change, while you figure out my television."

Leo heads into the bedroom as I go the other direction. He has a large television screen and about four remotes. I narrow my eyes, trying to remember what all of Leanne's look like and somehow that helps me. By the time Leo comes back, I've figured out how to look for movies and pick an oldie but goodie.

"Robin Hood?" Leo asks as he sits down on the couch. It's far smaller than the one in the living room, and dark grey. It goes with the rest of the aesthetic.

"With Kevin Costner," I say, sitting down beside him. He puts his arm around me, pulling me in close and I cuddle against his side. I doubt the film makes it more than twenty minutes in before I begin to fall asleep. Leo's heartbeat lulls me, and the long ass day finally is done and behind me.

Chapter 20

Fairytales

I wake up with a start, sweat covering my skin as I frantically touch my chest and stomach. Apart from the sweat, I'm dry. No blood. No puke. No semen. I'd felt like I was drowning again as hands held me down. The nightmare had persisted, and I swore I'd been screaming, but my throat feels fine. Once convinced I'm not covered in anything, I lay back staring at the ceiling. Hearing deep slow breaths beside me, I glance over at Leo who's on his back, sleeping soundly. His chest moves, expanding with each inhale and not a wrinkled brow in sight. Rubbing my eyes, I glance at the clock and see it's around 4 in the morning.

Wonderful.

I stare at the grey ceiling for a few minutes and already know I won't be sleeping for the rest of the morning. Quietly, I slip out of bed, pausing when Leo shifts onto his side to face me. His eyes remain closed, and I let out a breath of relief as I shut the bedroom door silently behind me.

I head into the kitchen, grabbing a glass of water and lean back on the counter. Not a lick of exhaustion hits me. Nope, instead my body buzzes, wary of the "potential" danger it had been in from the nightmare. I drink more, debating to slip out and go home. Except, one

I've already done that to Leo. Two, I don't want to be a dick after he put in so much effort last night to help me. Three…he has a better coffee machine.

I start making a pot, doing my best to be quiet as I constantly check his bedroom door. No movement. Once done, I head to his television room and find the television still on from last night. He wasn't kidding about not knowing how to work it. I go through the long list of movies, almost giddy at all the options. I have quite the collection but he has access to streaming services and channels. Such a waste for someone who doesn't seem to have any downtime. It feels like forever before I finally find something, deciding on a classic, even though I already own it. I need something cute and hopeful right now.

The beautiful animation begins, and soon Jacquimo is singing about impossible things. My nose scrunches in delight as I sip my coffee and watch the fairytale, settling in for a relaxed morning. The room is only illuminated by the screen and a small lamp as I watch, soon coming up on a favorite scene as Thumbelina and Cornelius start singing. I sing softly with them, the nightmare forgotten. I continue singing with them, humming until the end. As it finishes, I hear something off to the side and jolt when I turn toward the sound.

Leo stands just outside the doorway, watching me. I blink quickly, making sure I'm actually seeing him and then turn the volume down. I ask tentatively, "How long have you been standing there?"

"Long enough to learn you know the entire song by heart." Busted.

I nod toward the television and the coffee in my hands. "This is what I do when I can't sleep after a nightmare."

"Explains the stacks of movies." He didn't know the half of it.

He comes over sitting on the couch next to me. I pause the film, and gesture with coffee in hand. "There's more in the kitchen if you want. Uh, I didn't want to leave like a burglar in the night again. But since you're up, I can head out—"

"No, stay." Leo cups my face, placing a kiss against my cheek. "When do you have work?"

"Noon."

"You can stay here until then. Finish your movie. I'm going to my office for a bit, but I'll be back down to make breakfast. Don't leave." Leo's voice is soft, but there's a commanding tone that's not asking.

Knowing I'd just go home, have cereal or a leftover muffin and not much else, staying was probably more nutritional for me. And he does have Amazon Prime.

"Alright," I answer, and he gives me a warm expression. He kisses me, getting up and changing into some slacks and a long-sleeved shirt before taking a mug of coffee with him. The door shuts, leaving me alone in his apartment. Before the quiet gets to me, I go back to watching *Thumbelina*.

I finish the movie, and then play *Swan Princess*. It's a fairytale kind of day with heroes with brown hair and bad haircuts. You can't convince me Prince Derek's hair stylist wasn't trying to sabotage him. Once that film finishes, I get up and turn everything off as I try to busy myself in the kitchen. Except it's spotless. Guess not.

I wander around, walking over to the patio windows to see the first rays of sunlight. They reflect off the buildings, pouring over the park with a warm glow. Humming, I venture through his penthouse, looking through the few books he has, mostly literature classics like Hemingway, Austen, and Steinbeck. Turning away from the familiar names, I slide a little on my feet and glance down. I slip my foot over the hardwood surface, smirking. I try sliding a bit with the socks on, finding they have potential. Quickly going to the windows again, I step back and move forward to slide across the floor.

Hmm, not much space to gear up for a good run.

I look around the place, trying to find a starting spot. Finally, I head down the hallway, where a small stretch of rug is and discover my chance. I take a running start, stopping just as I reach the edge of the rug and slide almost all the way across the penthouse.

I pump my arms in the air. "Yes! Okay, this place has potential."

Swiftly, I go back to my starting position and do it again, skating over the hardwood floor. I erupt with laughter, feeling a sense of relief. I go off to do it again, running down the carpet when suddenly I see Leo coming around the corner.

It's too late to stop and my socked feet continue sliding, causing me to crash into him. He catches me as I collide against his chest, my hands scrambling before I clutch his shirt. I look up at him through my lashes with a guilty expression. His own is filled with surprise and a quirked brow. I've already been caught singing old cartoon songs, might as well lean into the curve.

"4 out of 5 for the socks," I rate.

He looks at my feet. "Why only four?"

"Lack of fuzziness." I hold a foot up.

"I'm relieved to have such an expert to comment on what socks I acquire." The tone in his voice is teasing, and I narrow my eyes at him. "Hungry after your expedition?"

"Don't get sassy on me, mister. And yes."

Finally, he smiles, bending over to kiss me. I wrap my arms around his torso, humming happily. Yup, very glad I stayed and didn't dip out. Heat rises in my cheeks and my body feels very aware as he kisses me gently, then steps away to the kitchen. "What would you like for breakfast?"

I smirk at him. "How about an omelet?"

He pauses, glancing over his shoulder with fondness in his gaze. I just know after yesterday, today will be good day. Even with a rough start.

A day can still be good after having coffee grounds dumped on you, right?

I gape at the coffee grounds covering my feet, creating a pile that takes up a corner of the kitchen. The bag in my hands is turned over and I see that someone has sliced the flap open once picked up. You gotta be kidding me.

"Autumn, what...*what* happened?" Yuki asks as she comes back from my exclamation. "Yuki, I'm sorry, the bag just opened and fell apart." I throw the bag away, going to brush off the grounds from myself.

"Shit, which bag was that?"

"Ethiopian, it was the last one."

Yuki grumbles under her breath, and we both hear the crowd outside getting busier. You'd think summer was the busiest for us but fall meant warm lattes again and seasonal favorites.

"I'll clean it up. Mabel should be here shortly."

"Don't go dropping anymore, Autumn. The owners were already complaining about cost and losing that much isn't going to make them happy."

"I know, I know."

"I'll take care of the front with Bailey." Yuki leaves as I snatch the broom and move the rug to start cleaning it off. How did I not see the bag was messed with?

Halfway through cleaning, Mabel comes in and blinks at me with shock. "What happened?"

"The bag just opened on me," I grumble.

"Things just really keep falling on you, huh?" Mabel quickly puts her stuff in the backroom, coming over to help me sweep as I get on my knees to get to the grounds that went under the counter space. Mabel goes still, and then asks quietly, "Was Bailey here before you?"

"Yeah, she helped open with Daniella and Yuki." Still, on my knees, I look up at Mabel almost feeling the question from her. She flicks her gaze toward the shop, back at me with a raised brow. "She wouldn't."

"I don't know, Autumn," Mabel says, helping brush away the grounds. "She's shown moments she's capable of sabotage. She did it to you twice yesterday, and now you're back here like Cinderella."

"Well, then someone better tell her the real ending of that story, otherwise she'll be surprised when she's a *foot* short."

Mabel snorts as I get to my feet, finish cleaning, and then go to the backroom to pull on a clean shirt. After yesterday, Leo gave me three shirts to keep at work. Man must be psychic. Mabel follows me in, raising both brows. I shake my head at her not to ask, pulling out my travel bottle of lotion and hold it up. She shrugs and nods with a knowing smile, taking it from me to lather on and I do the same up to my elbows.

"Maybe I should come in tomorrow."

"Don't," I tell her, giving an exasperated look. "You've been planning this with your mom for weeks, take the day off."

She huffs, and peeks over her shoulder at the shop. "Just promise me, don't be in a room alone with her. You're on her hit list, Autumn, I'm telling you."

A pang hits my gut, words similar to hers piercing through me. I clear my throat, giving a tight smile. Perhaps Bailey is more than pissed about yesterday, but she can't be any worse than what I've dealt with in the past. I could handle a jealous girl.

"I'll be fine. And I've got extra shirts now." I keep my tone light-hearted, holding up one of the shirts. "You should let Yuki know that you're here."

Mabel nods, heading out front as I take care of the kitchen. After a few minutes, Yuki comes back for some pastries, and she pauses before asking, "Can you come in a bit earlier tomorrow? Around ten?"

"Sure? Why?"

"Daniella needs to leave early and Sita can't come in. All I have left is you and Bailey." There's a pit in my stomach, and I ignore it as I nod. "Bailey will be in for her usual shift, but you'll have to close on your own."

"Used to it."

"Cool, and let's try to clear out the pastries and sandwiches," she nods towards the freezer where we keep them. "I don't want to throw all of that out."

I nod as she leaves, heading to the busy café.

In the words of many a hero…I have a bad feeling about this.

Chapter 21

The Long Haul

I've come to realize there's something worse than being stuck with Bailey for hours.

It's her not showing up at all.

Ten minutes after Daniella left, a sinking feeling inside tells me I'm shit up a creek without a paddle…stick…whatever the phrase is.

The next rush is about to hit and I'm alone working in the coffee shop. Orders are beginning to stack up as I try to run between making drinks, taking orders, and serving food. As more people show up for the Friday mid-day rush, I text Yuki with dread. It worsens when she replies that she'll try contacting Bailey, but I know I'm out of luck and on my own.

I'm half-tempted to text Mabel, but fuck that, her mom is finally getting better, and she needs time with her. I'm not taking that away. My brain goes into overdrive as I start setting drinks up, debating how to finagle this. I have another eight hours of working, presumably alone, unless Yuki can get someone in or Bailey has a lick of mercy in her.

Doubt it.

Finishing up a few drinks and finding a lull between customers, I pull out a piece of paper and quickly write. I slap the paper over the empty case where the pastries would be, saying that we're out for today, including all other food. I'll apologize to Yuki later. I brace myself for the long haul as I notice a group of women coming for the shop.

"Alrighty, come on, you know this shop like the back of your hand," I whisper to myself. The chime of the door is almost like a gun going off to start a race. My brain focuses, shutting out everything as I move from one station to the next, multi-tasking as I go.

I'm practically running from one thing to the next, mixing drinks even as I take orders and put them out near the register instead. There are a few complaints about there being no food, but I press on a smile, apologizing and saying it's just for today. Some grumble and others just order an extra drink. The latter is the worst part of it.

The first few hours feel like they should fly by, but with the number of orders suddenly, it's like time slows. Even with regulars trying to be encouraging, telling me not to rush as they wait for their drinks, which is a relief from others who complain about how slow I'm being, not at all caring it's just me. I check my phone from time to time, seeing no updates from Yuki and by the time the third hour passes, I say fuck it and text her not to bother.

I'm stuck between focus mode and pissed, knowing that Mabel is probably right. Bailey knew Mabel wouldn't be in today, the only one who'd be able to come in and save me. I shake those thoughts away, focusing on the lattes I'm making and cleaning one of the blenders. Given how long it takes to wash them *and* making fraps, I'm half tempted to say we're not selling those today either.

The afternoon drags on and my feet are beginning to throb, hating me as my stomach clenches from not being able to eat since before noon. My hands are dry and burned from accidentally grabbing hot metal, but I ignore it as I concentrate on the next order. The pangs will end in about an hour if I drink some coffee. Stay busy and I'll forget I'm hungry. Once the large line has disappeared, I pour myself a black coffee and down it swiftly. I then run to the bathroom quickly and return to clean my stations for the next round of orders. It's late afternoon when I hear the shop's door open again. I roll my shoulders back like I'm entering a boxing match as I hum *Redemption* in my head.

If Rocky can do it, so can I.

I finish hyping myself up and turn toward the register to see Leo with deeply furrowed brows as he glances at the sign I'd put out. Thank fuck, an easy drink. I start his Americano without speaking, relieved it's only him and the man who usually has a digital pad while following Leo around, but this time he has a phone to his ear.

"Does he want a coffee?" I ask, nodding toward Leo's guy sitting at a table, beginning to ring him up. "I've only learned Isaac's and Rudolf's, so you'll have to help me out here on a name."

Leo narrows his eyes for a moment, frowning, and answers, "His name is Owen. He handles most of my cyber security and accounts."

"Well, would Owen like a drink? I've finally got a slight break to clean the blenders, so please be nice and no frappes. Order those tomorrow."

"He only drinks plain coffee with some cream."

"Coming right up, then." I turn away, going back to his Americano and start to pour a cup for Owen.

"Are you the only one here?"

"Yup."

"Why? It's Friday, the shop is always busy."

"Just happened to be me today," I respond, bringing his Americano and the coffee over to the register. I ring him in, flicking my gaze up at a very stern and not so happy Leo. I sigh, and tell him, "7.50."

He still stares at me, almost glaring, but he does take his wallet out and gives me a ten. I give him his change as he asks, "Is anyone coming to help?"

"Nope."

"You're closing by yourself, too, then?"

"Yup." His expression visibly darkens, flicking his gaze to where the kitchen is. "You even think of coming back here or sending Isaac, Leonardo Durante Luciano, I will ban you from this shop."

My voice isn't loud, but I catch Owen looking up with shocked wide eyes. Leo's expression takes all my attention. His mouth becomes a thin line, while his neck muscles tighten, and the pinching of his brows worsen. Whether it's how I talked or the words used, the sudden switch of ire on his face is apparent.

Usually, I'd flinch at such a look, anxiety creeping up my spine that I did something wrong. Except I'm running off of caffeine, spite, and exhaustion. My head is clear enough to stand my ground with him, even if I know he's just worried or being protective. I may have down moments, like the other day, but like fuck am I some maiden in need of saving.

This time I will be a stubborn, independent woman stereotype.

"This is *my* job," I whisper harshly. "I got screwed over. Simple as that. I'm sure it's happened to you, and I'm *positive* you wouldn't want me intervening with *your* job, would you?" Thankfully no one else in the shop is paying attention to us, but his buddy Owen sure is. He's dropped his phone, watching us with caution. Right, gotta make sure the boss's girlfriend isn't embarrassing him in public.

Leo responds with a rough voice, "No."

"Exactly. Let me do mine. Please, Leo." My tone becomes gentler, trying to get him to understand I have to do this. Long hours, shitty coworker, or crappy customers...I like my job. It's the only consistency I've had for almost three years.

Suddenly, Leo's expression falls, and the harsh anger is gone. He becomes completely passive as he takes his two drinks and walks over to the table. Owen's face is unreadable, quickly moving his attention to Leo as he says something.

At that moment, three women walk in, and I busy myself taking their orders. Plastering on a smile, I take care of their three lattes and after placing them at the pick-up station, glance over at Leo. He sits with Owen, who slides a digital pad to Leo as he continues talking on the phone, not halting the conversation. I exhale sharply, before cleaning the blenders and replace coffee grounds. I make myself another coffee, sipping on it as I continue working. After an hour passes, I notice Isaac come in with a tight nod and replaces Owen, who leaves quietly. Another hour passes as, hopefully, the last rush of the day commences. Isaac disappears with the last of the later day crowd, but Leo remains. Evening begins to descend, and fewer and fewer people come in giving me some much needed time to clean and restock supplies. It's when seven hits, and Leo has not moved, that I know he's not leaving until close.

Stubborn man.

I could be mad that he didn't leave, but I *did* say not to help. Never said he couldn't linger. He sits at the table, making phone calls and using the device Owen left behind. When there's a pause between tasks, I feel slightly bad how rough I was with him and make another Americano. I walk over to put it down in front of him and he looks up at me, while on the phone. A small, tired smile is all I give him before going back to work without a word.

The last couple of hours are slow, and I feel like I can breathe. The shop empties more and more, until the last thirty minutes comes around and I make the executive decision to shut down early when no one is here, besides Leo. I pull the shades down, lock the door, and sit across from him as he hangs up the phone. My feet throb and my legs burn. There's a clenching, sickening pit in my stomach from not eating and mainly drinking coffee all day, plus a headache. I'm too exhausted to even be mad at Bailey. For now. I'll be furious tomorrow.

"I'm gonna still be here another 30 minutes," I say, rubbing my hand over my face. "Usually, Mabel takes care of some things so I don't have to, but with just me, it's gonna take longer."

"How long were you working alone today?"

I exhale sharply. No point in lying, I'll feel guilty about it two days later. "Since noon, but I started earlier with another barista, and uh, since it's me, I came in at 930."

"That's almost twelve hours."

"Don't remind me or my stomach is gonna get angry." And there's the signature furrowed brow. "Please, don't Leo. I know you're upset, but no one was able to come in to cover. It was last minute, and I could've called Mabel, but I wasn't going to pull her away from her mom today. Her mom rarely gets to leave her hospice care, and she's been getting better. And besides, I get all the tips. Woo."

The last little bit doesn't amuse him like it does me. I get up to finish closing duties in the shop, rambling tiredly to Leo as I do. "I appreciate you staying to keep an eye on me. The service industry sucks sometimes. Long days, and you sometimes do the work of three people. Yes, it's just a barista job or whatever, but it's mine. My parents never let me have anything of mine, always giving it to my sister, whether it was a bedroom, a car, or a fancy computer. Which, by the way, I could've used for my programing, but they didn't care. I'd bet your fifty buck tips they're still doing that for her. Doesn't matter. Apart from my movies and books, this is what I've got. You said your job was a part of who you were, well, mine isn't exactly… but it's important to me."

I continue rambling, not caring what I'm saying as I clean up the counter space. I pull over the tip jar as Leo comes to stand on the other side. Then I notice the chairs have all been put up . A breathy, amused huff comes out of me.

"You're right," he says. I slow down. "I almost overstepped, because I was angry you were left alone to do a job meant for multiple people. It's abhorrent to me that not even your manager was here to help. Although I know you can take care of yourself, you here alone with that much cash and supplies, if someone tried anything harmful , they'd have the advantage. Not to mention unruly, asshole customers."

"Knew that's why you stayed." I shake my head, laying out the tips. "Isn't that what Isaac is for?"

"Yes, but I couldn't leave you alone." I go still at the softness of his voice. "If anything had happened to you, I'd have never forgiven myself."

My gaze meets his, and the pinching hunger pain is replaced by a fiery sensation that warms through me. Although I'm exhausted, there's a sudden awareness within. My chest feels light while I stare at him. Leo brings his hand up, tracing his fingers along my jaw to under my lips, before moving his hand to cradle my face. He leans over the counter easily with his height, his lips gently press against mine. I close my eyes as my breath hitches, tasting the coffee and sweetness that's him. His tongue brushes over mine and I inhale deeply, opening to let him in as the heat in my core grows, pulsing down my tired legs. It's happening again, that feeling of arousal as I want him to touch me more, make the ache go away. Screw being tired and worn out, I craved for him to grab me and hold me close.

He breaks the kiss, leaving my heart pounding as he places another brief kiss at the corner of my mouth. He rubs his thumb over my bottom lip carefully, eyes almost smoldering.

I swallow hard, not sure if I can create sentences, but somehow ask, "Can I stay with you tonight?"

"Of course."

Even with the sudden heat on my skin and the fluttering in my stomach, there's a prickly feeling at the back of my mind. A warning and then a bout of uncertainty. My eyes become downcast, all good feelings slipping away. "Um, just…just to sleep."

"Autumn." He tugs on my face to look up. "You've been working all day. I'll take care of you. Just finish up so I can take you home."

I nod as he lets go, finishing collecting the tips and cleaning the last of the shop. It's another fifteen minutes before I have him follow me through the back door, locking up for the night. Leo places his hand at the small of my back, leading me down the sidewalk. My mind blurs as we enter the hotel, heading straight to the private elevator. Before I know it, I'm sitting on his couch, showered and with a plate of food from *Sole Blu* on my lap.

My phone chimes, and I get up to check it where it's charging on the counter. It's Mabel apologizing that I had a long, shitty day and that I should've called her. I text her I'm fine, and the tips were almost worth it. There's a voice mail from Yuki, too, and I check quickly, listening to her tell me to take the day off tomorrow.

There are no days off.

The dark voice in my head is cut off when I hear Leo come out of the bedroom, his hair damp from the shower. He rubs his hand over my shoulder, and I lean my head back, closing my eyes as he continues to massage my aching muscles.

"How do you usually handle such long days?" He asks softly.

"Heat up a hot pocket and fall asleep on the couch," I mumble, sighing against his touch. "On the worst days, I just go to bed."

"Without eating?"

I shrug nonchalantly. "I've been homeless and hungry before, surviving one day without much food isn't that bad. Four to five days, the pangs start to get to you."

His hands still.

I open my eyes, finding him staring at the counter with his jaw working. He blinks, bringing his attention back to the present. "What can I do?"

The small laugh I give is empty as I grab his hand, pulling him to the couch. We sit down and I curl my legs up under me while I give him a sympathetic smile.

"You've done enough. Helping me this week and being patient with me, more than I usually get. I don't know why I feel so out of it, but...you've done more than enough, Leo. I'm sorry I was so rude to you earlier, I know you were just trying to help in your own way, but I can be stubborn sometimes, too."

Leo's eyes are concentrated, flicking over my face as his brows pinch together. He lightly brushes back a few strands of my hair, remaining quiet as he threads his fingers through them. I'm not sure what he's doing, perhaps studying me, but his walls feel like they're back up again. Like he's holding in something. Then it hits me.

I haven't really asked how his week has been. He's just always so put together; I assume he's fine. He doesn't or won't open up unless he absolutely wants to. When he doesn't, even with his small tells, you can't always tell if something is wrong. Except right now.

"Have...have you had a bad week?" I ask, and his gaze meets mine. "I haven't asked how you've been and, shit, I'm sorry, Leo. I'm over here—"

"No," he abruptly says, pulling me towards his chest. I'm embraced by him as he settles his chin against the top of my head.

"Having you around makes it…it makes it easier. Do not apologize for things you cannot control or what I've offered and am glad to do. I'd rather be here, taking care of you than…than working or thinking of it."

I nod against his shoulder, moving my arms around to hug his torso, and burrowing in closer. Leo's chest expands steadily, breathing in deeply.

"Do you want to talk about it?" I murmur.

"No, it won't change anything." There's a finality in his voice, and I just nod again.

Okay, so we both have had a crap week from work. Guess it doesn't matter what class bracket you're in, shit still is unfair some days. But maybe I've gotten lucky for the end of the week.

"I don't have to work tomorrow. Yuki won't let me come in, I have Sunday off, too."

"Are you suggesting something, dear Watson?"

"Just a thought. We could do something to help escape from this week. I mean, you haven't seen *Reefer Madness* yet, and that feels like a crime."

He snorts, kissing my head. "I still have some business to attend to tomorrow, but in the evening…" he hums against my hair, bringing his lips down to my ear, "…I'll take care of everything."

My cheeks warm as I attempt to keep my breathing level. The heat down in my core, spreading to between my legs almost makes me rub them together with the sudden sensation. His breath over my skin makes it tingle and the feeling comes back. Tickling me with the idea of intimacy, to enjoy it again.

My voice is only a breathy response of, "Okay."

Chapter 22

Pearl Clutching Dinner

I saac stands at my door with garment bags in hand, while Rudolf is behind him with shoe boxes. When Leo told me to go home for the day to get ready while he finished with work before tonight's date, I figured it would be from my own closet.

Silly Autumn, Trix are for kids. Or something.

"Uh, come in," I say and almost giggle at how Rudolf has to duck under the threshold as I close the door behind them.

"He wanted to give you options for tonight," Isaac says, gesturing to take things into my room. I nod stiffly, raising a brow as I watch them put the items down on my messy bed. "There are jewelry options, as well."

"Is this his way of making sure we don't wear the same outfit?" I ask, and Rudolf snorts.

Isaac gives him a look, and he just gives him a shrug. Isaac responds, "We'll wait for you downstairs."

"Gee, my place is a mess, but not that bad." I walk to my kitchen counter, pulling out the stashed liquor. Both give a glance as I put out glasses for them, and say, "I don't mind you two staying up here, just no peeking."

"Boss would kill us if we even saw your ankle," Rudolf mutters under his breath. I stop, giving the big guy a questioning look. He smirks. "I want to keep my eyeballs. I'll wait for you downstairs, *bärchen.*"

"I doubt Leo's that bad," I respond.

"He's not," he says, winking over his shoulder before he leaves. "But I'm not leaving Jameson alone in my fucking car."

Isaac and I are left standing in my living room as he shakes his head. Clearing my throat, I ask, "Jameson? As in the whiskey or something else?"

"Person. You've met him briefly. He wanted to speak with you tonight. Nothing to worry over."

"Uh-huh." Old anxieties bubble up, like I've been caught in a trap or taking someone's cheese. Except, I'm not sure what cheese it was or who it would've belonged to. I ignore the feeling, gesturing toward the alcohol and ask Isaac, "You staying then? Risking your eyes?"

"After following you for several weeks, Miss Watson, I know *you're* the one I'm more worried about than the boss." We both share a smile and I disappear into the bathroom.

After taking a quick shower and blow drying my hair, I head into my bedroom and pull out the clothes they brought. There're several dresses, a few slacks and blouses, but most are cut low or sheer. Apprehension begins to yank at me, causing me to clench my hand while the other trails over the soft, silky material. Biting my bottom lip, fearful of exposing so much skin, I walk out in my bathrobe and find Isaac looking through my movies. My heart pounds in my chest, anxiety rising as he examines my collection.

"What are you looking for?" I ask, my throat feeling tight. Please be careful, please be careful.

He pauses, holding up *Howard the Duck*. "You actually watch this, Miss Watson?"

"Yeah, but maybe you'd want a drink first. Actually, could you be careful with them? I know it's disorganized, but they're important to me."

"Of course, Miss Watson." He puts the DVD down. I let out a long breath. "I apologize."

"Don't worry. You didn't know, and just call me Autumn. Please. You don't work for me."

"I'll try…Miss Autumn." I snort at him, and he gives me a half smile, glancing down at my shabby bathrobe. "Is something the matter?"

"No, but I just…" my mind scrambles to think of a way to explain the other panic dilemma, and I try to ignore the nerves in my stomach, "…Leo, you, or Rudolf will be with me the entire night, right? I won't be alone?"

His brows furrow. "Yes or Jameson." I raise my brows. "He's secondary security tonight."

"Ahh." Learned a new name, get a talk, *and* gaining another bodyguard? It's a big night.

"Is there something I should be aware of? Or tell—"

"No, thank you. Don't worry about it, I'll be out soon and dressed." I walk back into my bedroom, shutting the door and stare at the selection of clothes. Quickly, I pick something by instinct and a pair of low heels.

I choose a black halter-top dress with a high neckline that skims down to my sides, connecting in the middle of my back. The skirt is a hi-low, flaring out with light fabric layered in sparkles. The black heels make me teeter slightly, and I opt for even shorter ones. I still teeter, but it's easier and I don't think I'll fall over from lack of practice. Adjusting the outfit, I grab a small simple clutch that Trix gave me a year ago and ignore any jewelry. I'm barely wearing any make up, and the skirt and heels are already a stretch for me. My phone is put away, fully charged, and I check that I have cash and my debit cards. Last thing I grab is a deep blue shawl that's in the pile of clothes.

Coming out of the bedroom, I find Isaac reading the bottle of scotch I left out. He lifts his gaze, and they widen a moment as my heels click against the old wood floor.

"Miss Autumn, you look absolutely stunning."

"Far better upgrade from stained shirts and jeans." I glance down at myself, twirling a bit in place as I feel the flutter of the fabric around my legs. A spark of joy runs over me, and I spin faster to let the skirt flare out, obliterating the restless thoughts from before. A giggle escapes, forgetting that Isaac is even in the apartment. I stop, shaking my head at the slight dizziness.

I look up, finding Isaac staring at me. "I also like racing with fuzzy socks. More slippery the better."

He chuckles. "Le-...the boss said you do that from time to time. I haven't seen much of it shadowing you though."

"I'll have to step up my game." I gesture for the door. "Off we go? Or is Leo gonna make an elaborate entrance with a helicopter, flying us to...I don't know, Rhode Island?" Isaac flicks his attention to his phone and my eyes widen. "Please say no. I was kidding."

"You'll be staying in the city." He comes around, opening the door. "He'll be there when we arrive."

"Phew, so how fancy is this?" After locking up, I head down the stairs with him. "I'm guessing a lot, given the extra escorts, clothing, and all."

"Knowing the itinerary you've had with him before, fancier than others."

"Ah, so anything I should know?"

"Are you asking me how to act?" I pause on the stairs, glancing at him. He gives me a thoughtful, amused expression.

"What I should be prepared for. Such as...do I drink from certain glasses? Utensils? Ordering? Tipping?"

"He'll handle all money matters. Ordering, more likely he'll do so for the both of you. At this particular place, he has his usual for himself and other, um, well..."

"Dates?" Weariness comes over him, and I wave him off. "I know the man dated other women, Isaac." I start heading down the stairs again. My thoughts flit back to that first date, how he ordered for both of us. Actually, he's decided anytime food has been involved with our dates, including him cooking. "What's his usual for here?"

"Steak for him, and salad for his dates." I snort and Isaac softly chuckles as we reach the bottom. "Not appealing?"

"If we're eating at a five-star restaurant, I'm assuming that is…" he nods, and I continue, "…then I'm getting more than a freaking salad. That feels like a slap to the face of the chef and Nan would never forgive me, speaking of. Stay."

He blinks rapidly as I knock on Nan's door. She opens the door, and her eyes go wide, her hand coming up to cover her mouth.

"I'm off for tonight, and may not be back later, so no muffins in the morning," I tell her.

She nods quietly, pulling her hand down with a tender smile. Her eyes begin to glisten and takes my hand, then whispers, "You're wearing a dress."

There's happy relief on her face; eyes gazing over me with awe. A nod is all I can give her as she pulls me into a hug. It's been over four years since I've worn anything like this. To ever feel comfortable like this again. Relief floods me as Nan hugs me, believing I chose correctly.

"You feel safe?" I nod. "Good. Go and enjoy yourself."

"I'll see you soon." I kiss her cheek, stepping away to leave through the bookstore. Isaac follows behind, stepping quietly through the darkened shelves.

As I'm opening the door for him to walk through, I notice a curious expression on his face. "What?"

"Nothing, Miss Autumn, it's…hard to explain."

"Am I conundrum for you, too?"

"More so, not like those we're regularly around."

"We?" I shut the door behind us, locking it up and noticing a short limo parked down the block where Rudolf stands.

"Those who the boss is closer to," he says, walking beside me to the car. There's a slight autumn chill to the warm evening, and I pull the shawl closer around my shoulders. "Works with the most."

"The ones he at first didn't want me talking to?" His gaze meets mine a moment, and I raise a brow. "Well, given that Jameson wants a talk, guess that rule is changing."

"More than you know," he murmurs.

I'm about to ask what he means by that, when Rudolf opens the car door for me as we approach. I smile up at him. "Thanks, Rudy. Some wonderful gentlemen you all are."

He smirks with a wink as I climb in, Isaac right behind me. Once settled, I find Jameson a few seats away from me. It's the man Leo was with when I hid at the women's center, and then up at the country estate. I reach for a handshake, but he only looks down at it.

"I'm Autumn."

His brown eyes narrow a moment, before he takes my hand and shakes it. "Jameson."

The car begins to move, and I turn to Isaac. "Real quick, back to lessons."

"Utensil wise, start on the outside and work your way in." Jameson flashes him a look of disgruntlement. "If there's soup, spoon it away from you not toward. Less of a mess."

"Where were you when I dumped half a bowl on me?"

Isaac grins and continues. "When you've finished, place your knife and fork on the plate to signify you're done. Don't place your elbows on the table either."

"Noted."

Jameson's face becomes one of curiosity.

"If you leave the table, place your napkin on the chair. And perhaps, don't lick your plate when you're done."

"Yup, cause that'll scare the *lovely* ladies and gents—good food and acting hungry," I muse, leaning back in my seat. "Thanks. That helps. Now I won't be confused when I'm being thrown out into the street for putting a napkin on the table." Isaac chuckles.

"Leo would never allow that to happen," Jameson speaks, and I feel Isaac tense beside me. My gaze meets the laid-back gaze of Jameson, who lounges as if he owns the car. He assesses me a moment, like he's truly seeing me for the first time. "He'd shut down the restaurant if that came to be."

"You know for bikers, all of you have a pretty good understanding of etiquette. Wouldn't have guessed that, but then…wait, that's probably stereotyping." I scrunch my brows. "Okay, yeah, that's stereotyping. Sorry."

"We've heard worse." Jameson casually waves it off. "We all started similarly. Through the years of growth, Leo's companies and hotels; we've learned how to adapt to new social customs and rules. Comes with the territory."

"You call him Leo," I blurt and both men tense at the odd accusation. "He said only his friends do that. Don't act like you don't almost always call him that." I point at Isaac. He flicks his gaze to Jameson, clearing his throat. "You know you can around me, right?"

"That's not why," Jameson answers for him.

"Then why?"

They exchange a glance, and Jameson frowns at me briefly.

Isaac clears his throat again, "Miss Autumn, it's not our place to discuss."

"Fine, whatever roles you play, go ahead. I understand there's things I don't know about your world; how it works with a different hierarchy, but if you're more comfortable calling him by his actual name, please do that. Especially, if he's opening up about me speaking with you, because I'd like to know his friends. To know he *has* friends. Even if they work for him," I murmur the last part, but glance over at Jameson who cocks his head at me. "What I've seen so far, I'm guessing the only ones close to him are all of you—his security team aka his motorcycle club. If I remember right, bikers are like siblings, which may explain why he's so private, even about you all. But don't treat me like one of the women from before who wants to fuck his bike."

I settle back, playing my fingers over the other and clear my throat, realizing how forward I just was about something trivial. Pretty sure it was Jameson who was supposed to talk, not the other way around. And now Jameson stares at me with wide eyes. Isaac coughs under his breath.

Slowly, the tip of Jameson's mouth pulls up into a smirk. "For damn once, he found someone he deserves."

"More like his *coffee* found me," I mutter.

Jameson leans further into his seat, appearing impressed. "Alright, we'll address him as we deem appropriate. No pretenses."

The car stops, and Isaac steps out of the car. I stay seated, waiting for whatever he wanted to speak with me about. After a moment, he nods his head to the door.

"If you're late, and he knows it was my fault he'll tan my hide. We'll talk another time." He flicks his gaze over me, like he's assessing me again. "I've learned what I needed tonight."

Me and my fucking blunt rambling.

Pressing a smile, I nod and leave the car with the door shutting behind me. I take a deep breath, shuddering slightly and hope that whatever Jameson just determined isn't gonna bite me in the ass. I concentrate on the extravagant view before me. Before me is a large archway of marble with gigantic windows. Trembling begins in my limbs as I stare at the splendor of the place. I glance down the block, noticing the area we're in, which I've rarely ever visited or ever come near.

I doubt my jean jackets would suffice even on the sidewalk.

Isaac motions for me to follow, and I concentrate not teetering over in my heels or throwing up from the nervousness that's hit me. Inside, the floor is bronzed and there's red carpet. The spacious foyer even has a fountain. We walk up some stairs, until a doorman opens the doors, and we walk through a short hall into an elevator. I wait to see if others join, but they don't as we head up and up. I feel Isaac looking at me, but I keep my eyes on the shiny elevator with tall plants, pulling the shawl off. It seems like forever before the elevator opens, revealing a dimly lit restaurant filled with red velvet, deep purples, and bronze accents. Isaac continues leading me until we come to the maître d station, set at a spilt between two main aisles that circle around the room with seating. Steps lead down into the middle for more tables on a glittering surface and dancefloor, which people are *actually* dancing on. The drifting sounds of Italian singing hits my ears as I stare at the place. *Scent of a Woman* comes to mind.

I swallow hard against the dryness in my throat, feeling completely out of place. The maître d is wearing a black velvet vest, complete with a white button up, hair slicked back, and small moustache.

Okay, someone's punking me. No one better ask me about soup and flies.

Nervous giggles want to erupt with the anxiety building in my stomach. Isaac speaks with him a moment, and the man's face suddenly brightens, but…totally fake. Like *really* fake. Could've seen it a mile away.

"Good evening, Miss Watson. It's a pleasure to meet Mr. Luciano's *guest* this evening."

I should respond, but words don't come out. Instead, I force a smile, feeling my arms shake. My stomach plummets wanting the guy to stop looking at me like I'm not wearing enough clothing. I want to put the shawl back on. If I ran now, would I make the elevator before it goes down?

Come on, you can do this. Just another restaurant.

Anxiety starts to overwhelm me, the lavish set up pressing in. *I shouldn't be here. I don't belong here.* I swallow hard again, debating how quickly I can run if I take my heels off.

"If you'll follow me. Mr. Luciano is—"

"Right here."

The waiter moves, and my shaking stops with relief when I see him.

Leo's wearing a black suit, no tie, and deep maroon shirt. It feels like my heart stops as I watch him approach with a commanding gait. His gaze is smoldering, slowly dragging up my body to my face. I can visibly see him swallow harshly, brows furrowing with concentration as a hand flexes at his side. Seeing his reaction makes me blush as he comes closer, taking my hand to kiss it. Hazel eyes peer into mine and I forget about the world around me.

"You are breath takingly gorgeous tonight, dear Watson," he whispers.

"And you're simply dashing tonight, Leonardo Luciano." I smile at him, and his eyes glimmer.

He turns with a slight nod to Isaac, who nods back as Leo leads me to our table. He keeps a hand on the small of my back. The warmth easing the trembling anxiety out of me as I relish in his touch. We pass table after table with people bringing their attention to Leo as we walk, continuing until we reach the back side of the room near wide windows. A view of the city skyline glitters against the dark sky. He pulls my chair out, putting our backs to the windows, and I sit down. He leans over me, placing a soft kiss on my lips.

"Really trying to woo me, huh?" I ask a bit breathlessly as he adjusts his jacket in a fluid movement and sits down next to me, which makes my skin heat. Shit, the way he looks, he's freaking handsome in the candlelight and intoxicating, I may need to hold onto the table.

Leo hums, taking my hand and cocks his head. "Do you prefer this or the motorcycle when it comes to…*wooing*?"

My thumb moves over his skin, glimpsing at the place that minutes ago had practically given me a panic attack. It's sheer opulence, absolutely not what I'm used to. I give him a mischievous grin, and answer, "The motorcycle."

His brows shoot up. "Really?"

"Don't get me wrong, this is gorgeous, and I appreciate you making this happen after the past week, but…" my voice trails off, and I lightly rub my neck and drop my hand from the nervous tick, "…you never looked happier than when you were riding."

"I'm quite happy right now." His sultry voice makes my body jolt, eyes flashing to his as the smallest tug of a smile comes up on his face. He breaks the contact when the waiter comes by, straightening.

"Good evening, Mr. Luciano. It is a delight to have you again, and a good evening to your lovely guest, Miss Watson." Not sure how I feel about him knowing my name. He turns back to Leo, full attention on him. "What will we be having this evening?"

Leo opens his mouth, but I interject quickly. "Wait, I have a question."

The waiter almost steps back with shock, jaw slackening. Leo tilts his head at me with intrigue. "Yes, dear Watson?"

"Have you ever had anything here that *wasn't* your usual?"

He blinks once, peering past me for a second. I don't have to turn around to know Isaac is sitting in the room. *I'm never alone, even if it seems I am.* He wasn't kidding. Leo leans back, self-assuredly, and waves the waiter away without a word. The man practically stumbles away, clutching his chest.

"What were your thoughts?"

"Well, if you get something different from the usual, you may not want the same kind of wine. Unless it's a red that goes with anything, but you don't strike me as the sort. So, I thought we'd look at the menu…*together* and decide from there."

Leo tries to suppress a smile. "What if I wanted my usual of steak?"

I shrug. "Go ahead, but I'm not having salad, mister." I pick up the menu, beginning to browse and peek over the top at his bemused face.

He sighs, peering past me again and I look over my shoulder this time. Isaac and Jameson are at a table on the far side of the room near the entrance. They exchange a glance with each other as I turn back to Leo, who asks, "What did they tell you?"

"You're particular, but I already knew that," I say nonchalantly. "You have a desire to control everything, making decisions about meals falls under that. I'll take your *suggestions* with food because you have experience of cooking, but uh…" I put the menu down and purse my lips, "…why have a usual in a five-star restaurant? Wouldn't this place be the best for trying new dishes?"

"Try explaining the difference between shrimp scampi and lobster ravioli to, well," he starts, but clears his throat and shifts in his seat. He leans forward and finishes with, "uneducated individuals."

A giggle comes out and he quirks a brow. "That's what we're going with?"

"Would you prefer another name?"

"No, because not much else describes some people at times. I mean, I've had to explain the difference between lattes and cappuccinos for like thirty minutes. I get it."

"What is the difference?"

"More foam," I say deadpan.

Leo lets out a laugh, leaning back with an absolutely dazzling smile. I peek to Isaac and Jameson who watch in surprise. Isaac grins, leaning back in his seat as Jameson just stares. Leo's laugh subsides, nodding at me. "What are you feeling, Autumn?"

We read through the menu, and I listen to him explain dishes and we settle on something with scallops and a fish recipe. Leo orders a saffron risotto and something with chicken, which helps makes the decision of white wine for the table. Leo checks with me multiple times that I'm fine drinking some, and I assure him I'm good with a glass. It's light and doesn't remind me of past experiences, making it easier to swallow and not try reaching for the whole bottle. He clinks his glass to mine once the waiter scuttles off.

"How badly did I scare the daylights out of him?" I ask, sipping my wine.

"Quite a bit."

"Why?"

"No one interrupts, let alone speaks for me." The statement is almost harsh. I put my glass down, cautiously. "Except you."

"Why?"

He swirls his glass, taking a sip before he sets it down. "Any time you have, usually it's with good conscience or to explain yourself. Or I've done something absurd and I deserve to have my head bitten off to let someone else speak."

"I haven't—" A flash of trying to shove a door in his face comes back. "Never mind."

"Dear Watson." He takes my hand, bringing it to his lips. "Those in the past who've interrupted or defied me have done so with ill intent. Disrespect. Nasty means. You haven't. Not once, even when angry. And you've given me more patience, grace, and under-standing than most."

His other hand goes to the nape of my neck, stroking my skin and under my hair. Gently, he pulls me forward, lips meeting mine. My breath hitches as he kisses me. My stomach flutters then tightens while heat stretches over my body, tingling in delight. I clutch his other hand in mine, deepening the kiss as he takes a deep breath and strokes his tongue against my bottom lip. I taste the wine, not stopping my small, quiet moan. Leo holds my head still, diving deeper for a few moments before pulling away to place his forehead against mine.

"Fuck, how you intoxicate me," he rasps.

"Leo?" He hums, watching me attentively and calm joy spreads over me. "Thank you," I whisper, looking into those wonderful hazel eyes. "This week. Tonight. For everything. Thank you."

His eyes soften. There's a reverence in them, like those aren't words he hears often. He brings my hand back up to his lips, almost nuzzling it. He goes to say something, when I hear the waiter come back and instantly Leo's expression hardens to steel. He scowls, snapping his gaze to the intruder with warning.

The quick change over the fact we've been interrupted makes me giggle, and I squeeze his hand before he keeps sending a death glare to the poor waiter. Leo looks back at me, giving a softer expression meant only for me.

The waiter clears his throat. "Sir, t-there's a…an urgent call for you."

"It can't wait?" Leo asks, leaning back with a fearsome look. The waiter visibly gulps, shaking his head. Leo sighs, kissing my hand briefly before getting up. "This is what I get for…never mind. I'll be back."

"Okay, Terminator."

Leo snorts as the waiter quickly walks away.

I whisper as he leaves, "Speaking of, stop scaring the staff!"

He gives me a sly look, turning away to head toward the entrance. I watch him walk away, although my attention is *definitely* on his ass. And shoulders. And commanding stride. I mean, come on!

He passes Jameson and Isaac with a nod, who give him one back and they remain seated. I reach for my small purse, ignoring the people at other tables who glare at me for pulling out my phone.

Quickly, I text Isaac: **How many waiters has he made piss their pants?**

Isaac takes out his phone to check, and he freezes, bringing his sight to me. I wave my fingers at him with amusement. He shakes his head as Jameson looks at him with a disapproving expression, so Isaac shows him the text. Jameson makes a movement like he's trying not to laugh and juts his head at Isaac.

Isaac: **Lost count.**

Me: **Hell of a superpower.**

Isaac: **He's perfected it.**

I glimpse up at them and go off a gut feeling.

Me: **Can I have Jameson's number?**

Isaac stares at the text, then shows it to Jameson who takes the phone and texts: **Why?**

Me: **Back-up. In case Isaac is busy, cause I'm sure he has a life. Something tells me you're next in shadowing. Could ask Rudy instead.**

Jameson looks up at me, shifting in his seat uneasily as Isaac shrugs and gestures something. The other shakes his head, making a face.

Me: **I won't tell Leo.**

Jameson: **He'll be pissed from here til hell when he finds out.**

Me: **Why? Doesn't like sharing your wonderful disposition?**

Jameson looks up, meeting my gaze across the room with a glare. Leo and him could be brothers with that scowl.

Jameson: **He's very private for reasons.**

Me: **I promise to behave. No giving away secrets.**

He just stares at the phone for a couple seconds. So, I send another text.

Me: **Promise this is only for emergencies. Scout's honor, though I suck at selling cookies.**

Jameson: **That's girl scouts.**

Me: **Never made it in. Must've been the boy scout thing.**

He barks out a laugh, bringing his full attention to me with a faint smile. He shows the messages to Isaac who grins. They speak to each other, and Isaac types into his phone and I get a message of a new number. I send a text to it, and I see Jameson hold his phone up. I smile, going back to my wine and leaving them alone.

Relief settles me having the extra number. Anything left of my anxiety disappears and I breathe easy, settling into my seat as I stare out one of the windows. My finger trails around the rim of my wine glass, leaning my elbows on the table to continue watching the city lights.

I jolt, pulling my elbows off the table. I grumble, "Damn. Already broke a rule."

"What rule?" I startle, almost jumping out of my seat as Leo approaches. I clutch my chest, letting out a breathy laugh.

"Elbows on the table," I answer, and he quirks a brow. "Also got a crash course on *fine dining* etiquette."

Leo takes his glass, sipping the wine and places it down, then deliberately puts his elbows on the table, folding his hands under his chin. I give a mock gasp, clutching my non-existent pearls. "Scandalous!"

He smirks at me while I laugh just as the food arrives, which is beyond delicious. Our evening continues with talk and small smiles, all the struggles of this week wash away. I become enraptured by Leo, falling into the wonderful, serene world of his adoring gaze. The touch of his hand, which skims over my thigh, sparks a tingling sensation through me every time. Once again, I'm beginning to be filled with a desirable heat, flourishing with each touch and look. My mouth goes dry as I realize I want to try again. After all the patience and care and safety he's given me, I want to conquer my shadows. I want him to fulfill that promise of replacing every lingering touch of the past with his. Hold him and bring those desires to fruition.

Fall completely. Hazel eyes meet mine, and I think may have already.

Chapter 23

Green. Yellow. Red.

Alluring rumba music drifts from the dancefloor, and I look over to the middle of the restaurant where couples dance. I stare at the dimly, candlelit area, flickering shadows over the space. Remembering the last time Leo and I danced, I carefully bite my bottom lip. A shiver runs down my spine, recalling the strong hold of his arms. I'm lost in the past. For once, not terrified of it.

Leo pulls me back to reality as he steps into my line of sight. He holds his hand out, and I take it for him to lead us down the short set of stairs. More sensual Latin music plays and my breathing hitches as I realize what we're doing. Nervousness creeps up, the feeling of people watching and being on display. Leo keeps a firm hold of my hand, stopping shortly on the dancefloor. Murmuring happens nearby, and my gaze flicks to others staring and I'm ready to bolt again. Run for the hills.

Get out.

I'm pulled in by Leo.

My full attention is directed to him as a hand slips down the small of my back, his other keeping hold of my hand. Mine drifts up to his shoulder. We come in close as my chest brushes against his and there's butterflies in my stomach. Leo tilts his head down, close to my ear, and whispers, "Do you know rumba, too?"

I nod stiffly.

Leo kisses my cheek, pulling back to lead us into the first steps of the dance. I stare up at the man before me, following easily as the music carries through the space. Lights create shadows over his face, eyes darkening with smoldering concentration. My entire body begins to flush as we dance. I try not to close my eyes as his hips brush against mine, rolling as he dances. He moves to flare us out a little, slowly and deliberate, leading me back to his embrace with his fingers tracing down my back. His touch causes my skin to spark, traveling down, down to the apex of my thighs. My breathing becomes shallow as I glance up through my lashes, inhaling his aroma. Leo leads us away from the group of other dancers, into a darkened spot of the dancefloor overshadowed by a wall.

"Where did you learn to dance?" He asks.

"College. Took a class. Then it became this part time gig for a while."

"Did you compete?"

"No, just teaching at youth centers. Long before being a barista. What about you, Mr. Classic Heritage?"

"You remembered the model," he muses, kissing my hand in his. Oh, I feel like I'm on fire. "Part of my upbringing. Usual childhood aristocratic things. A few years ago, I decided to refresh my memory of the hobby."

"For how long?"

"Five months. Stopped due to hotels going up, putting my time towards those and other real estate." He spins me slowly to the side, bringing me back into the close frame. "Do you have a favorite dance?"

When his hand reaches my back, I swallow hard against the dryness in my throat. "Right now…rumba."

Leo's grip tightens. His expression changing into something ravenous as he takes a deep breath in. My hand on his shoulder digs into him more, trying to convey how much the need is pulsating through me. I bite my bottom lip lightly, focused on the movement of his neck muscles and chest. I'm not sure if what I'm trying to relay is working, until he dips his head down. He kisses me. Slowly, full of need and in worship. My tongue brushes over his lips, holding him tightly as I clutch his shoulder. Leo pulls away suddenly, and my eyes flutter back open as he whispers, "Are you trying to seduce me, dear Watson?"

"Depends. Is it working?"

His brows furrow, thinking, as his gaze flicks to my lips. "Autumn, are you sure? I'll wait—"

"I want you, Leo," I rasp, clutching his hand tightly as I feel myself shake. Nerves begin to fight against the building need of desire. "I want…I want to, uh—"

Leo places a hand against my jaw, stopping our dance as he strokes his thumb over my cheek. My eyes close, trying to force away the panic. My throat tightens, holding onto every ounce of good he makes me feel. Leo brings his mouth closer to mine, but doesn't kiss me, keeping a hair width away.

"What are feeling right now?" The heat of his breath washes over my skin as I open my eyes, seeing golden green. My mouth works, trying to find the words, but they don't come out. "Don't think of anything or anyone else in this room. Right now, in front of me, what are you feeling?"

His words wash over me as I lean into the touch against my cheek, breathing heavily. I peer into those safe eyes, now hooded with desire. They reflect back what I want.

"Like I'm going to combust," I whisper. "And how…how much I love your hand against my back. My skin. I feel safe. Wanted."

"Do you want to know what I'm feeling?" Another wave of arousal comes over me, flushing my skin as I numbly nod my head. He places a soft kiss at the corner of my mouth, and then brings his lips against my ear. Hot breath drifting over my skin. "Like no one else exists, only you. Every movement and sound you make, my entire body pulses with want. *Every* moment of your hold on me, your tongue, lips has driven me closer to ecstasy."

Gasping, my eyes widen as he breathes over my skin, causing a shiver down my spine. His hand on my back travels up with it, then back down as my muscles tighten. A moan catches in my throat as I lean closer for support.

"Leo," I plead.

"A few rules before we go further." He sways us a little, and I follow his small steps automatically as he lets go of my face to take my hand again. I stare up at him, unsure what he's planning. "One, we take this as slow as you need. No rush for the main event." He smiles softly and it helps some of my anxiety vanish. It's Leo. I'm safe. "Two, we'll use the stoplight method. Do you know what that is?" I shake my head. "I'll be checking in with you, which you'll respond with green, yellow, or red. Green is to continue, yellow is ease back, and red is full stop. No matter what we're doing. Understood?"

I go to nod, but he raises a brow which makes me smirk as I answer, "Yes, I understand."

"Very good, and last thing." He leans down, kissing my cheek. "Even if I don't ask or check in, you can say red. There'll be no repercussions, Autumn. We'll stop. I want this to be as enjoyable for you as possible. I meant it when I said all you'd know is pleasure from my hands, and I will do everything to uphold that."

"What about you?" The question falls out quickly.

Leo grins ruefully. "Don't worry about me, dear Watson."

He stops us, keeping his hand on my back as he leads us off the dancefloor. His stride is almost predatory and protective as he keeps me close, and his voice becomes a sultry darkness which strikes pleasure straight down to my core. "The pleasure I'm going to give you will be enough to satisfy my needs for a decade."

Excitement runs over my skin as we walk past Jameson and Isaac. Leo nods at them as they move past, Jameson to the maître d, while Isaac goes back to our table to retrieve our things. I go to say something, but Leo already walks us into the elevator and punches the button. The doors close, leaving us alone and I peek up at him. Strong focus is all over his face, and it makes me smile as he glances down at me. He cradles my face, kissing me fervently.

He growls against my lips, "I told you how gorgeous you are in this dress, correct?"

"Uh-huh."

"Good." He kisses me again. The complete mood switch of sweet, romantic Leo to smoldering, possessive Leo makes me giggle against his mouth. He breaks the kiss, pulling back with a small furrow. I gasp, slapping my hand over my mouth as my eyes go wide.

Why did I just laugh as he was kissing me?!

"I didn't mean to—"

"Fuck, you're wonderful." He wraps an arm around my waist, bringing me flush against his body to kiss along my neck and jaw. "Never stop being you. Every." Kiss. "Beautiful." Kiss. "Facet."

"*Now* who's seducing?"

He gives me a mischievous grin, stepping back as the elevator doors open. His hand stays on my back, keeping me close as he practically parts the sea of people we walk by. I avert my gaze from everyone, not wanting my stomach to twist when I see the surprise on their faces of who's walking past them. I concentrate on the touch of his hand, striding next to me and keeping me shielded.

We come outside and the limo is there already with Rudolf holding the door open.

"Thank you," I say, stepping in with Leo directly behind.

"Hotel," Leo orders, shutting the door. He presses a button, and a divider goes up between us and Rudolf. It shuts completely and Leo pushes another button, before reaching for me. He places a hand behind my head, pulling me close as he lays kisses upon my jaw to my lips. The moan I've been holding in since the dancefloor comes out, whimpering almost at the contact. The arousal continues to spur forward, and I hold on with everything I have to the growing feeling.

Leo pulls back, and says, "Check in."

Immediately, I respond, "Green."

He smiles, kissing me once again as I press myself further against his body. We continue to make out in the back of the car with his hands traveling up my thighs and back down. My breath is shaky with anticipation as the excitement builds, gasping when he clutches my ass through the skirt. "Check in."

"Green," I rasp.

"Good girl," he whispers, planting a tender kiss under my earlobe. I shiver at the response, and a small huff of nervous laughter comes out as my hands shake, clutching onto his shirt. Leo pauses. He looks at me with caution. "What is it?"

I clear my throat. "Uh, the…name, I didn't think I'd ever…" he raises a brow, "…ever like that. I liked that."

He smiles warmly, stroking my hair as he threads his fingers through the short strands. I hum and close my eyes as he massages the back of my head, while he kisses my neck softly. "Only I can ever call you that."

I grin as he continues the sensual torture, creating heat to flourish inside me. The car stops, and Leo looks to the front. Soon there's a few raps on the divider. Leo lets go, opening the door and steps out with me close behind. I inhale deeply as he helps me stand, keeping his hand in mine. We're in a parking garage, walking briskly inside and into a short hall, then the elevators. The entire hotel ambiance is quiet as we enter the private elevator, doors barely closing before Leo grips my hips, pulling me against him. He goes to crush his lips against mine but stops. He stares down at me, hazel eyes flicking over my features and down the rest of my body. Usually, with that kind of look, I'd shy away in shame or nerves. Except, with him looking at me like that, I don't feel that way. The hard desire in his eyes calm a moment as he traces a finger down my neck.

"Check in."

Realizing he's trying to slow down for me, I smile. Arousal strikes at my core, spreading over me. Safety blankets me as he carefully handles all of me, his attentive actions and words calming the nerves. "Green."

His forehead rests against mine, breathing deeply. I close my eyes. The moment of silence together almost ridding all the nervous trembling in my body. My lungs feel constricted as I inhale a long breath, smelling the alluring scent of his cologne. A hand travels up to the nape of my neck, holding me protectively.

The elevator doors open, and Leo walks me backward through the foyer, around the table to the door. My eyes remain on him the entire time, letting him move me and shut the door behind us. The clack of the door and locking sets off a prick at the back of my mind. It scratches in warning, and I ignore it, concentrating on the smoldering gaze before me.

Leo pauses, stepping back to shuck off his jacket and unbutton his shirt a little as I take a step back against the island. He doesn't let me go far, grabbing my waist to press his hips against mine. I feel his erection.

Oh, *fuck me*. Yup, that's the plan.

My sex pulses and I almost want to rub my thighs together because of it. Leo clutches the back of my head, kissing me deeply as he grinds his hips against mine. My entire body hums with desire as I reach up to grab his hair. There's a deep growl at the back of his throat as he moves us, and my back presses against the wall. Cold and hard.

It breaks the spell I'm under.

The chilled surface drives panic through me, almost smothering the heat that's been building for the past hour. Fear travels down my spine as my eyes fly open. Leo kisses me, encaging me with his body.

Trapped. I'm trapped.

I try to fight the oncoming terror of repressed memories that scratch and tear at me. My breath becomes heavier as I try to stay in the present. The warmth of Leo. The arousal. His hands…*his* hands.

NO.

He presses me harder into the wall. *Please don't hate me. Please.*

Breaking the kiss, I gasp, "Yellow."

Leo's chest heaves as he looks down at me with wide eyes, flashing between me and then to the wall. He curses under his breath, and my body starts to tense, awaiting the beating. Instead, he lifts me into his arms, wrapping my legs around his waist as he takes me away from the wall and into his bedroom. A hand caresses my back, sitting me on the bed as he kneels before me as his other hand clutches my face.

A different fear builds. I fucking ruined it. Of course, I fucking did. I grasp onto his hand and plead, "Please don't stop."

"Autumn."

"I want this...please, don't, *please*," I beg, reaching for him to come back. He starts to pull away and tears prick my eyes, stomach aching in guilt. I close my eyes, trying to will away the storm of emotions as I shake. "I don't want them to take this, too...please... don't hate me..."

"Dear Watson, look at me." My eyes stay screwed shut, not wanting to see disappointment in his. Leo moves his hand down my side, caressing me in a gentle manner. The movement makes me open my eyes slowly, finding his gaze. But there's no hate. "Give yourself a minute. I said all the time you need, it's okay."

I swallow hard, nodding my head stiffly.

"I don't hate you, never could, sweetheart," he murmurs, stroking his hand continuously down my side. "I'm right here, breathe."

I inhale deeply, and then again not daring to take my gaze away from his. It tethers me to reality, keeping me here along with his hand that lightly strokes my skin. The hand against my cheek, goes to the nape of my neck, holding me firmly, but gently. I take another deep breath, some of the anxiety dissipating with the slow, comforting touches.

"Good girl," he whispers. For some reason the moment he says that I relax further with a sense of security. His calming tone is a trance as he continues to caress me. "What triggered you?"

My mouth works a little, thinking. "Wall, maybe because—"

"Don't explain. Not now," he says quietly, coming forward to kiss my cheek and then the other. "Check in. Be honest."

I ease further into his touch. Soft. Firm. Lips against my skin. I swallow as the arousal begins to come back as I calm. "Green."

He pauses before he kisses me tenderly on the lips and I moan at the contact. My body starts to get more on track as I bring my arms around his neck, and he places his around me. He holds me close, deepening the kiss and I moan again with need. Leo pulls back enough to whisper against my lips, "Good girl."

I hum at the name as he kisses me again, but it feels cut short as he moves back to pull his shirt off. He then pulls off the undershirt, baring his nude torso. I blink quickly at the well-muscled body before me, coming face to face, finally with more of his tattoos. He's completely covered in them.

Dark ink travels up from his forearms to his shoulders, back down his chest, and disappearing under his pants. I notice on the right side of his chest are skulls piled up with fire around them. On the left side are roses and thorns, engulfed in more flames. Wire wraps around his arms with flowers, wilting and some blooming, along with knives. There're more images, filling in the empty spaces with red, black, blue, and yellow. Heavy lines with brutal designs.

Leo remains still as I bring my hand up tentatively to trace over the ink. He watches me carefully, waiting for my response, as I run my hands across his ribs. I press against the tattooed muscles, and he stands up fully as I do with him. I become enraptured with the art. What seems like a chaotic mess, isn't. It's carefully planned out as I see the lines connect and flow into the next, every image with a purpose.

I peek up at him. His eyes are closed as he shudders a breath as my fingers play over the ink. After a few moments, he opens them staring at me with burning want. Somehow touching the incredible ink and seeing the look in his gaze spurs on my courage.

I can do this. I want this. I want *him*.

"You're beautiful," I whisper, keeping my hand on his chest.

I'm not sure if I should've said it, wondering if I could take it back and replace it with something more masculine. Until Leo smiles gently, placing his hand over mine and pressing it to his chest. "Only you'd say that so earnestly."

I shrug, biting my lower lip as I step back and start to peel my clothes off. Leo stares at me as I strip, tossing the dress aside with only my underwear still on. Boxers. Leo's brows furrow a moment, and I think it's because of my stunning choice in underwear when I remember no one has seen me naked in years.

Self-consciousness comes over me, chilling me a little as I remember the scars along my abdomen and down my thighs. Not to mention the small burns across my chest. I go to move my arms to cover myself, but Leo stops me as he grabs my wrists gently. He lets go of one, tracing a finger down my side and over one of the surgery scars across my stomach. His gaze meets mine, letting go to lift my chin up to look at him.

The furrow is gone, and he says, "You're beautiful."

Hearing the honesty in his voice, I giggle, especially as he strokes my stomach again and it tickles. I bite my lip to stop the sound, but Leo just does the movement again and I can't stop the sound coming out of me.

"There she is."

He starts to lay me back on the soft bed, and I let him with a hard swallow as helps me take my heels off. Kicking his own shoes off, he stands and looks me over on the bed. "Check in."

"Green," I breathe out, staring at the tattooed torso.

A slight smile pulls at his lips as he kneels before the bed, slowly taking my boxers off. My breathing becomes heavy as his hands travel up my inner thighs toward my sex, and I begin to shake slightly. I gulp, staring up at the ceiling as tears prick at my eyes. Hot breath comes over my nether region and I clutch the sheets.

No. My mind spirals again, horrible nightmares slamming against the doors of my mind.

No. Clenching my jaw, I refuse to say it. I've already almost fucked this up. He'll hate me. They've *always* hated me. It's fine… it's fine…

I try to remain still, but my body rages against me with its shaking. Leo pulls away. "Check in."

I open my mouth, but nothing comes out. No. NO.

"Autumn, check in."

My mind continues to spiral as my chest constricts, struggling for breath. Tears stream down the sides of my face as I scowl, not wanting to give in to the tumbling emotions. I'm fine. *Quit being weak—*

"*Check. In.*" Leo empathizes, moving off the bed.

Fearful of the aftermath, I tremble more as I pinch my face together in pain. I choke out, giving in to the order, and rasp, "Red."

Leo is instantly on the bed, yanking me up and embracing me. He holds me close as I shake violently, trying to hide my face against his chest. He strokes my back, speaking quietly, "I need you to tell me. No matter what. I'm not angry. I need you to learn, sweetheart."

"I'm sorry. I'm—"

"No, shh, it's okay. We can stop—"

"No," I demand with a choked sound.

"I'm not going to push you, you called red. It's okay."

"No." I grit my teeth, taking a deep breath. I concentrate on his warmth. "I want this…*bad*, Leo. I want…I want my peace back again. To have *this* again. All of it. I want control of, of my own damn body!"

He continues to rub my back, holding me firmly as I cry against his chest. I clutch him, trying to focus on the security he gives me and the warmth. Gently, he kisses the side of my head. Pulling back, I refuse to meet his gaze. "Look at me, dear Watson." I swallow hard, looking up. "Good girl."

A strangled whimper comes from me as I lean more into his arms. That name, whatever magic he uses, helps keep me focused. Reminding me where I am. "Let's start with this, what makes you feel safe?"

Surprised by the question, I blink, thinking and say after a moment, "You holding me."

"Like this?" I nod. "You said before you liked my touch on your back. Anywhere else?"

"Neck."

He nods, looking down at me within his lap. He hums and a small smile rises on his face.

Leo puts a hand at the back of my neck, massaging into the base of my skull. My eyes flutter close as he kisses along my jaw, behind my earlobes, down my neck, and to my mouth. My breath hitches when his lips brush against mine, starting to kiss me with affection. I deepen the kiss as he presses his hand at my back, helping the heat rekindle.

Him. I want him. And every bit of pleasure he drives through my body, even with the storm of emotions inside. I fall deeper and deeper into his spell. I wrap my arms around his neck, while my lips feel swollen from the kiss.

He breaks off. "Check in."

"Green," I answer without second thought.

"Good girl," he whispers against my skin. I smile as my eyes close, feeling his chest rumble with a laugh. "You like that honorific, don't you?" I hum and nod. He nips at my earlobe, sitting me on the bed.

"We'll continue, but if you need, we will stop. No repercussions, Autumn, I swear," he says, stroking his fingers through my hair.

"Okay," I whisper.

I blink as he gets off the bed, removing his pants and then his briefs. My eyes widen at the sight of his bare ass, powerful thighs, and the erection that's not softened since I felt it earlier. And yup, more ink down his legs, even to his feet. My gaze moves up as he goes to the bedside table, pulling out a condom and lube. My stomach flips, but I bite back any words as he holds the lube out to me. "Put some on."

I take the small bottle, putting a bit on my fingers and feel the smooth, cool lube. I give the bottle back as he starts to put the condom on, and I slide the lube over my sex, shivering at the chill. Wiping the last of it on my thigh, Leo comes back to the bed and sits, gesturing for me to come over. He positions my legs to straddle him so that I'm hovering over his erection. I glimpse down at it and back up at him.

"Safe in my arms. You control how deep and how fast. No wall." He kisses the side of my mouth, squeezing my thighs gently to help maneuver my hips.

I take a deep breath, placing my hands on his shoulders as I stare into his eyes for a moment longer. Easing down, he slowly enters me, stretching me a little as I gasp. I pause, knowing it's been years and swallow hard. I slide his cock further into me, gripping his shoulders, and feel him hold my hips firmly.

My legs already begin to shake as I bring myself back up, and go back down, and then again. Tingling travels up my spine as his girth enters me fully, my muscles clenching around him as he takes sharp breaths. Arousal pulses as I wiggle my hips, his cock filling me.

"Good girl," he rasps.

I smile, turned on by how his chest expands with each breath. Spurred on by his expression of ecstasy, I continue the slow torture of moving up and down his dick. My legs tremble as I do so, not used to it, but determined to keep going. My own arousal and pleasure building as he strokes against my inner walls.

Going all the way back down again, we both moan as I bury my face against his chest. Leo flexes his hands on my hips, and I nod against his neck. He takes the cue, lifting my waist and brings me back down. I choke out a moan, circling my hips instinctively to feel more of him. I melt against his touch, holding onto him tightly. We continue the slow torturing movement. I grow used to him inside me, finding more pleasure with each thrust. After a while he checks in, and I reply with a breathy "green". He lays me down on my back, remaining within me as he encages me with his body. He pauses, watching my reaction from the position change.

There's warmth this time. His body around me. The soft bed. And I lift my hips, encouraging him to slowly thrust his cock inside me. Leo holds me close as he continues to move, and I feel him enter me deeper. A groan escapes, clutching at his back as he responds in kind. The base of my spine tingles, traveling up in a blissful sensation. I become aware of every movement and touch. Holding on, I see a sheen of sweat on his forehead and the concentration on his face.

More. I want more.

I gulp, and breathe out, "Harder."

He flashes a look, eyes hardening before he lets out a low growl. He slides a hand down my thigh as he moves to his knees. Holding my leg up, he drives himself deeper. His hands stroke over my skin, tilting my hips as he pushes into me. I let out a loud gasp, my legs coming up on their own to wrap around his waist, and I tug him closer. He grunts as he thrusts into me, and I moan. My eyes close as I clutch the sheets beside me.

"Look at me," he demands with a gentle tone. I do without hesitation, although my chest shakes at the intimacy of meeting his gaze. Instantly, I want to shy away, but his gaze holds me. His eyes are hooded with want. He thrusts his hips forward, causing my body to shiver as the pleasure builds and continues. "Good girl."

Those words create sparks which flicker at the base of my spine, striking to my core as he thrusts harder and deeper. I let out a choked gasp, keeping my gaze on him and watching as his tattoos move with his muscles. All of a sudden, I feel it. The building of an orgasm comes, making my muscles go tight as my legs grip around his waist. My eyes widen at the reaction, surprised by it. Holy shit.

"Leo," I choke out in a desperate moan.

"Stay with me...stay with me," he breathes out between each thrust. He moves a hand over my thigh, holding tight as he drives forward. I feel the base of my spine explode into a fiery spasm. My entire lower body flexes and releases as the orgasm falls over me. I grip his arms, throwing my head back as I let out a long, silent moan as the pleasure races over my body with bliss, muscles tightening.

I feel Leo come next as his muscles flex, letting out a long groan as he thrusts his cock one last time. We breathe heavy as I relax further into the bed, staring up at the panting man above me. His jaw slackens as he catches his breath, then carefully, he eases down, bringing me into his arms as a smile grows on my face.

Joy and pleasure, mixed with accomplishment, crash inside me. A few tears escape my eyes as I bury my flushed face against his neck, and sigh, "Green."

Chapter 24

Limited Secrets

Leo brews tea as I sit on the couch, wearing a comfy robe, somewhat dazed from the storm of emotions and orgasm. I'm not sure which I'm more surprised by. I'd expected sex to be good with him and maybe enjoy it, but *that* good? I can't even remember the last time I had an orgasm. An odd sickening thought with a bit of guilt comes up along that realization, making me pull my legs up. Okay, already trying not to feel overwhelmed from the orgasm, torrent of emotions and having sex again, let's not add shame.

Leo suggested moving to the living room to talk after sitting in silence for almost twenty minutes in bed. I'm definitely overthinking about what he wants to talk about. I watch not-so patiently as he brings over tea and scotch, sitting beside me and placing the ceramic mug in my hands. He leans back as I move to settle closer to him as he sips his scotch, while his other hand massages the back of my head. If he keeps doing that, I'm gonna melt into nothing.

"How are you feeling?"

"Do I answer with colors?" I peek up at him. Amusement flits over his face before kissing my temple. "Gonna presume we're past the color wheel stage."

"We'll still use it in the future, but for now we should discuss any hard limits you may know of. I understand what happened earlier, you may not have known—"

"Wait, wait." I sit up as Leo watches me with a careful gaze. "Hard limits?"

"Things you're not willing to do. Or soft limits, things you may be open to, but unsure about. I don't always have these discussions for sex, unless I know I'm doing harder scenes, but given your background I thought best to at least implement the stoplight method."

Wait… scenes? Limits? Wait, he said honorific earlier, too.

Gears turn in my head as I stare at him. Any anxiety I had is now gone, replaced by curiosity. Pieces fall together. Clues becoming clear as day. Offhand things he's said or done.

Oh.

As words jumble in my head, I blurt out, "Are you a Dom?"

His expression remains impassive. "Would that upset you if I was?"

That's a weird question.

I cradle the mug against my chest, finding it my turn to pinch my brows together. "Not at all. I don't know much about BDSM apart from friends who were into it in college. What I do know, it makes sense for you." Now his brows furrow. "Your need to control things. Ordering dinner, protection detail, safety precautions, private life…"

"That's not from being a Dom, that's…business and work." He clears his throat, sipping some of his scotch. "Or family trauma is it were."

"Doesn't being a Dom tie into that?"

"Not always."

A little confused, I ask, "Are you still one? Wait, I'm prying and sound a bit…um, if that's something you want, I may need more time—"

"Autumn." He places his drink down, putting his hand on my leg. "Most of my time as an active Dom was in California, while I was still in the other MC, who introduced me to the lifestyle. Although I've played while in New York, I've not done much in four years, due to work and not feeling comfortable with anyone."

"Is this what you were waiting to tell me? I don't want to force you to talk about it or share if you're not ready." My stomach twists, remembering my own skeletons and one of them that taps louder at the back of my head.

"No, this isn't that," he reassures me. "I was more open about being involved in BDSM out west, but here I've kept quiet due to… work and personal reasons. Not something I want my PR to deal with. But you, I'm not worried about knowing. If you want to learn more about it, then we'll talk. You forced nothing and I most certainly won't force you into it. That certain lifestyle is not a requirement for us, especially if it scares you."

I think about what I know of BDSM and it's not much.

"I'm not scared of it or upset if it's something you've done or do." I put my mug down on the coffee table, turning to face him and to take his hand. "You took more care with me than *anyone* in my life. Tonight, this week, and many other times. If BDSM is why or part of why that is, then I'm more than open to it. And I do know it's not a bad hobby or lifestyle, and won't hate you for it, but uh, why did you stop? If you found people in California, why not here?"

Leo releases a breath, kissing my hand. "When I started it was to help me through some stuff. To let go a part of myself, but soon I realized I didn't want that anywhere near the bedroom. That part of my life. The trust wasn't there."

"What do you mean?"

"I want to remind you, that my promises still stand. That I'll never—"

"Leo." I kiss his hand next, holding it tight. "I trust you. After tonight, I trust you more than anyone."

He nods, clearing his throat and takes another drink. I wait quietly, glad he's willing to talk after barely opening up at all this week. After a minute, he explains, "Most of who I rode with called it my 'controlled anger management,' and it worked for a short time. Looking back, it wasn't the best idea, but I was young. I wanted to inflict pain. Most call it being a sadist, but it was…different for me. The guilt became too much, what I was being expected and asked to do. There was no pleasure in it even with every submissive who wanted it."

"Why?"

"My family, well father, was specific in how he handled business and it bled into family life. Not just for me, but my brothers, too. I hoped BDSM would help with those challenges, but it worsened other fears. Although, deep inside I wanted to hurt people, I didn't *enjoy* inflicting pain on those I wanted to bring pleasure to. It's a fine line because those entering scenes like that, find their pleasure through pain. They consented. Wanted it. Except, I couldn't separate it as a Dom. It felt wrong to be the Top or Dominant others wanted from me."

"So…they expected pain from you?"

"Most, yes," he whispers, thumb stroking my hand. "My want for control is easily recognizable, and many think it fully transpires into the bedroom." He clears his throat, eyes flicking down to where he strokes my hand. "Play partners always came to me expecting a hard Dom. A harsh Master, as it were. Someone who would punish or humiliate them. In reality, that wasn't the kind of Dom I wanted to be."

"What did you want to be?"

"I consider myself a soft or pleasure Dom."

Given my lack of knowledge with the subject, my mind tries to make it make sense. I knew the basics like safe words, certain kinks, fetishes, and that people liked pain. I never quite saw the appeal of it. Being in abusive relationships, tend to make you steer clear of more utensils that could hurt you. But the way he talks about it, sparks intrigue. I've never heard of a soft Dom before.

"So, if I asked to be spanked? You'd say no?" I ask.

"It's not a hard limit, I'll say. I prefer not to, unless it's something you really wanted, then we'd work towards it."

"What about other things? I don't have a list, but I feel like I could make one." Books can help with that, right? Movies?

Leo smirks. Worry vanishing. "Then we discuss it. I can walk you through all of it, whether it's to be spanked or not."

"Given I had a panic attack about a wall, doubt you have to worry about that..." my voice trails away, frowning down at our hands.

Insecurity and embarrassment start to come back, realizing how much more experience he has. He's had years being in BDSM, then there's me—panicking about walls and him going down on me. My stomach clenches, knowing I should tell him the rest, but guilt and fear start to press down. I want to crawl inside myself suddenly.

I think to pull away, but Leo swiftly pulls me into his lap. Blinking at him in shock, he caresses his hand down my back, holding me close. Firmly, but gently, he eases my chin up to look at him.

"There's nothing to be ashamed of," he whispers. "Limits are limits. Whether you know them or not. You have a past that can create them, which can include items most consider ordinary. A hard limit is a hard limit. We steer clear of it."

"But you...I mean, won't you expect me... uh, want to..." my chest aches, squeezing with worry as I try to get the words out, "... give you, fuck..." oh, just say it! "...head?"

Leo briefly clears his throat, the line above his brow is deep with concern. "Autumn, I've already assumed *that* act is also a hard limit. It's fine."

My mind flashes to old conversations, being yelled at, chastised, and coerced. "Are, uh, are you sure?"

"Yes. I won't force you to do anything." The pressure doesn't let up with the shame, and suddenly, I'm filled with questions. Tears form in my eyes as I shake, pressing my head against his chest in attempt to make it stop. "You're safe, Autumn. I promise you; you'll always be safe with me."

More tears come mixed with relief and gnawing doubt. I'm unsure which is making me cry. "I-I don't know why...I'm sorry...I keep *crying* with you..."

"Never apologize for crying. You can always cry on my shoulder."

"Careful what you wish for," I say with a rough voice. He kisses the side of my head. We stay there in the quiet as the tears dry. Slowly, I can think without fully panicking. "I tried after the...you know what. But couldn't. Tried dating like I told you. But I was pressured, yelled at, or told to leave while being called names. I gave up after that, and didn't want to say red tonight because…because…"

"You thought I'd do the same."

"It was nothing you did. Just a consistent pattern before."

He inhales deeply, easing me back from his shoulder as he wipes away my tears. "Autumn, I care about you. More than anyone else in my life," he murmurs, meeting my gaze. "So, I think I can live without my dick being sucked for the rest of my days. I'll survive."

My heart skips a beat, holding my breath. Did he just…what?

"Leo, do you think this, you and I…?"

"I'm not saying this because we just had sex." He gives a half smile, while I half-heartedly smile back. "But I am certain I'm falling in love with you."

Breath leaves me all together, feeling like my gut was punched. Everything becomes fuzzy, staring into those hazel eyes which capture me. I remember every moment my heart lightens around him, how he makes me melt in his arms. How much I adore his smile, becoming more frequent of late, and the safety of his arms around me. The lines above his brow as they pinch together in thought.

"I think I am, too," I whisper.

His expression is affectionate, bringing his forehead to mine. "I promise you, my dear Watson, you'll always…*always* be safe with me."

For the first time, without a second thought, I believe him fully.

I kiss him, bringing my arms around his neck. I'm brief with it, enticed by learning more and curious as I ask, "Okay, tell me more about being a Dom."

Sunlight streams into the bedroom as I wake. Leo's side of the bed is empty.

Abruptly, I sit up. Panic grips me, heart racing that everything was a dream. It wasn't real and I'd been—

I see a piece of paper on the bedside table with my name on it, and I reach for it.

Dear Watson, hopefully you slept well. I didn't want to wake you, but I'll be back soon. An urgent meeting came up I couldn't avoid. Have breakfast, relax.

PS check the drawer next to you.

I open the drawer, smiling as I look upon a row of new fuzzy socks. The panic subsides, and I pull on a pair. They're beyond soft, and I grin as I get out of bed, and walk out of the bedroom. There's a noise from the kitchen, someone there who isn't Leo.

Choking out a scream, I scramble for the bedroom, until they turn around. Clutching my chest, I gasp, "Isaac! You scared me!"

He holds his hands up, one with a spatula in it. "I'm sorry, Miss Autumn. I didn't mean to startle you. I presumed you were warned I was here."

"Nope. I think Leo just wants to check if my heart is working." I tap my chest. "Good news, it is." I head towards the kitchen as he puts a mug on the counter, while I eye him. "That will only help you a little." I take the coffee, sipping it and it's like life elixir. "Okay, maybe more than a little. How did you know how I liked my coffee?"

"He told me."

"Course he did." I drink more, waking up as Isaac cooks breakfast which consists of eggs and toast. He looks comfortable being in the kitchen, yet I've never seen anyone in here besides Leo and me.

Screw it, I'll take the plunge before the coffee hits. "Have you done this before for his...sleepovers?"

Isaac pauses, glancing over his shoulder. "No."

I gesture around the penthouse. "So, whenever he's had someone over..."

"Please understand, Miss Autumn," he stops me, and I shut my mouth. "I won't go into his exploits. It's not my position to know or ask. What I do know, is that you're the first who's had breakfast here ever or any form of meal. And this is the first I've been allowed in here while you are. The other *individuals*—"

"Just say women, Isaac."

He clears his throat. "I apologize for being abrupt."

"Don't, I kinda walked into it."

"The women who've been here are told to leave before 6AM or are long gone before midnight. He's also never danced or dined them at his own hotel, let alone taking them to his estate in the countryside." He turns away and mumbles, "Or survived a car ride with Jameson."

Oh. Wasn't expecting that.

Isaac finishes breakfast, putting a plate before me. I reach for his hand, and he freezes at the touch. "I'm sorry. I didn't mean to come off as that, well, bitch of 'am I special.' This is all just very new for me, and this morning is…weird, after last night…" that's putting it lightly, "…I don't want to be imposing either. But thank you for breakfast."

His blue eyes ease, nodding his head, which prompts me to let go to eat as he cleans up the kitchen. I eat slowly, liking it, but finding I miss Leo's cooking. I may be a bit prejudiced on favorites though.

My mind fades to last night, our conversations went late with him talking about BDSM and our limits. The more we spoke, the more I became comfortable with trying again without so much issue. I felt less broken and used and ashamed of my past, like a whole new world had opened up. I'd been terrified to talk about sex and enjoying it again, but with Leo it felt right and easy. I became less fearful, which only opened the prospect more of falling in love with him.

After all that's happened in the past, was that possible for me? To have someone who listens and helps me through the hard moments? To love again? It felt possible last night.

I shake myself, coming back to the present as Isaac cleans out the frying pans.

"So, given talking seems allowed now, how did you meet Leo?" Isaac stops. "Or not."

He snorts, expression changing to deep thought as he finishes cleaning. He leans onto the counter with his own coffee in hand. "You *honestly* want to know that?"

"No, I'm secretly hoping you'll tell me where M is." We both smirk, and I shrug. "Sorry, but the Bond jokes come easy for you." He waves it off. "But yes, I do. You respect him. And I think he respects and thinks highly of you, too. Stern as he is."

"Could just be a job."

"Nah-huh, partner, don't believe that." I shake my head. "I've worked for people I've hated, doing the bare minimum because of it, while others I've gone over the top *because* I respected them. Maybe I don't do hotels or real estate, but I doubt it's much different. If you all were part of a club in California, knowing each other for about a decade, then there's *definitely* a story."

He grins, looking caught red-handed. "Got me there, but it's not that interesting."

"Try me." I sip with raised brows.

"To begin, I was born in the U.K, shocking I know." I feign a gasp, and he chuckles. "I grew up in London, going into the military for a short enlistment after university. After, I moved to California, after visiting for a few missions I was on. There, I met other veterans who were bikers, a pastime I've had since my teen years and introduced to a club, but decided it wasn't the place for me. They weren't honest in what they stood for nor an official MC either, so they got away with some things."

"Official?"

"Certain clubs go through a board, being recognized. I won't get into the politics, but those who aren't recognized are usually what media portrays mostly. The outlaw ones. In the US that is."

"Like *Sons of Anarchy*?" He nods. "Hmm, figured it was based on some truth."

"Very little."

"So, that's what they were like?"

"Almost. They had a code I wasn't comfortable with. After I left, one day I was out riding and stopped at a small bar off the coastal highway. A club came riding in, and it was Leo with his Crew, which also isn't fully recognized."

"Are those MCs illegal then?"

"No, just not part of the American Motorcycle Association or AMA. They go by their own rules and subculture, just like other biker gangs or MCs out there." I think I found a new subject to start researching. "He and I talked, offering me a position for security given the vast growth of his hotel franchise and other companies. He trusted bikers. Many of us in that original group are close, and he offered jobs to all of us. Financial security as it were."

I wonder if Leo protecting his private life so strongly wasn't just for him, then, but also for those in his MC. Definitely was correct on them being his friends, even if they did work for him, too.

"He did this with the others?"

"Basically. We're his…inner circle, as it were. The Crew. We all came from different backgrounds, and he created a safe haven. A sense of place and purpose. So, when he moved here, we all followed him."

"Why?"

"He values people and loyalty, which he'd worked over a decade for," Jameson's voice interrupts.

He stands in the front hallway in dark jeans, a button-up, and jacket slung over his shoulder. Isaac's wearing something similar. Have any of them heard of band t-shirts?

He sets a bag down, handing over a folder to Isaac, who takes it and glances over the contents. Without a word, he walks around the counter and heads toward the office near the patio.

"Excuse me, Miss Autumn." Yeah, something tells me I'm not getting away with just Autumn.

The door closes, and Jameson speaks as he grabs himself a mug of coffee. "Isaac spilling every secret about Leo?"

"No, and I wouldn't ask Isaac anyways."

"You say that now."

"No, I mean it, including not giving a shit how much money he has or getting a free vacation place," I interrupt, and he stares at me. "We haven't been around each other much, so I get that whole 'don't trust you' vibes, but I'm not here to hurt Leo in any way." His gaze locks with mine. "And I'm guessing *this* was the talk you wanted last night until I kinda told you off. Given the reactions, you care about him. Great. So, do I. But I'm not here to screw him over."

His face hardens. May have overstepped. Again. I'm getting punchier lately. I blame work.

Jameson grips his mug, stepping toward the counter across from me. Jaw tightening, his eyes narrow and a slow smile appears. "I was right. He finally found someone he deserves. You're more straight forward than him."

My eyes widen. Okay, not where I thought *that* was going.

"He said you have blunt moments, which balance out your, what I believe he called 'starry-eyed' moments?" He continues.

I bring up my leg to show off my feet. "I like fuzzy socks."

"I know. He wasn't the only one entertained that night," he smirks, and I blush a little, slightly embarrassed. "Better dancing I've seen in those rooms in a while."

"Drunk grooms don't do it for you?"

"Or business conferences with members who have twerking competitions, which are just fucking sad."

I listen, trying to locate the accent in his voice. Isaac's is clearly British, Rudolf is German I found out, but Jameson's has a lilt of Spanish dialect I've heard before. The other little newness is him swearing in front of me. None of Leo's staff have, always careful since I first started seeing him. Probably precaution to not upset my 'delicate sensibilities.'

I take my empty dishes to the sink. Jameson goes to stop me, but I wave him off as I do and clean them. I appreciate being taken care of, but I can reciprocate with other means. Even if it's dishes. Since making cereal is a freaking crime here.

Figuring we're done talking, I walk around him as I head for the bedroom with my coffee. Isaac I'm fine hanging with, Jameson I'm not sure of. Except, his voice stops me. "If Leo trusts you, then I will, too."

I stop and turn back. "Why?"

"He doesn't trust easily." He walks around the counter, leaning against it. "He'll take chances on people but won't trust them right away. Gives them the benefit of the doubt before passing judgement. They have to earn his trust."

"Like with Isaac, giving him a chance with the job and the biker club?"

"One way to call it I guess."

"The club?" He nods. "You're a part of it, too? Is that how you met Leo?"

"No, I helped him create it." I go still as he runs his hand through his dark hair, glancing at the office Isaac disappeared into. He nods toward the couch. I walk over, sitting with my legs under me while he sits on the far other side.

"Leo and I met in New Mexico."

"That's where he first moved to."

"First stop for both of us," he explains. "We were seventeen, had nothing to our names. Started working in this big hotel as busboys and cleaning, but back then my name wasn't Jameson." My chest pinches a moment as my brows raise. "It was Joaquin. I moved to America when I was fourteen with my family. Made it to Florida, kept going West and they stopped in Arizona while I continued. Changed my name soon after."

"Why?"

"My family came from Cuba for a better future and all, but things happen. And Jameson is more palatable to certain societies." His eyes meet mine, and I know he doesn't need to say more. I nod my head.

"That must've been hard."

"Leo and I became good friends. We wanted to make something for ourselves. So, we watched how the hotel ran, worked our way into management positions, made connections, and with Leo's background in business from his family we took over the hotel."

"Wait, what? How?" Trix and Leanne *never* mentioned this when they looked him up.

"Got lucky, honestly. Weren't even twenty yet, but the man who owned it was embezzling, so we made a deal. We got the hotel; he moves."

"How'd you even know he was?"

"Worked service, got the dirt on everyone." Okay, yeah, he's got me there. "We were behind the scenes, knew what could be found. Used it to our advantage to help our fellow coworkers, since we all were getting the short end of the stick."

"That's how the hotel 'empire' started?"

"Once the first one was set, we sold it." My jaw drops, and he smirks. "We wanted out of New Mexico, into a state with more potential and it was California. We used what we had to buy a small motel, built it up, and did the same with others. Each becoming their own small luxury hotel. They were reputable. We managed from the ground up, keeping close contact with anyone from cleaning to management. Then, we'd sell the hotel to the largest buyer."

"You were flipping hotels instead of houses," I gasp.

"Basically. Keeping good relationships with employees helped us retain good staff, which resolved into good reviews and PR. Next thing we knew we owned some of the most prominent luxury hotels outside of San Diego and Sacramento. I came in charge of management of the hotels, while Leo did the finance, investments, and relations with sponsors. Leo was smart. We created our own franchise, invested in real estate and air rights, controlling what we wanted after we stopped flipping."

"Real estate and air rights?"

"Fully owning in every way, not have someone dictate what we could or do it for us."

"Wait." I place my mug down, trying to make sense of all this. While I was trying to survive college, Leo was building the foundations of multi-million-dollar businesses. "You said us. Is all this yours, too? I thought Leo was the CEO."

"He is."

I grumble, rubbing my fingers into my temple. I need more coffee.

"I wanted financial freedom, but without the fanfare that came with it," Jameson explains. "I hated PR when we began, still fucking do. A few of the companies I co-own with him, but the hotels and other businesses are his. He just ensures I get my cut. But…Leo is the boss." His gaze meets mine. "In every way."

"You're not worried he'll screw you over?"

"No." He sips his coffee, looking out to the patio. "We're more than business partners. We're brothers. We started a business franchise and MC together, lived together, and fought together. It was his idea to branch into real estate and imports, buying within the U.S. to support everything locally. He could've built it alone easily, but he refused to leave me behind and I'm grateful. It was his since the beginning, I just ensure it stays his and protect it. Of course, when he moved here, I followed suit. No fucking way was I staying in California. It'll still be there, especially when you own private jets."

I snort at his little joke. How long until he was used to that kind of thinking? Over a decade I'd guess.

"Why tell me any of this?" I cock my head at him.

He brings his mug up, taking a sip before answering, "You didn't inquire about his secrets."

"Not to scare me off?" His brown gaze meets mine, and I can tell I'm not completely far off. I smirk. "Really are brothers."

Isaac walks into the living room, who makes quick eye contact with Jameson. There's a shared nod as he leans against the fireplace. "Jameson's behaving himself?"

I look between them. "Wait, that means Isaac works for Leo *and* you."

Isaac flashes a glance at Jameson, who ignores the question. Isaac answers, "Mainly just Leo. Although, none of us see him…fully like that."

The way they exchange glances, there's something they're not telling me. Probably won't. It's over a decade of relationships that I didn't want to pry into it. There's just one little thing scratching at the back of my mind. Anxiety pinching at me.

"One more thought. If everything was good out in California, business and the MC, why move here? *Back* to New York for Leo, that is?"

Isaac moves toward the kitchen, hiding his expression.

Jameson is the one who answers, "His family business was going under. He came back to help, and through twists of fate he became the sole proprietor of it."

"Because of his family, he came back?" Jameson nods slowly. I grab my mug, frowning. I couldn't imagine being forced back home because of toxic family, especially after spending so much time finding freedom. A chill runs down my spine.

I whisper, "Must have been hard coming back."

"It was at first."

"Visiting our past or encountering it sometimes, well, sucks. But, guess I did get to meet him because of it." Because of a lot of things, I've been able to.

"Leo never mentioned how you met," Isaac says, returning. "Would he be hiding anything from us?"

"If Juanita was there, perhaps," Jameson comments in a low voice.

"Well, she's kind of the reason why," I say with a shrug and they both give curious faces. "Her coffee spilled all over me. And his."

"And now you're…dating?" Jameson asks with confusion.

"Not how you start yours?"

"Not really."

"Well, I don't recommend, but I did have an apron on at the time. It was just a not-to-hot latte and Americano. I've gotten worse." Isaac barely grimaces. "But I jumped in front of him so *he* wouldn't get coffee burns."

"Wait, you *let* yourself get spilled on?" Jameson asks. Both their expressions are funny.

I start laughing. "In the past those wearing Armani or whatever hate getting coffee on them. Besides the foam was delicious and his face was hilarious. Completely stunned."

"Don't blame him," Isaac comments.

"It looked like I'd taken a bullet for him," I giggle harder, remembering his face. After a moment, I realize I'm the only one laughing and there's serious looks on their faces. "I'm kidding! Geez, ya'll don't like things spilled on you, huh? Not that bad."

Their expressions swiftly change, and Jameson stands. "Once had frying oil spilled on me, that hurt like a bitch."

"Fine you win this time." I point at him. "Don't think I'll go easy next time."

"Next time?" Isaac asks warily.

"Trust me, there's dishwater and kids puke in my future still because they thought it'd be fun to guzzle espresso for fun. I want to sue every parent who's ever let their child drink coffee before the age of ten."

"Careful how you talk about my culture," Jameson says with a smug expression.

I chuckle at him about to continue teasing when the front door opens. Leo stalks in with a sour expression, yanking his tie and jacket off. All his attention is on Jameson who meets him before reaching the kitchen.

"I won't fucking deal with their insolence anymore. Take care of Robinson and Dwyer before I do," Leo growls.

"Not budging?" Jameson asks.

"You've not fucking idea. I want a meeting later this week. Have it here, not there. *My* damn office." Leo's voice is dark, pushing a phone to Jameson who takes it and pulls out his phone.

Isaac goes to pass Leo. "Port check-ins?"

"Both teams. I want checks on every roster before this blows up," Leo orders as Isaac gives a gesture, walking out of the penthouse.

I watch curiously as he orders them about. Whatever meeting Leo was in, wasn't fun. He continues low whispers with Jameson, snatching a mug from the cabinet.

Jameson suddenly says loud enough for me to hear, "She's a keeper."

Leo freezes. He slowly drifts his gaze to me on the couch. I bring a hand up, wiggling my fingers at him in a wave. Realization flashes over his face, and I bite my bottom lip to keep from giggling at him. He really was so engrossed with his meeting he might've forgot I was here altogether. Or didn't think I stayed.

He scowls, brows furrowing as he glares at Jameson. "What did you tell her?"

"Or what she figured out?"

Leo's eyes widen, going slightly pale. "What?"

The panic on Leo's face makes me worried, and whatever Jameson is teasing Leo about, I don't like it.

"I already knew he was smart, you just confirmed those thoughts," I interrupt, getting up and walking over.

Leo's mug clanks on the counter. His brows pinch together, lines forming above them, and I do my best not to look like I'm laughing at him as he stares at me. I hide my smile behind my mug, seeing him relax more. Whatever morning he had, I don't want to make it worse.

"What did he tell you?" Leo asks.

"Told me how you met. How you started your *empire*."

"Not technically an empire."

"Other people do. I could say kingdom instead, but I don't want to give you a big head before I see the castle with the moat," I tease lightly.

Leo relaxes fully, smiling faintly. Jameson flashes him a curious look, cocking his head. He then hums, walking out without a word. Leo watches him leave, then turns back to me once the door closes. "Come here."

I grin, putting my mug down and go into his arms. He embraces me, holding me close. Hands moving down, he lifts me up onto the counter, standing between my legs as he kisses my neck and I begin giggling at the feathery touches.

"Sleep well?" He asks.

"Yup, and thanks for the socks." I hold a foot up, and he chuckles, kissing my cheek.

He stands fully, exhaling a long breath as I rub my hands over his arms. "Where to for lunch?"

"I just had breakfast," I snort.

"Thinking ahead."

I narrow my eyes. "This isn't when I say Italian food and then you fly us to Italy…right?"

A sly smile forms on his face. "Not today."

"*Not today.*" My eyes roll, and he chuckles before kissing me, causing me to melt against him once again.

Chapter 25

Rose-Colored Glasses

We went to a bodega.

After a laid-back lunch, we spent some of the afternoon at the bookstore. He was called away a few hours later, having meetings to attend to. Now it was hours later, and I've been laying on my bed for over an hour talking to him on the phone. Whatever last meeting he had wore him out, and it sounded like something had gone wrong. He sounded exhausted.

"Hey Leo?"

"Yes, dear Watson?"

"Do you ever get tired of being a CEO…being in charge, I guess? Like it just gets to being too much?"

He inhales sharply, quiet a moment before answering, "I don't think I've ever been asked that."

"Pretty good at asking first-time questions."

"Yes, you are," he muses. "I've made my decisions and am here now. I've told you before it's not something I could easily walk away from. Can't leave all those people behind."

"But what about you?"

"Me?"

"Yeah. Those people are important, but like I said, none of its you.

And what you want is important, too, not just the CEO part. What about what you want or *is* that all you want?"

"I mostly have what I want. The rest that's missing…I'm working on keeping it." His voice becomes low. "And you? What do you want?"

I stare at the ceiling, my chest feeling heavy. Suddenly, I want him more than anything here with me, lying next to me where the empty space is. My hand brushes over my blankets, beginning to hate the loneliness. "Working on it, too."

"I guess we can work together to obtain those things," he murmurs.

I'm not sure why I'm trembling at the sound of his voice, closing my eyes, and listening to his breathing on the other end. I struggle inside to ask him over. Have him stay here tonight, hating the distance between us. I can't get the words out, unable to ask.

I swallow hard, sitting up and rubbing my head. "You've had a long day, go to sleep, Leo."

"I'll talk to you tomorrow, dear Watson."

We hang up, and my phone falls to my side as I lay back down. I feel like I've fallen completely for him already. The more I learn about him, the more I want to hold tighter. Not let go.

Turning to my side, butterflies rise in my stomach as my mind wanders to the night before. His hands stroking my skin, his lips against my neck, and touching me with such reverence. His soothing voice like a melody in a storm. I curl up, swallowing hard as I try to sleep.

Late in the night, I wake up in a cold sweat with a gasping scream. My shirt is soaked and I shiver from the sudden chill. Throat hurting, I rub my head as the leftover fear wrecks through me. I try to regulate my breathing, going into routine. Quickly changing, I head to the kitchen and realize it's only 5am. I make coffee, then go through my stacks of movies and rearrange a few, putting some on the bottom before I find a Nick Cage film to pop in. Once the coffee finishes, I grab my mug and plop down on my couch to bundle myself under the blankets. *Guarding Tess* begins to play, and I settle in hoping that the nightmare isn't a bad omen for how my week is going to start.

———

I t was definitely an omen.

I stare at Yuki in shock. Her lips are pursed, arms crossed over her chest with an uncomfortableness that I've rarely seen before. I know she doesn't want to do this; I've known her for years to know. Except it doesn't smother the anger that's boiling in my gut.

"My last day here I worked almost a 12-hour shift, ten of those hours by *myself*," I say through gritted teeth.

"You didn't sell any pastries, lost that revenue and dropped coffee grounds."

"It was *one* bag." That was tampered with!

"I'm sorry, Autumn." Her voice is tight, staring at me with guilt. "I *have* to listen to the owner, there's nothing I can do. Daniella put in a report of misconduct concerning you."

"Daniella? The other day is the first time I've worked with her in *months*."

Yuki clears her throat, adjusting her stance awkwardly. "Baily filed a report, too, about misconduct and incompetence, including instances of dropping coffee all over you."

You gotta be kidding me.

"You're seriously firing me? Not even a warning?"

"It's enough for the owner to settle anything before it gets worse in their eyes."

I scoff, folding my arms. "Meaning before Bailey's *father* settles anything?" Yuki averts her gaze and I want to scream. "You're gonna placate her whims, after everything I've done for the shop?"

After everything, you're taking away my—

My stomach drops, hating this feeling of unworthiness and deceit. It didn't matter. What I've done here for almost three years, what I did *two days ago* to keep the cafe open didn't matter. This can't be happening. My insides twist, feeling history repeat itself. I can't be losing my job because of a jealous girl who fucked another employee in the back.

"I can't lose my job, Autumn. I—"

"But *I* can," I state coldly. Her shoulders fall, and I wish I could care, except I'm too angry. "Bailey can live without a job, while I can barely afford…you're really firing me? With no customer complaints, no issues in almost three years? Or at least change shifts so I don't work with her?"

Yuki swallows hard, glancing toward her closed door and speaks in a hushed tone. "I *tried*, Autumn. Bailey's father is a control freak, especially with her, otherwise I'd have fired her months ago. He holds stock in the shop." I stare at her, raging inside that the little bitch is getting what she wants. "I don't have references of jobs in the past for you, unless you ask to have the women's center—"

"No," I rasp, pushing my hair back. I can't involve them.

Yuki looks at me with pity, and I want to crumble under it as the air feels thin. Shit, what am I going to tell Nan? She'll be understanding, but I don't know when I'll be able to help moneywise. Sure, I can find another job, but due to my past, my options for jobs were limited.

"I'm sorry, Autumn," she says again.

I take deep breaths, trying to keep from screaming. "When do I—"

Yuki pulls out an envelope with my name on it. Yup, final paycheck. I take it, stuffing it into my back pocket as I look away from the pity in her eyes. It reminds me too much of other past mistakes.

"Gather your stuff, and I'll…see you around. For what it's worth, you were one of the best employees I had." Her voice is hoarse as I turn for the door. "If you need a reference—"

"Yeah," I mutter, walking out. I glance at the front where Bailey and Mabel are. Mabel makes eye contact with me, confusion on her face until I hold up the envelope and shake my head. Her eyes widen, flicking to Bailey and then to me.

She mouths, "What the fuck."

I shrug in defeat.

I go to the backroom, stuffing whatever I have into my bag and walk out the backdoor. There's not enough strength in me to say goodbye to Mabel. I'll text her later.

I stand next to the trash and stare up at the sky. A few short breaths, and I walk toward the other street and see Isaac in the coffee shop across the way, getting up to leave quickly. I walk down the block without him, grinding my teeth as the boiling anger in my gut rises. I stop not far from *Blue Java* and take a few steadying breaths, repeating a couple stanzas from *The Raven*.

"Miss Autumn. Miss Autumn." Isaac comes up behind me. "What's wrong?"

I'm slammed with more memories. Used. Expendable. Forgotten. Nothing.

Like fuck she's gonna get the last laugh, not after everything I've been through.

"You want coffee?" I ask roughly.

His brows scrunch. "Miss Autumn, what are you—?"

"Do *you* want coffee?"

He says tentatively, "Sure."

"Okay, please hold this for me. And you can stay closer than usual." I give my bag to him, walking right back to *Blue Java Café*.

I enter with Isaac close behind, his body tensing as I go to the counter like any customer. Mabel comes over with a disgruntled face, glaring at Bailey briefly, who merrily makes drinks. I place money on the counter, and order, "Two mocha lattes with caramel syrup. Large, please."

"Autumn…"

"It's okay, Mabel," I whisper, giving a tight smile. "Just sorry you'll be stuck with her."

She takes the money. "Gonna miss you."

"Same. I'll see you around."

"Finally get some shots together?"

"Sure." When she hands back the change, I grip her hand and she squeezes back. Heading down to the pick-up station, I make eye contact with Isaac for a moment, who watches in confusion. My gaze flicks to the back, seeing Yuki handling everything and then to Bailey as she finishes up the drinks.

She starts to bring them forward, then stops with a malicious grin. She puts the drinks down. "Last drink for the riff-raff?"

I smile brightly, and her eyes widen.

Moving to grab the drinks, I pretend to trip over my shoes and knock the drinks over. One splashes directly over Bailey's front, while the other spills across the counter and onto her pants and shoes, drenching her. She lets out a screech as coffee, foam, and caramel syrup drips down to the floor.

I feign shock, gasping with my hand over my mouth. "I'm *so* sorry. I *must've* slipped."

People murmur in the shop as Mabel holds back her laughter, covering her face. Yuki comes out, gaping at the scene.

"You *bitch*!" Bailey screams, fisting her hands like she's gonna swing at me. Isaac comes up behind me, falling into his role perfectly.

"Ma'am, is that any way to talk to a customer? She said she's sorry," he says politely.

Bailey sneers at him, making my anger worsen. I've grown used to my shadow of late, and the only venom she can spew is at me.

I fake a smile. "These things happen, especially with someone as *clumsy* as me. You know that, right? Don't worry about making any more, and here's a *tip* for your troubles." I take the first fifty-dollar bill Leo gave me, still tucked away in my wallet. A knowing look on my face, Bailey's goes ablaze.

The fifty is slipped through the wet counter, soaking up the latte.

Bailey glares at me, and I whisper for only her to hear, "He would've never wasted his time on you."

I catch a glimpse of Yuki, who still watches in shock. Mabel turns away, trying to control her snickering as others in the shop stare. I leave with Isaac close behind as Bailey complains loudly as the door shuts behind us.

My steps are heavy, stalking down the street. I mutter, "I still owe you a coffee."

"What happened?" He asks trailing me.

"I was fucking fired for stupid reasons after bailing out that fucking shop, and because in that damn girl's head, I *stole* Leo from her."

"What?"

"Damn jealous, privileged little weasel." I spin to face Isaac, who stops abruptly with surprise. "Do women always act like that with him? Like they own him or he's only worth his money or sex?" Isaac stumbles back at the verbiage, but I don't care, seething with fury. "How often is he used like a damn mine for them to dig their fucking claws into? He started from nothing. Left home with nothing and *that's* what he gets? He's a person! A fucking good, kind, and patient person! And all they care about is, 'how do I get his dick inside me'?"

"Have you ever sworn this much?" I glower at him. I head across the street to a small park to hopefully cool off. It doesn't look good on that front. "It's something he's used to."

"That doesn't matter, and actually don't answer those questions, because I may go back to claw her damn eyes out next. So, fucking *spiteful* and vindictive…I was fired because he didn't want to fuck her. Because I made her stop making *him* uncomfortable. *Bitch!*"

A few people glance our way, but I'm too angry to care.

Isaac grabs my arm, stopping me gently as he pulls us aside from oncoming foot traffic. "You were actually fired?"

"Don't tell him." I point a finger at his chest. "I know you're itching to."

"You just lost your job because—"

"No, not because of him. It was due to a rich daddy's girl who gets everything she wants. Who doesn't care about *anyone* but herself."

"He still should—"

"Isaac, I know it's your job to tell him what happens to me." I pull my arm from his grasp, bringing my voice down as I angrily rant. "Which may include me getting fired due to a possessive girl who laid claim on a man who didn't look twice at her, no, he did *once* and that was enough for her to harass him. Don't tell him because I will. I probably just made an enemy of a rich heiress to a law firm or she'll forget I exist after two days with a new victim. She'll probably fuck the next frat guy who takes his coffee from her. But if he finds out from *you* first, he's gonna come down here and either buy the shop, buy her father's law firm, or do something else outlandish."

Perhaps I should be madder about being fired in general, but I'll find another job. No matter how hard, I've done it before, I can do it again. I just hate that I lost this one over something like an annoying Greek tragedy. This particular anger was keeping other emotions in the background, to not think about the gut-wrenching past. In the back of my head, I keep hearing: *you deserve this, worthless, expendable, replaceable…I gave you everything!* The memory is shoved away.

Isaac watches me carefully, letting me catch my breath after a minute or two. I close my eyes, focusing on the noises around us.

He finally speaks, "You're probably right with how he'd respond."

I press my hand over my face. "How am I correct with that man every time?"

"You pay attention to who he is."

"Don't get smart on me," I warn, and there's a glint in his eyes, almost coaxing a smile from me. I take another grounding breath. "Don't tell him. I just need…"

"Coffee?" One step closer to me smiling. "Maybe tea instead? Early dinner?"

"How busy is he today?" I sigh.

"Unfortunately…very." Great, that means hours before I'll be able to talk to him.

I rub my temple, thinking how to spend the rest of my day. "I'll go home. I need to tell Nan. She needs to know I lost my income and won't be able to help with rent or bills, along with everything else to pay off…crud muffins. Well, at least my therapy is covered by the women's center, but I gotta talk to Nan…"

My voice trails off when I see Isaac trying to hide a grimace. I glare at him, and he clears his throat, "Actually, you won't need to worry—"

"He *actually* bought the damn building, didn't he?" Isaac barely nods. "That's it! I wanna kill something, shoot kneecaps, or lace out someone's innards into a rug." His mouth opens in horror. "What? Don't worry, I won't. I'm just...angry, frustrated, conflicted, and...gah!"

My head leans back as I close my eyes, trying to calm down as my heart races. I try focusing on the wind that grazes my skin, and the warmth of the sun. It's fine. You told him it was fine. Perhaps he didn't say anything 'cause it just happened or Nan was gonna tell me. Not my decision...not my...I feel like drinking.

I grab my bag from Isaac, throwing it over my shoulder. "I'm going home. Stay far enough back to keep an eye out for jealous women and creepy guys. But once I'm home, *you* go home. Got it?"

"I uh—"

"I'll be safe there. Trust me. I need space right now...a lot of it."

"Very well." I take the long route home with my shadow not far behind.

* * *

Nan sits behind the store counter with me, while I perch on a chair.

"Fired for 'misconduct' and not selling pastries because a rich girl didn't get the guy," I grumble. "Where did my life go wrong, Nan?" She chuckles, shaking her head which she's done a lot in the past hour. "Eh, you're right, still sucks."

"Young love is one thing, but young lust is something I'm too old to remember," she muses, patting my shoulder. "It was a good job while it lasted. But we knew it wasn't going to be forever."

"Yeah, but to be fired over a guy?" I fling my hand in the air. "He was almost covered in coffee because of her, practically harassed because of *her*. Should've dumped the entire espresso machine on her." Nan raises a brow. "She deserved it; I won't apologize."

"What's done is done. You can work here for a bit, give me

another vacation to go south. You know I hate the winter here, Georgia weather is better for my bones."

"Speaking of the *bookstore*..." I eye her a little, and she doesn't even look perturbed. "Did he buy the store?"

"Technically he didn't—"

"Nan!"

"It wasn't your decision, dear. It was between him and I, and well, I guess the ex-owner of the building." I put my face into my hands. He said he would, but I didn't think this quick or that Nan was serious! Wait, didn't I say no building? I can't remember. "It'll make things easier on me. On us."

"I know, Nan...I mean, I told him I'd be fine with it...mostly," I mumble through my hands.

"Are you not?"

"Let's say processing. Lost my job today, too, remember?" She eyes me a little, like she doesn't understand my inner dilemma. "Nan, admit it that it makes things odd, especially if I work for you now. Cause then technically I work for him."

Oh, great I'll live and work in a building he owns *and* go to therapy at a center he funds. So much for being independent. I go to smack my head against the counter, but Nan stops me.

"Now, dear," she says, breaking me out of my thoughts and handing me a chocolate chip cookie. Woman is sweetening me up. More conniving than Leo, I swear. "He owns the building, not the store."

I blink at her. "Not helping much here, Nan."

"I'm just saying, and it couldn't be helped."

"Explain, Lucy."

She pats her curly hair. "You know I used to be a redhead?"

"Nan!"

"Something...came up, it was easier for him to buy the entire building instead of just the store," she continues, and I stare at her. Don't like the sound of that, why would it be easier to *buy a building*? "I'm just a renter of his, mainly just for the bookstore. He determined the apartments fall under it in rent. We had a lovely discussion with his lawyers on cost."

I narrow my gaze, biting into my cookie. "How much?" She looks away. "Nan."

"Twenty dollars a month seemed fair." I concentrate on the cookie in front of me. She can't be serious. "We'll still pay bills, but the rest is taken care of."

I should be elated, hell I kind of was when he first brought it up. I didn't want her losing what was most precious to her all these years. She never told the finances, but I knew she struggled most months. And it's been my only true home in over a decade. Except, being jobless now, it feels like I'm living off of him. I didn't want to be no better than those who've gouged him for money. Used him as a bank.

"Sweetie, what's wrong? I believe he's trustworthy, and good owner—"

"I'm not worried about that."

"Then what?"

"What if he thinks I'm using him for his money? Yes, he offered and its business between you two, not my name on anything, but I don't want...I *never* want him to think I'm using him like that."

Learning about how he built everything with Jameson, it was more than just his livelihood.

"You'll work here. And *I* will pay you, not him." She takes a cookie. "You can help with my organization and security cameras. Maybe finally get those new shelves I wanted." I glance at the old shelves. Everything was the same since I first stumbled into the place during college.

Nan murmurs, "I think being fired was a good thing."

"Are you serious? You always said it was the best thing for me."

Nan becomes quiet, dipping her cookie into her tea. She chews it slowly before giving a long sigh as she stares out the front door. A couple walks in, which we greet before they browse. Once they're out of earshot, Nan whispers, "You only needed that job after what happened. It's time for you to live your life that isn't under the shadow from your past."

I swallow hard, staring down at the tea in front of me. "I loved that job though, Nan."

"There's better things to love," she says. "People and spaces that will love you back. Give you what you want."

"What if I still don't know what I want?"

"You'll have the time now. Without that job as a crutch." I open my mouth and she gives me a knowing look. "It was, dear. A counter to hide behind to heal."

Fine. It was the job I needed to feel human again, survive those first couple of months to remain busy. It turned into years. It gave me access to work overtime, not think, and give a purpose of some kind. Even if that purpose was coffee. It was better than nothing. It was mine though.

"Time to move forward for new things." She reaches for my chin, lifting it. "*Enjoy* life again. I know you were content, but you deserve more. This is the first time I've seen you smile so often, even better over a boy."

"Definitely not a boy, Nan."

"A mature man, then," she chuckles. The couple comes around and buys a few books, Nan smiles as she rings them out and they leave. "That young girl will learn her lesson soon enough, when she doesn't get what she wants *or* does."

"Doubt it," I scoff, and Nan quirks a brow. "Good thing or not, it's all unfair even to Yuki with her hands tied. Bailey will do this again and again, and she'll…honestly, I don't know."

"Some are born with rose-colored glasses, dear."

"Must be nice."

"Must be awful." I scowl at her. "Think about you at that age, how naïve. I don't like to think about what you went through, but what happened made you see the world through all its spectrum of colors. Awful thing, but more compassion after. You know different kinds of love and understanding because your glasses were ripped off…in the worst ways possible." She clears her throat. "Those with the wool over their eyes, they'll never open to new possibilities and have compassion for others. They're stuck. Watching the world from ivory towers with tinted glasses, blinded of consequence and responsibility, soon to be very alone."

I rotate the mug, watching the tea swirl. My voice is somber. "Do you think only trauma can get rid of those glasses? See what's on the other side?"

"I think experiencing both love and pain, knowing the difference between them is what rids us of them. The combination. My Finn learned from watching pain within his own family, and I think I did, too. How he and survived those early years of the bookstore. The decisions we had to make." Nan hums solemnly, touching the wedding ring still on her finger. "Yet, sometimes, even those who've suffered pain, have come out worse than before. They ignore and add more lenses to not see the truth."

She pats my knee, sipping her tea as she adds, "Perhaps, Leonardo is stripping away the last of your lenses...and you for him."

"Maybe."

Chapter 26

From the Chandelier

The frozen pizza in the microwave spins.

My eyes slip to the scotch on my counter. *Don't do it.*

I start pacing my apartment, and then go through movies on what to watch. I grab an 80s action flick when the timer goes off. I think of Leo as I take the pizza out, missing his cooking. Pausing, I glance at the late time. It's dinner and I haven't heard from him. That's weird.

Dropping off the pizza on the counter, I search for my phone and find it in my bag. Crap, I was supposed to charge it earlier, and it's dead.

"Really? You let that happen?" I mutter, quickly plugging it in. "Shit…"

After a few minutes, it lights up and there's three missed calls. All from Leo. Crud muffins! I try calling him back only to get his voicemail. I try again. Nothing. Panic starts to twist in my stomach.

I decide to call my back up, putting it on speaker as I grab my pizza. It rings a couple times and Isaac picks up, "Hello?"

"Isaac? My phone was dead. I just forgot with everything to charge it, I never let that happen and Leo tried calling me, but—"

"Hold on, Miss Autumn, it's fine."

"Is he mad?" My chest tightens at the idea, remembering how

worried he was the first time I missed his calls. "He won't pick up the phone, Isaac. He's not picking up. Why won't he pick up?"

"That's because he's flying down to Florida."

"What?"

"It was last minute, and he had to take his private jet down, concerning his hotel in Miami. He left a few hours ago and tried to contact you but when you didn't answer, well…" Isaac takes a moment and confesses, "…I've been across the street since he left, giving him updates on your whereabouts. Reminder I work for him, not you. His word is final."

I slump over my counter, pushing my late-night pizza aside. Yup, not hungry. "Crab apples, I'm sorry Isaac."

"It's quite alright, knowing your phone is working again, I'll be able to leave in peace. And, uh, crab apples?"

"Don't think too much on it," I murmur, rubbing my head. "He just…left?"

Oh goodie, not only was he not there when I woke up the morning after we had sex, but a day later he completely leaves the state. My self-esteem is rock solid…not.

"Everything happened quickly. I can't give more details than that," he explains, and I nod my head like he can see me. My brain spirals. Loneliness and shame come creeping back. Gone. I stare down at the tile. "Miss Autumn?"

The poem is recited in my head. Guilt and shame digs deeper into my bones. Alone.

"He's coming back."

Those words shake me, and I clear my throat. I pick at the pizza even as my stomach twists. Emotions roil inside me, pulling me in different directions.

"This had priority. It's just for work," he tries to explain.

"I'm not mad." Not at him at least. I grab the bottle of scotch. "He went to do his job. He's a freaking CEO, so I'm not mad he's taking matters into his own hands, doesn't surprise me one bit. He called; I didn't pick up. It's my own damn fault. And besides if you'd told me he stayed, *then* I'd be worried. Or ask if he was drunk or whatever."

"Then what is it?"

I stop pouring my drink, clinking the bottle on the counter. My head hangs down as tears try to come forward, fear and nerves bubbling inside. There's a prick against my neck, and I glance over my shoulder at the door. It's locked. I swallow hard and my hand itches toward my wrist. I'll be alone and I can't talk to him.

And it sucks.

"It's been a long day, and when you've had a long day, what would you want?"

I finish pouring my glass. "Depends, I guess."

"Well for me, lately, it's to have a certain someone around who makes it better."

"I can have him—"

"Don't. I can't be selfish right now. I can't tell him what to do. And I *can't* be mad at him for something he's *supposed* to be doing. Like I told him with my…ex job. I'm just frustrated from today." I push the bottle of liquor back into the corner.

"Is there something I can do?"

"No." I start bringing the glass to my lips, feeling my stomach clench at the smell.

"Don't."

The glass near my lips stops. I look over at the phone as my chest concaves. "What?"

"I have a good sense to believe you're going to drink. Don't."

"What did he tell you or did you get a dossier about me?" The silence is revealing. "Manilla folder, got it."

"I—"

"Shit, I can't even be mad about that." I put the glass down, sliding it away. I lean back with a huff. "Let me ramble so I don't drink un-responsibly."

"Very well."

"Leo has paranoia, I can see it. Between his security, how he handles his private life, and constantly staying in control. I'm surprised I've even been given so much trust with him already. Whoever broke his trust so much that he *needs* that much control, must've been a real piece of work. To seclude himself because he thinks he deserves it. Even his friend of almost twenty years was surprised how much he's opened up with me. Maybe that's why Jameson's protective, too. I'm humbled to be let in, but…fuck I know what it's like looking over your shoulder constantly. Not trusting anyone. Unsure what else people will take from you."

"He needs that control," Isaac murmurs. "You're the only one he's ever let fully in. Even those of us who are close, it took *years* to learn anything private about him. You…calm him. Give him something other than what he's built. So, what he gave us about you—"

"Isaac, I don't—"

"It was mainly superficial items like allergies, work schedule, where you live, or that you shouldn't drink alone. Safety measures for you." Okay, just simple stuff. Sounds normal for a bodyguard anyways.

"Google list then?"

"Basically. It was need to know for a select few of us. If it makes you feel better, we've done it for other hotel guests in the past. Although usually, requested."

"You know that's kind of scary, right?" I whisper, hoping the curiosity isn't heard in my voice. There's something in my closet I didn't want out.

I glance at the locked door again. I try to sound aloof, and ask, "That easy to find stuff on people?"

"Why I've been hired."

"Really are Bond, huh? Or maybe *you're* M."

"Not entirely, security is my specialty, but that comes in all forms."

"My hero," I sarcastically muse.

"Don't tell him you said that."

"I'll do my best." I get up on the counter, sitting as I stare at the phone across from me. A few minutes tick by, and Isaac doesn't get off the line.

"Do you feel better?" He asks.

"You're pretty good at the distracting thing."

"Part of the job."

"You have training in counseling or something?"

He chuckles. "A bit while in the military, thought I'd use it for police work one day."

"Then why this job?"

"Gives me purpose. Different than what I thought, but it does. Aside from being your bodyguard, Leo has been a good boss and friend to make it so."

"Glad you found something you like."

"You will, too."

My gaze moves to the knives on my counter, and I quickly squash those thoughts. I get up, grabbing my phone and plug it in closer to me as I sit and restack my movies. I debate actually hanging up, saying I'm fine, but having someone on the phone is comforting.

It's been years since I've called the suicide hotlines, but I remember how those voices helped in the early days. To just be heard.

"Wanna know something?" I ask.

"Well, tonight's slow, so alright." We both chuckle, and I take a deep breath, sitting back on my knees.

"I didn't think I'd live past sixteen," I begin and Isaac's breath hitches. "When I did, I decided to live, obviously, but each year got harder and harder. It was difficult with those thoughts never relenting. Never really thought about my future. To me, it didn't exist. I just couldn't see past this expiration date in my head. So, I lived day by day, enjoyed the things I liked and focused on them, no matter how silly I was told they were. Some hobbies bit me in the ass, I think, but others I'll never regret." I clear my throat, pushing a few movies around. "I picked my major on a whim, never planning to use it. Didn't plan to live long enough to. And maybe that's why I stayed in an abusive relationship for so long, I thought by the end it'd do the trick to finally reach that expiration date. Or I deserved it. But the littlest things seemed to…keep me around, like the next Nick Cage movie."

My mind wanders, remembering the long months after and how

little I held onto survival. Movies. Ice cream. A friend's laugh. A cup of coffee. My worst nightmare was in the hospital, not wanting to be alive anymore. If it hadn't been for Trix or Leanne I'd have pulled the plug.

"And now?" Isaac asks in a quiet tone.

"Well, that remains to be seen."

"I mean, do you still have that expiration date in your head?"

Scarface stares up at me, and I trace a finger over Al Pacino. "Been working on it in therapy. I've gotten better and healed some, but sometimes I forget how much longer the road is."

I stack the movie with the others, and place a few more children's movies together. I think of switching my viewing for tonight, when finally, Isaac says, "He's right about you."

"What?"

"You are an open book, unapologetically so. It's very much not a bad thing, Miss Autumn, it's almost refreshing, odd as it sounds to hear something so…"

"Sad?"

"Human." I sit a bit more heavily on the floor. "I've experienced quite a bit in my life, and I can …relate to some of the things you speak of. I'm grateful you decided to stay."

I swallow past the lump in my throat. Tears prick at my eyes, and I whisper, "Thank you."

Isaac inhales sharply and says, "Miss Autumn, I have an urgent call I must make. Please take care of yourself tonight, I'm only a phone call away. Or Jameson."

"Yeah." He hangs up.

My gaze goes toward the kitchen where the pizza and alcohol await. Rubbing my face harshly, I grumble at the thoughts in my head. It's been a while since I've had a night as bad as this, tumbling with all kinds of emotions. Fuck, did I really say all that to Isaac?

Now I really, *really* want to drink for all the wrong reasons.

I head over to the kitchen, flicking my gaze from one thing to the other. I'm about to say screw it with the scotch when my phone rings. I pick it up expecting Isaac.

"I'm pouring the fucking liquor down the drain, but if you tell me no ice cream we're rethinking your job position," I grumble, dumping the glass into the sink.

"Depends on the ice cream." I freeze when Leo's voice comes over the line.

My hands tremble, almost dropping the glass into the sink as relief hits me. I choke out, "Leo?"

"Hello, dear Watson."

"Leo, I'm so sorry. My phone was off, and I didn't realize it'd died, then you called, left voice messages, and I'm sorry I should've—"

"Autumn. Autumn, it's alright, breathe. Long as you're okay that's all I care about." I start sliding down against the cabinets to the kitchen floor, pulling my knees in close as I take shaky breaths and nod my head. "I apologize I left so abruptly, but it was—"

"I'm not mad, I'm not, just…" I take another breath, focusing on calming down and to behave. I realize my old defense mechanism has kicked in, and I tell myself he's not Steve. He's not going to berate or hurt me. It's Leo, just Leo. "I'm not mad, well, a heads up would've been nice, but it sounds like you didn't get that either. It'd be unfair to be mad at what you're supposed to be doing. You know? And my phone was dead."

"I'm also supposed to be taking care of you."

"Then I guess you'll have to do that when you get back, huh?" My voice comes out with a bit more sting than I intend. My throat closes, wanting to sob suddenly as I grip my knees. The combination of today's events, Leo gone, my suicidal rambling to Isaac, and now being triggered by a damn phone call is making my head and chest hurt.

"What's wrong, Autumn?"

I lean my head back, staring up at the ceiling. "Just tired is all."

"Your voice dropped and you mentioned drinking and ice cream…what is it?"

"Would you believe me if I said I missed you?"

"Yes."

"Then that."

"Autumn—"

"I don't want to talk about it right now. Perhaps I should, but not right now. I want to tell you in person not when you're over…which state you flying over right now?"

"Georgia, I think."

"I don't want to tell you while you're flying over Georgia. Nothing will change anyways whether you know now or later. Trust me."

"Dear Watson…"

"I'm fine. And you should know Isaac is doing his job far better than his first day," I choke out a small laugh. "I'll be fine. Don't need to worry over me while you're taking care of million-dollar deals for all I know."

"Except I want to worry about you."

"You can do that when you get back." Tears begin to fall down my cheeks.

I want to tell him that I want him here. In this damn kitchen scowling at the lack of food in my cabinets and the cereal I have. To tell him I want to be back in his penthouse, watching him cook and smiling. But I can't.

"My dear Watson," he says softly.

"You keep doing that."

"I enjoy saying it."

I smile as the tears drop silently to my knees, laying my head them as I listen to the small noises in the background of the plane. I think of what Leo would do if he was here. His arms around me, kissing my head and holding me like nothing could touch me. Not even my memories or nightmares.

Leo says quietly, "I'll be back. I promise you. I'm not running away, and I meant it the other night. *Everything*."

I close my eyes, taking a deep grounding breath. "I believe you whole heartedly….mister."

"Good, because I'm a man who keeps his promises, especially with you…my dear Watson."

Chapter 27

Quiet Libraries Bring Quiet Thoughts

Leo stayed on the phone with me just before he landed in Miami. When I mentioned Isaac and the "manilla folder," he apologized, explaining like Isaac had—just simple information for security purposes. It'd been compiled before our talk the day I knee-d Isaac. I wondered if that's what he meant the day we went riding, that he'd gone a step too far.

I didn't ask.

A part of me worried, but what was buried deep in my past was still buried. Or long gone. What mattered is that they hadn't found it, so I wouldn't give them reason to keep digging.

Nan awoke me this morning with muffins and coffee before work in the bookstore. Most of it I spent glancing over her security cameras, which I used to check every few days, but now only once a month.

Mid-way through the afternoon she sent me off to go relax or do something fun. Felt like a kid being told to go play outside. I called Leanne, telling her what happened and then Trix, both of them sorry I'd lost my job. Although, I'm not taking Leanne near *Blue Java* for a while…she'd pull Bailey's hair out. I'd help.

Both were working long hours, so no last-minute meetup, instead, I decided to distract myself with something else.

It's warm out as I hop off the subway, walking the last bit before I stop before the stone lions and smile. It's been years since I've visited the New York Public Library and figured it was about time I did. I climb up the stairs, navigating my way through the building and up more stairs as I wander through the Rose Reading Room. It's quiet as I step between desks, my feet carrying me through the vast space as I thumb through random books. Grabbing another, I hear something behind me. Turning, I expect to see Isaac, but he's not there.

My skin pricks, ticking at the back of my neck as my heart rate quickens. I check behind myself again, the library mostly silent apart from flipping pages. Putting the book back, I glance behind again. Nothing.

The keys in my back pocket press against my hand, then put the keys between my fingers as I make a fist. I walk toward a back corner of the room and hope to catch my shadow. I move around a smaller aisle, but nada.

He's gotta be here. Isaac wouldn't leave me alone with Leo out of the state.

Unless someone…no, he's fine. *He's fine.*

"Isaac?" I whisper. Silence.

The keys dig into my hand as I clench my fist. I briskly walk out of the large reading room to a smaller one. I listen for footsteps, rounding a corner of shelving and hear something scuff behind me. Glancing over my shoulder, I see a familiar face and let out a breath of relief.

Clutching my chest, I gasp, "Jameson."

He's back in his suit today, and his brows pinch together as he approaches. "Are you alright?"

"Now I am," I answer, putting the keys back into my pocket. "Say something next time. I thought I was being followed in a bad way." I rub my head, taking some steadying breaths as we move down the aisle.

"Sorry. You practically bolted from the room, and I came after you."

"I didn't bolt. Just…fast paced."

I pull a book out and finger through some pages. Jameson leans against a bookcase as I skim. After minutes of silence, I put it back and ask, "Where's Isaac?"

"Even he needs a break. Said that yourself."

"Thank goodness." I move a few shelves down, crouching to look at titles. "Glad Isaac's taking a break, but shouldn't you be in Florida with Leo?"

"Why should I be?"

"You practically co-own everything shouldn't you be with him? Rather than taking girlfriend duty?"

He snorts. "Someone has to keep an eye on things here. He'll be fine. Always better on his own."

Not as comforting of a statement he may think that is.

"Again, why are *you* the one here with me then? No offense, but it takes a bit longer to get a five-star review from me."

He smirks, "My breaks are different than others. I'm more hands on."

"Oh, goodie," I scoff. "Being my bodyguard is a break for you?"

"Better than meetings with others I wish I hadn't even spent two minutes with and…" he pauses, gaze meeting mine suddenly serious, "…thought we could talk."

Here I thought my best friends could put someone through the ringer with protective friend talks. Seems like Jameson has levels to his. Unless he wants to talk about the stock market, which he's out of luck there.

I stand up, crossing my arms. "About what?"

"I want you to understand why Leo is the way he is."

Oh, darn not stock markets.

"You don't—"

"Yes, I do." I shut my mouth. "He's my business partner and practically my brother. It's up to me to help him every way I can, that includes you at the moment." His brows scrunch, focusing on me. I nod for him to continue, leaning against the bookcase.

"He has precautions for a reason, which includes finding information on people and handing it over to individuals like myself to take care of matters. It's done for security reasons, given his position and influence. Even with you, there's no exceptions."

The man is blunt, I'll give him that. Honestly, I like it better than being told some fluffed up lie.

"I know. I'm not upset with him anymore." He frowns, tilting his head like I just said the sky is polka dotted. "He apologized and we talked. You didn't think we would?"

"No, but I—"

"But it's not your place, whether you think it is or not, to interfere with our relationship. Or what he and I discuss. *Security reasons* or not." My voice is soft, arguing with him. If he thought I was straightforward before, he's got another thing coming due to his own bluntness. Not to mention I'm pretty certain he's going to be the one to push my boundaries the most.

Jameson looks at me as Leo had the first few times we spoke. Surprise and questioning. Neither seem used to someone speaking bluntly *back* at them. Guess I shouldn't be surprised given their backgrounds.

"Leo's working on being honest with me, same as I am with him. When we have blunders, we talk like any mature couple should do. I understand why he did, and after yesterday, I *definitely* don't blame him if what I dealt with was a fraction of what he deals with regularly."

Jameson crosses his arms. "If you could explain."

I start walking down the aisle, glimpsing at the people sitting at desks and doing their work. I stop, skimming over more titles. "I'm angry about losing my job, duh, but it's just a job at the end of the day. Even if it meant a lot to me, but I can honestly find another without a co-worker out to make my life hell. Nan's probably right about it being time I moved on. Unfortunately, my life always seems to wanna take the hard road for change." I huff to myself, frowning at the books before me. "I'm more upset over the why. Jealousy and spitefulness are what got me fired, and I'm pissed knowing it's not the first or last time with her. I got lucky in the aftermath, someone else won't."

I pause, biting my bottom lip a little and look over at Jameson. "But I'm also mad for Leo. Angry knowing this has probably happened before and will happen again. Next time it won't be some jealous girl."

"How does—?"

"He's seen as a trophy, not human," I whisper, and Jameson just blinks at me. "I know that statement seems odd. He's a grown man who can take care of himself. People are shitty, and he's probably had his own share, but…I understand feeling alone in a crowd. Expecting to feel used. I know how that feels."

I avert my gaze, staring at a green book with gold binding. My fingers trace over the soft cover.

"You're right it's not the first time," he murmurs. "Comes with the territory when you're worth a shit-ton."

"Maybe because of that I *shouldn't* feel sorry for him, but I do. Money doesn't take those feelings away. Being poor doesn't take those feelings away. He spent over a decade building something because he's smart and knows how, yet he's exploited for his looks. A look *he* clearly curates for the public. Because he knows it works. I've seen how some of his *associates* act around him, sometimes background checks won't cut it. Not everything is saved on paper."

I decide to pull a green book out, not really looking at the reference material as I sit down with my legs crossed. Jameson looks around before sitting down across from me.

He clears his throat, and says, "I think you're a rare person to see it that way. Most would brush it off. Act like he doesn't deserve to have pity. He made his bed."

"Money, fame, looks, or whatever people want for 'checking boxes'…he's still human. A human who's trying. Knowing what I've been told about his past, what he's gone through and tried to make better, I find it infuriating that at times he's only being noticed for the wrong reasons. Maybe it's cause I see him in a light that others don't or maybe it's cause I know how that feels in some way. Only known as one thing, and it has nothing to do with what *you* wanted to be."

"How so?"

I shrug, closing the book and put it back on the shelf. "I have nightmares, anxiety attacks, and triggered by the weirdest shit sometimes. Sometimes that fraction is all people notice. That's all they ever see, even if I spent so much time trying to get better."

Jameson leans further against the bookcase, watching others near the desks. He whispers, "You have *actual* depression, don't you?"

"Compared to *fake* depression?" I smirk.

"Some do," he argues lightly. "Or seasonal. Or just plain sad."

"It's more than being sad," I say, tilting my head at him. "Depression is…it's like…this thing that feels like a shadow made of oil, thick and sludgy meant to drown you. It pulls you under into destructive emotions that are more complex than just sad."

His clears his throat as he keeps his gaze on the rest of the room, adjusting where he sits. "I overheard some of your conversation with Isaac last night."

"My phone bugged, too?"

"Not yours." He flicks his gaze to me, and I make an 'ah' face. "Most our phone conversations are recorded, a safety precaution due to dealings in the past and…present. As you said, some background checks don't cut it."

Okay, shouldn't be surprised.

"Then I guess you know I have PTSD, then."

"I wasn't going to assume."

"Not a secret, I just don't talk about the events because it's still hard. Not a great subject to discuss regularly. Well, apart from with my therapist."

"How long have you been going to them?"

A slight panic runs down my spine. *It's fine,* I tell myself. Not like it's a clue to anything. "Couple of years. But just her, no drugs due to…personal reasons. Was any of that in the 'manilla folder' handed out?"

"Not a folder in his defense, even if you're not mad." We share a small smile.

"Long-story short. Leo's trying. He treats me like I'm someone worth being around, beyond my personal shit and whatever else people see me as. I'll keep doing the same for him."

Jameson stares at me, his expression becoming serious. "I'll hold you to that."

"You'd be a terrible biker brother if you didn't," I smirk, turning away to look at the books. "Ever wander around these halls?"

"Not naturally a New Yorker, so I don't randomly browse through famous buildings."

"Hint. Not even *natural* New Yorkers do that."

I get up and so does he, following me as I walk out of the reading room and into the marbled hall. There aren't that many people here today, apart from clusters of tourists in groups touring the building. I pause near a painting, glancing at Jameson who stops beside me.

"He told me about being kidnapped," I abruptly mention, feeling him shift on his feet. "But I don't think that's why he doesn't trust openly."

Jameson only grunts, putting his hands in his pockets.

"So…given all we just talked about, who betrayed Leo to push him to have all these precautions? For you and Isaac to defend him so often? He's worse than Bruce Wayne half the time on being reclusive. Yet, he seems close to you and those in that original MC, someone must've crossed a hell of a line." Jameson side eyes me. "Just saying. Most of us become private for reasons."

He puts his hands in his pocket with a huff. "I'm not sure whether to be fearful of your intuition about him or amazed."

"We're in a famous library, let's go with amazed." Since, apparently, I can read Leo like a book.

His face scrunches together, rubbing his chin a little. I shift on my feet, waiting for his reply and wonder if I took a step too far. Again. I've not wanted to pry but given Jameson's full awareness of Leo's extensive privacy and him seemingly trying to shake me, it's made me curious. As I think about it, they *all* seem protective of him, and I don't believe it's just because he's their boss or CEO.

"Eight years ago." My thoughts stop as Jameson explains in a low voice. "Someone tried to convince him to come back for his brothers and family business. They blackmailed him. Everything we'd worked for was about to be destroyed. Hidden for years in privacy and almost gone in an instant. After...he became more careful to never allow it to happen again. A few we trusted were the ones who told his family where he was, using *very* personal relationships and private information against him. He wasn't the same after that."

I stare at the painting, the colors melding together as dread trickles down my spine.

"He was garnering attention though; wouldn't they have found out about him?"

"He changed his name, like me. Even with similarities, if they'd found out, it would've at least been on our terms. Could've stayed peacefully in California." The last part is barely murmured.

We're both quiet, staring at the painting like it's gonna add to the conversation.

Jameson turns toward me, cocking his head. "Alright, I won't pry into your relationship with him. But don't think I won't go easy on you because of that."

"I'm really not here to hurt him," I whisper, and his gaze softens. "Ever. Even if he messes up. I care about him...a lot."

"You're very forgiving. It's a breath of fresh air, especially in our area of work. Accusations on the other hand, never short of that."

"Well, therapy will do wonders," I snort, laughing to myself and head down the hall. "Want to get some dinner, Mr. Shadow?"

He makes a snorting laugh sound, shaking it off quickly. He nods, staying next to me as we head for the stairs.

"If it makes you feel less *targeted*, we all attend therapy periodically," he says.

"Really?"

"It helps us stay on our toes, due to some colorful backgrounds.

He can tell you more, but Leo's been somewhat consistent for six years."

"After the whole…?"

"Yes. And after other ideas didn't pan out. I won't say more, probably will get my ass kicked for talking as much as I have. Surprised I haven't from the other day."

"I'll act innocent. Been told I'm good at that." I wink at him, heading down the stairs. "But thanks for talking with me. It does make me feel better that ya'll are not afraid to get help if you need it. Tells me a lot about you."

"If you wanted another reason why we're loyal to him. After everything, good or bad, he tries to be better."

"Aren't we all?"

He pauses, and I stop a few steps down from him and look up. His brows are back to pinching together. Did he learn that from Leo or vice versa?

"I do wonder how you're so willing to understand, therapy or not, doesn't explain *why* you're so forgiving. So, why?"

"Really looking for that ulterior motive, huh? Or maybe you love my long-winded rambling." His face doesn't budge, and I shrug. "I have a bad habit of giving people chances and hoping for the best, even if I get screwed over in the end." His jaw tightens, while his eyes harden. "Much like my current job situation."

I turn away and hear him follow me down the stairs. There's a low vibrating sound, and I stop as he makes a face and pulls out his phone, reaching the first floor. He holds a finger up to me, walking towards a corner away from people.

The building's ambiance is quiet. I move off to the side of the hall as people pass. Suddenly, there's a prick at my neck. The odd feeling of being watched comes back, yanking at me to be on alert. A shiver runs down my spine as I look at Jameson on the phone, talking roughly, as I spin in place down the hall.

Quiet.

The prick continues to pull at my skin, goosebumps rising as my heartbeat quickens.

You're fine. All the talking about hidden pasts and trust is just—

I start turning toward the entrance when I freeze. I notice someone down the way. Dark blonde stubble and hair. He's wearing a brown leather jacket with jeans. Not quite a square jaw. My breathing is shallow as I stare at the man, moving between some couples.

Please don't let my past haunt me more ways than one.

It can't be him. No. They would've called. *They would've told me.*

Time goes still as I stare at the man who continues down the hall.

A hand touches my shoulder. I flinch harshly, jumping back into the wall as I stare up at Jameson, who appears confused. "Autumn?"

I clear my throat, looking back to where the man was, but he's gone. My anxiety runs rampant, screaming at me to run. Jameson looks down the direction I was. "What is it?"

"Nothing. Weird sound. Let's get dinner." I walk briskly for the exit, hoping I'm not wrong.

The water drips on Leo's penthouse floor, while the thunderstorm rages outside. Jameson and I are soaked to the bone. We'd gotten dinner, deciding to walk back to the hotel and it began pouring without warning. After Jameson made a call to Leo, and Chiari trying not to chuckle with me in the lobby, I now stood in my boyfriend's luxury apartment with a very wet bodyguard. While the other stands before us in shock.

Thunder cracks as Isaac walks over to a wall panel near the patio, pressing a button, which mutes the outside noise.

"This is why I don't go for walks," Jameson grumbles as he starts to walk back out. I can't help but giggle under my breath at his 'wet cat' behavior. "Make sure she gets everything she needs, otherwise he'll destroy your riding gear."

He walks out, closing the door behind him. I glance at Isaac who smirks. "Use whatever you need in his bathroom, and there should be some clothes in the left dresser for you. And I will not divulge how he got said clothes and sizes."

"Too late, already knew about it." Inside I was thanking Nan.

"I'll just make you some tea to warm up."

"I'll definitely take you up on that offer."

I head into the bedroom, dumping my jacket onto the bathroom floor and peel out of the wet clothes, pulling on the robe I've used before. I search for warm, dry clothes and find the dresser filled with more clothes in my size. Not a drawer, a *dresser*. I roll my eyes, and pull out the essentials of lounge pants, sweater, and ah-ha! Socks!

About to take it all into the bathroom, I pause and glance at Leo's walk-in closet. Tiptoeing, I go to peek at the large space, which is filled with suits, dress-shirts galore, slacks, and shoes lined up perfectly. It's all…pristine. It's so perfectly set up that I want to desperately mess it up. Angle one shoe or something. Move a hanger.

"Okay, leave his stuff alone," I chuckle to myself.

I get showered and dried, putting on the new clothes and head out to the living space. I glance outside, barely seeing the lights of the city as I grab my phone to text Nan I'll be staying here. Rain pounds against the windows while flashes of lightening streak across the dark sky. Well, damn.

The kettle begins to whistle, and Isaac takes it off. "I'll be here for a bit, but you should be fine here by yourself tonight. That storm is supposed to go on until morning."

"Not going swimming are you?" I ask, sitting at the counter as he brings me the tea. "Thanks."

"I prefer better conditions."

"Do you ever get caught in the rain while riding?"

"More times than I care to admit."

"Wet, grumpy bikers," I giggle, thinking about a soaking wet Leo, scowling.

The evening continues with flooding rain and thunder, while Isaac and I talk for a bit. Jameson comes back, less grumpy. It's another few hours before I'm tired enough to try sleeping, leaving the two in the kitchen with a wave. Before I close the door, I hear them whisper about shipments and clientele issues.

I stare at the bed, remembering Leo as his hands stroked my sides. Him pressing me against the covers and feeling the pulse of him inside me. Rippling tattoos. Shivering, I pull back the covers and climb into the large bed. I stretch out my arms and touch where he'd be, and then let out a sigh as I lay back and stare at the ceiling. The rain pounds against the window and I watch the storm. Slowly, my eyes shut, and I fall asleep.

I'm trapped.

Darkness captures me as screams echo, vibrating through my bones. I scream against the others, reaching for anything as forgotten pain comes rushing back. Tied down. Crashing glass. The smell of cigarettes. Pinned against walls...against the onslaught. Laughter. Wicked, vicious laughter.

Dirty blonde hair.

A shriek tears from my throat as I sit up, gasping for air as I clutch the sheets. Every muscle trembles, aching down my spine as I struggle to breathe. All I hear is the roar of the past as hands grab for me. Someone tugs at my arms, and I let out another scream that makes them let go. I grip my hands into my hair and sob against the pain that doesn't leave. Darkness drowning me as it doesn't relent like that night.

An unfamiliar hand touches me again, and I shout in horror, *"Red! Red!"*

The hand disappears, leaving me to rock and sob in the middle of the bed. Pain develops over me, the phantom leftovers of their torture and assault. I hold myself tight, screaming and wanting the nightmare to end. In the roar of my mind, I hear someone call out in a gentle voice.

"Autumn...Autumn."

No, not that name...not that name.

I shake my head, shivering as cold sweat coats my skin. I wince as another memory flashes of being held down, alcohol being forced down my throat. Phone calls telling me to stay. Hold on. I whimper against the painful memories.

I survived; I swear I survived.

"Autumn."

I shake my head and plead, "Red, red, red…"

I know the onslaught of sobbing and terror I'll have to endure for hours with no sleep. I sob against my legs, holding myself as I try to protect my body. Until something is pushed toward me and the sobs in my throat catch when I hear his voice.

"Dear Watson." A pitiful whimpering sound is all I manage as Leo's voice drifts to my ears. Shakingly, my hand reaches out and finds the phone. "Listen to my voice. If you can, say yellow if you can hear me."

I swallow past the lump, and whisper, "Y-yellow."

"Good girl." I choke out a sob at those words, continuing to rock in the darkness. A few moments later he recites *The Raven* with a slow tempo.

I concentrate on each word, saying the lines in my head with him. I clutch the phone close as I listen. My breathing calms, slowing into a steady pace, but the tremors don't stop.

Swallowing against the tightness around my throat, I whisper with him, *"But the Raven… sitting lonely …"*

Leo doesn't stop, speaking every line with me until we reach the end. I'm curled against a pillow, clutching the blankets as the cold sweat begins to dry on my skin.

"You're safe, my dear Watson. You're safe, sweetheart," Leo says quietly over the phone. It's the last thing I remember before I fall back into sleep, exhaustion overtaking me.

Chapter 28

Building Trust, Building Lies

The blankets are wrapped around me, practically tying me up. The phone is gone from my hands as I start to untangle myself. My head feels heavy, while my throat aches from screaming and crying. Once released from said blankets I sit up, glancing around the bedroom to the clock which tells me I slept a little. 8:30 without an alarm. New record for me.

It's still drizzling outside, rain pitter-pattering against the window. I get up slowly, stumbling a bit as I open the bedroom door and rub my eyes. Coming around the corner, I freeze.

I must still be asleep.

Leo's making breakfast, wearing a black shirt and jeans with a towel flung over his shoulder. Some tattoos are on display, glistening with sweat as he works over the stovetop. The smell of coffee drifts towards me. Maybe I am awake.

I start trembling, hoping that if I am dreaming, I stay the fuck asleep.

He can't be here. There's no way he'd be able to fly in last night.

Yanking at my hands and staring at the man, I take a few steps forward. He turns, setting down a skillet and his gaze finds mine. It's all I need to know this is real. I let out a choked sound of relief, moving without thought as I sprint for him. Leo's there to catch me as my arms fling around his neck. The shaking won't stop as he holds me close while I bury my face against his neck.

"Hello, my dear Watson," he whispers, his voice providing soothing relief.

I don't care how long time has passed. Every part of me ached for him last night and having him here crushes all those worries and fears. I cling to him, and finally grab his face to kiss him. His lips press against mine, reminding me of softness that I've wanted for almost three days. Leo steps back, leaning against the counter as his hand strokes up my spine.

Almost gasping for air, I loosen my hold and he kisses my cheek. I move my arms around his torso, looking up at his handsome face. "How are you here? The storm last night was brutal."

"It calmed enough to fly in this morning. Plus, a pilot who's just as stubborn as I am." I swear if it's Rudolf, I'm looking to see what other things that guy can drive.

"I couldn't be away from you another night," he says cradling my face.

Tears form in relief and pure happiness. I smile weakly, putting my forehead against his chest as I deeply inhale his scent. His gentle strength is what I needed.

"I missed you," I whisper.

"I missed you as well." He massages the back of my head, enticing a quiet hum from me.

Some of the shakiness disappears as reality sinks in that he's here. I'm not alone. He's back. He didn't leave forever. I go to step back, but he keeps me where I am, and I grin against his shirt. He places a kiss on my head, breathing in deeply.

"What are you cooking?"

"Not cereal." A loud snort leaves me, and he chuckles. He lets go of me, gesturing for me to sit at the counter to wait. "Since I'm back, it's time I make sure you eat properly."

"I ate..." my voice trails off as I sit and he quirks a brow, setting down a mug of coffee, "…frozen pizza counts as food. It's not that bad."

"True, it's not marshmallows in milk," he retorts, going back to the stove.

"One day, I'm gonna get you to eat it. Just you wait, mister." I take the coffee, sipping it as I watch him make breakfast. I glance at the rain that still comes down. "Was, uh, things taken care of in Florida?"

He responds briskly, "Yes. What needed to be done was. Those I trust will handle the rest."

The question bubbles in my chest, wanting to ask if I'd cost him anything. Am I to blame if something goes wrong because of a damn nightmare? Guilt suddenly makes my stomach clench, wondering if I should apologize. He's already helped so much. But then, I didn't ask for him to come back early. Yet, I still feel guilty. I hold my tongue, swallowing hard as I watch him.

Leo glimpses over at me, then says in a steady tone, "I made my decision to come back early for you because I wanted to. Everything was handled. You cost me nothing, Autumn."

My mug stops at my lips. I've gotten so good at recognizing his tells, has he caught on to mine? Probably.

I put the mug down, letting out a long sigh. The guilt still festers, so I decide to distract myself with the next inevitable subject. And be honest where some of the anxiety came from. Isaac probably did tell him about me being fired.

While keeping my gaze on my coffee, I say, "I was fired the day you left."

Leo tenses and goes still.

Oh. He didn't know.

He sets things aside and turns the burners down, then grabs his coffee while leaning against the opposite counter to look at me. "What happened?"

I explain everything, including the reasoning behind it with Bailey and practically threatening Isaac not to tell him. No need for him to get chewed out for clamming up like I asked. My shadow gets brownie points for keeping his word. Lastly, I tell him that's why I wasn't my best on the phone call the other night. Leo's jaw tenses as I talk, keeping a mostly neutral expression, but his brows still furrow. Not wanting to stay on the subject of being fired, I bring up my talk with Nan and him buying the building.

Leo sighs, putting his mug down. "I thought you said you were fine with it."

"You buying the entire building was a shock, even though I'm sure you could buy the entire block if you wanted. It just came out of nowhere to find out with all else that happened, and from Isaac. And I did say *bookstore,* not the entire building. But hey, tomato, tomato," I mumble the last part.

"I planned to tell you when I got back from Florida. Discuss what happened with you. The paperwork was finalized the day before I left." He watches me carefully, brows furrowing together. "I wasn't hiding it from you I swear."

"I know."

"I *was* intending to only buy the bookstore, help Nancy, but the previous owner wasn't...wasn't who I thought he'd be." He turns away, checking the food.

The odd, uneasy feeling I got when Nan spoke about it comes back. "What do you mean?"

He keeps his focus on the food, answering with a stern voice. "Remember that Nancy is a smart woman, but stubborn. From your reaction and question, then I assume she didn't tell you the entire story. For that...I'm sorry."

My mug clacks against the counter. I stare at him as he looks over his shoulder briefly.

I ask worriedly, "Leo, what happened?"

"Nancy *should've* owned the bookstore and the apartments due to a deal with the original owner that her late husband made, but it seems an *interest* rate was enacted after his death to keep the space under their control. Due to this and a skewed contract that was drawn up *after* Finnigan's demise as well, she was barely months away from losing the bookstore as 'collateral.' It would've been soon that you and she would've been told to leave. Even your contribution towards bills or rent would've never been enough. I'm surprised she's stayed afloat this long."

I gape at him. "She told me everything was fine. That it was... how was she paying for all that?"

"Ever since Finnigan's passing, she's presumedly been using her life savings and his life insurance to pay off what she could to keep the place."

My stomach sinks as I stare down at the counter. She lied.

"Wait, some of the things you just said...don't exactly sound legal," I whisper. Leo pauses, looking over at me and my stomach twists.

"I won't go into the details, but you're correct. What and how he did things were not legal, and Nancy knew." Oh gee, I may end up being sick this morning. I want to yell at her or cry.

"Why, why didn't she tell me?"

"She was trying to protect you," he answers. "She hoped to figure something out, but that man was a scumbag. Instead of dealing with more issues that would start a police investigation, which Nancy didn't want, I went over his head and bought the entire damn building. Including, the next two down the block. He's completely irrelevant now. Her debt has been paid and I made sure she got her life savings back and the money she lost from Finnigan's life insurance."

Holy fucking crud muffins.

"Leo," I rasp.

"Allow me to explain, and I will be direct with you." Blinking at him, I nod faintly. "I'm the sole owner of the buildings, everything has been paid for and handled financially. Legally. Nancy and I made a deal for rent that seemed appropriate to her for the apartments and bookstore. She refused sole ownership of the property; I think out of shame for what happened. But she did allow me to pay her back after what was taken from her. On some level, for a while, she knew what that man was up to but couldn't fight him. That's why she came to me, asking for advice and we devised a plan for her to keep the bookstore and your homes. However, I'll allow taking rent from her, I won't from you. There is no possible way I am taking money from my girlfriend to live in a building I own."

He takes a sharp breath, moving things off the stove and onto plates. I stare down at the food as he puts it in front of me as he continues.

"You've spoken of wanting to work fulltime at the bookstore, to give Nancy more of a retirement and you can do that now. *Nan's Bookstore* is still hers, so it wouldn't be my money paying you. I don't want you to think I own you in any capacity, this was a decision between me and her, as involved as you are in her life, you are not when making decisions about her finances and business. Please understand I had no intention in trying to control yours and what you want to do, but I was doing what I thought was best to allow Nancy and you not to be tossed onto the street."

My jaw goes slack at his stern tone, looking at him almost frozen. He stands before me and flicks his gaze toward the food and back up to me. "It's going to get cold."

Because of course that's what he's worried about.

Here I was worried he thought I was using him when he was thinking practically the opposite.

"Leo, do…do you know what you've done?"

His expression becomes serious. "I know exactly what I was doing, Autumn. Nancy and I conducted a business deal, which developed into me doing what I excel at, which is finding promising real estate to invest in. I've helped many small businesses stay afloat. I've made far riskier deals and contracts than buying a couple damn buildings from a landlord who didn't deserve them, stealing from people until their homeless."

I blink, waiting for my brain and body to scream and tell me to run. His strict tone, although similar to another in the past, doesn't illicit the same fight or flight response. I can tell he means me no harm. Leo sounds like…well, me when I told him it was my job.

He's right about it being a business transaction that didn't inherently involve me. Nan owned the apartments, not me. All I did was accidentally introduce them after holding a knife at Isaac. Leo knew real estate; he knew handling business ordeals. I didn't. Outside his hotel franchise, he was CEO of multiples companies. Easily, he could've done this without me knowing. Fuck, I didn't even know about the women's center until Trix brought it up, who knows what else he owned in the city. In my head, this cost him, but to him…it was another Wednesday afternoon.

I decipher the emotions swirling inside me as I try to recognize each. Mostly relief for Nan. I'm mad with her, but I know she's always tried to take care of me, to give me a home. Nan being Nan, didn't want me to worry. She knew enough about my past, what I went through. Oh, but she is getting a scolding later.

After a few long minutes of me trying to figure out what to say, Leo moves. His business persona falls, covering his face with his hand. "Autumn, tell me what you're thinking please. Tell me if I crossed a line—"

"Thank you." He drops his hand with a surprised look. "What you did…you didn't need to. If Nan and I had to move, we would've survived. I've told you I've been homeless before, I could do it again, but I wouldn't want…" I shake my head, trying not to think of her in the soup kitchen with me, "…you could've said no, especially when you learned illegal things were happening. Walked away. But that bookstore is all she has left of Finn. You saved it for her."

"Even if you were kept in the dark? That I didn't tell you everything?"

"I didn't tell you I got fired day of." I shrug weakly. "And I do thank you for trying to tell me, even if Nan didn't. She's the one who lied, not you. I'm mad at her for not telling me the truth. You…I told you to help, but things didn't go as planned. Not your fault she was being grifted."

His brows remain furrowed, staring at me, confounded. The familiar expression, less stern now, makes me smile softly. Leo shakes his head, running his hand through his hair.

"I'm not saying I hoped you'd be mad, but I honestly thought you would be angrier."

Grabbing the fork next to my plate, I stab the potatoes for a bite. "Because you didn't tell me right away?"

"That you'd think I was trying to buy or impress you. Control your life by doing this or that you may think you owe me."

"Like pulling a white knight?"

Leo exhales sharply, nodding as he comes around to sit beside me. He drags his plate toward him but pauses before eating. "You confuse me at times."

"Coming from the one who flew from Florida because I had a night terror. Pretty sure this entire dynamic is confusing." I gesture my forkful of eggs between us. His expression doesn't change, staring down at his plate. Leo still doesn't move as I take a few more bites. "Would it help if I explained *why* I'm not mad? Least with you?"

Leo comes out of what stupor he's in, glancing over and gestures for me to continue before finally eating his breakfast.

"The only reason I can think for being mad at you is pride," I start. "Bruised ego that you helped Nan, but that kind of pride sometimes gets you nowhere. It's what got me homeless in the first place. Been there, don't want to go back. If I *really* didn't want to live there, I can move. Not a wild concept. Unless you tell me I can't."

"Of course not."

"See? Not controlling, just really...*really* weird, awful circumstances. And I know *now* to take help when given. I don't mind you helping because I think back to the times when I should've, and it could've saved me a lot of pain."

Leo chews his food slowly, tensing a little at the mention of me being homeless. He really doesn't like that subject.

"And Nan and you are right, it's between you two. You didn't keep me completely in the dark, you did warn me weeks ago. I don't think you're gonna kick me or Nan out. But my threat of toilet papering your hotel will remain if you screw her over." He quirks a brow at me, and I give him a half smile. "Plus, you do show affection with physical stuff sometimes. Pretty sure, buying a building is up there."

"You show affection by being present," he says suddenly. I'm taken by surprise by the comment. "You don't do *things*; you take time and give your attention to people. Understanding them instead of judging, even with someone like me who uses…*stuff* or money."

I reach over, putting my hand on his knee. "Leo, I think you've been the most attentive person I've met. You care about those close to you, who you trust in. Sometimes, well, the things you do are seemingly outlandish or extravagant, but it's what you know. Unlike some I've met, I don't think you forgot what it's like to have nothing, even if brief." Leo's face relaxes, becoming gentle almost as he puts his hand over mine. "I can see you haven't forgotten every time I mention being homeless."

He inhales sharply, bringing his hand up to cradle my face as his thumb strokes my cheek. "I just want you safe. This is the only way I know how."

"I'm learning that." I turn my head, kissing his palm. "And I appreciate it, but let's both work on not putting Isaac in the middle anymore. We're gonna give the man worry lines soon."

He smirks. "Could make it be Jameson instead."

I pull away and point at him. "Careful, we bonded while you were gone. So, watch out or I may get those dirty details on you."

A flash of an odd emotion flits over his eyes, catching my attention, but it's gone quickly as he gets up for coffee. "If you do feel left out, I can just discuss with you on whether I should buy *Blue Java Café*."

"Let's hold off on any more building buying, because I literally told Isaac you would try," I grumble, hitting my head gently on the counter.

"I won't," he says as he sits down again, stopping me from hitting my head again. "I have standards. Bookstores are where I draw the line…for now."

He lets go of my head as I smirk at him. "Beginning to wonder if the whole losing my job thing must be something that has to happen to date the rich guy. Part of a screwed fate. And weirdly enough, *that* was the one thing you didn't get involved with." Cause I wouldn't let him.

Leo grimaces, putting his mug down. "Technically, I was due to—"

"Stupid jealousy," I mutter and *this* time I am a bit angry. I stab into some eggs and catch Leo looking at me with interest. "What?"

"Well, I do believe I've found something that makes you mad," he muses.

"Okay," I say, putting my fork down. "What *she* did was controlling, manipulative and bitchy because she didn't take in *anyone's* thoughts or feelings except her own." I flit my hand in the air with frustration. "It's people like *that* who use their privilege for stupid shit, screwing others over. Like the fucker who was swindling Nan. Their little worlds go around with no regard to anyone."

I also hate that Mabel is now stuck with Bailey.

I scowl at my mug, anger flickering across my skin and up my spine. People are suffering out there and Bailey's using people like freaking barbie dolls. Leo was trying to help an older woman keep her livelihood and home.

He chuckles under a scoff, trying to hide a smile. I narrow my eyes at him. "What?"

"One of the few times I've seen you angry, so please continue," he muses. "And it's not directed at me."

"Glad you're enjoying this." I roll my eyes at him. About to go back to my food, I pause. "You don't think it's ridiculous I'm complaining about a small job like that?"

"Job is a job. It was important to you and needed, which gives good reason to be angry. Being fired effects more than just you. I've reacted worse in situations about losing contracts that I needed. No matter how small."

"You?" I scoff. "Lose your shit?"

"It can happen," he says in a quiet tone.

"Leo, you may be stern and serious at times, but you have very good control over your emotions."

"You don't think I can get mad?"

"Oh, I know you can. I've seen glimpses, but there's a difference between being angry and losing one's shit. You out of control? Don't see it."

Leo gives me a faint half smile. "Well, I won't prove you wrong… or right."

We go back to having a quiet breakfast, and after a few minutes I grab his free hand without looking over at him. "Thank you for coming back."

He squeezes my hand. "No one can keep me away from you."

I peek over, giving him a small smile and he returns it. As we continue, we move into some small talk like the weather. Once we finish, I help him clean-up the dishes and find the dish soap gone, including other cleaning things as Leo puts dishes into the dishwater.

"Do you have a cleaning lady or something?" I ask, wiping down the counter.

"Yes, they come in weekly." He peers over his shoulder to me. "You don't think this place is pristine by magic, do you?"

I mean…maybe?

"You've just never mentioned them, and I haven't seen anyone here besides Isaac and Jameson. For some multi-millionaire, I've not seen many who work for you." The ones I have, keep their distance unless they're yelling about shoes.

I fold the towel, stepping back to let Leo reach over to grab something. My eyes go to his muscles, flexing beneath his shirt. There's a rising heat in my stomach as a tingling sensation ripples over my skin as he moves again, smirking at me with calm mirth. The little expression makes the heat worse, deepening into my core with needy arousal.

"I'm careful who I have around you," he responds finally.

"Afraid I'll make them start dancing in hallways or participate in sock skating races?" I ask with a wide smile, trying to ignore the want of grabbing and pushing him against the counter.

"Exactly that."

He turns, gently moving to kiss me. A moan grows in my throat, but I keep it from coming forward. My chest tightens, wanting him to hold me and bring me close. I want to feel his skin against mine, have him encase me with his body heat. Leo steps away, walking around me.

I gulp, "Leo?"

"Yes?" He pauses at the counter.

When his hazel eyes meet mine, suddenly shyness overwhelms me. Although there's a warmth in my lower stomach, striking and almost making me squirm as he looks at me, I can't say anything. Anxiety rears its ugly head, stopping me from asking to have that intimacy again.

What if I said the wrong thing? What if he doesn't want me? The last time we had sex wasn't perfect and the morning after was bizarre on most accounts. I mean we just got done discussing him buying the building I live in, doesn't seem like great foreplay.

"Autumn, what is it?" Leo breaks me from my runaway thoughts.

I wave my hand in the air lightly. "Never mind, I was confused about something."

"What about?" He walks toward me, and my heart thunders in my chest.

Son of a nutcracker. I think quickly, grasping for anything that doesn't include *hey, wanna have sex* or *fuck me on the counter?* My gaze flicks to the calendar, and…

"Therapy. I forgot I had it today."

"You do? What time?"

"Around 2 or 3," I mumble.

"Don't remember? That's odd for you." He quirks a brow.

"Been a long week." I narrow my eyes at him. "Some of us forget things, unlike perfect hotel CEOs." I walk past, pushing down the arousal in my gut. My skin tingles as I brush past him.

"I'm far from perfect, Autumn," he says quietly.

"You're perfect to me." I'm about to make it into his bedroom, when he grabs me from behind, pulling me against his chest. I gasp as he holds me, pressing his face into my neck and kissing it affectionately. The heat inside me flashes, and a moan wants to break free at his searing touch. I hold onto his arms, keeping myself still from rubbing against him.

He whispers into my ear, "And you're perfect to me, my dear Watson."

"Don't you have an empire to run?"

"Already you're trying to get rid of me. Is it because—"

"Just want to get ready for therapy. I've got to check in with Nan, too, and I think I have a lunch date—" I ramble, and Leo stops me with a kiss as he turns me around. The moan inside worsens, melting against him as my legs become unsteady.

Leo caresses the side of my face, pulling away. "I was teasing. You clearly had plans, and me coming back early or not, you should keep them. I just want to see you tonight. Pick you up for dinner."

I nod with a tight smile. He watches me a moment, flicking his eyes over my features before he releases me.

He's back early *for* me, and I want to spend more time with him, including sex. But I don't know how to ask. The night of the date, it felt easier with the music and dancing. It felt different than now when we just had breakfast. This territory I've no idea. The fear of saying the wrong thing or doing it wrong paralyzes me. Last thing I wanted was my anxiety to ruin it again, to lose all other chances. Maybe I'm a coward. For all that talk on communication and being honest, here I am keeping secrets and not speaking what I want.

Leo isn't the one keeping me in the dark.

I am.

Chapter 29

Old Habits Die Hard

The car pulls up to the curb, half a block from the women's center. I barely notice due to staring at Leo in confusion. "What? How was he found?"

He holds my hand firmly, stroking his thumb over my wrist. "The bounty hunters I hired found him, but what matters is that he's been prosecuted. My lawyers are very good at what they do. I promised you I'd have it handled, and he'd never hurt you again. He won't."

During the drive, Leo told me about my attacker from weeks ago had been caught. I'd briefly forgotten about him. He was sentenced to prison on other counts of assault, apart from me. I think Leo sued him for damage to his hotel property, too. I didn't have to be there to testify against him. Thank fuck. Last thing I wanted was a phone call from a detective I didn't want to hear from. Or be in a courtroom.

I shake my head, pressing my hand against my forehead. I'm still processing shit from this morning and the lack of sleep.

"I have *very* good lawyers, Autumn, he won't get out." He squeezes my hand lightly. "Mine have to be, and I wasn't going to let him near you again. I already saw what he did to you and could've done worse."

"I appreciate you handling it, thank you." Leo kisses my hand, lingering it near his lips. I smile, pulling my hand from his and point at his nose. "But don't think I'm some delicate flower. I can still pack a punch need be."

"Isaac and I are very aware." He grins faintly, but it falls when he flicks his gaze to Rudolf in the driver's seat. "About Isaac—"

"You still want me to have a bodyguard?" I finish, tilting my head. Leo gives me a guilty expression. Yeah, saw that coming a mile away.

I exhale sharply, looking out the window at the familiar block. A sense of relief hits me. The guy is off the streets, away from me, thanks to Leo…again. The influence this man has is astounding, but then I've never been in a position of power like him.

But I've been around those who have.

Anxiety flickers at the base of my spine, coiling deep from the past, but I drown it out.

Long gone. It's all long gone. And he's not them, not *him*. He's never acted like any of them, and even the small thought of those men, I can agree easily he never could be.

"Few rules," I say. "I get more space while with friends, he goes home when I reach my last subway stop, and he's gotta teach me how to make a proper cup of British tea." Leo raises his brows. "I can be negotiable about the subway stop."

Leo leans forward, kissing me and then speaks against them, "Deal."

I open the door to hop out. "See? Compromise and negotiation. Totally can do it."

"You really want that tea, don't you?"

Standing outside the car, I lean in and smile. "I want to know his secrets."

"Then take over the world?"

"Well, that's always the plan Pinky."

"I'll pick you up for dinner." Leo leans back in his seat, and then says with a very fake, thick British accent, "My dear Watson."

I laugh, closing the door and jog toward the entrance of the center as the rain drizzles. I step into the lobby, shaking myself from the light rain and head upstairs. Trix is about to walk out as I enter the reception area.

"Oh! Autumn! I'm so glad I caught you before I left." She hugs me, and I give her a tight squeeze. I notice the bright blue eyeliner sweeping across her eyelids, complimenting the scarf wrapped around her head. "Did your session move?"

"Dr. Wilson has been trying to add more time between them," I say, walking into the waiting area and Trix walks back in with me. "Unless I really fucked up my timing."

"You? Doubt it." She smiles, and then rubs my arm. "How are you? I know it's only been a few days since you lost your job, but that's gotta be jarring."

"I'm alright, and I'll talk to Dr. Wilson."

"Good. Are you and Nan gonna be okay?"

I bite my bottom lip and nod. Yeah, I don't want to have a long conversation with her on why. "We'll be fine. I'm gonna be working at the bookstore helping her, but I need to have another friend date with you and Leanne soon."

Trix smiles brightly, squeezing my arm a little. "Yes! I've missed you and her, work has been…well, yeah. We need to have lunch, though I can't today."

"Meetings?" I ask, stepping aside as someone with bright purple hair and piercings walks out of another office and scoots past.

"You've no idea. Maybe dinner tomorrow or the next day?" I nod and she glances at the clock. "I've gotta go, but I'll see you soon and we can talk. Love ya."

"Love ya."

Trix leaves, and I sit in the waiting room and lean back, holding myself close. It feels like the past two weeks have been a dream, and reality is just now knocking on my door. My mind spirals, anxiety spiking as I try to decipher what's real through the sudden changes. It's a lot. Like, *a lot*. All kinds of things that Dr. Wilson and others have warned me to be weary of like my job, relationship, where I live…

I put my hands in my face, grumbling.

Dr. Wilson's door opens, startling me as I look up at her. She walks out, putting folders on the counter and then gives me a reassuring smile. She gestures to the door, and I walk in to sit on the familiar couch.

The doc settles in across from me, and asks, "How are we doing?"

I tumble into the long couple of weeks from the issues with Bailey, losing my job, panic attacks, dates with Leo, and figuring things out with Nan at the bookstore. I even explained Leo's and my first-time having sex. I barely give much detail about our talk after, feels too private to share. She's quiet as I tell her about the night terror, and Leo coming back early. She jots a few things down on her pad, tilting her head as I finish.

"He sounds like someone who can help you feel secure," she comments.

She's no idea. Didn't tell her about the building buying.

"Yeah." I nod stiffly. My tone is tentative as I stare at the carpet.

"Do you not like where the relationship is going?"

I clear my throat. "It feels surreal. Like, I don't understand how I could fall so easily. To feel this stable and someone having my back, even when I keep expecting them not to. Can people find stability like this? Be this supportive? He's already certain this is long term, I thought you needed more time to know."

"It has been a few months. You're entering a stage where you'd be discussing goals within the relationship." She puts her notepad down. Oh, goodie. "Is it not a goal of yours?"

"I don't know, I mean, I like him… *a lot*, and appreciate everything he does, but this fast? Isn't this fast? It felt fast with Steve, what if it's the same—"

She holds up a hand and I clam up.

"Let me suggest a scenario. When you met your friends, were you quick to trust and love them?" I nod a little. "You mentioned the first time in the dorms with Leanne you knew she was going to be important to you. The same with Trix."

"Well, yeah."

"People fall in love at different speeds. There's no wrong in feeling comforted by someone. We do it with friendships, family, and other supporting relationships. Trusting someone doesn't have a time stamp to reach before you feel it. And we fall in love with platonic partners and friends at fast rates, yet we rarely think about it. But, romantic ones, we're more trepidatious because there's more at stake of showing our true selves. Being vulnerable. Any masks we have fall away."

"Isn't it dangerous to just give yourself over to someone so quickly?"

"Yes, but so is starting anything new. Although, your view may be skewed due to your past trauma, so it's understandable to be cautious. Not to mention your parents." I avert my gaze, staring at the coffee table. I tended to ignore my childhood memories, and I *really* hope she doesn't want to start prying today. That part of me no longer exists. "Giving ourselves over to someone is scary. Trusting someone is scary."

"I trusted Roger," I say suddenly.

"Different circumstances." Her voice is soft, and I look up. Her face is almost blank, watching me. "And he did help you. The best he could, especially in the situation you were in."

My jaw tenses as a prick ticks at the back of my neck.

"Sometimes I'm not so sure," I murmur softly.

She clears her throat, adjusting in her seat. "Let's stay on topic. We've agreed that's in your past, let's focus on your current relationship for it to blossom. It does sound like it is and that he's helping you."

I swallow hard, pushing away the ticking anxiety and memories. She's right. It is the past, completely dead to me. Including my family.

"It's okay then?" I ask, focusing on Leo instead. "That I could be falling in love?"

She laughs under her breath. "Yes. There's still work to be done, but it sounds like you've been improving. I won't chastise you for having feelings. Even with your worry, I can tell you want this to work. Otherwise, you wouldn't have brought it up at all."

I wring my hands, staring down at them. A question haunts me, following me like a plague. "What if I make the same mistake again, like Steve?"

Dr. Wilson goes still.

"End up…like I was?" I murmur.

"Autumn. You've been improving these last few years. You've taken long strides in healing; going out in public, maintaining better coping skills, and recognizing your growth. Panic attacks or not, you've conquered a bit. I know it can be hard not to, but you won't move forward if you allow your past to dictate who to trust."

"Thought it was supposed to give you insight."

"Yes, but if we only listen to mistakes, we'll only repeat them. Carry them with us."

"Right…baggage," I mutter.

"Which we all have, even if yours may seem heavier than others."

I sigh, leaning my head back to stare at the ceiling. "It's just that… it was hard without Leo, and I was so fucking relieved to see him. Maybe I'm getting too attached already, and fearful of falling into similar patterns. Like give up my freedom for that sense of comfortability."

"If I think you're in that same pattern, I'd tell you. Thus my job," she says, picking her notepad back up. "But in this relationship, you've held your ground, stated boundaries, and communicated your worries. Besides, missing someone we care about is normal. Feeling better that he's back, isn't wrong."

A small smile comes over my face as my mind flashes to this morning.

"I can just exist around him without effort," I whisper. "I can talk without a filter, blurt weird things out, just be me. It doesn't feel real at times even when he doesn't understand fully." I pause, blinking a few tears away that have worked up. "But he tries, in the only ways he knows how. He accepts me, doesn't balk or argue or hate learning about…from me."

"Sounds like you're building a friendship." She starts to write something down, then stops. "Have you told him about your past?"

"Just about that night."

"Nothing else?"

"No." I shake my head vigorously. "I'm hoping I never have to."

"As for right now, I'll agree." I meet her gaze hesitantly. "Although there could be pieces of it you *could* tell him." I shake my head again. "It's just a suggestion."

I hold myself close, not liking the topic being brought up at all. Most of the time we avoid it, surprisingly, at least over the past year the most. My stomach twists as I remember the smell of smoke and burnt drugs.

I trust Leo, and I'm falling in love with him, but I couldn't divulge my shadows to him. Not that part. Not to anyone. The idea of subjecting him to any of it, what I had *decided* to endure and stay within, it felt too much. There were secrets I even refused to tell Dr. Wilson about.

"You know, it was easy with Steve at first, too," I murmur, and Dr. Wilson watches me closely as I start to rock and recite two stanzas in my head. Fuck, how long has it been since I spoke about him with her?

"Autumn. Remain calm."

I inhale deeply and let the words out. "It was easy because I could lie or hide things. I mean, we were young and agreed to anything in the beginning, fearful of saying the wrong thing. Never fought. Always believed everything was fine. Both a little lost, helping the other, but...not like how Leo helps. Looking back, I realize how much Steve wouldn't let me just...*exist*. There had to be whys and explanations, because if he didn't understand it, he'd ignore me or berate me like I was dumb. Like I was wrong to be myself."

"Does Leo make you feel that way?"

"No." I laugh under my breath. "It's like he's fascinated *with* me, but not in a bad way. He wants to know, but he doesn't need to know. I feel the same with him."

"How so?"

"Everyone can sense how strong he is, powerful even," I say, wiping the stray tears away. "You can feel it when he walks into a room. He's particular, suave, thoughtful, intelligent…and it just surrounds him like this aura. When he looks at me, there's a version of myself I see in him, weirdly enough. We both bury things we don't want seen, protecting ourselves. Except, he rarely allows himself to smile, laugh, or be open because of it. I learn more about him each time he does."

She gives me a small smile. "Sounds like he's opening up more often when he's around you."

I shrug. "Maybe. It is amazing when he does. When he smiles, shows me something he enjoys, or teases me." My throat clears, and I notice the rain has stopped. "It's like watching a sunrise. I don't know what I'm going to get, but there's going to be light. And I don't want to miss a second of it."

"Maybe that's what he sees in you. Perhaps, you both finding a sunrise within each other."

I hum, nodding a little as I continue staring out the window. She folds a paper on her pad, catching my attention as she places it gently on her lap. "Let's not keep your entire past off the table just yet, let's focus on your communication and coping skills. So, those sunrises get stronger and more frequent."

"It's really okay to feel this strongly about someone then?"

"Love happens every day, and I don't think any form of it should be overlooked."

———

Puddles fill the sidewalk as I make it back outside. I look down the way that leads towards the subway entrance and the park. Glimpsing into the sky, it's mostly clear with some clouds. Not ready to go home and face Nan about her lying to me, I head for the park. I also need a walk after that session.

Three to four times is a charm, right?

There are fewer people out due to the storms, and I head across the street. My eyes flick over to a vendor, almost looking like someone of years ago.

Steve and I in the beginning hadn't been bad. Just young. But as his addictions became worse, so did he. I'd stayed in hopes of helping, getting him out, and believing I could change things. Except, I had no idea how far that rabbit hole went. The fact it took me almost being killed, battered into barely being human to reach my breaking point, doesn't give me much faith in myself. What does that say about me? It wasn't the abuse, homelessness, drugs, and alcohol… it'd been that torturous night. A part of me still blames myself for it. There was a pain that hasn't really healed. I'm not even certain that piece of myself could be healed. Or forgotten.

An exasperated sigh leaves me as I walk down a path, most of it empty of people. I run my hand through my hair, trying to let go of what haunts me, leaving it behind. A few joggers pass me as I come to an overcast of tree boughs, lined with benches.

Gradually, my skin begins to crawl as my hairs stand on end.

"Just Isaac." My pace doesn't change. The unease doesn't relent, traveling over my skin. "Come on, just walk in the park *for once* without panicking."

An alarm blares in my head, screaming that someone is coming. Watching.

I stop at a bench, sitting down to give myself a reason to look where I'd been. I don't want to alarm Isaac if my anxiety has decided to be a pain per usual. Peering down the way, I don't see him. My eyes rove over the area, not finding him anywhere. I lean, searching down the other paths.

No sight of him.

My heart begins to race. I gulp against my dry throat. Where's Isaac?

I know I told Leo for him to hang back, but he shouldn't be invisible.

I'm slammed with nerve wracking fear, trembling as I fall into a panic. What if they found me? What if they found Isaac, grabbing him? I brought him his demise by shadowing me. My eyes flash to the small crowds, searching for anyone out of the usual as they stroll.

Trying to be calm, I stand and reach into my pocket to pull out my phone. Fingers trembling, I start dialing, but stop when realization hits that if they've gotten Isaac...it's too late. If he's not there, I'm fucked. My stomach twists as I turn down a path, hairs rising as a chill runs down my spine. I've memorized the park in the past, and pieces of it start coming back.

They're following me.

Coming around a corner of a path, I sprint. My shoes splash through puddles as I run, racing like a bat out of hell. I clutch the phone, going through my head on who to call. Should I call *him*? Would he pick up?

Bolting around another turn, there's a shout behind me. It's familiar and I slow down, spinning as Isaac runs for me. Relief hits my body as I gasp, flinging my arms around him when he's close. He startles, putting an arm around my shoulder as I heave.

"Miss Autumn, what happened? Are you alright?"

"I'm fine...I'm fine," I whisper against his chest.

He's fine. He's okay.

I feel his head move, looking around before carefully moving us out of the middle of the path. We reach a bench, and he sits me down and pulls out his phone. My hand snaps out, grabbing his wrist. "Don't call Leo."

"You just ran through the park, I need to—"

"I had a panic attack. It happens. I didn't see you and..." *thought you were taken,* "...and I panicked."

He narrows his eyes. Isaac pries my hand off his wrist gently before putting his phone away. "Why would you panic that I was gone?"

I gulp, trying to decipher my thoughts. I can't tell him the truth. Fuck Dr. Wilson's suggestion. I don't want any of them near those of my past. They're too dangerous.

I shake my head, running my hand through my hair. "Old habits die hard."

Isaac barely relaxes, sitting next to me. "Are you sure it was nothing else?"

"Positive." I see nothing out of the ordinary down the path. The prick against my neck hasn't subsided completely, which only makes my stomach twist. My skin tightens, even if I feel safer next to Isaac. I force myself a smile at him, and he scrunches his face in uncertainty.

"I think it's time I go home. Even if I haven't threatened you with a knife yet," I try to joke.

"Miss Autumn, you'd tell me if something was truly wrong…correct?"

I swallow hard and nod. "Yeah. Same with Leo."

Isaac watches me a moment. He finally relents, standing with me. "Let's get you home then."

"Just in case of another panic attack, why don't you just walk beside me?"

"Of course."

Each step further away from where I'd run, the sensation of being hunted vanishes. The twist in my stomach though, doesn't leave until we're out of the park.

It's official, that place is my bad luck charm.

Chapter 30

Keep on Believin'

Journey's best hits fill my apartment as I clean. My depression of a singular night resulted with a mess in the kitchen, living area, and clothes strewn about my bedroom. Plus, wet towels in the hallway. Must've crawled there.

I focus on restacking my movies after Leo texted me about an hour before saying he'd be late. So, I've cleaned the best I could.

In only a Pink Floyd t-shirt, shorts, and socks from Leo, I sit cross-legged reconfiguring and stacking the DVDs as music plays. Rom-coms versus thrillers, action films by decade. Checking the time, I figure I have another fifteen minutes before I hear from him. A favorite song plays as I get up. Journey sings about the lonely and I smile, spinning in place on the old hardwood floor. Going to my bedroom, I demonstrate some epic 70s dance moves.

Okay, maybe not *totally* epic.

Grabbing a hairbrush, I use it as a microphone and sing as the chorus comes. I point at my wall, singing my heart out. My feet slide around the apartment as I dance to the song, and skate through my galley kitchen and then my living room space.

"—love's unfair!" I belt out, dancing around my couch. "Ask the lonely!" I start to spin in the same spot, dancing to the beat. The fourth or fifth time around, I notice Leo leaning on the doorframe.

I scream, tripping over my feet and fall over my couch. Movies scatter around me as I land on the rug. I groan as pain laces through my side.

Leo is instantly beside me. "I didn't mean to scare you."

He helps me sit up, and I wince at the faint throb across my side and butt. Shaking myself a little and the ache already subsiding, I glance at the mess of my collection. Every damn time. This is probably why people put them on shelves. Smarty-alecks. At this point, I should just leave them in their haphazard piles.

I look up to see Leo's worried expression. His brow is deeply furrowed, eyes intent on looking me over. My mind is transported back to when we first met. He's giving me the same expression, which borders more on uncertainty as I begin to giggle. He attempts to keep his composure, but after a minute he's smirking.

"Here I thought you were hurt." He runs his hand through my hair, placing it at the nape of my neck. "And I was going to offer a kiss to make it better."

My laughter fades, but my smile remains as he leans down to kiss me. A hum releases from my throat as I reach forward, wrapping my arms around him. He tastes divine and smells even better.

Leo deepens the kiss, skimming his tongue over my bottom lip and my own tangles with his. My body starts to feel hot as my stomach tightens with anticipation and want. I can practically feel the muscles down below clench, remembering the feel of him inside me.

He breaks the kiss, leaving my body wanting and a bit confused at the loss. I blink as he asks, "Just your everyday dance session then?"

"I *was* cleaning."

"You have an odd and, yet fun way of cleaning. Not at all surprising with you." He stands, stepping back to take his jacket off and folds it over the back of the couch. The heat across my skin heightens when he does, while I watch his back and neck muscles flex.

I'm staring. Hard.

I know I'm staring unabashedly, especially when he brings his attention back to me.

"I have a couple standing reservations—"

When his voice abruptly stops, I'm brought out of my haze. Blinking quickly, and swallowing hard, I mentally shake myself. He looks at me curiously and asks, "What is it?"

"Nothing." I get up and act like I'm brushing myself off. "Must be the cleaning fumes." I move past to the kitchen, busying myself with folding towels that I'd thrown to the side.

He's quiet behind me, and I keep my focus on the task. I'm unsure if my voice is revealing my tells. I peek over my shoulder, and now he's the one staring. Except his gaze only gives me butterflies as the arousal makes me feel flushed.

"You were saying about reservations? Should I wear bejeweled jeans then?" The playfulness in my voice isn't where I want it to be.

I'm shaking as I grip the towel. The coiling need to be touched, held, and have him pressing inside me worsens. I've never felt this strongly before for sex, and I'm unsure what to do. I mean, I do, but how the fuck do I get there? We're supposed to have dinner, so I should wait…right? Or do it before? Is that fine? What if I panic again and then we miss dinner all together?

Mentally, I'm spiraling, while my body is spiraling that Leo isn't touching me yet.

I try to get a grip on my thoughts, but just feel lost and unsure. What if he doesn't want to? Oh my…fuck, what if he doesn't want to, well, fuck?

Leo moves, making me go still as he brings me flush against his chest. The hardness of his body against mine. I swallow hard. One of his hands trails down my arm, causing me to drop the towel as he takes my hand. His breath floats over my skin as he whispers against my ear, "Tell me what you want."

My throat feels dry as a shiver runs down my spine. I'm blushing as I try to speak, "I…uh, Leo, don't we have…"

He brings my hand up, kissing the palm and then my wrist.

"You've told me to talk to you. To be honest. Do the same with me, dear Watson. Tell me what you want."

"I don't...I don't know how," I whisper.

"All you have to do is ask." Warm breath moves over my neck and my spine straightens. A whimper catches in the back of my throat, wanting to press my back further against his chest. He kisses the palm of my hand again, lingering with his lips against my skin. "I can tell you want me, but you need to tell me. I won't risk false signals. Never with you, my dear Watson."

I move my arm up, finding the short stubble along his jaw. The hold he has around my torso is firm, but gentle as he keeps me close. He lets go of my hand, running it down my side, while his other finds my hand against his face, stroking my wrist.

"What do you want?" He asks again.

Nerves flare, and I'm half tempted to push him away and run to the other side of the room. That part of me feels faint. The rest wants him. It wants this and more of the good feelings that come with being with him. Pleasure. Ecstasy.

I swallow harshly against its dryness and answer, "You."

"How do you want me?" Nervousness flits over me, not knowing if I can say it. I'm not even sure how I want him. My body tenses as my hand starts to fall from his face. He catches it, wrapping it around my upper body with his arm. I'm fully trapped by him.

Another warning flits over my brain, but Leo brings his head close to my ear and says tenderly, "Breathe, sweetheart. You're safe. Remember you can say red anytime."

His words make the worry vanish, and a sigh leaves me as I lean more into him. I feel his arms, hugging me like a safety net to catch me. I close my eyes, taking a few deep breaths as his thumb continues to stroke over my wrist.

"Sex," I rasp. "I want sex."

"As you wish, dear Watson."

Leo steps back, bringing me with him and I feel him bump against the other counter. An arm remains snaked around my waist, hugging me firmly as if he's keeping me grounded. His other starts to bring my arm up again, placing my hand at the back of his neck.

"Don't be afraid to tell me what you want. Just like check-ins. With or without prompting from me," he murmurs against my hair. "All of it tells me how to be with you…please you…pleasure you."

His words drift over my senses. I close my eyes, feeling his hand trail down my arm and caress my side. Lips are pressed against my neck, softly kissing me as he travels to behind my ear. A whimper comes out of me, almost missing the first check in.

"Green."

"Good girl." I shiver at the response, elation making me smile.

"Take your shirt off," he orders gently, giving me space to do so.

I slowly obey, breathing heavily as he unbuttons and removes his own. His undershirt is easily removed too, just before he pulls me back to him. The heat of my back meets his chest, and it stokes the fire within, skyrocketing for more. I sigh as he wraps an arm around my waist, holding me flush against him.

"Better than a wall?" He whispers.

Oh, fuck yes. "Uh-huh."

I tilt my head back, turning enough for him to kiss me and he does. I open for more, tasting him as his tongue meets mine. The moan I've wanted to let loose since this morning, almost bubbling up since then, releases with need. Leo breathes out, which makes me shudder against his hot breath. Leo lingers, continuing to kiss me as I hold onto the arm around me.

He takes my arms, raising them above my head to place around his neck. He becomes the barrier between me and the hard surface of the counter, becoming a haven as the last of my worried thoughts disappear. One of his hands move down, skimming over my skin around my breasts, down my stomach, and to my upper thigh. I gasp as his fingers move closer to my sex, causing him to break the kiss.

"Check in."

"Green." His fingers rove under the waistband of my shorts, traveling to the apex of my thighs. Odd emotions come up, unsure of the light touching sensations. A few muscles in my stomach and legs tighten, uncertainty coming back. Leo's other hand moves, going to massage one of my breasts, which makes the nerves lessen.

"Keep your arms where they are. I'll keep you upright but remain here." There's a sultry seduction in his tone. I nod in response just before his fingers brush over the folds of my sex.

My breath hitches as he starts to rub his fingers over me, lightly and with a gentle caress. My arms tighten around his neck, swallowing hard as he moves his fingers, and then his thumb circles my clit. The hand on my breast squeezes, while he inserts a finger inside me. I inhale sharply at the small intrusion, arousal rolling over me from his tender caress and him slowly penetrating me. I grip onto him as he works me leisurely, thrusting his finger at an agonizing pace.

He's going slow for me. I know he is. He's taking his time as he squeezes my breasts again, circling his thumb over the nipple and flicking it lightly. My breath catches as he flicks it. Below, his finger presses deeper inside.

"Leo," I whimper.

"Tell me, sweetheart."

"More." He adds a second finger and I gasp. His fingers move, scissoring and then hooking inside me. "Fuck...fast-faster, please."

He kisses my neck, complying with my request as his hand moves quicker. I moan, hanging my head forward as he pumps his fingers harder. Leo buries his face against my neck, bringing my head back up to lean against his shoulder. He continues to rub and circle my nipple as he clutches my breast. Sensations vibrate throughout my muscles from all different areas as he works me into a jumbled mess of blissful emotions. I'm not sure if I can take anymore until he says against my throat, "Good girl."

That damn honorific about undoes me.

My legs tremble as tension in my lower back grows, pulsating through me and it feels like my skin tightens at every touch. I feel hot, flushed as I pant and hold onto him with all my strength to keep from crumbling over. Leo abruptly lets my breast go, wrapping his arm around my waist to tightly press my sweaty back against his chest. I let out a whimpering moan as he presses my clit harder and thrusts his fingers up hitting the right spot.

It hits me like a tidal wave. The orgasm explodes up through my spine and down my legs as they shake. The rest of my body tightens, before trembling from the onslaught of pleasure, hanging onto Leo as my breath seems to stop for a moment. Everything releases as Leo starts to ease his movements, working me back down as he holds me against him.

"Are those towels clean?" I nod. He pulls his hand away, grabbing one of the stray towels on the counter. He wipes his hand off, and then between my thighs from where I apparently…

Well, that's new. I didn't just come…I *came.*

There's a wetness down my thighs, and I fidget due to it. Leo soothes me, kissing my neck as he cleans my inner thighs. Tossing the towel off to the side, he brings my arms back down, then turns me so I can lean forward against his chest.

Leo rubs my upper arms lightly, and over my shoulders. "Check in."

"Emerald," I murmur.

He chuckles under his breath. "Is that a special shade?"

"It's the 'only you could do that' shade."

"Really?" He asks, placing a hand under my chin to lift my gaze to his. Smoldering hazel eyes greet me. "Is that what you wanted?"

I stare at him. Then, finally, realize what he's asking.

Amazing as that was, it's not *him* inside me. My chin begins to quiver, and I try to keep it from doing so. Leo strokes his thumb under my bottom lip. The hand at my back brushes up my spine and back down again, helping me take a deep breath.

"Not…entirely," I whisper.

Leo glances down my body, and I almost want to fold up into nothing. He asks gently, "You did say sex, didn't you?"

"Yes."

He smiles, leaning down to kiss me and the anxiety disappears at the tender response. He says against my lips, "Good girl. Thank you for telling me."

My heart skips a beat and for some reason, I think I want to cry. I'm almost distracted by the emotion, until Leo lifts me up, wrapping my legs around his waist as he walks us out of the kitchen to my bedroom. Thank goodness I cleaned.

He sets me down on the bed and instructs, "Shorts off."

And we're back to Dom-y Leo.

I watch as he unbuckles his belt, which brings my attention to his erection. How did I not feel that earlier? Wait, how long has he been hard? Also, how is he making taking his pants off hot? That feels unfair.

"Autumn."

I look up at his smirking face and a giggle escapes me. I slap my hand over my mouth. Of all the times to laugh, doing it while he's taking his pants off is not the time! Son of a biscuit!

My arms involuntarily shake as Leo comes closer, and I almost flinch for the repercussion. He smiles affectionately at me, then leans down, removing my hand from my mouth and kisses my cheek. He steps back, gesturing at my shorts. I do as he says as he drops his briefs, but not before pulling a condom from his pants pocket. I raise a brow at him.

"Always ready for any situation," he says with a cocky smile.

"Should I ask how long it's been there?"

"No." He rolls it on, and I hold my breath, seeing the sight of his cock in front of me. My mind flashes back to last time and how I freaked out. I've come close tonight, and so far, Leo's been patient with me, helping me stay in the present. I push away the other thoughts, but every time I shove one away, another wants to come back.

I'm pulled to reality when Leo asks, "Check in?"

"Green," I automatically response, eyes meeting his. His smoldering green and golden gaze helps calm me as he moves toward the bed.

"Lay down on the bed, keep your eyes on me."

I do as he says, my breathing heavy as he approaches and grabs my hips. A small gasp comes out as he strokes my skin, and my hips move upward on their own. Leo has a concentrated expression as he tugs me toward him, positioning himself between my legs. A hand moves up to the apex of my thighs, slipping a finger inside me. I gasp as he strokes me a few times and then guides his cock to my entrance. He brushes his fingers one more time before thrusting forward.

A long moan is my response as he enters, filling me as I've wanted since this morning. Fuck, since that night on the phone with him, wanting him here doing this. My muscles tighten around him as he pushes forward, then pulls out and moves back inside me. Leo groans quietly as he goes a slow, steady pace. He doesn't go to the hilt yet, taking his time as he circles his thumbs over my hips.

"Leo." Suddenly, he thrusts until he's all the way in. I choke out a breath, clutching the sheets next to me. My legs already start to shake, hips involuntarily pushing up against his.

He doesn't move, staring down at me as he gazes over my body and to where we're joined. They flick back up to mine. "Check in."

"Green."

Leo takes one of my legs, pulling it up to hook over his shoulder. The new position makes my body tremble all to the way to my feet as he begins to steadily thrust. I grip the bedcovers, holding on as every drive forward feels like he's going deeper and deeper. His hips move fluidly at a constant pace before he grabs my other leg, placing it over his other shoulder.

My body tenses, unsure about this position and my hands move to find his on my thighs. Leo adjusts himself, then pulls out almost completely before slamming his cock back inside. The new position makes everything tighter, hitting inner walls and brushing up against other nerves. My entire sex pulses as I stifle a moan as he thrusts heavily.

Throwing my head back, I shake as the pleasure courses through me, and the heat ignites down my spine. I bite down onto my lip, trying not to make any loud noise. Leo leans forward, and I gasp as he deepens his cock inside me. He puts his hands on the bed beside me, groaning as his hips grind forward. My hands begin to shake, moving to place them over his.

"Don't be afraid to make noise," he says. I swallow hard, staring up at him as he places his forehead against mine. "You're safe. Focus on me."

He pulls out a bit, driving back forward which almost causes me to scream loudly, but all I can get out is a quiet one. I throw my head back and Leo kisses my neck, my arms reaching for him. He takes my legs off his shoulders, moving to press his chest against mine. Leo holds me close as my own arms wrap around him. I bury my face against his shoulder, gripping him tightly as the pleasure builds again.

I do as he says, focusing on him and the feelings he elicits inside me. The heat climbs, enveloping me and taking hold as the orgasm starts to come closer. Ecstasy skitters over my skin. The bottom of my spine tingles as the pressure builds. I heave for air as the orgasm rips through me and makes my entire body tense. Leo grunts into my shoulder, letting out a long groan as my body begins to untense, but then tenses again. I gasp loudly, muffled against his skin as I cling to him, struggling for breath.

As my muscles relax, I breathe heavily along with him as we come down from the blissful high. Leo repositions himself to not fully crush me, falling to the side as he keeps me connected with him. A smile forms on my face as I place my head against his chest, while he kisses my temple. Minutes go by as we lay there, and I begin to absent mindedly trace my fingers over the lines of his tattoos. I'm entranced by the artwork of roses and fire when realization dawns on me.

I whisper against his tattooed skin, "I didn't have a panic attack."

He kisses my head again. "I'm proud of you."

There's a lightness in my heart as I hear him say that. My fingers continue tracing his ink, moving to one of the skulls. "Did this mess up your plans?"

"Never," he says quickly. "If you're ever in the mood for sex, just tell me."

"I was just, well, scared of saying the wrong thing. And maybe, you wouldn't want to because..." my voice tails off, and Leo shifts under me, but I keep my sight on his chest, "…last time didn't go as planned. And what if it happened again?"

"Most times these things never go as planned," he says softly. "But we talked after, and I told you it was alright. I wasn't lying to you, Autumn. We'll keep going at whatever pace is comfortable for you."

"Seems unfair for you."

"Not at all, because I'll have you in whatever capacity you deem me worthy of."

I finally lean my head back, finding an adoring expression on his face as he strokes my hair back. "You really do have this habit of saying the sweetest things or smooth lines, you know?"

"So, I've been told by a curiously, wonderful woman of late."

"Oh, do I know her?"

Leo smirks, kissing me and then pulls out, getting up to discard the condom. He goes to clean up as I sit on the bed, bringing my legs in close, hugging them as he pulls his boxer briefs on. He gets back onto the bed, tugging me into his arms again.

"Although original plans have been changed, I still need to feed you," he says, threading his fingers through my hair.

I scowl. "Well, now I don't wanna leave. Besides, how am I supposed to walk normally after that?"

Leo chuckles, his chest vibrating. "You're gonna give me a big head if you keep talking like that."

"Oh, yeah, 'cause we can't have the hotel mogul getting *cocky*."

"A tragedy. How about I cook some dinner?"

I snort loudly, "Yeah, you're not gonna like what's in my fridge and cabinets."

"Am I going to need to teach you how to, at the very least, keep sufficient supplies that aren't frozen?" Not if he says it like that.

He looks down at me and I peek up at him with a small shrug. "Frozen pizza and hot pockets are a staple food. Same with frozen burritos."

"They are not."

"Right up there with cereal." Leo grunts, eyes narrowing at me for mentioning the retched stuff. "Fine, how about delivery? When was the last time you had subpar Moo Goo Gai Pan or Lo Mein?"

His expression falls and I start laughing. He sighs in defeat, and I grin wide, knowing I won this round. Leo attempts to be a bit stern, but his façade falls when he brings his mouth against mine and mumbles, "I choose where. I'll have it delivered."

"Okay, mister," I mumble back, then throw my arms around his neck and kiss him deeply.

A minute later, I hop off the bed and almost fall over from jumbly, numbish legs. Leo helps me stand and I scowl at him. He chuckles, getting up and grabbing his phone. I tug on sweatpants and a loose Lynyrd Skynyrd t-shirt. I walk out to the kitchen, snatching up the discarded clothing and used towel, tossing them into my hamper. I start some hot water for tea, while Leo comes out of the bedroom only in his underwear.

This is the first time he's been here late or may sleep over. Crap, I've got nothing for him to wear. Maybe, one of my old band shirts could fit him. Okay, I doubt even one of my towels could fit around his waist.

I go to open my mouth, but he opens the front door and glances over his shoulder. "I'll be right back." He walks out as I stare at the partially closed door. I'm in the same place when he comes back with a small black duffle bag in hand. I blink at him with wide eyes.

"Either you had that stashed in your car or you've got one hell of a service," I comment.

He stops. "I didn't want them coming up to your apartment, but the food will be delivered to the doorstep if that's okay."

"Yeah, sure, the back doorway is usually where the delivery guys come in."

He nods once, disappearing into my bedroom. I hum, looking back at the front door and shake off a weird feeling as Leo comes back out a few minutes later in lounge pants and a shirt. "Food should arrive in 30 minutes."

I open my cabinet, taking out the stashed scotch bottle and grab him a glass. His brows go up as I put it down in front of him. "Since you're willingly staying in my tiny apartment and having takeout, you can have this. Not Dewar, sorry."

"Are you sure?"

"Yeah. Probably not gonna drink it anytime soon. I'll stick with tea." I flick my hand in the air, checking the kettle. "You can even pick a movie for us to watch while we eat."

"*While* eating?" I turn to see his perplexed expression. I smile mischievously and nod. Has he never heard of TV dinners? Oh right, he abhors frozen food.

I point at the mess of movies, cocking my hip. "Go pick a movie, mister. Might be best you only choose from the stacks closest to the couch." He raises a brow. "Trust me, you're not ready."

He sighs, heading over and I snicker under my breath as he looks down at my collection. I finish making tea and pour him a drink. Frequently, I check on him as he sifts through the cases. I grin when he picks a classic film, well, I think it is and nod in approval. I hand over the drinks to him, putting in *Face/Off* and snuggle him on the couch. About fifteen minutes into the movie, I can tell Leo may be regretting his choice. Later there's a knock on the door, and Leo gets up to grab the food. I presume it was picked up by one of his personnel from what I see of their attire.

The suit is a giveaway

Leo ordered Chinese, and I'm surprised he ordered couple of my favorites as I bring out utensils. I'm cool with the container and fork, while he prefers a plate and chopsticks. Perfectly balanced.

I'm content eating my orange chicken next to Leo, who seems good with his rice and beef. It's late by the time I feel myself drifting off to sleep, leaning against his chest with container still in hand. I'm barely coherent as things are taken from my hands and carried to bed. A blanket covers me, tucking me in as the grogginess takes over. My body and brain are exhausted from the past few days, reaching for sleep.

Through the drowsy fog, I hear movement and a door opening and closing. There's a muffled sound, seemingly far away as I fall further into my pillow.

"Keep the perimeter secure," Leo's voice is soft. "Keep them there...*keep them there*." There's a creak and the door closes, footsteps in my living room. "Find me those names. Don't care. Don't leave a trace. *No* trace."

My body tenses at the strictness of his voice, but then I hear him come into the room and the bed dips with him carefully pulling me into his embrace. Too tired to care, I relax into his arms with a sigh.

Whatever I may have heard, it disappears from memory as I fall asleep.

Chapter 31

Devilish Tattoos

My eyes snap open, body tensing. A small ray of light comes in from my bedroom window. There's a tightness around my chest, almost making it hard to breathe as I sit up and rub my head. Beginning to groan, I stop when I find Leo laying on his stomach beside me, head turned away. He sleeps deeply, and I notice it's still pretty early. Taking a few steadying breaths, I'm able to calm and my heart doesn't pound in my ears.

I debate stepping out of bed to go start some early-bird coffee and a movie, when my gaze catches the sight of Leo's back. I've not seen the entirety of his back tattoos yet. He's shirtless with the blanket barely covering half his back.

Curiosity taking hold, I lean over and pull the blanket down a bit more to examine the, well…masterpiece.

Wings are tattooed across his back, almost taking up the entire expanse of it, folded down his sides. They're leathery like a bat's or like pictures I've seen of Wyverns. They're tattered with holes and rips like they've been through a storm and darkly colored. There's a sword pointing down between them directly on his spine. The hilt reminds me of a medieval sword, made of silver and bronze, but the blade itself is bathed in blue flames. Beyond the wings is a fiery landscape of smoke, ash, and jagged cliffs. As I pull back the blanket a bit more, I can see just above his tailbone the start of dark flames rising up with bones stacked like a wall. Skeletons and other creatures dance along the wall. The design takes up his entire back. My eyes flick to see a glimpse of the other tattoos that don't match this style, disappearing to his front.

I stare down at the artwork, mesmerized by the shapes and how realistic it appears. Slowly, I trace my finger down the edge of the sword, and then realize what the fiery landscape may be.

Hell. Leo has a hellish landscape tattooed on his back.

It's done like one of those Renaissance paintings: gruesome, detailed, and bold.

My fingers move to the wings, moving along the bone structure. Maybe a devil's or demon's. I flick my gaze to Leo's head, his dark hair swept over as he sleeps quietly. I continue to trace over the lines of the artwork, finding that even with the daunting theme, it's beautiful. I can't seem to take my eyes off of it.

Whatever had scared me out of sleep is long gone, and I find myself distracted with Leo's body art. What usually takes a movie or two, I've been able to find peace with only a few minutes.

Leo makes a small noise and I freeze just before he murmurs against the pillow, "You seem to have quite the fascination with my tattoos."

I snatch my hand back, looking at where his head is. "Sorry, I didn't mean to wake you."

"Don't stop." My head tilts as Leo moves to face me a little. "It felt good."

I scoot closer, pulling the blanket down more until I see the waistline of his pants. My fingers follow the flames, stroking his skin as I follow up his spine to the sword hilt. Leo hums, and I smile as I feel his muscles relax.

"How long did this piece take?"

"Several sessions. Quite a few hours each."

"Sure is a commitment," I say softly, moving my hand over one of the folded wings. "But it's really pretty."

"Pretty?" He adjusts, moving his hand to stroke my leg.

"Yeah. Unless, you'd prefer I say it's ruggedly awesome or something?"

"Describe it however you want, but I don't think I've ever had anyone call my tattoos that."

"Seem to do that a lot with you," I whisper, flattening my hand over his shoulder. Hidden within the ink I feel scars. Stroking my hand over the wing, I bring my head down and kiss where I feel one. Leo tenses a moment, relaxing as I place another soft kiss in the middle of his spine where the blue flames meet the hilt of the sword.

Moving my hand up to his shoulder blade, I lay my head in the middle of his back and feel the warmth of his skin against my cheek. My hand snakes around his waist holding onto him as I continuously trace over the ink.

"You really do have enough tattoos for the both of us," I say quietly, soothed by the rising of his torso.

"Do you want any?"

"Not sure," I answer.

"If you ever want any, I know an artist."

"Eh, we'll see. Right now, all I have are scars." My voice is soft, remembering the physical leftovers of my past across my abdomen and scattered across my body. One in particular sticks out, reminding me of what I still haven't told him yet.

I should. I shouldn't keep it secret, but I can't seem to open my mouth to tell him. The words don't bubble, instead plummeting into my stomach. Body tensing as I shut off the anxious thoughts, I decide not to tell him. We've only been dating a few months, and just started having sex, it's fine. I can wait and explain…yeah. It'll be fine.

"Autumn?"

His voice brings me out my thoughts, and I exhale before leaving a quick kiss on his back. "I'll start the coffee. You'll have to deal with no fancy equipment though."

Pulling the blanket over him, I get off the bed and head to the kitchen. My apartment is partially cleaned. The mess I would've expected from ordering in isn't there. The movies have been restacked, though not in order, but they don't cover my carpet. The counter is cleared and has been wiped down.

Huh. I'm not particularly a very messy person, but there's always something on my counters. No matter how hard I try those movies always end up escaping across my floor. Guess it's not just Leo's cleaning staff who keeps his apartment pristine.

I start making coffee, unsure why there's a small pressure against my chest. Coffee pot brewing, I run my hand through my hair and scratch my head a little.

"Are you alright?"

My body jolts, jumping as I turn around to see Leo on the other side of the counter. He cocks his head, careful eyes flicking over me as I clutch my chest.

Letting out a long breath, I response, "Yeah, just not a morning person honestly."

"You always seem to be at my apartment." I wrap my arms around myself and shrug. "Was it something I did or said?"

My gaze shifts up, finding his signature furrowed brows with worried eyes. Instantly, I feel guilt. I wave my hands in front of me. "No, no! You're fine. It's not you, it's me. Oh, crud muffins, *that* doesn't sound cliché at all."

I groan, holding my head. Great. Not having a fantastic morning and I'm making him believe it's *his* fault. He's been fucking wonderful, and not just because of, well, the fucking.

Leo's footsteps are quiet as he comes closer, grabbing my hand and removing it from my face. His other goes to my chin, tilting my head up.

"Talk to me, dear Watson. Was it something I said about you getting tattoos? You don't need—"

"No, no," I mumble, shaking my head and put my forehead against his chest. Leo puts his arms around me. "I woke up from a nightmare, I think, sometimes I just jolt awake. Makes things fuzzy. Little things can make me anxious."

He places a kiss on my head. "Do you need a movie?"

A half-hearted chuckle comes out of me. "I was going to, but then

I got distracted by devil wings."

His arms become stiff a moment, and he whispers, "Did the tattoo scare…what I mean is—"

"No." I lean my head back, looking up at him with confusion. There's still worry in his eyes, brow furrowed further with concern.

Did he really think the tattoos would scare me off? He did pause the first time he was fully naked, but so had I. He does have some intense images, but I wouldn't say they scare me. I've no doubt the tattoos are part of his lifestyle from being a biker. Most of the art is reminiscent of those I've seen bikers have with heavy lines, dark colors, and the 'stereotypical' designs of skulls, knives, and flames.

"Leo, I do think they're pretty. You've got some…descriptive images, but they're really well done and beautiful." I shrug, trying to give him a small smile. "You don't scare me one bit."

His expression remains stiff, deep in thought as he strokes a few strands of my hair back and then traces my jawline. When his palm is almost against my cheek, I lean into his touch, closing my eyes with a deep breath. The pressure within my chest vanishes.

We stand there silently as the coffee brews, bubbling as it comes close to finishing. Leo doesn't move, keeping still with long controlled breaths. I open my eyes to see his closed, still with a furrowed brow, but now with a deep frown.

I don't know what's wrong. The small traces of pain on his face worry me. I reach up, placing my own hand against his cheek and his eyes snap open. I get on my tip toes, carefully, to kiss him. Leo's breath hitches as my lips touch his. He grabs the back of my head, keeping me still as his tongue brushes with mine.

A spark flutters up and over my skin as I press further for more. Tingling from arousal, I wrap my other arm around his torso to bring him closer. Leo's arm tightens around my waist, lifting me up completely as he places me on the counter and steps between my legs. We continue kissing as my legs clamp around his waist and my skin feels flushed all over my body.

I've never been one for morning sex, but gah damn, did I suddenly want it.

I want that frown on his face to disappear. I want him as close to me as possible to make my own worries vanish. Whatever courage I have, it surges through me to continue. My hand goes to the hem of my shirt to peel it off.

Leo breaks the kiss as I maneuver, not so sexily, to take my shirt off and he places his hand at the back of my head, gripping me tenderly.

"Check in," he whispers.

"Green."

His other hand skims around my waist, then tracing a finger under my breast. My breath hitches, shivering at the light touch as I start to bite my bottom lip. My eyes flick down his front, seeing his pants already tenting. Well, that boosts my ego slightly.

"What would you like, dear Watson?"

"Sex," I say bluntly, and that frown is quickly replaced by a smirk. He tries not to laugh at my quick response, eyes lighting up. "See? I'm learning."

"Yes, you are, sweetheart."

Leo trails his hands down, coming to the waistline of my pants, tugging at them. I bring my hips up, and he slides them off, but keeps me sitting on the counter.

"You want to do it here?" I ask.

Leo rubs his hands up my thigh, slowly until he's mere inches away from my sex. One hand goes back to tracing the underside of my breasts, lightly caressing my skin.

"Do you want to move?" He asks.

"Uh, no it's just...the coffee is there, and I don't know when, I mean, what if—"

He quickly picks me up, causing my legs to move around his waist as he turns and sets me down on the other counter. I let out a soft yelp at the cold surface, hugging Leo close to me for his body heat. He kisses my neck, moving his hand back down toward the apex of my thighs as he continues to stroke my skin.

"Leo, what are you...oh, hello!" Leo's finger brushes through my sex, moving up over gently where my clit is, just before he inserts it slowly. My arms tighten around his neck, while his hand squeezes my breast and flicks a thumb over my nipple.

His hand slowly pumps in and out of me while his thumb circles, moving unhurriedly over my clit. My breathing becomes rapid at the languid movement, reminded of what he did last night, working me up in a gentle rhythm.

"Only pleasure from me, my dear Watson," he murmurs against my ear, hot breath falling over my skin which causes me to shiver. He adds another finger, beginning to hook and scissor them inside me, pressing inside as my muscles tighten. "Always. I swear."

My legs start to shake, trying to clench him harder as he continues to thrust his fingers, circling his thumb as he goes and pressing up. A whimper comes out of me, and I bury my head against his shoulder as I let the wave of bliss and ecstasy travel through my body.

I rasp, "I'm safe. I'm safe with you."

Leo pauses for only a moment, his hand stilling as I feel his body go tense. Almost like the moment didn't happen, he goes back to thrusting his fingers inside me and brings his other hand to the nape of my neck. He keeps me in place as he continues the slow onslaught, beginning to pick up speed as my breathing becomes more ragged and my legs tremble around his waist. His thumb pushes harder against my clit, moving upward and it's what breaks the damn. My entire body becomes rigid as I come, and I clutch Leo hard as I gasp for air against the onslaught, feeling my entire sex pulse. He continues moving his fingers, bringing me down from the high as I lean my head against his shoulder.

Leo pulls his hand away, wrapping his arm around me and picks me up again, taking me to the couch this time. He lays me down on the cushions, giving me a quick kiss.

"Stay here," he instructs against my lips. He leaves and I remain where I am, staring up at the ceiling.

See? Not that hard, Autumn. Start kissing the man, that seems to get the ball rolling. Noted for the future. I'm gonna need a journal for these notes I'm supposed to keep track of.

Leo comes back, pants off and with a condom ready to go. I smile up at him, and a small grin comes over his face as he leans down over me. "Good girl."

I beam at him as he strokes his hand down my thigh, bringing my leg up as he starts to position himself. "Check in."

"Green." My response is quick, reaching up to grab his shoulders. He chuckles at my enthusiasm, going easy as he enters me all the way. I swear my heart skips a beat while I try to catch my breath. I may become a morning sex person.

The fact I'm enjoying sex at all feels like a damn miracle.

Leo starts to thrust his hips, keeping one hand on my thigh, bending against his side while the other keeps him up by holding the couch. He brings his forehead against mine, breathing heavily. My hips push up on their own accord and he groans, driving himself deeply inside me.

I try to bury my face against his neck again, kissing him. Moans are tempted out of me as he continues to thrust, his pace becoming harder and harder. I tighten my leg, hooking it onto the small of his back, which allows his cock to sink deeper. Leo grunts, suddenly grabbing me and swings me up onto his lap as he sits down on the couch. My hands grab anything they can, which is the back of the couch as Leo clutches my hips and pulls me down onto his cock. There's sweat over his brow, and he breathes heavily, kissing my neck.

"Check in, sweetheart."

I almost giggle. Finding it endearing that even with him sweating, almost frantic to continue and on the brink of coming, is still checking in. "Green."

Without another word, he lifts my hips and brings me back down hard. He groans as I wiggle my hips, circling them. My own groan of satisfaction comes out as my muscles tighten around him. Leo lifts my hips, slamming them down a few more times before I feel myself come again, muscles spasming as I hug him tightly.

Leo lets out a grunt, groaning against my neck as his hips undulate against mine before stilling finally. His chest rises roughly as his arms move around my torso. I lay my head on his shoulder, getting my own breathing under control as I smile softly.

"Two in a row, no panic attacks," I murmur.

He hums, stroking my hair back before massaging my scalp. "Good girl."

I give a sigh of content, rubbing my face against his shoulder. Pride flits through me, knowing that not every time will be without a panic, but the last two times going well…feels eons better than years ago. Even months ago.

His hand strokes down my back, and after a few minutes as the sweat on my skin starts to cool, I shiver. Leo grabs one of the blankets from the back of my couch, pulling it around me and keeps me still on his lap. I giggle at the fact that he won't let go, tucking my arms against his chest.

"How long can you stay?" I ask quietly.

"I've got all morning with you." I hum, snuggling closer and he chuckles. "Although something tells me the same dilemma of last night will reoccur this morning."

I scrunch my brows, pulling back to look at him. "You better not mean the movie. Nick Cage is phenomenal."

"I'm talking about your pantry."

"Oh, we're fine there." I shrug, and he narrows his gaze. "I have cereal."

Leo groans. I start giggling at him. "I'm not entirely against cereal, but I'm certain the kind you have is what I'm against."

"Oh, definitely."

"Then how about we go out for breakfast?"

"Haven't even used my stove yet, and already don't like it, huh?"

"It's the lack in your pantry."

"Pretty sure I have frozen waffles, too," I tease.

He places a hand above my hip, squeezing playfully. "I'm also against your lack of nutrition, dear Watson."

"You know I survived fine before you." I cock my head at him. "And there's nothing wrong with frozen food *or* sugary cereal."

"Then answer me this. Would you prefer your store-bought waffles or my cooking?"

Ohhhh, he's playing DIRTY.

I scowl at him, and a small, smug smile starts to grow on his face. Conniving man. I lean my head back dramatically. "Fine, mister. You win this time."

Leo tugs at my chin, and I bring my head down for him to kiss me. I smile against his lips. I'm glad he's no longer frowning and even my own anxiety is gone. I break away and look up at the time. Guess it's not that late to go over to the hotel for breakfast. It's not like I have a job I *absolutely* have to be at, I'm not even sure if Nan wanted me to work a full day today.

I think I hear creaking outside the door and my eyes widen. Oh, no.

Leo tilts his head at me. "What's wrong?"

"I think—"

There's a knock . "Dear, are you awake? I thought I heard something up here."

Oh, no, it's an 'old-biddie' muffin morning. I agreed that Nan and I would talk this morning about the whole lying thing.

Leo flicks his gaze to the door, not at all perturbed that there's only a door between Nan and us sitting on my couch naked. With him *still* inside me.

"If we stay completely quiet, she'll come back in ten minutes," I whisper against his ear. Leo starts to smile, looking smug as he pulls the blanket up more. I will smother him with a pillow if he makes a noise.

The door handle moves again, and I hear the lock beginning to turn.

"Nan, no—!"

Door opening, I press myself against Leo who doesn't look concerned about the situation at hand. Nan freezes with a plate of muffins in one hand and her other on the doorknob. She blinks rapidly in surprise.

Never have I ever felt like a caught teenager then this exact moment. I'm a grown woman in my own apartment, on my own couch, sitting naked on my boyfriend's lap. Who hasn't pulled out yet. My therapist is gonna be *thrilled*.

Leo looks over at Nan, keeping his arms around me. He smiles nonchalantly like he's wearing jeans and watching *The View*. "Good morning, Nancy."

Quickly, she schools her expression and clears her throat.

"Well, I didn't know you had guests over, dear," she says in a calm tone, then flashes her gaze to the blanket covering me. And now *she* looks unbothered by the situation. "Are you staying for breakfast?"

"Depends what it is," Leo answers. "We were just discussing it."

They are not doing this right now.

"Muffins. Raisin and blueberry ones." Yup they are. Do neither of them know shame? Of course not. They bought a building under your nose, Autumn!

"Sounds far better than sugary cereal," Leo says, keeping the blanket in place. "If you could give us a few minutes to get dressed."

"I'll just set these over here." She walks into my apartment, setting the muffins down on the counter and goes back to the doorway. "I'll be back with some jam and butter, too. You have fifteen minutes. Behave yourselves."

Nan walks out, giggling under her breath as she closes the door. My gaze goes back over to the counter where the muffins were placed, and I immediately start laughing. Leo grunts, getting me off him as I fall onto the couch, holding my sides. Laughter takes over the embarrassment, realizing where she put the plate.

"Oh, *now*, it's funny?"

"I…she…" I try catching my breath, finally getting the words out, "…she put the muffins where you fingered my muffin."

I almost fall off the couch laughing from the ridiculousness of it. Leo soon joins me with his own, throwing his head back. Giggles overwhelm me as I look over in teary eyes; his smile is the largest I've seen since riding the bike. I can't help but feel absolute joy being part of the reason why.

Chapter 32

Cheers to Friendships

It's a warm autumn day. The umbrella over our table shades us from the shining sun, peeking through clusters of clouds. It's a nice change from the on and off rain for the past week. It's been almost two since Nan walked in on Leo and me.

I took my extra key back from her.

Since then, Leo and I've had sex, but he usually initiates. The few times I've tried since that morning, I chicken out, get distracted, or worry if it's the wrong time. Leo has learned more of my tells, leading me toward his bedroom or mine. Thankfully no major panic attacks, except calling yellow a few times, such as last night when we discovered floors are apparently a trigger, too. Leo said it was probably just hard surfaces against my back. So, of course, I cried for thirty minutes out of shame. Leo didn't like that, so he made dinner and we watched *Gone in 60 Seconds* to help me feel better. It worked. Mainly from shock, cause *that's* the Nick Cage movie he likes.

I'm brought out of my thoughts from the night before when Leanne clinks her water against mine. She comments, "Bookstore life is made for you."

"Sturdier schedule, and a wee bit better than making coffee for rude customers." I grab the cappuccino I ordered. "Honestly nice to just drink it."

"And no bitchy coworkers," Leanne mumbles. I give her a look, and she raises her brows at me. Yeah, that's a large plus.

"Unless Nan has a bad day, but I think she'd still give you cookies," Trix comments, leaning back in her seat with a smile.

Yeah, but Nan hasn't fully left my partial shit list for lying.

"I'm surprised you decided to have lunch with us, figured you'd be knee-deep in a new book," Leanne says.

"In between series at the moment, but enough about me, what about you two? I've barely gotten any life updates. Thought ya'll only get this busy closer to the holidays before the new year."

"Or it's because you're busy with your hot boyfriend," Trix teases, wiggling her brows.

"Should've known you'd leave us for someone as handsome and rich as him," Leanne adds.

I'm sure they're joking, and not actually jealous, but unease trickles down my spine. My face falls. Leanne quickly notices, taking my hand and smiles warmly. "We're kidding, hun. We're happy for you, really, it's just we finally get to tease you a little about it. Right, Trix?"

"Of course! Keep the heat off my back," Trix laughs half-heartedly. "Besides, not much to joke with when you found a guy who listens and respects you. Like does he have a sister?"

Leanne and I share a look. I ask, "What happened to the girl you were seeing?"

"Yeah, Jackie or something." I point at Leanne for saying the correct name.

Trix sighs, swirling her glass and shrugs. "Didn't work out…in my favor."

"Well, that sounds ominous," Leanne notes.

"What happened?"

"Let's just say some people aren't that informed of certain histories." I chance a peek at Leanne, who shrugs that she has no idea.

"Definitely ominous now," I mention.

Trix scoffs, putting her glass down. "She kept asking about what plantation parties were and wanting to know if they still existed." Oh, shit. "And then kept talking about wanting to see that new film *Django Unchained* when it comes out in December. Little *too* heavily."

Leanne snorts in disappointment, shaking her head.

"She wouldn't listen to me on why it made me uncomfortable, so I ended it."

"Sorry," I tell her.

She waves a hand in the air. "Annoying, but unfortunately not the first time. Maybe I should try dating older women, unless Leo has a brother, then I may rethink my options."

I hide a cough behind my cappuccino as Leanne chimes in, "Both is always good."

"Gives options," I add.

"Says the bi-woman and straight one sitting across from me," Trix laughs at us.

Leanne puts her arm around me, pulling me in close as she ruffles my newly trimmed hair, and I giggle at her. It needed to be cut a little.

"We also know how *terrible* women can be, since we are a part of them," Leanne jokes.

"Especially during PSL season." I grimace and we all laugh. "*That* part I don't miss working."

Trix waves her hand in the air for the waiter, then asks them, "Can we have a cheesecake with three forks?"

"We're sharing?" Leanne asks.

"Cutting down on sugar intake," Trix says as the waiter leaves. "Just like my dating life."

"Oh, don't give up yet," I say.

"Yeah, look at her." Leanne gestures toward me. "Wasn't looking and he just waltzed right into the coffee shop. Sometimes fate just has to intervene. Give it a moment."

I smile to myself over the waltz comment. I should get him to sneak out to the ballrooms again.

"Well, maybe my fate will bring the cheesecake," Trix says, grabbing her drink. "In the meantime, I'm just gonna focus on work. The classic excuse."

"Ah, yes can't allow that to go out of style," I smirk. She grins back.

"How are those new propositions coming?" Leanne asks Trix, while I sip my coffee.

"First stage was accepted. Proposals for the scholarships anyways. Columbia is more willing, but NYU I may have to push more…or just plain convince. It's a long shot, but I'm hoping they take the idea for the new centers. I just wish they wouldn't give me so much red tape to cut through."

"They giving any reason?" I ask.

Trix makes air quotes. *"Finding space."*

"Ugh, *that* response," Leanne groans.

"Why is that universities can never find space for that, like student learning centers? Yet always have new buildings for sports or their business majors?" I ask.

"Do you really want me to say it?" Leanne mumbles over her glass, and we both sigh. Right, the money makers.

"Wait, what about collaborating with the library? Could they help?" I suggest.

Trix shakes her head. "They already have rooms and spaces for the LGBQTIA+ community. Not really in their realm to focus on the impoverished or domestic violence."

"Medical center?"

"They have a women's health center, apparently that's good enough," Trix grumbles, taking a long drink. "Except it's not just women who get placed in those dangerous situations."

I purse my lips, trying to think of ideas to help. Trix has spent years trying to create temporary living spaces for those leaving abusive homes or relationships while in college, especially during winter and summer break. Somewhere to have security and to focus on education. Boosting funding for scholarships or helping students pay for school was usually the compromise she got. Helpful, but not if you're unsure if you'll live to be in class the next semester.

"You need a big name to put their name on it," I murmur. "Publicity, so it looks like they're doing a good deed. Isn't that how those sports centers go up?"

"Basically," Trix sighs. "It's frustrating, because board members think just having the ability to take domestic calls or having trained medical staff will do it all, but there are still other issues. It's the aftermath where things can go sideways. An *actual* space for those affected, allowing them to get their education in peace. Not worrying about where to go if they can't afford a dorm room. Those first few weeks getting people out and providing independence are crucial. Such as—"

Trix stops, eyes landing on me. She reaches across the table, giving an apologetic look. "Hun, I'm sorry, I shouldn't have to explain any of this to you."

"It's fine, Trix." I squeeze her hand, smiling a little. "I'm grateful you care so much, and willing to put a lot into helping others."

"Tell me if you want me to stop."

I shake my head at her. "Go on and vent. I'm fine. I get it, how annoying it can be…I remember. So, go on."

She gives me a reassuring squeeze, letting go as the cheesecake comes around. We start to dig in as Trix explains more of the issues she's dealing with at work. We're almost finished with dessert as Leanne talks about work next, and the upcoming challenges for the semester.

I can't help smiling at them, proud of how far both have come. Leanne never thought she'd get this far into education, but it makes me happy to see her doing something she loves. And Trix, well, she was made for helping others. Over the past three years a lot has changed, but mostly for the better.

"We should go out!" Trix suddenly exclaims.

And some things never truly change.

"Where?" Leanne asks.

"There are some new clubs I've heard about. We can go and have a girls' night."

"Would be nice before I start going to bed before ten. I swear, I'm ready for the nursing home some nights." Leanne takes the last bite of cheesecake.

"Can we get bunkbeds?" I giggle.

"Long as I get bottom bunk."

"Fine, but I'm getting a slide."

We laugh together. Trix rolls her eyes at us. "Come on, just a small girls' night. We haven't tried in forever."

"Sure, but tonight is my only full free night without an early morning. Otherwise, wait a month," Leanne responds.

"Then tonight. It's only like two, plenty time to get ready."

"Are you sure?" I ask.

"It's a weekday. It'll be less busy. And you've been doing great lately in public." Trix grabs my hand, smiling large. "We won't be out until like three, promise. We're not that young anymore. Just some drinks and dancing like we've got midterms in two weeks."

"Good, 'cause I value my sleep." Leanne points at Trix.

"We know, grandma," I tease. Leanne winks at me.

Even though I'm joking with them, anxiety twists in my stomach. I ignore it, not wanting to submit to the damn emotion. Crowds spike my panic attacks at times, and clubs tend to have those. They ignite memories I wanted to long forget; nights I want erased. I didn't want to give up a good time with my friends because the past haunts me. Besides, Trix is right. I've been able to handle panic attacks easier, even with a bump in the road a time or two.

I can do this.

After the past month, I deserve to have a night out with my best friends.

"Okay, but I'm wearing jeans and no heels," I finally answer. Leanne gasps as Trix lifts her hands in victory. "Alright, not *that* astonishing I'm agreeing."

"Kind of, but are you sure?" Leanne asks.

"Can't stay cooped up forever, right?"

Trix pulls out her phone, going through a few clubs for us to try, and we decide on one that a couple of her friends have recommended. We set a game plan, deciding to all meet at Leanne's to gather before our night out. Once we pay our bill, we go our separate ways.

I head down the street, texting Isaac about the plans for tonight. May be a good idea not to give him a panic when he realizes I'm not staying home tonight. I roll my eyes at his response about needing to tell Leo. Not at all surprised, I give him the go ahead as I head down into the subway. Once on the train, I stay off to the side and pull out a stashed book from my messenger bag. Skimming through the slow burn romance, I chuckle at the characters who continue to fight through their sexual frustration. The train stops, and I get off as my phone starts to buzz.

Quickly flashing a look at the screen, I grin and answer, "That was faster than I thought you'd be."

"I was in a meeting," Leo responds.

"Oh, well that explains the five-minute wait," I tease, heading back up to the street. "Or Isaac isn't as quick as he says he is."

"Autumn, you know I'm not going to tell you what to do." I snort loudly. "Meaning, I try not to impose while suggesting my opinion, including reigning in my want for control and sometimes obedience. Others are not privy to such restraint, only you. Better?"

"Fancy talking today, huh, stud?" He snorts next. "And least you admit it, took weeks, but here we are." I giggle, leaning my head back to feel the sunshine.

"I just want you to be safe. You don't respond well with crowds."

"Don't forget the grass."

"I was refraining from mentioning it."

"Leo, don't worry, I'll be careful. Trust me. My friends are always responsible, even when having fun."

"Why haven't I met them yet?" My steps falter on the sidewalk, straightening myself. Didn't see that one coming.

"I thought you wouldn't want, well, I thought maybe you wouldn't be interested. Since I know you don't spend time with, well, people unless its work, and I didn't want to make you…uncomfortable."

"Dear Watson, if they're important to you, then of course I'd want to meet them. With or without my need for solitude, which you've noted very early in our relationship. I'm aware I'm a loner most days, even with my own small group of friends. It's my decision in not having many friendships, but that doesn't mean I won't learn of yours."

"Does that mean I get to meet yours soon?"

"You've already met a few."

"So, do all your friends work for you?"

Leo clears his throat over the line. "My world is a bit different, seemingly strange to most outside of it. But yes, all those I consider friends do work for me." Sure, not at all strange.

I hum, remembering how Isaac and Jameson talked about coming to New York with him. Apart from what they told me, I don't know much about how loyal bikers are to each other, but I'm guessing a lot. They did come across the country with him. And Jameson *technically* doesn't work for Leo.

Okay, it's strange.

"Does that mean I get to have tea with Rudy? Cause seeing him holding a teacup would make my week."

"Who's Rudy?"

"Rudolf. Your driver for anything and everything apparently."

"You call him Rudy?"

"He said I could."

"When?"

I rub the back of my head, unsure why it matters. "The first night you made carbonara," I say quietly.

"Ah," Leo hums, seemingly fine with that answer. "We'll set up a time for your friends, not *Rudy*. Perhaps dinner in the next week or so."

I smile, feeling a joyful feeling spread through my chest. "I'd like that."

"Most of my work is done for the day, I could see you—"

"No way, mister," I laugh coming around a corner. "I've gotta get ready, which means taking forever at Leanne's. I'll keep Isaac updated, and you'll get a 'fun hangover' girlfriend call in the morning."

"Are you saying I may not see you tomorrow either?" He clearly doesn't understand what happens the day *after* a fun night. Stay in, watch bad tv, and eat Cheetos.

"It'll make it better when I do see you? Right?"

There's a sudden muffled sound as Leo covers the phone's speaker, voices sounding distant with closing doors. Although I can't tell what he's saying, I can hear his aggravated tone. I grin, knowing full well his work is definitely not done. How he finds time with me while managing everything he does, I've no idea.

"Apologies, apparently I'm not done." His tone is rough and agitated. Well, shucks, now I wanted to see him to just give him a hug.

"Even without me, you better stop working long enough to relax a bit," I say as I stop outside the bookstore's door.

"I only relax when you're around." The quiet, melancholy of his voice makes my heart clench. For a moment, I think about cancelling my plans. Before I can second guess tonight, Leo says, "Call me if you need anything. Absolutely *anything*. Have fun...my dear Watson."

A set of words grow in my chest, wanting to tell him suddenly. If only to finally admit it or to help ease the concern in his voice. Except, I can't. The first time saying it shouldn't be over the phone. "Have a good night, Leo. Bye."

I hang up, staring down at the phone in my hand. A harsh swallow goes down my throat, realizing those words have only flourished in my heart. Next time I see him I will.

Against all odds, I'll tell Leo I love him.

Leanne and I lean on each other as Trix pays the taxi driver. She then leads us toward the bar she's been talking about for most of our taxi ride. Neon signs flash and there are other blinking lights in tandem with the rest of the loud noise of the never-sleeping city. It's early, barely being 9pm. We pass a few women wearing tight clubwear, high heels, and jingling jewelry. Most seem to be closer to our ages, all of us going out before the college students who will start descending later.

I'm wearing jeans, flats, and a long-sleeved shirt with a loose vest. Leanne is wearing shorts, a halter top, and booties, all with sparkles. Trix wears a dress that flares out above her knees, wearing a dark scarf bejeweled with green gems. We finally get to the bar, and I hook my arm with Leanne's just before flashing our IDs to the bouncer.

He smiles, nodding, and gestures for us to go in.

My thoughts trail away as we enter a room filled with a strong bass, pulsing lights, and the noise of people getting drinks. The place isn't packed. You can see the floor and there's tables and spots open at the bar. Why did we never come early before?

Trix takes my hand, guiding us to the bar. They get cocktails as I stick with water, while Leanne finds a great spot to sit. The club starts playing songs that were popular in our college years. I'm not sure if they're still popular or the DJ is calling us out on age. Leanne clinks her glass against ours, "Here's to a great girls' night out!"

We laugh as we begin to head out to the dancefloor. Other song favorites fill the place such as *Pon de Replay, One, Two Step,* and *Hollaback Girl*. People scream sing with the music as lights stream over us. The busier hours of the club about to commence as more people enter.

There's a ticking at the back of my neck, and I frequently flash my gaze to the entrance or back exit. Each time, there's nothing suspicious. I'm sure that Isaac is nearby, or another bodyguard. I concentrate on Leanne's or Trix's smiling face every time I feel overwhelmed or worry nags at me.

Just a normal club. Everything's fine.

We continue dancing, taking small breaks to quickly bounce from one table to the next, before they're all gone. I'm more relaxed, holding onto the cheerful high as we sing our lungs out and dance with each other. I twirl with Leanne, and then Trix. Leanne calls over the music about getting a drink, and Trix nods in agreement.

"I'll head to the bathroom then," I tell them. They can replenish on liquid, I needed to let some out.

"Want company?" Leanne asks against my ear.

I waver her off. "Get your refill! Before the kids come in!"

We glance at the door as much younger people enter and she gives me a playful distressed look. I giggle at her, heading for the bathrooms.

There's a short hallway that splits off, one veering toward the left for the bathrooms, while the other to an exit and other doors. I almost stumble into a group of girls who giggle loudly as I pass them and make it to the short line.

I lean a shoulder against the wall, waiting for the bathroom line to move and pull out my phone. Checking messages, there's only one.

Have a good time, dear Watson.

I smile at the simple text, half-tempted to call him. There's laughing again as more girls leave the bathroom. Yeah, a bit too loud for a phone call, I'd get drowned out. I put my phone away, sighing when it's my turn. Getting relief for my bladder, I wash my hands, and ease my way past the next group of girls coming in.

On the way out, I have to press myself against the wall for *another* group of girls to come past. Really am the odd one out. Maybe I should've brought Leanne with me. I chuckle to myself, when suddenly there's a tickling sensation along my spine. Warning of danger tugs when a breeze of cool air of the outside brushes over me. With it, comes the scent of smoke.

My head becomes encased in fog as I smell the familiar cigarettes and cheap gin. Time feels like it slows, completely drowning out the voices of the women leaving the bathroom with their rowdy banter. My breath slows, hearing only the deeper voices down the other hall as I struggle to breathe. Flash of other nightclubs. Dark hallways.

No. No…

Men speak behind me with voices that bounce off the walls in contrast of the club music. There's a tightening around my chest, lungs burning as recognition sets in with a punch to my gut. Another speaks, while one laughs.

Elm Jed

I know that laughter.

Slowly, I turn toward the voices, hoping to the very depths of hell that I'm not this unlucky. Not after years of staying hidden. Not after so much I've put to move forward and survive. After everything I endured, please no. I hope, fucking praying, to whatever deities above or below that my anxiety is fucking with me.

The fear becomes lead in my stomach as my gaze comes upon them in the dim lighting. Others stand with them, holding up cash as they exchange it for a few small baggies. Their faces forever etched into my brain, driving horror through my bones as realization sinks in. In this small hallway, illuminated by cheap lights, stand three of the men who brutally raped me.

Chapter 33

RED

I can't breathe.

I can't *fucking* breathe.

Seven men are gathered at the back with a couple of girls, all huddled over packets with pills and white dust. Cigarettes hang from some of their mouths, and the smell of that damn brand hits me like a wrecking ball. I can't tear my eyes away as they talk.

One notices me, looking me up and down before licking his lips. Vomit claws its way up my throat from the way he looks me over. A scream wants to be let out, knowing that kind of predatory look. I've felt it before…from *him*.

Another turns. He follows his buddy's gaze ,and I can taste what I had for supper in my mouth. I remember those eyes. Sharp jaw, dark stubble, and almost black eyes. His gaze skims me over like the other, smiling as he curls his lip with a sickening smile. My stomach drops and I gulp hard, trying my damndest not to puke all over the floor. He begins to step toward me, and flight finally kicks in. *Run.*

I stumble back, turning away as I clutch the wall as I head for the club. I hear laughter behind me, and someone comments on me being drunk.

Finding me later.

Throat tightening, I choke on my breath as I struggle to breathe. I stagger forward, squinting at the lights that are now too bright as the music tries to drown out the shrieking, roaring in my head. Time slows as if I'm moving through molasses to get out.

I'm shaking, uncontrollably. Aiming for the bar, I search for Leanne and Trix. Find them.

Get out.

GET OUT.

After what seems like forever, I find them at the end of the bar. Flashbacks slam into me, making my head swim and stomach twist. Pain laces over my sides and down my legs, remembering that night as I launch my hand forward to grab for Leanne's hand. She quickly catches me as I try to steady myself, but almost spill her drink as she grasps my arm.

"Hun, what is it?" She takes my shoulder, trying to get me to look at her. When I do, her eyes widen. "What happened?"

"Babe, what happened?" Trix asks, soon beside me, too.

"Out," I rasp. "Out *now*."

Without another word, they hull me after them out of the club and onto the street. Hoping the fresh air will help, it doesn't, not enough as I start to hyperventilate. I gasp for breath. My heart pounds loudly in my ears. Horrible memories slam into me, and I bend over, clutching my stomach as I stumble. They help me move to a brightly lit alley not far from the bar.

The roar in my head overpowers their voices. It drowns out the city noise as I hear the screams again. The pain. Laughter. Horrors that had felt never ending. All of it comes rushing back like I'm in that hospital bed again. Trapped. Left for nothing.

Leanne tries to help me stand, but I end up hitting the brick wall with my back. The contact snaps the last of my restraint as I feel the cold, hard surface.

I let out a strangled scream, crumbling to the ground, "No!"

My shoes hit water, soaking them as I curl into myself, gripping my knees tight as I shut my eyes tightly. My muscles shake, gasping for air as my senses become fuzzy.

"Autumn, hun, listen to my voice." Trix speaks in a soft tone beside me. "What happened? This isn't normal for you."

"I-I…can't…"

"Breathe in through your nose, you're okay," she tries to soothe me.

"Miss Autumn!" Through the wailing noise in my head, I hear Isaac's voice and the slamming of boots. "Miss Autumn!"

"Hey! Who are you?" Leanne asks. "Don't even think of coming—"

"I'm employed by Mr. Luciano and have been tasked for weeks to keep eyes on her," Isaac explains. "This is my ID, and here's our text message exchange we had earlier today. She told me where she'd be, per an agreement for my job."

Leanne argues, "Wait, that happened weeks ago. Why are you—?"

"Bodyguard," I rasp between struggling breaths. My lungs hurt as my head pounds, tears streaming down my cheeks. It hurts…everything hurts.

"You actually know him?" Trix asks. I nod my head.

"That's her phone number, and her texts," Leanne says. "Fine, you're clear."

"*What* happened?"

"Okay, before you go accusing with that tone, *bodyguard*, we don't know," Leanne states bluntly. "She went to the bathroom while we were getting drinks. She came back when the panic attack started. I thought it was due to the crowd, but this isn't normal for her. This reaction is too severe."

As Leanne explains, another small scream comes out of me as a phantom pain crushes me. It twists into my stomach, further down until my legs start violently shaking. They punched me. *There.* I cry harder, holding myself as I attempt to fight off the memories to no avail. Reality slips further as my throat burns.

"Autumn…" I don't respond to Trix, "…hun, what caused this?"

My chin quivers, breathing heavily as my mouth works out each word. "They're…here. Back…back hallway. They're…*here.*"

"Who?"

"*Them.*" There's a grit to my voice, making Trix go still next to me. "The *men...*"

"What?" Leanne asks in horror. "Are you sure?"

I sob against my chest, nodding as I remember the one looking at me. I don't think they recognized me, which gives some relief but also anger. Until I recall one stepping towards me. "There were d-drugs. Said...they'd find me...me later—"

"Shit," Trix swears.

"Who is it?" Isaac asks.

"The men who, damn it...I need to go double check," Leanne says. I whimper, begging against my sobbing for her not to. I don't want her near them. None of them.

"No...no..." I shake even worse. The pavement slams against my hands, and I choke out a sob, fingers digging into the concrete.

"I'll go with her, Miss Autumn," Isaac offers. There's a silent moment and shifting of feet. "We'll check. Do you know how to help her?"

"Yes, just go with Leanne," Trix answers quickly. "She knows what they look like."

Trix is left with me, stroking my head as I rock. My stomach feels like lead before I feel my mouth water and my throat tightens suddenly, the need to hurl overwhelming. So, I lean over to do just that. Trix rubs my back as I sob through the vomiting, then dry heave after my stomach contents have spilled to the ground.

It feels like I've lost control of my body, heaving for everything to come out. The shaking worsens, beginning to make my muscles ache as my head pounds. I sit with my back away from the wall, leaning against it on my shoulder, facing away from my puke. I rock again as Trix goes to reach for me again, but I flinch and almost swipe at her. She eases back, talking soothingly as she crouches next to me.

"Breathe. You're okay, hun. Just breathe." Even as she talks, telling me I'm alright, my mind still wars within.

I can't escape. They're hands are on me again. Using me. Battering the last of my body with malicious laughter and burning cigarettes. I whimper when Trix stands up, noise coming from down the alley.

"It's them," Leanne hisses. "Isaac saw the drugs, and one of them had a gun tucked into his pants."

"We need to call the police."

"Isaac's contacted someone already, and on the phone with another. Doesn't want to spook them into disappearing or worse, shooting up the club. It's filled with people now and knowing their history…" Leanne's voice trails off.

The roaring in my head hasn't stopped, spiraling out of control and I groan in agony. Although they're trying to be calm, I can hear the fear in their voices. If anyone knows what those men are capable of I do. My fists hit the puddle, clenching through the pain.

"What do we do for her?" Leanne asks.

"Hope this passes soon to get her home," Trix explains. "And make sure she doesn't harm herself, but if this continues or worsens…we need to take her to the hospital."

"Trix, we *can't*."

"We may have no choice. I'm not letting her hurt herself again—"

"Miss Autumn," Isaac calls out through the darkness. Footsteps come close, stopping nearby.

"Don't touch her. I think she's having flashbacks; she's already almost hit me. She'll get more violent to protect herself, and trust me, she *will* hurt you. She doesn't know where she is," Trix explains briefly.

My mind flashes to the hospital bed, tossing and tearing out IVs, and hitting nurses. *"Restrain her!"*

I curl further inside myself as Isaac approaches, kneeling before me at a far enough distance. He whispers in a calm voice, "He's coming. Leo will be here soon. I need you to stay with us, Miss Autumn."

A strangled sound is my response, nodding barely as my chin quivers. Isaac stands, informing my friends of the situation as my brain fuzzes out. I hear snippets, passing in and out of flashbacks and thinking one of the men is them. There's talk of seven people. Guns.

Warning bouncers. Voices collide as I struggle, scratching my fingers into the concrete, feeling the pain against the grit. Anger and fear warp together as I sit in the puddle, soaking through my shoes, pants, and underwear.

Abruptly, there's a screech of tires and slamming of doors. More voices come as I rock, concentrating on the bumpy, hard surface beneath me. Then I hear him. His voice carries over, and a harsh, violent sob releases from my throat. Fearful it's not real. *He's* not real.

What if I never got out? What if the nightmare never ended? What if they—?

Hard steps come forward, and I see black boots with jeans cuffed over them. Crouching before me, there's a shirt and black leather jacket. I can't seem to pull my gaze up further from his chest. Fearful it's all a trick. That my memories, good ones, are being ruined by the old. Until Leo's soft voice reaches my ears. "Check in."

"Red, red, red," I repeat over and over again, shaking my head.

"I'm here, dear Watson," he says gently, and I stop repeating the word, choking out a sob. "Look at me, sweetheart."

The small order pierces through the dark fog that's developed around me. My eyes finally move up, finding his. Worry lines his expression, but he's calm and collected. His voice is steady when he states, "Good girl."

I whimper at the name, reminding me where I am.

I'm not in the hospital. Not in that apartment. Not trapped. He's real. Leo is real.

"What the fuck did he just say?" Leanne asks.

"Stay back." I hear Jameson's voice.

"Touch me, and you'll see why that's a bad idea, buddy," Leanne warns.

"I said stay—" The shaking worsens at the raised voices, and I flinch as Jameson's gets angrier. Leo's expression goes rigid.

"Stop," he orders, and the arguing halts. "It's an honorific meant to ground her, which it has in the past. You can ask her about it later."

"Wait, did you just say honorific?" Trix asks.

"Again, we'll explain another time," Leo says calmly, keeping his gaze on mine. "Breathe, I'm right here, sweetheart. You're safe." Tears roll down my cheeks, but I finally take a long breath in. "Leanne. Trix. Go with Jameson and Isaac, tell them everything you know. They'll handle the situation. I'll take care of her."

Leanne begins to protest, "No way. Not about to leave her—"

"Do as I say, Leanne," Leo interrupts.

"Now, the hold the fuck on—"

"Please." He finally breaks his gaze with mine, looking over at her. "I promise she'll be safe with me. I'll have her contact you tomorrow. You have my word, but whether you agree or not...she is coming with *me.*"

There's a pause. I grip into my jeans, shivering harshly as I stare at the jacket. Finally, Leanne says quietly, "You take care of her, and have her call me."

Shoes scuff before Leo brings his attention back to me.

"You're safe," he states again, and I nod barely. "I'm getting you out of here, but I need to touch you, okay?"

"Y-yes."

"Good girl." Leo moves forward carefully, wrapping an arm around my shoulder and I flinch hard. He hushes me softly, then brings me against his chest as I start sobbing violently again. Once his warmth seeps into me and I smell his cologne, knowing it's him, my arms wind around his neck. I bury my face against his shoulder, clinging to him. He hooks his other arm under my legs, strokes my hair with other before cradling my head against his chest. He starts to stand, and I hold on, but his embrace keeps me firmly against him with a strength that eases a tiny part of me.

"I've got you. You're safe, dear Watson."

He walks me out of the alley to a car. Opening the door, he leans in and places me in the backseat. When he pulls away, I curl back into myself on the leather cushions. Leo leans back, and there's more voices all in lower octaves.

"What do you want done?" A deep voice asks.

"Clean-up protocol. Chesty, inform the others," Leo informs.

"What about—"

"Take care of them," Leo orders in a dark tone. "You know what those fuckers did to her."

"Fucking gladly," Rudolf responds, walking away.

Leo gets into the car with me, hauling me into his arms and placing my head under his chin. The door slams shut, and the car moves, making me flinch as the cold sweat makes me shiver. Not to mention being drenched from the butt down.

"Penthouse, Animal," Leo instructs.

"Got it, boss," they reply. "I'll call the doorman. Enigma's arriving with backup."

"Good."

Leo brushes my hair back as I lean into him, phasing in and out of the present. The ride is a blur as Leo attempts to talk to me. Or I'm just hearing voices. My lungs hurt from crying, screaming, and dry heaving making it difficult to breathe.

The car finally stops, and Leo keeps me in his arms as he carries me out and into an unfamiliar venue. Everything feels bright with gold plating, and I hide my face against his shoulder as he walks through glass doors.

"Mr. Luciano, everything is set," an older male voice greets.

"No disturbances, Xavier," Leo responds harshly. "Everything goes through Owen or Mila."

"Absolutely, sir," they respond as Leo enters an elevator.

The doors shut, and Leo speaks quietly, "We're going to keep using the stoplight system. You don't need to explain anything. Green for yes, red for no, yellow for maybe or you don't know. If you can't talk, nod your head for yes and squeeze my hand for no. Do you understand?"

I nod and say with a hoarse voice, "Green."

"Good girl." I sink into his arms more; safety encompasses me as the doors ding and he walks me through a short foyer. I'm too deep within my brain fog to know fully where I am, but I'm aware enough to know we're not at the hotel.

He walks me through a hall and into a living room area. He places me on a soft couch, pulling away to take his jacket off and to sit beside me. The wetness on my skin makes me shiver again and my toes feel clammy. Leo pulls a blanket from somewhere, placing it over me.

"Did you drink alcohol?" I take his hand and squeeze it. "Just checking, given you puked. Do you want food?"

"Yellow," I whisper.

"A drink?"

"Yellow."

"Do you want me to take you home?"

Fear presses at my chest, being alone in that apartment and the quiet…the knives…

"Red, red…" I say, squeezing his hand tightly.

"Alright, not leaving." He squeezes my hand, then reaches over carefully to stroke my hair back. "I needed to make sure. New clothes?"

"Green."

"Shower?"

"Green."

"Let's start there, then." He scoops me up, blanket and all as he carries me to a bedroom and then into a bathroom.

I hug his neck, glancing at the spacious place of mostly chrome and black with dark tiles. He sits me on the toilet, moving to turn the shower on, and leaves briefly to come back with clothes in hand. Sitting it all on the counter, he crouches before me and cups the side of my face.

"Do you want me to stay here while you shower?" Automatically, I squeeze my hand in his. "Okay, but I'll be right outside. Not going far. Take however long you need, but if you need me, shout red, okay?" He instructs gently.

He leaves, closing the door behind him.

For a moment, I just sit there holding myself, staring at the tiles. The shower heats up the entire bathroom, beginning to create fog on the glass. After what seems like a century in my head, I get up and peel my clothes off in a gruff fashion. I practically toss my socks and flats across the room before I dump them in a corner. Shivering and aching, I move to the shower and walk into the hot water. Steam surrounds me as I take a deep breath. Hot water hits my skin, making me shudder against the downpour. I hang my head, letting the flow of it stream down my head and plunge to the floor, racing for the drain. Opening my mouth, I take deep breaths as I feel the water run over my face. My hands move out, steadying myself against the walls as another wave of sobs passes, camouflaged in the shower's water.

It feels as if my years of therapy are going down the drain, too.

Frustration bubbles up against the leftover fear and pain. I'm angry. They saw me and didn't recognize me. I should feel grateful. I should feel relieved, knowing all those plans put in place years ago worked. But I'm furious.

I'm angry I'm like this and they got to live on like nothing happened. They're still doing what they had done three years ago. They were unperturbed. They weren't *broken*.

I fist my hand, slamming it into the tiled wall beside me. A throbbing sensation travels through my fist and up my arm, distracting the awful thoughts. I hit the tile again. Then again. My bones ache as I sob, gasping for air against the hot water pouring over me.

"Bastards..." I rasp, choking back tears, "...those fucking...monsters."

I hit the wall again, concentrating on the pain that strikes after. My hand flexes, hurting from the hard hit and I notice the redness beginning to form. I inhale deeply, trying to calm back down as the sobs dissipate.

Don't do it. Don't.

My hands drop to their sides, head pounding as I remain staring at the swirling water. I focus on the drain, beginning to feel numb. I'm so focused on the water; I don't hear Leo come in and only do when he reaches into the shower to turn it off. He stands there with a towel in his hands, holding it open for me. I swallow hard, my throat tight as I stare at the man before me. Water drips down my face, dripping onto the floor.

"They didn't recognize me. I'm dead to them." My whispered

confession is weak, and Leo's gaze darkens. "They beat me…raped me, destroyed me. I'm left broken because of them…"

"You're not broken." His tone doesn't match his rigid expression; it's soft, tender, and…loving. "Let me dry you off, sweetheart."

I step out of the shower and into the warm towel. He wraps me in it, bringing me into the middle of the room. He grabs another towel, drying my hair and then the rest of me. He checks in with me a few times, before moving to certain body parts and I only nod numbly each time. I feel like a shell, exhausted and the leftover of a woman who once existed.

He gets me dry, pulling me into a robe and ties it on to keep me snug. He then picks me up, carrying me to the kitchen and sits me on the counter. He gently holds my face, tilting my head up to look at him.

"Ready for some food?"

I nod.

His thumb strokes my skin, and I lean into his touch. His other hand stays on my thigh, caressing my skin gently. Hazel eyes ground me as I focus on him checking me over, then flicking his gaze to the kitchen.

"I can have something brought up or I can make you something." I can only shrug, but my chin starts to quiver. Fuck, I feel like a wreck. "I think I know what you'd like, will pasta suffice?"

I nod.

"Good. No getting cereal or microwave pizza tonight." I give him a faint smile, and his gaze lightens a bit. "You can sit on the couch while I cook. I'll be right over here. Tea first, help settle your stomach."

Leo starts to move, but I grab him abruptly. He pauses, questions flitting over his gaze. In a scratchy voice I say, "Thank you."

He leans forward, kissing me on the forehead. Picking me up, he takes me over to the couch and tucks me under a different blanket. He strokes back my damp hair, then moves to the kitchen. Not long after, he comes back with some tea.

As I listen to him work, I watch the flames in the fireplace that he's turned on. It flickers before me, crackling as I watch light scatter shadows over the large penthouse. Leo speaks low, and I glimpse over to see him wearing an earpiece as he's cooking. The fireplace takes my attention again as the last of the shivers and trembling subsides. My muscles hurt like I've been hit by a truck.

My head is still foggy, unable to concentrate as sleep knocks at me, except the idea of closing my eyes terrifies me. I'm afraid of the nightmares tonight. How bad they'll be. I remember how horrible they were the first months after, how I never slept and would sleep on my kitchen floor or living room clutching random pillows. I try concentrating on listening to Leo cook. Not long after, he brings over two plates of pasta, placing them on the coffee table with some bread. He sits beside me, encouraging me to eat and drink some water. I'm quiet, mostly watching him as he takes care of me. Again.

I can't even feel guilty with how shitty I feel already.

Throughout the small meal, my chest aches for a different reason than earlier. I want to cry due to the safety I feel. The care is almost overwhelming after being alone for so long, struggling to find any ground. It's unfamiliar, but with Leo it feels right.

We finish, and he clears the mess before pulling me into his embrace. I lay my head against his chest, listening to his heartbeat.

"I've had everything cancelled tomorrow," he tells me. "I'll spend the day with you."

"I'll be fine." Hopefully.

"Much as I want to believe you, and I do, but I still want the day with you," he responds quietly, kissing my head. "I've called Nancy to let her know where you are. Your friends have been escorted safely back home. You can call tomorrow, so, they don't believe I kidnapped you."

"I think you kind of did."

"They'll have to accept it then. I won't relent easily, especially with you." A weak chuckle leaves me. "We can spend the day at the bookstore or stay here. Maybe watch more of those old movies of yours, whatever makes you comfortable."

Tears fall from my eyes, even though I have no clue how there's any left. I bring my hand up, trying to wipe them away. Leo leans back with concern, grasping my face and tilting my head up. "What is it? Do you need—"

"It's just…" I swallow past the tears and ache in my chest, "…no one, other than…I, no one has ever…"

"Autumn, it's okay," he whispers.

"I shouldn't have gone out," I partially cry. "Why didn't I just stay? I should've—"

"You didn't know. And they would've never been caught either. It's fucked that you stumbled upon them but going out is nothing to feel guilty about. You were just spending time with your friends."

"You don't hate me?" His brows furrow, and I glance down at the shirt he still wears. I look at the leather jacket thrown off to the side and the boots in the hall. "You were gonna go upstate. To ride."

"Yes, I was."

"And instead… fuck, you came back to, to *this*." I gesture weakly to myself.

"I'd rather be here with you."

I shake my head. Shit. I blink harshly against the tears that start to come. I fucked up, I fucked—

"Look at me, dear Watson," he says, gently tugging on my face. I find his hazel eyes and he brings his face close to mine. "*You* give me peace and happiness. No one or a bike is going to keep me away. I'll *always* come for you. Next to you is where I'd rather be, don't doubt that. None of this is your fault, sweetheart."

The ache in my heart worsens. My hands tremble as I clutch his hand and say the words I wanted to for days. "I love you."

Leo goes still. I swallow hard, whispering, "I know this isn't the best time…and I'm coming out of shock…or, but…"

He kisses my temple tenderly, making me quiet. "You have no idea how much I've wanted to hear that," he murmurs, pulling away enough to look me straight in the eye. "I love you, my dear, dear Watson. I swear I'll always protect you with as much vigor as you're tried to protect what's left of my heart. Whether you knew it or not."

I hold onto him, settling against him, but shiver once again Leo pulls the blanket over both of us, remaining in each other's arms as the night wears on. Flames flicker as he gently strokes my back, keeping me in the security of his arms.

In the quiet, and unsure how long it's actually been, I whisper again, "I love you."

It's a softer confession this time, and he presses his face against my hair to answer, "I love you."

Listening to his heartbeat, I start to drift. His arms dip around me, cradling me to carry me to the bedroom. I'm placed on possibly the softest bed I've ever been on, snuggling further into the covers. He doesn't join at first, and dread begins to rise as my sleepiness wears off in terror. The bed dips, and he gets into the bed with me, taking me into his arms. The panic vanishes, replaced with love. Exhaustion tugs me into sleep. Within the protective barrier of Leo, who holds me close, he keeps the nightmares at bay.

Chapter 34

Come Morning Light

I'm warm.

Releasing a sigh, I stretch under the soft blankets as I blink to light streaming in. I glance around my surroundings. I'm in a large bedroom with black and grey walls, dark furniture, a gigantic walk in closet, and plain decor. Rubbing my eyes, I sit up and feel someone move beside me. Suddenly, I remember where I am and how I got here. Leo's penthouse. I'm pretty sure I'm in his *actual* home.

Leo sleeps with slow, even breaths. My gaze shifts down to watch his chest rise and fall, once again not wearing a shirt in bed. A small smile forms on my face, beginning to think that's what he prefers. No complaints here.

I bring my legs in close, leaning my chin on my knees. The terror is long gone. It's been replaced by the morning peace, what smells like fresh air, and the pure delight I feel watching him sleep. There were no nightmares. I'd slept, after one of the worst panic attacks I've had in years…I slept. Somehow, Leo kept away the nightmares, even after being with me through my manic tears.

And then my grin broadens, remembering I told him I loved him.

I reach over, running my hand through his hair, feeling the soft strands. He rustles in his sleep, humming as I do it again. He rolls over onto his back, inhaling deeply before opening his eyes as I peer down at him.

"Tattoos fascinating you again?" He says in a rough morning voice.

"Well, you're just too darn *pretty*, mister," I tease. He smiles gently, pulling me down against his chest. I sigh against his skin while listening for the faint beat of his heart.

"How did you sleep?"

"Really, well," I laugh under my breath. "No nightmares, which I thought there'd be an onslaught. So, thank you."

"For what?"

"For chasing them away." I tilt my head, looking up at him. "You've got some special powers there."

"Highly doubt that." His smile falters a moment. "Just know aftercare well."

"Is that what that was?" I prop my chin on his chest. "How you knew what to do? Not just last night, but the other times, too?"

He strokes my hair, massaging his fingers down to the base of my neck. I close my eyes, humming at his touch. "Panic attacks and, well, BDSM scenes aren't far from each other in a sense."

"How?"

"Both create heightened emotions. Whether considered positive or negative, too much of any, being overstimulated, can be dangerous. Especially if not properly cared for." He sighs abruptly, laying his head back. "Isn't this a wonderful conversation topic before breakfast."

"Well, I did ask." I sit up, stretching my arms out. "So, let's go make breakfast."

"*I'll* make breakfast," Leo emphasizes, getting out of bed with me and tugging me into a hug. "We're in my place, so no marshmallow cereal or muffins, dear Watson."

Before I can argue, Leo kisses me as I wrap my arms around his neck. He pulls away, grinning smugly.

"Fine, you win today."

He glances over the robe I'm still wearing from last night.

"There are clothes you can wear in the closet on the right side. If you need more, tell me. I'll go start on a *real* breakfast."

"You know I'm gonna start thinking you're against my food choices," I joke as he grabs a shirt, throwing it on and winks at me before leaving the room.

I roll my eyes at him, standing up and groan. My back muscles hurt, along with my shoulders, and thighs. I rub my hands over my shoulders, venturing toward the large closet. His bedroom here is very similar to the one at the hotel, but it's wider with, unbelievably, more dark tones.

The closet isn't a freaking closet. It's another damn room.

I stop, looking down the line of suits on one side, more shirts hanging in the back and lined with drawers. There's a padded bench in the middle and a mirror near the back. Carefully, I run my fingers over the expensive jackets, coming to a vanity area with more drawers and I open one that has watches. Another with neatly folded socks. Pursing my lips, I come to the other side of the closet and find a few sweaters my size hanging up. There're shirts, too. More drawers within the wall, and I open one to find pants my size.

"Is this the rich version of 'don't worry I have a condom in my back pocket?'" I comment, shaking my head and grab a light sweater, and lounge pants to change into. "Gotta talk to him about this. It's like having a private shopper, and never being there when they shop."

Before walking out of the bedroom, I peek into the large bathroom I'd been in, yet barely remember. Yup, black and grey scheme. I walk out into the short hallway, glancing at a few doors across from the bedroom. I make my way to the living room, which has a fireplace across the way made of black stone. The walls are a light grey with couches to match. Like his other place, the walls are undecorated with a few bookcases and shelves to my left that are practically bare. Peering past, I see tall windows to a wide patio. In the far corner, near the patio doors, are wooden double doors to, maybe, a sunroom? Directly across from me is another small hallway and I see stairs.

Not yet curious for the rest of the penthouse, I look over at the kitchen on my right. It's massive. A huge island is in the middle with a stove top built into it. There's a two-stack oven against the wall alongside a large refrigerator. Modern lights hang down from the ceiling, giving the space an elegant look.

How does the hotel luxury apartment look tiny compared to this place?

The layout is extremely similar, but it's as if it was overdrawn with tiny differences. And somehow, I miss the hotel. Even mostly being an open concept, I feel like I could get lost.

Quietly, I enter the kitchen space while Leo moves around, setting up next to the stovetop. He smiles warmly while I approach the island.

"Does this place have two floors?" I ask, sitting on a barstool.

"Yes, but the second floor is mainly just an office, workout room, and some bedrooms. Extra space is all."

"So, guessing your home was a castle…wasn't far off," I say tentatively, and he raises a brow at me. "This place is huge, Leo."

He sighs, turning away to the counter. "It is."

"Remember how I thought the other place was, um, lonely?" I ask cautiously, and he peers over his shoulder and nods. "Scratch that. I get why you're over there all the time. No offense."

Leo suddenly chuckles, placing a mug of coffee in front of me. I give him a half, innocent smile as he touches my hand briefly. "I know this place is quite a bit…boring. But now you see why I've never brought you here before. Among other reasons."

"Well, if you're a minimalist, you're living the dream." I glance over my shoulder at the sparse living room, filled with dark, brooding colors. He could at least add a plastic plant or something. "But, I know you're not, so may I suggest a new decorator? Like the one who did your estate?"

"Same one."

Shut…up.

"I told them I wanted nothing in my way, keep it simple, since I'd be working all the time. I've never kept much in the city, rarely have people over, and this is what it came to be."

"Didn't think about adding a fake print of Monet? Couple more books? Macaroni art?"

"You've seen how busy I can be, Autumn. When I'm here I rarely give attention to any of it." He starts whipping eggs. "No point in letting those things waste away."

"Okay, maybe I called you out on working too much in the beginning, but if you prefer the hotel apartment more, why not sell this place?"

"Precautions." Leo's tone is serious, focusing on cooking. I decide then to stop with my questions about the place. It's barely eight in the morning and I'm giving him the fifth degree about his home. Again.

Taking my coffee, I sip the delicious drink and look past Leo to the fancy coffee maker on the far counter. It looks more complicated than what I had at *Blue Java*. He continues making breakfast with only the noise of the skillet sizzling. He expertly makes French toast, putting a few slices on a plate for me as he starts on a plate for himself before finally coming around to sit next to me.

After we both had a few bites, my curiosity takes over. "Since breakfast is being had…" he quirks a brow, catching my gaze and nods with an amused smile, "…about scenes being emotional highs? Like meltdowns?"

"They can have a conglomerate of emotions. The human body can take a lot. And scenes are very similar to, well, panic attacks from emotions that can range from pleasure to pain, sometimes both. Its adrenaline being raised for the emotional well-being; your body's response whether to survive, incited by bodily need or not, or triggered by outside factors. Does that make sense?"

"Uh, yeah, mostly. Never really thought of it that way before. Increased emotions, whether you intend for them to happen or not can be overwhelming. Even being happy or being sad or angry."

"Exactly, no matter what, afterwards there's going to be drop. The sudden loss of those emotions whether its fear, joy, pleasure, pain can be damaging or can be good. Body's natural reaction to a loss of a drug essentially."

I think a moment, tapping my fork on the plate, while Leo smiles at my inquisitive face. A thought pops up. "Or like after riding a roller coaster, getting off and realizing you didn't die."

He chuckles. "Yes, you feel a somewhat drop after a good roller coaster."

"And aftercare is helping through that?"

"Aftercare should be given when anything like that occurs," he explains, putting another piece of French toast on my plate. I grin at him, stabbing at it.

"Are you telling me what I should expect if we ever visit an amusement park together?"

"Maybe," he smirks. "But what you went through last night is a normal response to an abnormal situation, including that emotional drop. You had a panic attack with flashbacks, needing assistance during and for the aftermath that would come when your brain and body realize the danger has left. Oddly, it's not far from how very, *very* intense scenes in BDSM are." He pauses, jaw tightening a moment before flicking a glance toward me. "Not that I'm diminishing what you went through, but they're comparable with different, well…"

"Reasons." He nods, watching me carefully. I shrug a little. "Good to know the stoplight method works in other situations. When it happens again, may be easier than last night to find reality again."

Leo makes an odd noise before taking a bite of his food. I watch him as his brows furrow, clearly thinking hard about something. I take a few more bites, finally putting my fork down.

"You know it'll happen again, right?" He stops. "I know I've had other meltdowns, panics with you, but PTSD and shit like that doesn't really go away. It wasn't the first time for me, being that bad, it's gotten easier the last two years, but—"

"I know." His tone isn't strict, but sure. I stare at him. A voice deep inside wants to tell him. Everything, what I've done, but I can only stare at him. He takes my hand, stroking his thumb over my wrist. "Autumn, I understand this is what you endure some days and nights. I'm not unaware of it."

"Last night was different," I whisper. "It was…the worst I've had in almost a year, and I don't want to feel sorry or shame, but—"

"Then don't." He cups my cheek. "I meant it when I said I love you. That means *all* parts of you. Just as I hope you'll love me, all my parts, too."

"Well, you've not scared me off, so you'll have to try harder," I tease, but his expression doesn't relax. I hold his hand against my skin, being less playful. "I love you, Leo. Every part."

The smile I receive isn't bright or filled with amusement but nervousness. I want to ask him what's wrong, but he leans in and kisses me softly. His lips caress mine, making me hum as his hand moves to the back of my head. His tongue brushes over mine, and I press a bit harder, tasting the coffee and maple syrup on his lips. He ends it, placing a quick kiss at the corner of my mouth, and then goes to finish eating breakfast.

We eat in silence for a bit before I break it.

"Should I ever do the same with you? The stoplight method?" I reach for my mug, and he gives me a side glance with full on brow furrow. "Meaning, if you ever have a bad day, maybe my jokes don't land, be less blunt? Ease up on rambling? I don't want to be the only one to have check-ins, feels unfair."

His brows shoot up, surprise flitting over his face before he nods slowly. He shakes off the expression.

"Sounds like a plan." Finally, he smiles warmly, and it relaxes me.

Except I frown. "Wait, does this mean I can use it for weird things like if you ask me what to eat?"

"You can't say yellow," he chuckles.

"Rude." I pout playfully. Leo grins, and I reciprocate. He goes to eat, and I'm thankful for our breakfast talks. Whatever the horrors from the night before, the world always seems less harsh with him beside me.

The thin green sweater, jeans, and converse are a perfect fit. Can't even be surprised at this point, especially when Leo hands me a jean jacket with multiple pockets. Oh, the man knows the way to my heart!

I still raise a brow, taking the jacket. "I need to go through the closets, plural mind you, of what you've gotten me."

"Why? You've liked everything so far." He pulls on a leather jacket over his button-up.

"As much as I appreciate the clothes, I may not wear everything and some of it could be donated."

He adjusts his jacket, moving gently to tilt my chin up. I give him a look that I'm not relenting, and he sighs, "Another time." He kisses me until I smile. He pulls away with a satisfied smile. "Today is not that day."

"Did you just quote Aragorn at me?" He takes my hand, leading me out of the penthouse. I roll my eyes, and he squeezes my hand.

I decided on a leisure day, starting off at the bookstore with Nan. I called her this morning, after I called Leanne and Trix. Both were relieved and a smidge upset, but glad I was okay along with wanting to ask a million questions about Leo and his guys that showed up. It took longer to convince Leanne that I was fine, promising I'd give more details in person later this week. She agreed eventually.

We head into the elevator, and he presses the button, keeping his hand around mine. I look up at him. "So, plans for after bookstore?"

"Whatever you want to do." His gaze is relaxed. The events of last night feel far away, like a long nightmare passed. My body is still sore from the violent trembling, hitting the pavement, and the shower wall. Otherwise, I'm fine, including for another idea for today.

I scrunch up my face. "How about riding?"

"Really?"

"Yeah. Make up for the plans you had."

"You don't need to—"

"And I'd love to go riding with you again," I quickly add.

He smiles faintly. "Very well, dear Watson."

The doors open, revealing a reception area so high end, I gotta blink several times to see if it's real. There's a concierge desk to the side with a doorman, who nods as we leave through the opulent glittering golden and bronze walls. Leo escorts me through shiny doors to the already waiting car where Rudolf stands.

"Morning, Rudy." He nods with a small smile, then opens the door for me. I stop before getting in and look up at the big buy. His eyes flick to Leo. His expression is unfaltering with pleasantness though. "Thanks for any help last night. I appreciate it. And if you were planning to ride or take time off, too…sorry if I ruined your plans."

He gives a small nod. "No worries…" he pauses, the corner of his smile lifting a little, "…*barchën.*"

"I'm gonna figure out what that means one day, *Rudy.*" He winks and I giggle at him, finding the gesture endearing. I peer back at Leo, who's passive expression is back, not at all shifting even as I give him a questioning brow raise.

I climb into the car, buckling in while Leo takes a moment to whisper something low to Rudolf. He nods, before walking toward the driver side of the car as Leo gets in next to me.

Leo is quiet, holding my hand again as his fingers stroke my skin. Silently, I watch him for a few minutes, noticing his usual tells that something's bothering him. Wasn't me talking to Rudolf, was it?

"Something wrong?" I ask.

He forces a not at all convincing smile. "Business matters. I'll try to keep them away today."

"Thought you cancelled everything?"

"I did." Leo looks away. There's agitation and a bit of anger in his voice, strained almost. The moment passes, and he brings my hand up to kiss it. "You have nothing to worry about."

"Uh-huh, that's *exactly* what people say when they don't want you to worry. I should know, do it often enough."

"Yes, I've realized, dear Watson." His expression becomes less rigid, and he gives me a knowing look. I roll my eyes at him, leaning into his side and putting my head on his shoulder. His breath hitches a moment before settling back, relaxing into the seat.

When we get to *Nan's Bookstore*, the woman herself is inside with a plate of cookies and coffee. She and I talk, discussing what happened, and I skip a few details. She doesn't press hard for info, keeping neutral throughout the conversation, which I'm grateful for. We've barely been there half an hour before Jameson comes in abruptly, needing to talk with Leo. They excuse themselves, walking out of the bookstore. I watch them, seeing another car beside the one we arrived in, and I see Isaac and Owen, too.

"When he said he cancelled everything, it was hard to believe he'd be left alone entirely," I murmur, grabbing another cookie from Nan's tray, then walk around to sit behind the counter with her.

"Has he always been this busy?" Nan asks, typing a few things into her computer.

"Past week kind of busier than usual, but not too bad." I lean back, watching the men talk with strict expressions. Jameson appears worried, but mostly angry. Maybe that day off wasn't going to be as easy as Leo thought.

I sigh, "Five bucks he has a meeting or something else to attend to."

Nan gives me a knowing smile as I nibble the cookie. "You know him too well."

"I know his work ethic," I comment, shrugging my shoulders. "Know how much he cares whether he says it or not. Even if we were supposed to have a leisure day, I'm not mad if he goes. Don't think I'd mind recalibrating on my own anyways. I appreciate the help, but still weird, you know?"

Nan hums, glancing outside to the men next.

I continue talking, "And can't be easy being in charge of so much. I mean, it was a pain getting like six drinks together while cleaning machines."

"Hardly a suitable comparison." Nan laughs at me, grabbing a stack of books and I go to help her. I finish my cookie and follow behind.

"It's all I got to compare." She gives me a look. "Okay, okay maybe not, but still…close enough." We put the new books away on their shelves, rearranging a few. We're quiet as she organizes another shelf, and I peek through the window.

I tell Nan in a whisper, "He told me he loved me."

Nan stops. She turns, giving me wide eyes filled with surprise. "And…do you?"

"Yeah, and told him, too."

"Oh, sweetie." Nan hugs me tightly, whispering in my ear, "That's wonderful."

Not sure if it's her tender tone, but there's an ache in my chest and an odd twist in my stomach. I brush off the anxiety, following Nan back to the counter.

The door opens and in walks Leo without the others. I can see his jaw muscles are tight, stress lines appearing on his forehead. His gaze meets mine and I already know Nan owes me five bucks.

"How long will you need?" I ask as he stops before me, reaching to rub my arm gently.

"Few hours. Something came up about our…international contacts. And something personal." His voice is rough, and I narrow my gaze at him. I ignore the tickling feeling going up my spine. Just leftover jitters from last night is all.

"Hotel?" He nods. "Okay, I can wait there until you're done."

"No. Stay here. There's no point to have you come all the way down there, too," Leo argues.

"But once you're done—"

"I'll come pick you up." He cups my face, cradling it with reverence. "We'll head up to the countryside and stay the night at the estate. I'm sure Nancy will be fine with you gone for a night or two."

"Stay the week up there. Get some relaxation," Nan comments, flicking a look to Leo. "Fresh air will do you both good. Clear your head, Leonardo. I think you need it."

"Perhaps," Leo says, flashing a look to Nan behind me. "I'll come back for you, Autumn. Have some time with Nancy, then we'll have all the time together."

I inhale sharply, nodding with a soft smile. The tenseness in his voice and the hold he has on me, concerns me. He's rarely like this, and the times he has been weren't good. I know he feels guilty for leaving. Or whatever is going on *is* something to fret over.

Not sure what else to do to help, I reach up and bring him down to kiss me. His mouth crushes mine. Leo grips the nape of my neck, holding me still against the harsh, hungry kiss. I stifle a moan at the back of my throat, remembering we're not alone. I pull away before he does and smile more genuinely up at him.

"Go on, Mr. Hotel Empire," I tease, letting go and step back for him to leave. "You owe me cereal, now though."

He narrows his gaze. "Don't push it."

"Oh, come on, at least fruit loops! There's fruit in the name."

Leo starts to turn for the door and stops, looking at me with such sweet tenderness. "I love you, dear Watson."

I tilt my head at him, smiling larger. "I love you, too."

The door jingles as it closes behind him. Nan comes over to pat my shoulder.

I ask her, "Was Finn like that?"

"Take forever to leave for work?"

"More like guilty about working."

"Years ago," she says with a faint smile. "But we learned, and he gave me the bookstore to keep busy. After retirement he cooled down, somewhat. Always like being busy. Those who thrive building businesses, whatever it is, never can fully escape it, I think. Certain lifestyles are harder to leave than others, no?" Nan turns, nodding her head toward the back. "By the way, my back-alley camera is acting up again. It wasn't recording the other night."

"Because I fixed it to only record if there's any movement."

"Oh, well, then you better show me how to turn that off." I shake my head at her.

For the next few hours, I work in the bookstore, hearing nothing from Leo. It's almost one by the time I really start to worry. Deep in my gut, I know something's wrong. He was already off in the car ride and that conversation with Jameson didn't look good.

Another hour goes by, and I decide to go to the hotel. My patience wears thin, and I'll feel better being closer to him. I give Nan a quick hug, telling her I'll call her soon and head for the subway. Taking the route I used for work, I sit down at one of the few available seats and my legs start to bump up and down.

He's fine. This isn't the first time he'd taken longer than he thought.

I check my phone, and fidget with my wallet in my jacket. A few stanzas of *The Raven* are repeated in my head just before I get off the train and leave the station. I cross the street, staying on the other side from the coffee shop and walk through the thrall of afternoon crowds. I keep my gaze away from *Blue Java*, not able to look at it. Maybe I'll try to visit Mabel another day, but now I had a mission to find Leo.

Once inside the hotel lobby, I notice it's not so busy. I check my phone, realizing it's just before usual check-ins. I begin heading to the private elevator, when I realize I don't have a key card or access without one. Sighing, I head toward the reception desk, thankfully, finding Chiari.

"Miss Watson, good to see you," she greets me.

"Hi Chiari, I haven't seen you in a bit. Although usually you're working the later shift."

"Next few weeks my hours will be changing quite a bit due to some upper management issues. Double time as it were until they're resolved," she replies succinctly.

"Getting paid for that right?" I ask a bit jokingly. "Cause I can *totally* talk to the boss…"

She chuckles, waving her hand in the air. "Don't worry, I'm being compensated. I appreciate the concern."

"Double checking." I shrug. "Plus, I get having shifts switched and manager issues." It's been almost a month since I've been fired, and it still stings thinking about it.

"Thankfully I'm one of the managers," she muses, typing into her computer. For a moment, she pauses to glance toward an older man dressed splendidly and wears a nametag before disappearing down the hall with two cleaning staff.

"Trouble in paradise?" I ask.

"No, just high time with cleaning and preparing for guests. Our head butler here is wonderful at what he does, but he's a bit..." she hesitates, glancing around and leans forward, "...strict in how he does things, you know?"

"Ohhh, yeah I get that. Is he at least good?"

"The very best, which makes it harder to argue with him." She fake grimaces and I chuckle alongside her. "That reminds me, Mr. Luciano never mentioned you'd be here today."

"Oh, well, I wanted to come and..." my voice trails off when I notice Chiari's bright, calm expression disappear. Her eyes flicking past me.

I turn slowly, seeing a group of men walk into the lobby. All are wearing dark suits. One of them wears a pinstripe with slicked back brown hair. He's built like a freight train, large with bulky shoulders which don't seem right in a suit at all. His skin appears rough, tanned as if being in the sun too long. Two of them give leering looks at some women walking out of the lobby. All four come up to the reception desk, and I quickly move to the side as my skin crawls, keeping my distance.

Chiari greets them in a calm tone and small smile. "Good afternoon gentlemen." She pulls out a card, handing it to pinstripe dude. "You'll remember where the elevator is."

One of them behind the first takes the keycard instead, then looks me over. I don't squirm under his gaze, but damn do I want to. Warning bells go off in my head, but I'm certain these guys won't try anything while in the hotel. Hopefully.

He quirks a brow at me and scowls. "Checking in?"

"Could say that," I reply.

"Not quite dressed for this establishment." He makes an amused expression of disgust. "Unless you're staff."

I give him a cheeky grin. "Nope...just laundry day."

He partially sneers, and the pinstripe man frowns at him. I feel like I should know pinstripe dude, maybe he's come into *Blue Java* in the past. Mr. Pinstripe gives me a nod, walking toward the elevators with the others. Once gone, Chiari lets out a long breath and shakes her head, typing into her computer.

"Every time with him," she murmurs.

"I get that." Her eyes snap up to me, staring with surprise. "Used to deal with asshole businessmen a lot. Wall street guys really don't give a crap about others half the time. One time even Leo had to step in. Some are good, but…most are like that."

Chiari relaxes and nods with a tight smile. "Asshole is one way to put it."

I snort under my breath, and she quickly regains her composure, beginning to walk around the reception desk. "Mr. Luciano is in a meeting, but why don't I—"

"Chiari! Chiari!" Someone yells her name softly, and she stops as a young man comes up and whispers something in her ear. She nods and waves over another clerk to take over her spot as the young man leaves.

"Apologies Miss Watson, I have to handle some matters. Please wait for Mr. Luciano upstairs," she says as the new guy comes over.

I give her a short wave before she disappears. I glance at the name tag of the receptionist."Hi, Nick. I'm Autumn and need to wait for, well—"

"I heard," he interrupts, giving a stern, untroubled look. Alrighty then. Glancing at the computer, he types something and scans a card before handing it to me.

"Thanks," I murmur.

He waves me off and I head to the hallway toward the private elevator. Hopefully none of the men from before are around, and I exhale sharply as I scan the key card and the elevator chimes as it's called down. I wait, glancing up at the ceiling and cameras overhead, then down to the normal elevators where a few people get off. The doors finally open, and I walk in, but before I can press the button for the penthouse, the elevator starts moving. Scrunching my brows, I see the button for the top office floor light up.

"Oh, come on, he gave me the wrong card, *shit*," I mutter, glancing at the plastic. I press the button for the apartment, but it doesn't do anything. Crud muffins, I'm heading straight to Leo's office floor. Not what I was hoping on surprise. "Oh, come on. Please don't let me be *that* girlfriend."

Minutes pass slowly as I watch myself ascend until the elevator finally stops, opening the doors to a hallway. I walk out, glancing around the dark auburn walls with a few pictures of the city skyline and harbor. Down the left, the hallway continues toward doors and what appears to be more offices, which seem deserted. The right stops a bit sooner with large double doors which are shut. Directly ahead of me are another set of double doors, and one of them is ajar. No directory anywhere, but double doors usually mean conference rooms. Right?

I should turn around, go downstairs, and ask for Chiari. Or wait in the lobby. Or go find an empty ballroom. I glance behind me as the door shuts, elevator already going down. Great. I'll have to wait.

I press my fingers to the bridge of my nose. "Not the day I was hoping for."

Dropping my hand, I head toward the double doors, and poke my head in. My brows scrunch as the other door eases open, hoping to find someone I know. With that thought, I pause.

I don't have my shadow.

By now, Isaac would've surely stopped my butt from getting this far. I groan to myself, muttering, "Because I was at the bookstore. Well, I *really* thought this one through, huh? That's it no more surprises, except now I feel like a snooping, idjit girlfriend."

I lean against the door, and it opens completely, making me stumble not into a conference room, but a large office. It has grey carpet, dark wooden bookshelves with two couches facing each other and at the far end is a gigantic desk. Behind it is a wall of window, which reveals a massive sight over the city skyline. I explore a bit further, seeing that I'm already in 'invading girlfriend' territory, might as well make it worth it. At the far-left corner there's an opening that continues into another room. Everything is unadorned and empty of anything personal.

Undoubtedly Leo's office.

"Okay, stop prying and go downstairs," I tell myself, but curiosity wins as I'm captivated by the view outside. I move towards it, staring at famous buildings, and the vast sky of blue and fluffy white clouds. It's gorgeous. My hand presses against the glass, amazed by how lovely it all looks from here.

"With a view like this who needs paintings?" I whisper, smiling at the wonder of the city I've grown to fall back in love with. "Okay, it's *really* time to go."

As I pass the desk, something catches the corner of my eye and I freeze. There are folders with photos attached. My breath seems to stop, staring down at a manilla folder with a specific photo on top.

It's me. Working in the coffee shop.

Almost three years ago.

Chapter 35

She's a Little Runaway

Run. Get out.

My insides scream at me as my hands tremble, tracing my fingers over the glossy photo of me. It's a security camera shot from the side street before I disabled it. Faint bruises line my face, hair shoulder length and dark brown from an awful dye job. I swallow harshly, pushing the photo aside to see another of me perhaps weeks after, leaving the police station. My stomach jumps, fear wrenching my gut.

It worsens as I move the photo and see more folders underneath, labeled with my current name. My chest constricts making it hard to breathe. I joked about the manilla folder, but didn't there'd be an *actual* one or he'd gone this far.

My heart beats loudly, pounding through my head. I push aside more of the papers, terror gripping me as I skim lines of what they found, and a small bit of relief rushes over me when I see what they found. It's all there, the background I concocted, pieces of my old life before this one. The new one I weaved. Not a trace of who I used to be exists in the file, only the lies I conjured up.

Just Autumn Watson. Only her.

That relief is soon squashed when I flick my gaze to the others, seeing names I don't recognize. I flip a file open, revealing someone's rap sheet, a familiar face in a mugshot with a red X over it. It's the man who chased me, making me run into the hotel. The next page is someone else, same red X. And then another. People I don't know labeled with "deceased" and red X's. My stomach twists and I want to vomit, remembering finding folders like these in a different office a lifetime ago.

"No…" I gasp and see a folder with a name I *do* know.

I tear it open, horror coiling its way through my body as I stare down at the contents filled with the pictures of the men who assaulted, raped, and brutalized me years ago. The three I saw at the club all are clipped together, and I see notes scribbled to the side. I practically fling the photos aside, frantically reading the papers attached and find the drug deals, police involvement, and their confessions of murdering me. Their probation. Bail.

How did Leo get this? How did he get *any* of this?

I stumble back, staring at the paperwork strewn across the desk as blood pounds in my ears and my stomach clenches.

My mind grasps for any explanation. I frantically search over it all, making a mess of his desk, trying to find answers that doesn't make me want to hurl. Finally, I see the only personal item I've seen of Leo's since we met.

A sleek platinum picture frame borders a small photo of Leo and a younger man. It's from years ago, but Leo looks almost the same. The younger man is smiling, his arm patting Leo's back. His jaw is similar to Leo's along with the golden undertone to his skin, but his hair is brown along with his eyes. I know that face.

It's him. Matteo Marchetti.

Even though I only met him once, I remember the kid. I remember him following his eldest brother around. Memories flick by of his brother who he trailed behind in the clubs…in the bars…the shipping docks.

And that's when I finally see it. The tiny resemblances on Leo's face. Pure horror makes me freeze, screaming in my head. Realization sinking in.

Family. Brothers. One overseas and one put away.

Leo's older brother is the mafia boss I sent to prison.

Gabriel Cesare Marchetti.

"He changed his name, like me."

"Fuck." I pull out my phone, panic driving me as I send out a coded message to my contact. Next, I send one to Nan and Leanne, warning them that I may have been compromised and need to disappear. I tell them both I love them and to stay safe as I start running for the door.

A confirmation text comes from my contact, I search through my settings, and then turn my location off. I rush to the elevator, punching the button to go down and watch it slowly rise up.

"Come on…come on," I plead under my breath. I needed to leave as quietly as I can. I can't raise any alarms.

The doors finally open, but then I hear Jameson's voice drift from the office I just left. "Autumn? Chiari just rang up—"

There's movement as I rush into the elevator, slamming the button for the doors to close. I turn to see Jameson through the office doors, staring at the desk and snapping his head toward me. His eyes widen as I press my back to the elevator.

"Autumn, stop!" He yells. I press five buttons at once, watching him run for me as he tries to make it in time. Hurry up, you damn doors! "Wait! Autumn—"

They shut just before he reaches me. I exhale sharply and attempt to focus. There's no way I can just walk out, Jameson will call security to come stop me. He knows I know about their involvement with the mob. Worse if they find out *my* involvement.

The elevator dings, opening to the floor of Leo's apartment. Oh, sure, *now* it brings me here. I remain where I am, gulping and wondering what to do as I stare at the foyer. The flowers on the table. Where we first had sex. Where he helped me, took care of me. Picked me up and kissed me. Held me.

My walls come crashing up as I shove it all away, making myself numb as the doors close again.

"Keep it together. You know the plan. Get out…get out first."

Quickly, I go through my phone's maze of folders, accessing my scrambling software and enter a code. I flick my gaze to the elevator levels, and then up to the security cameras as red lights turn off. First step down.

The doors open, and I race out as determination battles with my anxiety, but my stubbornness and need to survive overwhelms everything else.

I run down the hall, turning the scrambler off on my phone as I race to the stairs for hotel guests, slamming through the door as I turn the scrambler back on and go down a couple flights of stairs. I jump the last ones, crashing through the doorway for the next floor and come across cleaning staff who stare at me with shock.

"Sorry, forgot something in my room," I say, skimming past and sprinting toward the other end of the hall to the other set of stairs. There are shouts from the cleaning staff as I head down the black carpeted steps, heaving short breaths as I reach a familiar floor number. It's the one I stayed on the first night here and had begun to memorize the hotel's layout.

The scrambling software on my phone is turned off just as I go through the door. *Keep fucking with their cameras,* I tell myself hoping to confuse them on where I am. Depending how good their software is, I have about 2-5 minutes before those cameras turn back on. I know I can't just go straight down, rookie mistake.

I reach the elevator finally, pushing the button and hoping it goes faster. I hear shouting down the way, and there are people on the elevator as it opens. I switch out with them, turning the scrambler back on as I punch the doors to close. All the camera red lights switch off.

I hit the button to go up two floors, and then hit random floors after. The doors open, and I wait, watching for any movement as I flick my gaze to the security camera just outside the elevator. I stay where I am as the doors close and go up another floor. It stops, and I run down the hall toward the staff stairwell. Coming into the stairwell, I hear voices far above me and far below.

Swearing under my breath, the voices below me disappear, but those above are slamming doors open. I keep going down, reading the signs briefly as I finally get to the ballroom floor, my thighs and feet burning.

Keep going. Get out.

I run down the hall, racing toward the *Coliseum Ballroom*. I yank it open to find people setting up for a conference, and I apologize as I race through the large space and head toward the back doorways. Once through, I move down a hall and more stairs, knowing it'll take me to my next step to escape.

The kitchens.

Before sprinting through the swinging doors, I peek through the windows and see workers going about their business. There's no sound of those coming after me, and I take that as my out as I go through the double doors and weave through the cooks and waiters. Some yell at me for getting in the way, just as I jump onto the service elevator with two delivery guys who frown at me.

I shrug, acting exasperated. "Can you believe my manager tried to get me to work an extra shift, *again*? Not worth the pay. Got shit to do, ya know?"

One of them nods, and grunts, "Tell me about it."

We go down, and in those precious seconds, I catch my breath. The doors open, and I hurry out passing cleaning staff and aiming for the loading docks. I push the last door of the hotel open, racing out into the shadowed back alley and loading dock for delivery trucks.

I continue running down the alleyway, breathing hard as I run the opposite direction of my final destination. I don't slow, jumping through the crowd like a maniac as I approach the nearest subway station. People yell and grumble at me as I go down the stairs, pausing long enough to glance at where the train is going before I scan my phone and jump on.

Remaining standing even with tired legs which are trembling, I pull up an app, make an account and input my emergency card info as I purchase last minute train tickets. Whether tracking me or not, I can't take any chances. Nor will I make it easy.

I buy a train ticket, leaving Penn Station for Cincinnati, Ohio. I glance up at the subway stop coming up and get ready to start running again. Once the doors open, I hurry through the small station and go up toward the street. Coming into the sun, I go back a block or two where I came from but veer off to another subway station away from the hotel. Once there, I head down the steps and wait with the crowd for the train. My feet ache as I fidget in place, keeping myself busy with buying another ticket for Chicago from Penn Station. Both trains are set to leave around the same time.

Once the subway train arrives, I delete my travel history on my subway app of the last few days. I get on, and I swear my body screams in relief when I sit in one of the few available seats. I watch people between checking my phone and turning off everything that may help track my location. It feels like forever before the train finally arrives.

The crowds are getting heavier as I weave through them to the subway entrance. The sidewalk is packed with people as I start jogging toward a storage locker facility not far from Penn Station. Double checking I'm not being followed, I slip inside and begin searching through the locker labels. Finally, I find the one I've been paying cash for the past year and a half. I take out the small backpack, checking the contents and the pouch filled with cash. I then yank off the jean jacket Leo gave me and stuff it into the locker.

For a moment, I pause, taking a deep breath.

You can do this. You can do this.

Throwing the bag over my shoulder, I quickly scramble the security cameras, checking as the lights go off for a few moments as I pass through like I was never there. I leave the building, coming back out into the city crowds and head down toward Penn Station. Once I'm close enough, I turn the phone location back on and hurry into the station. My head is on a swivel as I approach the ticket booths, checking in for one train and moving to another for the second. The crowds lessen as those rush for the platforms. I move away from the people, staying close to the wall. My hand taps on my thigh, waiting and watching.

Just as the train for Cincinnati starts to leave, I turn my phone location off again, and run through the station toward the bathrooms, evading the security cameras the best I can. Rushing into the bathroom, I pull out clothes from the bag. I yank off every piece of material Leo gave me, putting on a long shirt, leggings, jacket, and running shoes. I fit on a blonde wig, pulling on a beanie to hide the awful wig line and put on some cat-eye sunglasses. After shoving the other clothes into the bag, I start walking out, but peek around the corner for anyone. It's empty with the recent boarding of passengers, and I quickly run into the men's bathroom to toss the bag into the trashcan.

My head dips down as I check my surroundings, as I begin to leave the station, there's a prick at my neck and I look up. Near the exit, I see a couple of men in suits, hurrying into the train station. I almost stumble when I see the large man leading them.

Rudolf.

My heart pounds frantically, feeling my face pale as I continue walking, trying to act normal. I see him search through the crowds as the others aim for the platforms. I gulp, noticing there'll only be a few people between him and I. My hands shake as I shove them into my pockets, head lowered as they get closer.

One of the men on his phone, passing me. "Train has already left."

Rudolf responds, "Not Chicago. We can still catch—"

Before I can lose my shit, I disappear into the crowd, peeking over my shoulder as I see Rudolf pause. Turning away, I quickly leave the station and begin the long trek toward the ferry. Constantly checking that I'm not being followed; that Rudolf didn't actually notice me. Once sure I'm good, I breathe easier.

Fucking close one.

I delete the scrambler software from my phone, not letting anyone get a hold of that shit, and then the rest of the traveling apps. I double check that my location is completely off. Numbers are quickly blocked as I notice five voicemails. Jameson. Before I cave into guilt, I finally turn my phone off.

After what seems like forever, I reach the ferry and pay for my ticket at the booth in cash.

I'm able to get on before it leaves, feeling wobbly as it starts to move, and I run to the bathroom at the back of the boat. I yank off the wig and sunglasses, then stare at my reflection, hating the exhaustion in my eyes. The fear. Very familiar, old fear on my face.

I pull the beanie back on, throwing away the wig and sunglasses. The sun begins to descend as the ferry crosses to New Jersey. I stay huddled up against the boat as I watch the city become smaller. A crushing weight covers my shoulders as I watch my home I've fought to keep gets tinier. Tears threaten to fall as my heart wrenches.

Don't spiral. Not yet.

Once we arrive at port, I hail a taxi. I fidget in the back, my body shaking as I smell the inside of the car and the feel of the faux leather. Shit, come on, you're fine. You got out of the city.

The driver drops me off near an entrance of a park, and I pay him in cash before I watch him leave. I walk the distance he already drove, looking at house numbers in the neighborhoods of picket fences, backyards, and porches. I continue for several blocks, turning away from cul-de-sacs before finding the right street. The sun is close to setting when I find the brown painted house, walking past the tall wooden fenced-in front yard that leads to the back. The porch has a swing, white trim to compliment the house's scheme surrounded by dying potted plants. There's a vintage Chevy car in the driveway, repainted since the last time I saw it.

I knock on the door, trying not to fall into a panic attack. The door opens, revealing my old handler.

Detective Roger Caltz.

"Get inside." He ushers me in, shutting the door behind me.

His house is filled with pictures of fishing boats and landscapes of Canada. His living room is to the left with large-cushioned furniture and a new television, while to the right is his kitchen. My mind starts to go numb, wanting rest as tears start to press at my eyes. I slump down onto the couch and tear the beanie off my head. Fucking thing itches.

Roger comes around, sitting in front of me in the other chair. His skin looks more tanned since I last saw him, a bit aged probably from more time fishing. He's only in his mid-thirties, but you'd think early forties. His short blondish hair is spiked a little, cut shorter than it used to be, but his dark brown eyes haven't changed much with their downturned sides. I notice he's got a small beer gut now.

"What the hell happened?" He asks gruffly. "Do you know what—"

"Why didn't you tell me there was more than one brother?" I interrupt, breathing a bit erratically as more of my reality sinks in. The questions want to spill out as anger begins to bubble under the fear of the past few hours.

"What?"

"Gabriel has more than one brother!" I yell suddenly, balling my hands into fists as I stand up. "You said it was just Matteo. You fucking lied to me, Roger!"

He narrows his eyes, standing up quickly. Instinctively, I flinch. "Why? Who saw you?"

"At this point, I don't know." I hold my chest, which aches. This was the last place I wanted to be, but it's all I had left if I became compromised. *He* was all I had left. And I don't know if I can go back, even as my stomach twists violently at the idea of Leo hurting me. "I may have been found out, months ago, who knows. Could they have known it was me? *Any* of the other crime bosses, captains, whoever was left?"

He shakes his head. "Fuck sakes Sarah, if this is because you're having a meltdown—"

"Could they have known?" I yell at him, ignoring the jab. I'm *not* fucking crazy. "Did his brothers know it was me who put Gabriel in prison?"

"Course not!" He shouts, flinging his hand out and I flinch again. "Look. Everything was worked out with me and the FBI, no way could they've known it was you. Even if they did, you're already dead to them. Your background is so fucking clean and neat, even guys from my old precinct believe Sarah Marie is dead."

I grimace at my old name, hating it more than ever. I tremble, digging my fingers into my thighs. "Is Gabriel still in prison?"

He crosses his arms, shrugging. "Course he is."

"Could Steve rat me out?"

Roger scoffs, walking away to his liquor cabinet. "He definitely thinks you're dead. Besides, he'll keep his mouth shut to stay in max, which keeps him from being shanked. His record states he raped and killed you, along with those other charges. Even without the murder charge, he'd die in the first 24 hours if he goes back to general pop. Your ex-boyfriend is smarter than that, least when it comes to his own life."

I sneer at the term he gives Steve, true or not, it's the tone in his voice that makes me want to punch him. Why? Why did I come back to him?

Because you have no one *else. Nowhere to go.*

"None of them know you're alive," Roger grumbles, pouring himself a shot, and then pours another and holds it out for me. I just stare at the amber liquid, keeping the puke down as I smell the cheap whiskey. "Himself and the others think they murdered you, not that they're actually in there for drug running and roughing you up."

I want to scream at him, feeling myself slipping as I remember who I was long before. I start to pace, ignoring the drink in his hand, so he takes it and knocks it back. My hand grips at my hair, trying to make sense of what I saw.

Perhaps, I could go back. No. It's too late. Jameson knows I know. And what I saw, I *know* what I saw, and it wasn't *normal* business dealings.

"You gonna tell me what happened?" He asks.

I evade his question, almost gaslighting myself that I didn't see any of it. To let Roger just call me crazy and be done with it all. Go back to New York and chance it. And then an uneasy prick crawls up my spine.

"Why did you help me get a job a *block* away from them?" I ask.

"What are you talking about?" He questions, narrowing his eyes. "They rarely use that firm anymore, actually Matteo sold it couple years ago."

"Not what I'm talking about," I hiss at him, and he glares at me.

"You could've told me there was another brother, or that he was at least back in town a block away from me!"

"Matteo is in Europe," Roger dismisses, pouring another glass. "He has been since he took over, spending most of his time in Italy. Contacts at Interpol believe he's in cahoots with the mafia there, but there's been no—"

"Not him, the older one." My heart squeezes, not wanting to say his name, but I rasp out, "Leonardo."

He pauses, giving me a look of scrutiny. "You talking about *the* Leonardo Luciano?"

"Yes."

Roger stares at me, putting his glass down as he scrutinizes me. "Not part of the game, that I know of, for years. He hasn't even been a Marchetti for over a decade. Fifteen years ago, he left, and hasn't shown any signs of being involved when he came back to New York. That fancy fucking hotel of his was Matteo's, but he bought it legitimately, just like everything else he owns. Trust me. We checked. He's come up clean."

I stare at the ground, replaying the folders and sheets in my head. The Xs on the photographs on the desk. The dates. The names.

When Roger speaks again, his voice is almost ominous, prompting me to snap my eyes to his. "Is that why you're here? You found something that Luciano is connected?"

"I don't know." In my gut I knew I did but wasn't willing to fully admit it…yet. Not after everything I did to escape the mob, I couldn't have just waltzed right back in. Could I?

Everything comes back like a surging waterfall. The money, security teams, being watched, snippet of conversations I barely paid attention to, his "precaution" penthouse, his seclusion, and others obeying him. *Scared* of him. All of it I contributed it to being CEO of multiple companies, his gruffness from being a biker, and knowing how to remain calm in situations from being a Dom, but in reality, I'd been wearing rose-colored glasses.

"Sarah."

"It's not Sarah," I grind out, clenching my fists as my arms begin to shake. "It's Autumn."

"Fine, what did you find?"

I gulp harshly, my voice coming out shaky. "I saw folders of people; some I knew from the mob and random others all marked as deceased. There was a folder on me, and he had this meeting at the hotel where these men showed up…they came into the hotel and… fuck, fuck…"

How could I have been so naïve!?

I was better than this. Smarter than this.

I fall onto the couch, unscrambling pieces of the past few months. Snippets of what I saw and heard, but none of it concrete apart from the folders I saw. Roger is quiet as I connect the dots more clearly that Leo is heavily involved. I don't know what his role is, perhaps he's a hitman or takes care of business here while Matteo is in Italy. Or he has his own cut or is an underboss or takes care of cleanup…I don't know.

Roger shakes his head, finishing another whiskey. "Shit, he's probably been involved as a silent partner. Probably took over parts after Gabriel was taken out. This fucking changes things, he's already powerful enough."

"I was fucking blind, I should've…damn it, he knows about Nan and Leanne—"

"You send them your code?"

"Yeah."

"Then perhaps Nancy was smart enough to close up the book-store and head south. Can't say much for your friends, but from what I know about Luciano he's not vindictive like Gabriel. They may be safe…for now."

Leo wouldn't. Deep down to the core of myself, I can hear his words of promise to never hurt me. I cling to that little piece. He'd never touch them. But then I remember what his brother did to those who disobeyed him, and flickers of that anger were in Leo, too.

I rub my hand over my face, heart racing as my stomach feels like I swallowed hot lead. My body remembers the ache from last night, trembling as I struggle to keep still. A migraine starts, making it hard to think and I want to sob at the possibility that these past few months were a lie. I fell for a lie once more. Had I fallen for the devil again? Except this time, this one has more power. This one *owns* the building I live in.

"If he finds out about my involvement…" I mutter, staring up at Roger with tears forming in my eyes, "…I'm dead. I am *dead*."

"You're not—"

"I'm why his brother is in prison!" I scream at him. "I cost his family's business millions, imprisoned over a dozen high ranking captains and underbosses. Not to mention shutting down half a dozen warehouses and two of Gabriel's kingpins. The biggest bust was because of me! He will take that personally, they all do!"

Panic writhes inside as another thought forms. I can't say it, keeping it to myself.

I'm why he came back.

He left, escaped, and I put away his brother…making him come back. To stay. My memory flits to the tattoo on his back, and I choke on a sob. He'll blame me. He may already.

"Calm down," Roger orders.

Anger spurs forward as I sneer at him, standing up on shaking legs. "Easy for you to say. You weren't in hell for over a year with an abusive partner, homeless, lost *everything*, and then get gang raped—!"

"We took care of it! You did your job!"

"No! It *wasn't* my job! I died that night!"

"*Calm the fuck down*!" He bellows, pointing at my chest. My entire being flinches, fighting back tears.

The pain of those years come rushing back. Those first few weeks after, pretending to be dead, while feeling it. Alone, stuck in a hospital bed. *Nothing* to my name because I'd given it all already. Sarah Marie Mitchell died the night she crawled into that hospital, and Autumn Watson was brought to life a day later. Once again, I was back to nothing.

Worse. If the mob gets a hold of me, those who survived the

sweeping bust I'd caused, I'd be worse off than that night. I'll wish I was dead. I can't go back. I can never go back home. My safety was gone. All of it was stripped away in a blink. I had no protection. None.

"Sit there and get your shit together. Fuck sakes, you're better than this." Roger's cold tone makes my eyes prick with more tears. "We'll take care of this. Stay right here, I have to make calls. We'll have to be discreet. Go after him silently and finally catch the last of those Marchetti bastards."

Roger walks out of the room as I sit down on the couch, rocking back and forth as my body trembles. My mind spirals as the coldness of loneliness sets in. I wrap my arms around me, wishing it was Leo's. But the arms I wished for most may want me dead. Or worse.

I mutter under my breath as hot tears pour down my cheeks, "Red…red…red…"

Several times I try to recite *The Raven*, but for the first time in years, the words feel hollow.

Epilogue

Leo

Their screams are ignored while their dicks lie unattached on the floor. Leo pulls out his revolver. Quickly, a bullet strikes each of their heads as they plead. Everything quiets in the cold, tiled room as the men lay sprawled out in their blood. Leo's lip curls, hating this room, but today he felt justified and that eased the anger boiling in his veins.

"Monsters," Leo mutters under his breath, putting the gun back into his side holster.

The soundproof room was layered with material to easily take any stray bullets or mess with a back door to get rid of the "trash." Said trash were the fuckers who raped Autumn years ago. It was easy to nab the men after Leo's Crew showed up.

Leo could barely sleep last night, glancing at Autumn often with rage for her. He could hardly concentrate as he received more news this morning about others he had to take care of, pulling him away from her. Since he was already here, might as well get rid of the fuckers. Make them hurt before they left this world forever.

"Should've let them bleed more," Isaac comments from behind. Leo turns, giving him a scowl. He shrugs, unperturbed by his boss's menacing expression. All his Crew were used to it. "Make them eat their own cocks."

"Not patient enough."

Leo walks over to the wall panel, pressing the button for the cleaning staff to come and get rid of the bodies. "They didn't deserve another breath."

"Won't argue with you there after reading their damn profiles," Isaac scoffs, glaring at the three bodies. "Bastards even brutally killed a girl three years ago."

"You're right, I should've shoved their cocks into their mouths," Leo mutters, yanking his bloody shirt off and putting on a new one as they walk into the small prep room before the private room. "Send away the others. I wanted my meetings cancelled."

"You may want to reconsider—"

"I don't care. My day has already been ruined," Leo interrupts, putting on his leather jacket. "They won't lose money over that fucker's screw up. No one does even if Matteo *actually* comes back. Besides, Gabriel is secure."

"Even after Florida?"

"Those officers fucked up." Leo turns on him, frowning deeply. "My brother stays there, tell them that. Just cover our tracks and connections."

Isaac nods once. "I'll tell Owen and Julio to take care of it."

Leo turns, pushing the door open into the short hallway just as the cleaning crew arrives. One of them, Alba, an older woman with dark hair pulled back, gives him a knowing look. Leo pulls out an extra hundred-dollar tip for his favorite cleaning lady and gives another to the young redheaded woman following her. Two men follow behind them, disappearing into the prep room.

The doors close and Leo pauses, noticing the doors to his office are open. Who the fuck opened them? He glances over at Isaac, "Why is—"

Suddenly, Jameson comes out of the office with eyes ablaze. They stare at the man who looks frantic.

"What is it?" Leo asks. If something else keeps him from Autumn today, he's going to burn down a damn building at this point.

"She knows," Jameson answers. "Someone gave her the wrong fucking card key, and she came up to your office. Leo, she saw everything on your desk. Autumn *fucking* knows."

Leo's chest caves in, time slowing as he stares at his oldest friend. His worst fear slams into him. No. "Where is she?"

"Gone," Jameson chokes out, face crumbling into anger. "She had an exit plan."

"What do you mean exit plan?" Isaac asks.

"Somehow she disrupted most of our security feeds and we couldn't catch her in time before she left the hotel." Leo stares down at the floor, reality not yet sinking in. She can't be gone. "She's on her way to either Cincinnati or Chicago. Ringer is trying to catch her before she does."

Leo remains silent, slowly moving his gaze to the inside of his office where his desk lies. Jameson comes up, but freezes with wide eyes as Leo snarls, "Find her. Track her location."

"Trying to, but—"

"Fucking find her…*now*."

His world crumbles around him. Tonight, he was going to tell her, everything about who he was. Explain why he had to lie to protect her. And now she may already be out of New York.

Jameson leaves, slamming through one of the office doors down the hall as he gets on the phone. Isaac moves to join Jameson, pausing to tell Leo, "We'll find her."

Leo remains rooted in placed as Isaac walks away.

Images of the woman he loves flashes before his eyes. This morning. Last night. She can't be gone. The very thought of her getting hurt, and that he can't get to her makes him see—

"My dear Watson," he rasps, gripping the door frame. It creaks under his grip as he says in a broken, rough voice…

"RED."

Autumn and Leo's Story

Continues in...

My Forgotten Demons

Leonardo's secrets have been revealed,
but the first of Autumn Watson's have only begun to unravel.

Or should we say…Sarah Marie

Books Also by Elm Jed

<u>Paranormal Mafia</u>

Mafia, Murder, and Mayhem Series

Vinny the Vampire & Me

Sweet Cheeks & Her Mob Boss

The Wolf Boss & His Darling

Memories of the Underground: Volume One

My Dear Watson

My Forgotten Demons